D0239925

F/2163393

THE COURT-MARTIAL

THE COURT-MARTIAL

John Hollands

ROBERT HALE · LONDON

First published in Great Britain 2009

ISBN 978-0-7090-8738-0

Robert Hale Limited
Clerkenwell House
Clerkenwell Green
London EC1R 0HT

www.halebooks.com

2 4 6 8 10 9 7 5 3 1

Typeset in 10/13pt Sabon
by Derek Doyle & Associates, Shaw Heath
Printed in the UK by the MPG Books Group

This novel is dedicated to the memory of my late father,
Douglas Leslie Hollands

Author's Note

The Court-Martial is a work of fiction. Although names of Korean hills, towns and villages, various military units, and real events, are mentioned, they have often been changed in terms of timings and locations to enhance the story or to save possible embarrassment. Likewise, military titles and jargon have in places been simplified for the benefit of those unfamiliar with military matters.

PART ONE

Second-Lieutenant Robert Wilson

CHAPTER ONE

Second-Lieutenant Robert Wilson leaned against the deck rail of the troopship *Devonshire*, waiting for a first glimpse of the Korean coastline. Reveille had not yet sounded over the ship's Tannoy system and the only others on deck were the usual collection of keep-fit fanatics. To Wilson, it was an intensely moving moment. Just as his grandfather had watched the Table Mountain loom out of the haze on his way to the Boer War, and just as his father had first sighted Gallipoli, so he was now searching for Korea.

Wilson was nineteen. He was tall, nudging six foot three inches, with a remarkably mature body: broad, muscular, and athletic. His face was handsome, chiselled in well-defined lines, skin smooth and fresh. He had a mop of unruly brown hair and a ready smile, the type of smile which won him easy friendships.

So far, life had been kind to Wilson. At school, his mediocre performance in the classroom had paled into insignificance on account of his outstanding ability at rugby and cricket; and in an establishment where leadership was judged purely on physical accomplishments success came automatically. He saw the Korean war in simple terms. He was not interested in the reasons for it. Nor did it concern him that millions of people had already died in the conflict, and that millions more would probably join them. To Wilson the war was merely the inexorable roll of fate. In personal terms it was an opportunity to prove himself, to turn his temporary national service commission into something permanent. By excelling himself he could secure a recommendation for a short-service commission, from which a regular commission would follow naturally. His failure to pass the Sandhurst exam would no longer matter.

His thoughts were disturbed by a subdued cheer from several officers further along the deck. 'Land ahoy!' one of them shouted. Wilson scanned the horizon. There it was: Korea. He waited until it was clearly defined and then hurried below decks to break the news to his cabin mates . . . at least, to his real cabin mates, David Barclay and Albert Dring. George Saville, the fourth member of the cabin, was someone Wilson chose to ignore.

When Wilson burst back into his cabin, Barclay and Dring were getting dressed. George Saville was a familiar bulge beneath umpteen blankets, still sound asleep. 'Are you fellows coming on deck to see us dock?'

'You bet!' replied Barclay. 'Mustn't miss an occasion like this.'

As the *Devonshire* edged into Pusan a morning mist was swirling around the surrounding hills and for the first time since leaving England they felt a cold wind. Pusan was soon revealed as a battle-scarred slum. Major buildings were heavily pitted by shrapnel marks and bullet holes, and in the residential areas houses were nothing but shacks.

As they tied up alongside, an announcement over the Tannoy told the three officers that as soon as the *Devonshire* berthed they were to proceed to the Movement Control Officer at the Pusan railway station. They were to travel north without delay to join their battalion, the Home Counties Borderers. They snatched a quick breakfast and then collected their kit together. When they arrived at the gangway on C-deck a military police sergeant said: 'Right, gentlemen. You'll find a duty jeep waiting on the quayside to take you to the station. Good luck.'

They strode down the gangway, kit bags on their shoulders. As they set foot on Korea, there was a ragged cheer from above. They looked up and saw that a group of their friends had gathered on the promenade deck to see them off. They waved back and walked off down the quay, heading for the duty jeep, the start of their journey into the unknown.

Second-Lieutenant George Saville was among those leaning on the deck rail, but no cheers came from him. His presence was purely accidental. He was on his way to breakfast when he chanced upon the group. They welcomed him into their midst and there was an immediate outbreak of banter. 'Bit early for you to be up and about, isn't it, George?'

'Couldn't sleep for that bloody Tannoy.'

'Wish you were getting off as well?'

'Not likely, old boy. I'll stick to the geisha girls in Japan.'

There was the usual laughter that greeted Saville's remarks. He had joined the *Devonshire* at Singapore, destined for the newly formed British Commonwealth HQ in the Japanese ex-naval base in Kure. He was a soldier who could only have been spawned by national service. Militarily, everything about him was a disaster. He was short and fat, with bloated jowls and a backside like an over-inflated football. He wore spectacles with pebble lenses and was completely non-physical in everything he did, even though he was an infantryman in the Duke of Wellington's Regiment. Three generations of his family had been to Eton, Oxford, and then served in the Duke's. Not that George Saville intended to stay in the Duke's like his male predecessors. He was a qualified lawyer and as soon as his national service was over he intended to join a well-heeled partnership in the City of London.

On joining the *Devonshire*, Saville had made an immediate impact. Until then the voyage had been dull and spiritless, but his musical talents changed everything. Within a day or two he took it upon himself to organize impromptu concerts in the officers' lounge every evening after dinner. He took up permanent residence at the *Devonshire*'s dilapidated upright piano and then, between playing and singing popular ballads, he would call upon other officers to step forward to do party-pieces; and all of a sudden evenings became full of songs, jokes, and laughter. Not that everyone approved. Some preferred the quiet life. Among them were Saville's cabin mates. They found his behaviour irksome, and they dreaded that he would call upon them to perform in one of his concerts.

The night before they reached Hong Kong, Saville duly singled them out, urging them to contribute something to the entertainments. When they declined there were mild jeers and cries of 'Shame!' from other officers. Saville repeated his challenge a couple of nights later, this time taunting them: 'Not thought of anything to do yet?'

Later, Wilson took him to one side and told him to lay off. Inevitably, an explosive argument ensued which gave rise to a personal vendetta. The animosity between them became common knowledge and when they were drawn against each other in the semi-final of the ship's chess tournament interest in the clash ran high. Chess was Wilson's sole claim to intellectual brightness and he encouraged the support of his friends, keen for them to witness Saville's comeuppance. As it turned out, Saville made him look stupid. He had him in checkmate in five moves and then added insult to injury by announcing to all those watching: 'A purely routine opening ... known among the Hastings fraternity as "The Fool's Farewell".

As Saville watched his three cabin mates load their kit into the duty jeep, he didn't wish them ill. Indeed, he felt sorry for them. He was certain that in a year's time, when they re-embarked on a trooper bound for the

UK, they would be in a very different frame of mind. He didn't bother to wave to them, knowing that any gesture on his part would only be ignored. He was about to carry on to the dining-room when the officer next to him said: 'Don't know why they're in such a hurry. The Argylls and the Borderers are already on the Yalu. It'll be all over before they get there.'

'That won't stop Wilson,' said Saville. 'Knowing him, he'll start up his own war. Wilson and MacArthur against the Chinese. And God help the Chinese.'

Saville turned away, his thoughts on his breakfast. As he clattered down the stairs to B-deck he caught the delightful aroma of fried bacon and burnt toast and he recalled the deal he had done in the small hours of the morning with the *Devonshire*'s catering officer. In return for being allowed to do his impression of Greta Garbo, he had promised Saville a 'full-house' for breakfast: eggs, bacon, bangers, liver, tomatoes, mushrooms, baked beans, and a couple of slices of crisp fried bread. Saville couldn't wait to get stuck in.

CHAPTER TWO

Major Roy Middleton began to shiver violently. He did his best to control it, but it was impossible. All day he had been telling his men in Dog Company that coldness was a state of mind, that if one adopted a positive attitude one hardly felt it. Now, the charade was over. He was so cold that he had no option but to clamber into his greatcoat. Then he pulled his Balaclava over his wavy hair. His Balaclava was the best piece of gear he'd got, even though it was atrociously baggy and featured yellow and black stripes. It had been part of a parcel of knitwear sent by the Hackney Wick branch of the Townswomen's Guild. Middleton was well aware that it made him look like a wasp, but with the temperature nudging -12 degrees Fahrenheit he was past caring what he looked like.

Middleton sidled towards the corner of the tent, trying to avoid attention. He felt the eyes of Jordan and Corporal Turner following him. He knew who would be the first to speak: Turner, his company signals corporal. 'Getting chilly, sir?' Middleton smiled lamely, unable to think of a suitable reply. 'So much for the power of positive thinking,' mused Turner.

Nothing more was said. They knew Middleton was duty-bound to try to minimize the cold, but the truth was that unless they were issued with proper winter clothing they would freeze to death, quite literally. Dog Company had already had five cases of frostbite. It wasn't so bad for those in company HQ. At least they had tents to shelter in, but the rifle platoons were living in the open, with the ground so frozen it was impossible to dig in. They had broken so many pick handles that Colonel Wainwright had sent Middleton a terse note stating that unless the breakages ceased forthwith, no more picks would be issued. Middleton replied with an equally terse note, saying: 'In that case, don't bother. We don't break them on purpose.'

Dog Company had never been one of the colonel's favourites, but after Middleton's response they plunged even further in his estimation. It had always been the same with Middleton. His sympathy towards the other ranks always got him into trouble. He often tried to be a disciplinarian, but it never worked. He just didn't have it in him. Middleton walked to the far end of the tent and drew aside a strip of canvas which partitioned off his private quarters. In one corner was his camp bed and in the centre was a table on which he kept his drinks. He sat down and poured himself a gin. In eleven years of almost continuous active service he had never felt so depressed. Korea was the worst campaign he had ever known and Dog Company was in a hell of a mess. He should have taken a firmer stand long ago, but he hadn't. He had procrastinated in his usual way.

Middleton drained his glass, trying to convince himself that it wasn't his fault. It was fate. How else could one explain the coming together in 12 Platoon of four of the most notorious troublemakers in the army? Three of the hard-cases – Fogarty, Chadwick and Gaunt – had been posted to Dog Company straight from Colchester Detention Barracks. The fourth – McCleod – had been transferred from the Argyll and Sutherland Highlanders.

Middleton poured himself a second gin. He was aged thirty-three but looked older. Not that his extra years did him any harm. He had an aura of maturity, strength, and competence. It was a deceptive sheen that won him early promotions and helped him to bluff his way out of many scrapes. Middleton finished his second gin as quickly as his first. He realized he shouldn't have any more, but he poured another anyhow. He didn't give a damn. He needed something to see him through a bad patch. The recent incident involving Mr Carter was the low point of his career. Fogarty and his two mates, Chadwick and Gaunt, had been responsible, of course, even though they'd got away with it and the whole incident had been glossed over and was now forgotten. All three were a pain in the neck, yet curiously Middleton couldn't help liking them. Whilst they were responsible for most of the company's troubles, they were equally responsible for the good times; 12 Platoon's amorous adventures were typical. In the advance north from the Pusan Perimeter, 12 Platoon had enjoyed the favours of practically every young female they had come across. Along the length of the Korean peninsular there was a narrow corridor littered with cheques Fogarty had issued in payment for their sexual exploits. They were all duds: Williams & Glyn's cheques which Fogarty had stolen off the corpse of Mr Mitchell, their original platoon commander.

Then there was the highland dancing. That had made Dog Company the envy of the battalion. Whenever they spent a night in a safe area, 12 Platoon turned the whole thing into a carnival. McCleod had once been a piper in the Argylls and it was his greatest joy to change into his highland uniform and organize the dancing. There had been evenings of memorable revelry, the main feature being the way the Korean women and girls appeared as though from nowhere and joined in, the weird music a siren call to them.

Middleton had enjoyed those evenings as much as anyone and it was one of his greatest regrets that they had got out of hand. The trouble came through a clash of personalities. When McCleod joined them from the Argylls, shortly after they'd arrived in Korea, Fogarty and his pals had made a great fuss of him, but when Fogarty – the natural leader among the hard cases – realized he was losing the limelight, the friendship became strained. Fogarty wanted sidekicks like Chadwick and Gaunt, not a rival.

As the popularity of McCleod's highland dancing increased, so Fogarty looked around for ways of putting the Scotsman in his place. His first step, predictably enough, was to encourage the Korean women and girls to try to see if he was wearing anything under his kilt. The final confrontation came when they were billeted in a bombed-out school in Seoul. Once there was a good crowd of locals, Fogarty organized a posse to pounce on McCleod to de-kilt him. The upshot was that McCleod was left naked from the waist down, fully exposed to the women who screamed and laughed with delight.

The incident gave rise to unmitigated hatred between McCleod and Fogarty and there was no more highland dancing; McCleod's bagpipes hadn't been seen or heard since. It was all so typical of the hard cases, reflected Middleton. One moment a delight, the next an absolute menace. After the Carter incident he had recommended to the colonel that they should be split up and transferred to different companies, but Colonel Wainwright would have none of it. 'It's no good trying to shuffle off your responsibilities, Roy,' he said. 'Problems must be sorted out at source, by good leadership. What 12 Platoon needs is a first-class platoon commander. And it so happens that we've got some replacement officers coming soon. One of them, a young Scotsman named Wilson, is quite outstanding. Put Wilson in charge of 12 Platoon and you won't have any more trouble.'

*

That had been three weeks ago. Since then the Borderers had fought their way to the approaches to the Yalu River. Now, nothing had been seen or heard of the enemy for six days. Sometimes Middleton wished that they would reappear. There was nothing worse than their present predicament: freezing to death on top of windswept hills with nothing to do. It was true that there had been recent improvements in their lot: fresh American transport and a hundred Korean porters. These men were unarmed but equipped with 'jikkay' frames, wooden constructions like open haversacks on which they could carry weights of anything up to 300 pounds. It was a big joke in Dog Company that within an hour of the porters arriving McCleod had purloined one of the frames for lugging his kit around.

The porters were used mainly for carrying 42-gallon drums of petrol, and the sudden availability of this precious liquid brought partial relief to the problem of the cold. Open fires sprang up everywhere, but these created a fresh problem: one of personal cleanliness. As men stood over them, they became so engrained in thick, black, smoke that they soon resembled black and white minstrels.

Middleton finished his gin and returned to the main section of company HQ. He looked at his watch. 'Not much of a superman if he can't turn up on time,' said Corporal Turner.

Middleton turned, affecting puzzlement. 'Who are you talking about?'

'Mr Wilson. He's over an hour late. If he's so shit-hot he could at least turn up on time.'

'Who told you he was shit-hot?'

'The grapevine, sir. Everyone knows all about him being the answer to the 12 Platoon problem.'

'The 12 Platoon problem,' laughed Middleton. 'What 12 Platoon problem?'

Turner snorted with derision. 'Come off it, sir. We all know that this fellow Wilson has been earmarked to sort things out.'

'You don't even know that I'm going to give him 12 Platoon. There are two officers coming, you know. Mr Barclay as well.'

'Maybe. But I'll put a fiver on Mr Wilson getting 12 Platoon. The grapevine says that this Mr Wilson is some kind of sporting superstar. But if you and the colonel think that's sufficient qualifications for sorting out the likes of old Foggy, Chad, Gaunty, and Smokey McCleod, you're in for a hell of a shock.'

Middleton also thought the colonel was making a big mistake. No young, inexperienced national service officer was going to control that lot. His own idea of splitting the hard cases up would have been far more effective.

Middleton looked at his watch again. 'Well, I'm not going to waste my time arguing with you, Turner. May as well do something useful.'

Middleton went back into his personal quarters. He delved beneath his camp bed and brought out a worn exercise book. The book was famous throughout the battalion. It was known as 'the manuscript'. It was Middleton's hobby. He wrote pornographic poetry: dirty lyrics to well-known songs, and extra verses to smutty classics like Eskimo Nell. He wasn't much good at it, but he enjoyed himself and it helped to pass long hours of waiting. He laid the book open on the table and settled down on a hard, wooden chair. Ever since the death of Mr Carter, the manuscript had been going very slowly. For ten minutes he stared at the last entry without a decent thought entering his head. In sheer frustration he called out: 'What the hell rhymes with tart?'

'Fart,' called back Turner without any hesitation.

'That's no good.'

'Why not? It rhymes.'

'Because tarts don't usually fart.'

'Course they bloody do. Tarts are no different to anyone else.'

'Well, it's no good, anyhow.'

'I give you some smashing rhymes but you never use them.'

'Oh, shut up, Turner.'

Middleton searched in vain for inspiration. In desperation he committed pen to paper, using the word 'start'. Then he paused, debating whether it would be better to say, 'The tart woke with a start', or 'The tart woken with a fart'? He opted for 'fart' but he didn't tell Turner.

He was still struggling with the next line when a jeep drew up outside. He got up, crossed over to a small slit in the side of the tent, and peered out. Usually, he didn't give a damn what his platoon commanders were like, but with so much talk about this wonder-boy Wilson, he just couldn't wait to see him. As the two young officers jumped out of the jeep he had no difficulty in picking him out. He was certainly a big fellow. Middleton made no effort to go out to greet the two officers. He merely watched with cynical amusement as they edged into the company office. As he heard Barclay exchanging words with Turner, he returned to his chair and pretended to be busy with the manuscript. When the canvas strip was drawn aside, Middleton looked up, contriving great surprise.

The surprise shown by Barclay and Wilson was anything but contrived. They had never dreamt that they would serve under a company commander wearing a Balaclava with yellow and black stripes. Nevertheless, they saluted smartly.

'You must be Barclay and Wilson? Welcome to Dog Company. Come on in. I'm confronted by a bit of a problem at the moment so you'll have to excuse me if I seem preoccupied. See if you can help me. I'm writing some new verses for the 1930s song, "These Foolish Things". I need a new line to replace, "Oh, how the ghost of you clings".'

There was no response from either Barclay or Wilson. They hadn't the faintest idea of what he was talking about. Then Turner called out: 'Christ, sir. At least explain to them that you're writing dirty lyrics.'

Middleton smiled uneasily. 'Ignore Turner. They're not dirty lyrics. Just risqué. Anyhow, I need a substitute for "Oh how the ghost of you clings".'

Wilson still had no idea of what was going on, but Barclay rose to the occasion. 'What about this, sir: "Oh, how my old man stings"?'

'Excellent!' cried Middleton. 'First class. What about that, Turner?'

'Very good, sir. An intelligent officer at last.'

'Jealousy will get you nowhere, Turner,' chortled Middleton, writing the words down swiftly, as though frightened they might slip away. 'The next verse starts, "A cigarette that bears a lipstick's traces". Very tricky.'

Middleton's eyes lingered on Wilson, as though challenging him to respond. Wilson stared back, his mind a void. Barclay saw no problem. 'What about, "A cast-off Durex bearing lipstick traces"?'

'Fantastic,' enthused Middleton. 'Did you hear that, Turner? We have a genius in our midst. Better than Mr Carter.'

'I heard, sir. But what about telling them who gets 12 Platoon?'

Middleton ignored the remark. He was too busy writing down the new line. 'Next one . . . "An airline ticket to romantic places . . ." ?'

Barclay thought for a moment and then suggested: 'How about: "Those gentle probes into receptive places"?'

Middleton stared back, as though in disbelief. 'Perfect . . . spot on!' He went on picking Barclay's brains until they'd completed a new version of 'These Foolish Things'. 'By jingo, this is going to be a bloody classic,' he enthused. Then he closed the manuscript and slipped it beneath his camp bed. 'Well done. Most helpful. And as I said before, you're both most welcome to Dog Company. And before I forget to mention it, you'd better both come back here around eight-thirty for some dinner. Then you can meet Edwin Dolby, the other platoon commander. And we can all have another go at the manuscript. But you'd better have a drink first. Here, I say . . . I've been neglecting you, keeping you standing like this.

Pull up a pew each.'

Barclay and Wilson pulled up chairs and Middleton poured them gins, plus another for himself. As he handed them out, his attention focused on Wilson. 'And you must be Wilson? The athlete? Tossing the caber, and all that?'

'Yes, sir. But putting the shot, not tossing the caber.'

'Really? I wouldn't know the difference. Doubt if I could toss a pancake, but never mind. As I say, welcome. We've been through some pretty tough times recently, but despite a few casualties the company is in pretty good shape. The only real problem is winter clothing. But you'll get by. We improvize somehow or other. And you've both got excellent sergeants—'

Middleton smiled cheerfully. He usually said a lot more to his new subalterns but this time he judged that the least said the better, particularly about the Chinese bodies found among the enemy dead at Sinanju. 'Mr Wilson, I think you'd better take 12 Platoon—'

'Told you so,' called out Corporal Turner.

'—Mr Barclay, you take 10 Platoon. Both good platoons—'

'What exactly is the position with the enemy, sir?' asked Wilson.

'The enemy? You mean why aren't there any shells and bullets flying around? Don't worry, they'll come soon enough. You'll find that war is ninety-five per cent waiting and then ten per cent chaos.'

'That's a hundred and five per cent, sir. Bloody impossible.'

'Mind your own business, Turner.' Middleton glanced between his two subalterns. 'Ignore Turner. He's an idiot. Anyhow, Wilson, to answer your question, the Gooks are out there somewhere. If they turn up, just shoot the bastards. It's as simple as that out here. They just charge straight at you. So we just pop them off. Any more questions?'

Neither Barclay nor Wilson replied. With answers like that, Wilson decided it was better to wait to find out for himself.

'Good!' said Middleton. 'Then Jordan can show you to your platoons.'

Jordan led the way to the top of a narrow valley, There, the path divided, with two gullies cutting through the hills on either side. 'If you wait here, Mr Barclay, I'll take Mr Wilson to 12 Platoon and then call back for you.'

On the far side of the gully the landscape was very different. The ground fell away smoothly into a broad valley. A third of the way down the hill several open petrol fires were blazing away, each surrounded by a tight knot of men. One fire, in the centre of the position, was particularly large, with at least fifteen men gathered around it.

'Sergeant Sykes!' shouted Jordan.

'Hello?'

The reply came from a short man in his early thirties. His greatcoat fitted snugly and beneath his woollen skull cap he had a typical army haircut. He was the only man on the hill with any pretence of cleanliness, let alone neatness. The rest of them were filthy, with highly coloured knitted garments pulled on over their battledresses. Many wore balaclavas like Middleton's, although none so gaudy. Without exception, the exposed parts of their bodies were blackened by soot from the petrol fires.

'Here's your new officer, Sarge,' shouted Jordan. 'Mr Wilson.'

None of the men in the platoon looked round. It was so unnatural it was clearly deliberate. Sergeant Sykes sauntered over and when he reached Wilson he saluted casually. 'Pleased to meet you, sir.' He spoke with a soft, well-educated voice, a far cry from the usual croak of a square-bashing NCO. The other thing Wilson noticed was the hardness of his brown eyes. There was no friendship in them, not even interest.

'You'd better show me what the form is then, Sergeant.'

'Right, sir.' Sykes took a few steps towards the fires. 'Stand-to. Ready for officer's inspection. Move yourselves!'

The men left their fires very reluctantly, their sullen attitude in keeping with their appearance. Wilson watched them with mounting irritation. 'We'll start with platoon HQ, sir,' explained Sykes. 'I'll only name one or two men. Just the hard cases. We've got one or two lads who are a little difficult to handle. Best to leave them to me. The main trouble out here is that there are no punishments left. Just being here is the ultimate punishment.'

Platoon HQ consisted of three narrow trenches, with one man in each. One had an 88 wireless set, the second a two-inch mortar, and the third man, the platoon runner, a Sten gun. Sykes introduced Wilson to his new batman, a young national serviceman named Gregg. He was in the middle trench with the 88 set. Then they passed down the hill to the forward sections. Each time they reached a fresh trench, Sykes said: 'This is your new platoon commander, Mr Wilson.' They all regarded him curiously, but the nearest Wilson got to a welcome were nods and grunts. The last trench they came to was no more than a natural hollow in the ground, occupied by three men. They were regulars, in their late twenties, all sporting built-in sneers. Sykes introduced them as Fogarty, Chadwick and Gaunt.

'Glad to be with you,' said Wilson.

There was no response.

Sykes and Wilson returned to platoon HQ. 'Stand down!' shouted Sykes.

Men made for their fires again, running to get good positions. Wilson noticed that Fogarty, Chadwick and Gaunt ambled along as though nothing in the world would hurry them. When they reached the main fire the group around it parted, allowing them pride of place.

'You'd better brief me on the general situation, Sergeant,' said Wilson. 'For a start, why are the slit trenches so shallow?'

'The ground, sir. It's frozen so hard that it breaks all the pick handles.'

'And these fires? Not very wise in a forward position, surely?'

'Normally, they'd be suicidal. But here things are very different. The North Koreans never shell us or snipe at us, so we can either sit here and freeze to death, or burn petrol to keep warm. This is our sixth day on this hill and all we've had to eat is bully beef. So don't expect things to be normal.'

Wilson listened carefully as Sykes expanded the point. He was very articulate but Wilson wasn't fooled. He knew a string of excuses when he heard them. His scepticism showed and Sykes concluded by saying, 'Let me put it this way, sir. The first thing any new platoon commander would do is order the men to wash and shave. But we haven't had any new razor blades for two months. Water is strictly rationed and it takes about an hour to boil it in our bill cans. And we're down to our last scraps of soap.'

They lapsed into silence, watching the men below as they laughed and shouted, using the inevitable foul language. At length, a man moved away from one of the fires. He went a few yards, groped about beneath his voluminous clothing, undid his flies, and urinated. It was so cold that when his urine hit the ground it froze and started to form a stalagmite. Wilson stiffened with disgust. 'Why isn't that man using a latrine? Call him over here.'

'McCleod! Over here. At the double!'

McCleod looked up in surprise. He went on urinating for what seemed an eternity, until the stalagmite was in danger of reaching him and becoming an icicle. He made a long job of readjusting his clothing. Finally, he sauntered towards them. He was tall and looked too old to be an infantryman, well into his middle forties. He wore a greatcoat and on top of that a patched duffle coat, a relic of countless Atlantic convoys. He was incredibly dirty, easily the dirtiest man Wilson had spotted so far. When he reached the slit trench he saluted sloppily, a cigarette dangling

from the corner of his mouth.

'Get rid of that cigarette,' commanded Wilson.

McCleod removed it but cupped it in his hand, ready for future use.

'Did you hear what Sergeant Sykes said?' demanded Wilson.

'Aye, sir,' replied McCleod in a highland accent. 'He called me over.'

'He ordered you over here at the double. Go back down the hill. And when you reach that revolting pile you've made, double back here.'

McCleod trotted down the hill with an unhurried gait. The rest of the platoon had heard Wilson's raised voice and were watching every move, highly amused that he'd picked on McCleod first. When McCleod doubled back up the hill they cheered derisively, most of all Fogarty. He yelled: 'Come on, Smokey. Get a move on, you old Scottish git!'

When McCleod reached Wilson he was panting hard, but his cigarette was back in place, as though glued to his lower lip. 'Get that filthy cigarette out of your mouth. Throw it away. Have you any idea of what you look like?'

'Aye, sir. Much the same as everyone else.'

'Well, get properly turned out. And why didn't you use the latrine?'

'No one ever does, sir. Not for a slash.'

'Well, you will from now on. And so will the rest of the platoon.'

McCleod saluted and turned away, lighting a fresh cigarette as he went.

'I won't tolerate that kind of behaviour,' Wilson said. 'It's disgusting.'

An evening haze rose from the floor of the valley and drifted towards them. 'Time to get ready for the night, sir,' said Sykes. 'I'll get the fires put out. We put a couple of standing patrols out in the valley to give early warning of any activity. And between now and stand-to the men go back to company a section at a time for their evening meal.'

Wilson surprised everyone by doing a weapon inspection. The only trouble he encountered came from Fogarty, Chadwick and Gaunt. As he inspected their weapons they watched him with mocking smiles. They realized their reputation as hard cases would have preceded them and they were waiting for Wilson to make ingratiating remarks. Young officers always did. They were amazed when Wilson said nothing. He knew the golden rule with hard cases: ignore them whenever possible.

Eventually, Fogarty – a short, chubby-faced man – felt compelled to make his presence known. 'You've started on the right lines, sir. About time someone got a grip of that Scottish pillock, McCleod. Fancy pissing over the hill like that. Only a Jock would do a thing like that.'

They all laughed. They knew from battalion gossip that Wilson was a Scot. Wilson still said nothing. He merely handed the barrel of their Bren back to them and passed on. The last slit trench Wilson visited was McCleod's. The Scotsman was alone. As Wilson approached he threw his cigarette away. Wilson went over his Bren carefully. It was immaculate. 'You're obviously a Scot, McCleod. How come you're in an English regiment?'

'A wee bit of trouble in the Argylls, sir. I was transferred.'

'How do the Borderers compare with a Scottish regiment?'

'They dinna compare at all, sir.'

'My father was in the Black Watch.'

McCleod smiled, revealing teeth either black with decay or stained yellow by nicotine. 'I heard you were a Scot, sir. But I dinna believe it. You dinna choose to be in a Sassenach mob, surely?'

Wilson laughed. 'Only to make sure of getting to Korea. Once I've got my short-service commission, I'll be off to the Black Watch.'

As Wilson completed his inspection, McCleod said: 'That business earlier, sir. I'm sorry. It willna happen again.'

'Good. Seems we Scots aren't fully appreciated around here, McCleod. Perhaps we'd better show them how it is done.'

'Aye, sir. That willna be difficult.'

The first sign of trouble came with the sound of bugle calls. Everyone listened intently. When they persisted, Sykes jumped out of his trench and joined Wilson and Gregg. 'That's ominous. It's what we've been told to expect if the Chinese show up. Gregg, let company HQ know.'

Before Gregg could send the message one of the standing patrols came on the 88 set. 'Dog three. Bandits approaching. Over.'

Sykes grabbed the field telephone and cranked it. As he did so, more bugle calls sounded, a lot nearer this time. He turned to Wilson. 'You'd better make sure all the sections are ready for action, sir.'

Wilson felt numb, astounded by the prospect of an attack on his first night. He sprinted down the hill and then around the sections. As he urged them to be ready, he was amazed by their calmness. When he got back to platoon HQ, Sykes said: 'Major Middleton says all forward companies have reported activity. He's got the Gunners standing by with a stonk across the valley.'

'That should sort them out,' laughed Wilson.

'Don't be too sure of that, sir. There's only one battery within miles of us.'

More bugle calls sounded right across their front. They were followed by long bursts of small-arms fire from Brens and Stens. Finally, Wilson heard the distinct rattle of Chinese Burp guns for the first time. When the Stens and Brens went silent, Sykes said: 'That's enough for our lads. Gregg, get the major to put down the stonk as soon as possible.' Then Sykes turned to Wilson. 'Come on, sir. We'll go down to meet the standing patrols.'

When they got to the forward sections the standing patrols were already back, most of them out of breath and clearly shaken. One of the patrol commanders, Corporal Higgins, was bent double, his hands on his knees. 'They're like a bloody football crowd, Sarge. We'll never stop that number.'

Sykes wheeled round on Wilson. 'Get Gregg to tell company they're in at least battalion strength. And to call in the Vickers on their DFs.'

A nearby voice came from their right. 'Let's bug out now, Sarge.'

'You run when I run, Fogarty. And then make bloody sure you can keep up. I won't be hanging around for the likes of you.'

As Wilson got back to Gregg, the artillery stonk screamed overhead and landed a hundred yards or so into the valley, each explosion a skywards surge of rainbow colours. Wilson settled into his slit trench. Activity was increasing all the time. At the rear, 155mm guns kept coughing and barking, and ahead of them the valley was soon criss-crossed by a crazy pattern of tracer bullets as the Vickers machine guns opened up on defensive fields of fire. Next, the battalion's 3-inch mortars blasted away and within a short time it seemed as though the battle was being joined by every conceivable weapon, like the instruments of an orchestra being coaxed to a crescendo.

The hill on their left – Barclay's hill – suddenly sprang into life. Small-arms fire spluttered. Then it steadied, gaining momentum. Finally, it took on desperate urgency, with individual flashes clearly visible and voices spearing through the darkness, human cries of anguish and warning, screams of fear and elation, together with banshee-like yells from the Chinese as they advanced up the hill amid fresh bugle calls.

It was battle as Wilson had imagined it. A boyhood fantasy come true.

The shells passing overhead began to diminish and Wilson suddenly felt terribly vulnerable, dreading that his first night in the line would end in a fiasco, a humiliating defeat. More flares went up from the 2-inch mortar. They hissed into the sky and as they burst into brilliant light the whole area assumed an uncanny but terrifying beauty, with the few shells still landing blasting through the mist, lightning jabs of dazzling colours shooting upwards, spraying deadly shrapnel far and wide.

'Keep watching your fronts,' roared Sykes above the din.

Suddenly, there they were! Wilson knew he would never forget the sight of his first Chinaman. He was a small, shadowy figure in a quilted uniform: a human smudge. He was plodding up the hill as though he had started off too fast and was already exhausted. He was looking down at the ground, concentrating on his footholds instead of the possibility of being shot.

Very soon he was shot. Wilson saw no details. The man simply slumped forward on his face. There were no cries of terror, no gestures of despair, no writhing about. One moment alive, the next dead.

Then the same thing happened to others following behind him. As Wilson saw man killing man for the first time he could hardly believe it; but he felt no sympathy or sorrow, only relief and elation. He shouted, 'Keep firing! Keep firing!' and then he noticed with alarm that no matter how many of them fell, it made no difference. Following in their wake were literally thousands of others. Their numbers were awesome: a solid mass of men. Long, deep, waves of them were piled up one behind the other, disappearing back into the mist. They were going down so thick and fast that those coming up from the rear were stumbling over the bodies, slowing their advance appreciably.

Then the Chinese returned their fire and Wilson heard the dreaded crack of bullets passing his head. He heard the rustle of undergrowth as bullets landed around him, and spouts of frozen earth spat at him as bullets hit the ground. The Chinese kept rolling forward and as they got nearer their fire became more accurate. Their gentle trot suddenly became a desperate sprint and Wilson could see their gleaming bayonets. He had to restrain himself from leaping up and running. Sykes suddenly appeared at his side.

'Send a message to HQ,' he yelled at Gregg. 'We're bugging out.'

Gregg didn't respond. He slumped backwards, shot through the head, leaving a mass of tattered flesh and glimpses of gleaming, white bone. 'Get the 88 set off him,' ordered Sykes. 'Then pass the message back. I'll get the forward sections to bug out. The others can cover them.'

Sykes ran down the hill and Wilson struggled to remove the headset from Gregg. As he pulled at it, his fingers slipped among the raw flesh. Only stark necessity enabled him to wrench the headset free. He sent the message, but there was no response. In desperation he turned to the platoon runner. 'Go back to company HQ. Tell them we're pulling out.'

More flares went up and Wilson saw the forward sections evacuating their trenches. The firepower of the platoon slumped alarmingly so Wilson shouted at the rear section, urging them on. A Bren burst back into action and Wilson resumed firing his Sten. The Chinese were only thirty yards away and their small-arms fire was now consistently accurate. As the forward sections dashed back up the hill Wilson saw several of them fall, but there was no chance of helping them. The rest sprinted past. As they disappeared, Sykes rejoined Wilson. 'Set up a Bren in the gully. Cover everyone else. Then scarper.'

Wilson followed Sykes back up to the gully where a Bren group was already in position. Wilson lay down beside them and threw grenades. In their searing flashes he saw several men fall, but they made no lasting impression on the Chinese. The leaders were now only twenty yards away, funnelling in towards the gully. The Bren reached the end of a magazine and before they had time to reload, Wilson shouted: 'Run for it!'

They didn't need telling twice. Wilson followed them, sprinting through the gully and plunging down the reverse slope. When the Chinese burst through the gully they fired hopefully down the hill, but their bullets passed harmlessly overhead. The men in front of Wilson ran on like wild animals, leaping and bounding, zigzagging crazily to make difficult targets. Wilson looked back twice. He heard more bugle calls and lots of confused shouting, but there was no sound of the Chinese crashing through the undergrowth after them.

The night was still bathed in artificial light. Flares kept bursting overhead and at battalion HQ a huge fire was raging, giving a pink glow to the sky. By the time Wilson reached company HQ the Bren group had disappeared into a scene of chaos. Men were running about in all directions like headless chickens. The orderly tent was lying on the ground like a vast cowpat and beside it were several men on stretchers. Some were obviously dead. Others were crying out in pain and fear. In the centre of it was a 15-cwt truck and Major Middleton's jeep. Company Sergeant Major Randle was trying to organize the loading of the wounded on to the truck but he was getting nowhere. He was shouting and cursing hysterically. Every time men ran past the truck he shrieked at them, demanding to know where they were going, but no one took any notice of him. Corporal Turner was at the steering wheel of the truck and Middleton was standing nearby. When he saw Wilson he hurried over. 'I got your message. We're heading for the south bank of the Ying Dang. The Gunners will hit this area any time. Keep in touch with your 88 set.'

'It's gone, sir. Gregg was killed.'

'Never leave your 88 set behind. I'm getting these wounded men loaded and then I'm off. You make sure everyone else gets away.'

Wilson and Middleton jumped to one side as the 15-cwt truck lurched past. Randle was standing in the back among the stretchers, still yelling at the top of his voice. There were only two stretchers left on the ground and Wilson helped to load them on to the jeep. The major then leapt into the driving seat and sped away. Wilson looked around. Apart from men running down the road in the wake of the jeep, the entire area was suddenly deserted. He had a quick look around to make sure no one else was left and then followed after the others. Two hundred yards further back he came across a lone Bren gunner lying in the monsoon ditch. It was McCleod, complete with his jikkay frame on his back, sticking up like a great hump. 'Any more to come, sir?' McCleod yelled to Wilson over the noise of the shells.

'No. I'm the last. Where's the rest of the platoon?'

'Bugging out as fast as they can, sir. Let's catch them up.'

Wilson and McCleod set off and soon caught up with the rest of 12 Platoon. They were strung out in sections on alternate sides of the road, marching at a brisk pace. McCleod dropped in among the men of his own section and Wilson ran on to the head of the platoon and rejoined Sergeant Sykes. Without looking up, Sykes said: 'Still with us then.'

CHAPTER THREE

The Borderers kept marching south at a cracking pace. Platoons followed one after the other in blind faith, hoping and trusting that someone, somewhere, knew what was happening. When they'd covered several miles they were ordered off the Main Supply Route and took a track across the hills. It was difficult terrain and slowed their progress, but within an hour they came to the banks of the Ying Dang. There were no bridges and the covering ice soon gave way, forcing them to wade across a platoon at a time, the water up to their chests, their weapons at the high port. The cold reduced them to new depths of physical distress. Once across, they fanned out into an all-round defensive position. Then they lay there for what seemed like eternity, cocooned in ice and literally frozen to the ground. Eventually, the order came to press on, and they marched harder than ever, feet squelching in their boots, their ice-covered greatcoats like ton weights, their wet trousers chaffing their legs; but not a man complained, all of them knowing it was their only chance to generate warmth and their only hope of survival.

Several hours later the Borderers were deployed around a cluster of hills overlooking a major road junction on the MSR. One road led off to Sinanju on the west coast and the other north to Tokchon. North Korean infiltrators had already sprung an ambush on the junction and the battalion's orders were to make sure it didn't happen again. They had to guard the junction until the Republic of Korea 3rd Division completed its withdrawal from Sinanju. Then they were to join the retreat, acting as rearguards.

Now 12 Platoon was on a hill directly overlooking the junction. The wind swept down on them remorselessly, its mournful note howling like a wild animal. Their wet clothing became blankets of ice and the cold was so debilitating that time all but stood still. Men shivered convulsively, convinced they would be unable to endure it much longer, but they did: they had no alternative.

Wilson tried to keep his mind off the cold by watching the chaos raging below them. The scene was surreal. It flickered in sepia like an old film. The headlights of vehicles coming down the road leading to the junction cast long, eerie shadows which alternatively half-hid and then half-exposed glimpses of bedlam. Evidence of the North Korean ambush was everywhere. In the paddy fields around the junction were hundreds of bodies, civilian and military, united in death. Almost as numerous were the wrecked vehicles, ranging from three burnt-out Sherman tanks with corpses protruding from their turrets to a multitude of farm carts with family groups lying lifeless around them.

The ambush had taken place hours before, but in its wake came what seemed like the entire civilian population of the north. There was hardly a family that had not piled vital possessions on to their farm carts and started on the long trek south, knowing that however hazardous their journey might be, it would be better than living under a Chinese occupation. For mile after mile farm carts were inextricably tangled up with the military traffic and when they converged on the junction they congealed around the ambush site like a massive blood clot, everyone intent on only one thing, survival.

In retreat, the ROK 3rd Division was totally out of control. Their officers had grabbed the speediest vehicles and dashed south hours before, leaving their men to their own devices, a mere rabble scrabbling along as best they could. Most of them were on foot, but others were trying to make good their escape in semi-broken-down trucks and jeeps, many with tyres shot out, running on wheel rims. They came down the hill, approaching the junction at ridiculous speeds, lights flashing and horns blaring. When they found their way barred they tried to bulldoze their way through, using their vehicles like bumper-cars, heedless of the people they knocked down or ran over and crushed.

The farm carts of the refugees were slow and cumbersome, with solid wheels and screeching axels. They were pulled by hand, with young women between the shafts. All of them were loaded to bursting point, with the old folk sitting on top. The dreaded South Korean police were out in force and in an effort to keep things moving they manhandled carts off the road to make way for the military. They delighted in up-ending carts into the monsoon ditches and surrounding paddy fields. The old folk were sent flying from the top of the carts and then, as they lay there, injured or dying, their families rushed around in despair, screaming hysterically.

If the refugees on foot were reluctant to move aside the police beat them with rifle butts until they fled into the paddy fields. No arguments were tolerated. If belabouring didn't bring instant obedience the refugees were shot and left in the road to be trampled or kicked aside in the stampede. Wilson kept a count of the number he saw shot. They totalled fifteen.

The mad rush south took hours to diminish. First the military vehicles petered out, then the troops on foot became confined to stragglers and walking wounded, most of whom had donned civilian clothes stolen from dead refugees, hoping that this would save them if they were overtaken by the Chinese. Eventually, even the refugees began to thin out. Darkness returned and a gruesome finality settled over the scene. Gradually, even the moans of the wounded, the creaking of spinning wheels on upturned carts, and the wailing of ghostly figures searching among the dead faded to nothing. Only the howling wind remained. War had passed by.

When dawn broke the Borderers were on the march again. Their pace was slower now. They plodded in silence, the last of a defeated army, but they remained alert and well spaced, one of the few disciplined units left in an ignominious and cowardly retreat. It was snowing hard, the wind at their backs, pushing them along helpfully. They passed many harrowing sights. During the night such things had been half-hidden and vague, little more than shadows and shapes, the cries for help muted, seeping out from a void; but in daylight everything was laid bare in hideous detail. They passed through village after village which had been razed to the ground by the retreating South Korean army. Nothing had been spared. Towns, villages, and even isolated farms had been raided, pillaged, and sacked, vindictive acts of revenge aimed at making life impossible for any inhabitants who survived.

Lying in the debris were corpses in all manner of mutilation, some with exposed intestines, some with missing limbs, even decapitations. Yet some of the dead looked solid and sound, simply asleep, having met their end by a single bullet. As Wilson led his men past these gruesome sights, he reflected that the dead were the lucky ones. Those to be pitied were the wounded. Like the corpses, they were covered in snow and freezing solid, stuck in odd postures, all knowing that they had no hope, some facing it in stoic silence, others pleading for help. The Borderers pretended not to see or hear a thing. They knew there was nothing they could do. Their orders were to keep going, to stop for nothing, for once a popular order.

At approximately 0930 hours 12 Platoon, last in the battalion order of march, was ambushed. Wilson was at the rear of the platoon, making sure that everyone was keeping up. Without warning, the sound of Burp guns filled the air. It was only when Wilson heard Sykes yell: 'Take cover!' that it dawned on him what was happening. He flung himself into the monsoon ditch. He was only just in time. Bullets thudded into the bank directly above him. For several seconds he kept his head pressed against the side of the ditch, listening to more bullets passing overhead. Not far away, he heard the cries of a wounded man. By the time he recovered himself sufficiently to peer over the top of the ditch, most of 12 Platoon were returning the fire.

The North Korean infiltrators were behind a bund running parallel to the road, two paddy fields in from the road. Wilson was still sheltering in the monsoon ditch when some of his men came dashing towards him. McCleod was at their head, his jikkay frame rearing about on his back.

'Come on,' yelled McCleod. 'We'll outflank them. The others will cover us.'

Things were happening so swiftly that Wilson had no option but to follow. He saw McCleod jettison his jikkay frame as they continued along the ditch. Before long, they drew level with a bund which ran at right angles to the road, into the paddy fields. The rest of the platoon were still engaged in a small-arms exchange with the North Koreans and across the road the flashes of the Burp guns were quite clear.

'Cross the road in threes,' commanded McCleod. 'Then along that bund until we're opposite the bastards.'

Without hesitation three men sprinted across the road. Then another three. Wilson went with the last group. Once they were across, McCleod led the way behind the bund. They were soon level with the North Koreans, having outflanked them in a minute or two. McCleod and Wilson peered over the bund. There were twelve of the enemy. They were still firing, but increasingly pinned down by the accuracy of 12 Platoon's fire.

'Take them quickly, lads,' ordered McCleod. Wilson saw his men checking their weapons and fixing bayonets. 'Straight into the charge, lads . . . go!'

As one man they leapt over the bund, down into the frozen paddy field, and charged straight at the enemy. They were firing from the hip, shouting for all they were worth. The North Koreans were caught in two streams of fire. They panicked. They jumped up and ran. Only one of them fired at the assault group, but his bullets went high as his body jerked under the impact of bullets.

The men of 12 Platoon stopped firing as soon as they saw the assault group going into their charge. Wilson and his men kept blazing away until they had run right through the enemy position. Then they flung themselves to the ground, ready to cope with any further trouble. When nothing more happened, Wilson and McCleod got up. They approached the enemy bodies warily, looking for signs of life. When convinced they were all dead, they relaxed. They waved to the rest of the platoon and those on the road gave them a loud cheer.

Wilson was the last to get back to the road. As he saw Sergeant Sykes approaching, he said: 'Twelve of them . . . all dead—'

'Twelve?' laughed Sykes. 'McCleod just said there were twenty-five.'

'Well he's a bloody liar. There were twelve.'

'Not any more, sir. I've just been on the blower and told the major there were twenty-five. But don't worry. Main thing is that we've only had one wounded. Phillips. The major is coming back to collect him.'

Wilson hurried over to Phillips. His legs were covered in blood. His trouser legs had been slit up the seams and one of his mates was applying field dressings. Major Middleton soon came speeding up in his jeep. Wilson went over to him. 'Twenty-five of them?' queried Middleton, clearly not convinced. He knew that lying meant nothing to 12 Platoon. 'You sure?'

'Quite sure, sir,' lied Wilson.

'Aye, sir,' chipped in McCleod. 'Mr Wilson is quite correct.' Middleton and Wilson turned, surprised to see McCleod standing behind them. 'To be honest, sir,' added McCleod, 'I made it twenty-six. But the odd Gook willna make any difference.'

Middleton ignored McCleod. 'Sounds like a copy-book attack.'

'Aye, sir,' agreed McCleod, 'Mr Wilson moved with remarkable speed and decisiveness.'

Middleton swivelled round angrily. 'Bugger off, McCleod! This has nothing to do with you. Get back to your section.'

McCleod slunk off, smiling to himself as he lit another cigarette.

'We'll soon have Phillips sorted out,' continued Middleton. 'It could be that we're already cut off. Anyhow, get your platoon ready to move off. We could be in for a long haul. It's the usual old story, I'm afraid. . . . The PBI.'

'Right, sir.'

'Do you know what that means?'

'The PBI? The poor bloody infantry. That's the oldest joke in the book, sir.'

Middleton drove off in his jeep, muttering: 'Cocky young bastard.'

They kept marching all day. Their only rests came when other companies were ambushed. Apart from that, they kept trudging forward, heads lowered into their greatcoat collars, backs covered by scales of frozen snow. Inevitably, they became tired and hungry. Men began to grumble, cursing the army for the way they were being treated. Wilson was so sensitive to this that he took frequent trips along the length of his platoon to encourage his men, but he only succeeded in antagonizing them further.

Then, much to everyone's surprise, they came across a ration truck. It was parked around a sharp bend in the road, waiting for them. The food and drink worked wonders on their morale. Chirpy conversation flourished and there was general banter about the foul-up of the retreat. A battalion cook serving food out of the back of the truck was full of himself. He was so relieved to have survived some real action the night before that he never stopped describing how they'd been attacked from the rear by North Korean infiltrators, and how the MT Section, with all their brand new American trucks, had been set alight and the adjutant shot dead.

No one in 12 Platoon was impressed. If anyone had to get shot, it struck them that the adjutant was a good one to start with. The cook wasn't deterred by their indifference. 'Well, did you hear about the lads this morning who wiped out twenty-five Gooks?'

'That was us, you git,' responded Fogarty. 'But there were far more than that . . . thirty or forty at least.'

'Really? The bastards at battalion never give you full credit, do they?'

'What do mean? You are one of the bastards from battalion.'

Sykes was sitting on the opposite side of the road from Wilson. He smiled across, as though to say, 'There you are. I told you so'.

Wilson didn't respond. He was watching Fogarty. The man never stopped shouting his mouth off. He had a ripe, Cockney accent and he sneered at everything. Whatever was said, he either topped it with an outrageous boast or cut it down with biting sarcasm. Wilson found him physically repulsive, in some ways reminiscent of George Saville. The most off-putting thing about him was his habit of going up behind others, grabbing them around the waist, and then simulating sex, calling out: ' 'Ello, darlin'. 'Ow about a length?'

Fogarty was still holding forth about the morning's ambush. 'I got ten myself. Surprise, my son. That was the secret of our success. Surprise!'

As he spoke, Fogarty returned to the back of the truck for more tea. When the cook was slow to serve him, he shouted: 'Come on, you skiving bastard. Get a move on. The Chinks could appear down the road at any moment.'

The cook called across to Sykes. 'That true, Sarge?'

'Bloody right it is.'

As though acting on a prompt, Sykes replaced his mess tin in his haversack. Then he ordered everyone back on to the road, ready to move off. The cook bustled about in the back of the truck. As far as he was concerned, Sykes's order hadn't come a moment too soon. He secured his tea urn and yelled to the driver: 'Start her up! We're off.'

When the driver tried to start the engine all he got was a feeble groan.

'Ready to move off,' shouted Sykes.

'Hey, Sarge,' yelled the cook. 'The battery is frozen up. Give us a shove.'

'Shove it your bloody self,' advised Fogarty. 'You ride in it, you shove it.'

Sykes ordered several men to give the truck a push, but however fast they pushed it, when the driver let the clutch out, it slithered to a halt. With each failure there were fresh jeers from Fogarty, backed up by Chadwick and Gaunt. They never stopped scoffing.

Wilson decided things were out of hand. He ordered the entire platoon to give the truck a push. They got up a really good turn of speed but instead of the engine firing, the truck went into another skid, with the front wheels slithering into the monsoon ditch. There were more jeers, and Fogarty appointed himself as the authority on how to retrieve the situation.

Wilson had had enough. 'Everyone back into their sections,' he ordered. 'Sergeant Sykes, get the men ready to move off.'

The driver stuck his head out of his cab. 'What about my truck?'

'Leave it.'

Everyone stared at Wilson in amazement. They all knew that given time they could get the truck started. As the driver jumped out of his truck, ready for a confrontation, Fogarty chipped in again. 'Quite right, Mr Wilson. You tell the silly sod. High time someone got a grip of these sods from battalion.'

'Get your spare can of petrol out,' ordered Wilson.

'Burn my truck? You must be mad. All it needs is a bloody good push.'

The rest of the platoon watched with amusement. They had often seen young officers get themselves into awkward situations, but whereas most of them backed off, Wilson clearly had no intention of changing his mind. As the driver continued to protest, Sykes detailed men to give the truck another push; but Wilson would have none of it. 'What do you think you're doing, Sergeant? Get those men back where they were. When I decide on something, I do it.'

'Right, sir. I'll bear that in mind.'

Whilst Sykes got the platoon on the move, the driver splashed petrol over the truck. Then he joined Wilson and Sykes thirty yards down the road. Wilson removed a grenade from his belt. He pulled the pin out and threw it as hard as he could. It went straight through the windscreen. The truck went up like a bomb, an instant inferno. Then 12 Platoon, led by Fogarty, gave a great cheer and marched off in high spirits.

Colonel Wainwright was delighted with their day's march. They would have done even better if it had not been for several ambushes, but even they brought compensations. They had been dealt with in an exemplary manner, especially the biggest of them, which 12 Platoon had swept aside. The colonel realized, of course, that in many ways they were fortunate. Unlike other retreats he'd known, they hadn't been harassed from the air, or by artillery. Not that the latter was likely to hold off for much longer. Divisional intelligence had concluded that the slowness of the Chinese to follow up their massive breakthrough was due to bringing their artillery forward. At a hastily convened orders group, Colonel Wainwright told his company commanders that whilst the Chinese attack had relied upon surprise, future attacks were expected to rely on close artillery support. He smiled sourly when Middleton said: 'Hopefully, their artillery will be less successful than their surprise.'

Middleton soon regretted his little witticism. The colonel retaliated by giving Dog Company the worst job in the next phase of the retreat. At dusk, they were to take up a defensive position in three villages along the MSR with Able, Baker and Charlie Companies deployed in the surrounding hills to protect their flanks. The three villages to be occupied were each separated by about half a mile and the reasoning behind the plan was to re-establish contact with the Chinese and then to resist their advance with sufficient determination to give the impression of a major stand. As usual, Middleton's greatest concern was the handing out of the dirty work. The platoon in the first village was going to take the brunt of the attack, especially since it was expected to do considerably more than engage and withdraw. Once it had been forced out of the village it was to join forces with the platoon in the next village and help to defend that as well, then fall back to the third village for a full company defence.

When Dog Company got within two miles of the first village Middleton ordered a rest. He found a suitable spot to hold an orders group by the remains of a thatched barn. He pulled his jeep into the shelter of a wall and got Turner and Jordan to lay out ground sheets between the jeep and a wall so that the platoon commanders had a sheltered spot in which to sit.

Edwin Dolby of 11 Platoon was the first to arrive. He was tall and thin, all angles and protruding bones, with rimless glasses. He flopped down on a ground sheet and complained to Turner and Jordan about his feet. They showed no interest. Sergeant Evans of 10 Platoon arrived shortly afterwards with CSM Randle, and Wilson brought up the rear. Middleton made no attempt to introduce Wilson to the others.

'Where is Mr Barclay?' Wilson asked generally.

Middleton looked up. 'Barclay? Haven't you heard? He was killed.'

The blood drained from Wilson's face. He stared at Middleton in dismay. It just didn't seem possible. All day, Wilson had been looking forward to swapping yarns with Barclay about the attack, yet all the time he was dead.

'Was his body recovered, sir?'

'I'm afraid not. Officially, he's listed as missing.'

Wilson knew that they were all watching him. He tried to remain impassive but he couldn't stop himself from swallowing hard several times.

'Had you known him long?' asked Middleton.

'Since prep school, sir.'

'Oh, I am sorry. But I'm afraid these things do happen.'

'Yes, sir.' Wilson remained calm but he was thinking, *my God, that's it! Middleton says, 'These things do happen' and that's the end of it?*

'We'll have a statement about casualties later,' said Middleton. 'In the meantime, we'd better press on.'

'Don't forget the ration truck, sir,' prompted Corporal Turner.

'Oh yes! The ration truck. It seems battalion's ration truck has mysteriously disappeared. Anyone know anything about it?'

Wilson was so engrossed in his thoughts about Barclay that Middleton's question escaped him.

'No one know anything about the ration truck?'

'The ration truck, sir?' asked Wilson, coming to at the last second.

'Yes. Know anything about it?'

'Yes, sir. I destroyed it.'

There was a burst of laughter in which Middleton did not join.

'Destroyed it, Wilson?'

'Yes, sir. Blew it up.'

There was more laughter. 'Blew it up? Why, for Christ's sake?'

'It was hopelessly stuck, but it won't be of any use to the Chinese.'

'Bugger the Chinese. What about us?'

'Well it was well and truly stuck, sir. The battery was frozen solid—'

'Then why didn't you get in touch with me?'

'There was no point. You couldn't have done anything about it.'

'But that's the battalion's last truck.'

'Well, I can't help that, sir. It was completely stuck.'

'I doubt if the colonel will see it like that, Wilson. You don't have the authority to go around blowing up War Department property.'

'What shall I tell battalion, sir?' asked Corporal Turner.

'That it's been blown up . . . what else?'

'I just wondered if you would like to use a euphemism? If the colonel hears the term "blown up" he'll blow up as well. And what about the driver and the cook? Were they blown up as well? Or did they escape this holocaust?'

Dolby and Evans laughed. Middleton looked anxiously towards Wilson. 'They're all right, aren't they?'

'Of course, sir. They're with my platoon.'

'Good. Then send them back to battalion right away.'

'They'll get a real heroes welcome,' observed Turner.

Middleton continued with the orders group, explaining his plan for the defence of the three villages. Deliberately, he didn't tell them that a fresh ROK unit was standing by to relieve them, nor that there was a half-promise of American transport being laid on to evacuate them. The colonel had stressed that neither was guaranteed, so Middleton judged it best not raise false hopes.

As Middleton spoke his eyes flickered around the platoon commanders. He didn't know what Wilson was thinking, but Dolby and Evans were an open book, praying they wouldn't get the first village. 'So that's the plan. The order of march will stay put until a mile before the village. Then 12 Platoon will pass through 10 and 11 Platoons, and 11 Platoon will pass through 10 Platoon. . . .'

'Excuse me, sir. . . .' Everyone looked at Wilson. Middleton was obviously irritated. 'Sorry to interrupt,' continued Wilson. 'But wouldn't it be easier if we left the order of march unchanged? My platoon could take the first village and it would save a lot of time and confusion—' Wilson became aware of everyone staring at him. 'I'm sorry, sir—'

'No need to apologize,' laughed Middleton. 'Everyone is free to volunteer. Stay as you are by all means. That means 12 Platoon in the first village, 11 Platoon in the second, and the 10 Platoon in the third. But I would emphasize that all villages are to be defended stoutly. And each retiring platoon must stand and fight at the next village. Understood? Good. Then let's get moving.'

CHAPTER FOUR

There was still an hour's daylight when 12 Platoon reached the first village. Wilson posted his men in defensive positions and then did a thorough recce with Sykes. It wasn't until they reached a large house at the end of the village that they came across the villagers. They were huddled together on the wide verandah of the headman's house. They were mostly women and children, with just a sprinkling of old men. In the centre, swaying gently to and fro in a rocking chair, was the village elder. He had a wispy beard, white robes, and a comical little top hat secured by a chin strap.

The villagers were sullen and anxious. For several weeks they had escaped the ravages of war, but all day long they had watched with a feeling of impending doom as the defeated UN Forces poured back through the village. They were in the combat zone again and they knew that whoever appeared next, their only hope of survival was to co-operate. From the verandah they watched every move of Sykes and Wilson.

'Best to take over the headman's house, sir,' said Sykes as they completed their recce. 'We can take it in turns to come down to keep warm and get a hot meal off the locals. But we'd better make sure they're friendly. I'll get Fogarty. He speaks the lingo. It comes from chatting up all the women – Fogarty!'

'Sarge?' Fogarty was close at hand, expecting the call. As he went forward, so did the rest of his section. They clustered around the raised verandah and peered at the Koreans through the wooden slats. Fogarty negotiating with the Koreans was always good for a laugh. Wilson, Sykes and Fogarty went up the steps of the verandah, with Fogarty ogling the young women.

'Plenty of crumpet, Sarge!' One of the elderly Korean women suddenly grabbed Wilson's sleeve, recognizing him as the officer. She pleaded with him hysterically. 'Blimey, sir!' exclaimed Fogarty. 'Don't fancy yours much.'

Sykes took hold of the woman and guided her back to the others. 'Get to work on the old man, Fogarty. Get a decent meal out of them.'

For the next fifteen minutes Fogarty went through a ritual, persuading the Koreans to co-operate, using his own brand of 'Gook talk', a strange mixture of international expressions, English slang and obscenities, mixed with Korean words. Halfway through it all, Sykes nudged Wilson. 'I can't stand any more of this, sir. You hang on here. I'll go and take a look around the hills.'

Fogarty's negotiations ended with deep bows all round and the headman thrusting open the doors of the house in a gesture of hospitality. Wilson went inside and found it spacious and very simple. There was a central living room with bedrooms at each end. Extended along the back of the house was a lean-to shelter crowded with goats. They stank appallingly. At the far end of the living room was a primitive cooking range with a metal chimney. Several women were already bustling about, making initial preparations for the meal.

When Wilson returned outside he looked up into the surrounding hills and saw Sykes striding around. He decided to join him. 'It's a good defensive position, sir,' said Sykes. We'll keep clear of the village and have everyone in the hills, split evenly each side. The Chinks will come straight down the valley, with patrols ahead of them in these hills. So we'll drive them back down into the valley. That will be our killing ground. And once we've got them down there, the Gunners can bring down a stonk. Then scarper. But we'll put a Bren group at the far end of the village to stop the Chinks charging straight through. McCleod's the man for that. He can hold them for a time and then put up a Very light for everyone to scarper and RV behind the village.'

Wilson agreed to Sykes's suggestions and when they got back to the village he established his HQ in one of the bedrooms. He reported back to company HQ over the 88 set that they had settled in and then made arrangements for the Gunners to stand by with a stonk across the entrance of the village using the code word 'Bulldozer'. Next, he called an orders group. It was his first and he was delighted with how it went. When his section commanders dispersed, they led their men into the hills to prepare their positions.

Darkness closed in. Stand-to was called. As usual, their high position meant they took the full blast of the wind and after only a few minutes Wilson heard men shuffling about, trying to keep warm. When the order came over the 88 set from Middleton to stand down, Wilson told his batman, Shaw: 'I'm going to the headman's house. Contact Sergeant Sykes and tell him to send down the first batch of men for their meal in about a quarter of an hour.'

Wilson ran down the hill and when he got near the headman's house he heard laughter. He strode up the steps of the verandah and barged in. Several Korean girls were clustered around the cooking range and in the middle of them, holding court and the source of the merriment, were Fogarty, Chadwick, and Gaunt. 'What are you three doing here?' demanded Wilson.

'Helping to prepare the meal, sir,' replied Fogarty. 'We always do.'

Wilson accepted the explanation. Fogarty turned on the girls in mock anger. 'Hubba hubba, girls! Tocksan sake for officer-san.'

The girls giggled uproariously, well and truly under Fogarty's spell. One of them hurried forward, offering Wilson some sake in a small earthenware bowl. She bowed as she handed it to him and he waited until she looked up again before accepting it. She was very pretty with large, brown eyes. When she realized he was studying her, she smiled sweetly.

'Here, watch it, sir!' cried Fogarty. 'She's spoken for. But if you fancy any of the others, just let me know. I'll fix you up, no trouble.'

The doors of the house suddenly burst open and the first batch of men streamed in. Fogarty immediately took control. 'Keep the noise down, you ignorant twits. This is a respectable house. And good grub. So just behave.'

McCleod shuffled to the front to inspect the cooking. Then he scrutinized the young girls surrounding Fogarty. They didn't meet with his approval. 'You're just lusting after these heathen whores, you Sassenach bastard.'

'Just keep a civil tongue in your head, Smokey. Otherwise you won't get any. It's everyone's favourite – goat stew! And out here they make stew the same way as the Arabs do. They put the bloody lot in. So if you happen to see an eyeball staring up at you, Smokey, I don't want any of your Scottish moaning. Just swallow it down like a good 'un.'

'Laddie,' said McCleod in a cold, measured tone, 'if I get anything that remotely resembles an eyeball I'll stick it straight up your Sassenach arse. Then you'll see the Chinks as clear as day as you run for your miserable life.'

Wilson stood back and watched as men were served with sake by the Korean girls. They flirted with them outrageously and the voice of Fogarty was never silent, warning them to behave themselves and making it clear which of the girls had already been earmarked by himself and his mates. The sake soon had an inevitable effect. It gave them a glow of general well-being. They relaxed. To be warm again was fantastic. Conversations flowed and laughter rang out. To start with, Wilson stood alone, but before long Corporal Higgins joined him and when Wilson explained the trouble he was expecting over the destruction of the ration truck, others joined them, anxious to hear the details. There was nothing 12 Platoon liked better than adding to their notoriety. Soon, there was a happy, chattering, group around Wilson. Men competed with each other to tell him about their experiences in Korea. Yarns about the hard cases abounded. To start with they concentrated on their sexual exploits, but then they went on to McCleod and his enthusiasm for looting. They told Wilson about the liberation of Pynongyang and how McCleod had prowled the city, searching for things of value, eventually coming up with what he claimed was a genuine Ming vase which was now wrapped in cotton wool and stored at the bottom of his kitbag. Inevitably, their prize story was about the highland dancing and how it had led to the bitter feud between McCleod and Fogarty. Whilst they talked, they encouraged the Korean girls to keep topping up Wilson's earthenware cup and he soon felt his head spinning. He suddenly warmed to these men. He became aware of an intense feeling of comradeship. This was what he had hoped for. To serve in a platoon where the men were truly 'his' men: men with whom he shared hardships and triumphs; men with whom he would be proud to serve and even shed blood.

'Stew up!' shouted Fogarty. 'Come and get it.'

Men rushed forward, seeking an early place in the queue. Once they'd been served, Wilson collected his. It had a very dubious look about it, but there was no eyeball staring up at him. After a time, Fogarty shouted: 'Second helpings! Come on, Mr Wilson! You're first this time.' As Wilson moved forward Fogarty turned to the girls and said: 'Mr Wilson number one officer-san. Number one tocksan jig-a-jigger!'

The girl shrieked with laughter and flung flirtatious glances in Wilson's direction, eyeing his powerful frame with approval. As Wilson returned to the centre of the room, McCleod joined him. 'He's no right to talk like that about you, sir. He's nothing but an animal. Out to ravish these young lassies.'

Wilson refused to be drawn. 'Are you clear about your role tonight?'

'Aye, sir. You dinna have to worry about Jock McCleod.'

As McCleod spoke, Wilson was nibbling tentatively at his stew. He was concentrating on the more wholesome-looking pieces of meat. At length he came across a large lump boasting squiggly veins. He prodded it tentatively, scrutinizing it. Then he cut it in half, which did nothing to allay his suspicions. Nor was McCleod reassured. He was watching Wilson's progress more closely than Wilson himself. When Wilson forked the lump out of his mess tin, about to eat it, McCleod suddenly grabbed his arm and exclaimed: 'By Christ! A bollock!'

Wilson dropped the meat back into the mess tin with alarm.

'FOGARTY!'

McCleod shouted so loudly that everything came to a standstill. Everyone stared at the Scotsman. 'FOGARTY! You Sassenach bastard! You've given Mr Wilson one of yon billy goat's bollocks—'

'And bollocks to you, Haggis—'

The men roared with laughter.

'Congratulations, sir,' continued Fogarty, as chirpy as ever. 'The most delicious part of the animal. Give you years of virility. As for you, Haggis, don't worry. They come in pairs. You can have the other one.'

Without reference to Wilson, McCleod plunged his hand into the mess tin and grabbed one half of the of offending testicle. Then he leapt forward, sweeping men aside. The Korean girls screamed as he ploughed through them. There was a murderous gleam in his eyes, as though the final reckoning had come. Fogarty tried to edge away, sheltering behind two girls, but McCleod was too quick for him. He grabbed him by the throat like a terrier killing a rat. Fogarty was no match for McCleod and the Scotsman's vice-like grip on his throat made him gasp for air.

'Open up wider, you Cockney bastard,' yelled McLeod.

As Fogarty's mouth fell further open, McCleod thrust the meat into it. Finally, he used his free hand to clamp Fogarty's jaw shut and held it tight until the Londoner swallowed. Only then did he release his grip, shoving Fogarty to one side with contempt, making him sprawl at the feet of the Korean girls, coughing and spluttering, fighting for breath.

'Just see what that does for your virility, you Cockney runt!'

The men cheered with delight, as did Wilson. As Fogarty stood up, still clutching his throat, McCleod stalked back down the room, a hero.

Half an hour later Sykes and his men went down for their meal. Wilson returned to platoon HQ and lay on the frozen earth beside Shaw. The outline of the surrounding hills was clear, but the valley below was as black as soot. The more he peered into it, the more his eyes ached and he suddenly became conscious of acute tiredness. His mind began to wander and he thought about the girls in the headman's house. Some were really attractive. He could have had one of them. Fogarty had offered to organize it for him. He just had to say the word. Yet he knew he never would and he wondered how desperate he would have to become before he summoned up enough courage to have a woman.

On the hour, Wilson told Shaw to do a routine wireless check with company HQ. Then he went around the platoon. His final check was on McCleod's Bren group. He had only gone a few yards past the headman's house when he was challenged. He answered and moved towards the men. 'There should be three of you here,' he said. 'Where's McCleod?' 'Over at the headman's house. We take it in turns to shelter in the lean-to.'

Wilson doubled back to the headman's house. The smell of the goats was as strong as ever and after he'd followed the line of the lean-to for a few yards he saw a speck of red light, a burning cigarette.

'McCleod! What are you doing in there?'

'I'm no skiving, sir. Just keeping warm.'

'Well get back to your position with the others.'

'There's something you should see, sir . . . that bastard Fogarty.'

Wilson pushed his way through the goats. As he got to the wall of the house he could see several chinks of light coming from cracks where the wood cladding took over from the mud walls. McCleod guided Wilson to the planks and Wilson peered through a crack. It was like looking into the very lowest type of brothel. He couldn't have imagined a more degrading scene.

Sykes was lying on his back on a bedding roll with a naked girl straddled across him in a sitting position, moaning with pleasure as she rode him. Fogarty was standing at the far side of the room. He had his back to Wilson, his trousers crumpled around his ankles, exposing his stubby legs and chunky backside. His arms were extended in front of him, resting against the wall, and pinned between his arms was the girl he'd been flirting with all evening. She was sitting on a chest of drawers and although Wilson couldn't see much of her, she was obviously naked. He could see her face over Fogarty's shoulder. She was smiling and giggling as she teased him, denying him immediate entry.

Wilson's initial reaction was one of revulsion, but this soon turned to fascination. His eyes flickered between Sykes and Fogarty, hardly knowing where to look for fear of missing an intimate detail. Fogarty's girl was now perched on the very edge of the chest of drawers, her legs wrapped around him, her ankles locked one over the other. Fogarty's buttocks were contracting and then relaxing as he pumped away with animal-like abandon. She was going with him, almost slipping from her perch in her anxiety for more of him inside her. Her round eyes were wide open and the rest of her face was distorted by a frown of endeavour. Then her frown lifted and her expression burst free, her teeth gleaming as her mouth fell open. As her orgasm approached she cried out, gripping Fogarty more urgently than ever, desperate now she was on the threshold that those magical moments should not escape her. Then she froze, her legs locked around him. She let out a great cry of joy and relief and a look of utter disbelief engulfed her. The scene was etched on Wilson's mind for ever. It was destined to haunt him.

The first incoming shells landed on the surrounding hills. Their blast shook the flimsy house. Wilson was so engrossed in watching Sykes and Fogarty that he only became fully aware of what was happening when they literally tossed their girls aside. Sykes's girl landed on the floor with an undignified bump and Fogarty's girl was sucked off the chest of drawers and ended up on her knees, in front of him. For an absurd moment they all stumbled about. Sykes groped around for his clothes. Fogarty reached down for his trousers. At his feet his girl was so voracious for more of him that she grabbed his swollen and glistening member, only for it to slip through her fingers like a tablet of wet soap. She grabbed it again and was still grappling with it when Wilson felt McCleod pulling at his shoulder. 'Quick, sir! We must away.'

More Chinese shells crashed down on the hills. Wilson rushed round to the front of the house. The men were vaulting over the verandah balustrade and sprinting towards their section positions. Sykes and Fogarty were the last to emerge. Sykes hesitated in the doorway, shouting back at the Koreans, urging them to flee into the hills. As he turned away he saw Wilson. 'What are you doing here? There will be thousands following this up.'

'I know—' Wilson was about to confront Sykes with what he had seen, but the words died on his lips. Sykes was already sprinting towards his sections. Wilson lost no time in doing the same. When he was halfway up the hill the range of the shells shifted. They passed over 12 Platoon and homed in on the village. Wilson saw several houses take direct hits, their thatched roofs bursting into flames. He saw the villagers running off in panic, scattering in all directions, screaming hysterically. Then the headman's house took a direct hit. The roof caved in, only to be blown straight out again, flaming thatch leaping into the air and fanning out like an extravagant fireworks display.

When Wilson reached platoon HQ the shelling stopped. Everything went quiet except for the crackling of the burning village and the cries and moans of the villagers. Wilson waited for the first signs of the Chinese. Within minutes there were bugle calls and then one of his men at the top of the hill yelled: 'Here they come!' As the Chinese appeared over the crest of the hill, Wilson's men fired long bursts, stopping the Chinese in their tracks. Those who weren't shot fled into the valley. It was just as Sykes had predicted. A flare went up from their two-inch mortar and Wilson saw exactly the same thing happening on Sykes's side of the valley. The Chinese were forming a solid mass on the floor of the valley. Then they began to surge forward towards the village.

Wilson shouted to Shaw to call for 'Bulldozer'. Then he urged his men to direct their full firepower into the valley. Very soon the MSR and the surrounding paddy fields were scattered with corpses. Those who survived kept going towards the village, closing in fast. Wilson began to despair of the artillery stonk arriving in time. Seconds later, McCleod's Bren group opened up, a sure sign that the Chinese were threatening to sweep through the village.

Then 'Bulldozer' screamed in, smack on target.

It was over very quickly. For a little over two minutes it was as though they were sitting on the edge of an erupting volcano. When the shelling stopped and the smoke and flying debris cleared there were no signs of the Chinese. There was a long, eerie, silence. Then McCleod's Bren group opened up again, using single shots as Chinese survivors broke for cover. No flare went up from McCleod. The plan had worked perfectly.

'Best to bug out now, sir,' said Shaw.

Wilson took his advice. It took a while to organize the withdrawal. Men saw little need for urgency. By the time they had rendezvoused with Sykes's men on the MSR and were picking their way through the Chinese dead more bugle calls sounded. Very soon, a second wave of Chinese appeared out of the darkness; 12 Platoon came under small-arms fire and they dashed forward, seeking cover in the ruined houses. Several men were hit. Wilson saw Shaw go down, his back riddled by bullets. He stopped to help him, but he was already dead. Wilson left him and rejoined the others in their flight.

He soon found himself back at the headman's house. The verandah had been flattened. Splintered planks were sticking up at odd angles and there was a sickly smell of burnt flesh. The only sign of life was a demented goat darting about, butting anything that was left standing. Flames were licking about the shell of the house and in their light Wilson saw several villagers lying under the debris. They were all dead. He made his way to the far bedroom. The girls Sykes and Fogarty had cast off were still there, both dead.

When Wilson returned outside, Sykes, Denzil, Gaunt, and McCleod's Bren group were behind the remains of the front wall of the house. They were watching the Chinese as they entered the village. They waited until a large group were in the open and then cut them down with a hail of bullets. For a time they had great success, but the Chinese knew the principle of fire and movement and whilst some of them brought their Burp guns to bear on the house, others dashed forward, one group leap-frogging another. From nearby houses, other 12 Platoon men broke from cover and made a run for it, heading for the second village. For a time, Wilson's group covered them. Then Sykes yelled: 'They're away. Get ready to run!'

Bullets raked across the rubble in front of them. A chorus of ricochets screamed out and splinters of wood flew like spears. Sykes turned to those beside him and shouted: 'Go!' Sykes and Wilson fired two more bursts and then followed them. In the race back along the MSR, Wilson surged ahead of the others and was the first to reach the second village. 'Don't shoot!' he yelled out in warning to 11 Platoon. Then he watched as his platoon ran and stumbled past. Some were wounded, several in a bad way. Sykes was last in.

'RV at the end of the village,' ordered Wilson. 'I'll join you there.'

Sykes acknowledge the order and hurried on. Wilson went in search of Dolby. He found him in the last house with his sergeant and several others. Dolby was pacing about the room. 'I suppose there were thousands of the bastards? Why we can't just bug out, I'll never understand.'

'Well, I wouldn't stay in the houses,' advised Wilson. 'They'll shell hell out of them. Just like they did in the first village. Sergeant Sykes reckons—'

'Sykes!' exclaimed Dolby. 'That bastard has just buggered off—'

'I told him to RV at the end of the village.'

'Well, this is the end of the village and he's buggered off.'

Wilson ran out into the night. He soon spotted Sykes. He had regrouped the platoon on the lower slopes of a hillock on their left. Wilson hurried over to them and confronted Sykes. 'I told you to RV at the end of the village.'

'If we stay with that idiot Dolby we'll all get killed.'

'Rubbish! Get ready to move back to help them.'

'We can't, sir,' protested Sykes. 'I've just checked our wounded. We've got so many we need all the men to help them back.'

The argument got no further. Shells began to fall on the village and Sykes's opinion was so clearly vindicated that he automatically took control. 'We'll put two men in charge of each of the wounded to help them back. The rest of you go up on the hill and give covering fire as 11 Platoon pull out.'

Wilson was left with eight men, including two Bren groups. One of them was McCleod's. He led them up the hill, keeping at right angles to the end of the village. He soon found an ideal spot among large boulders. He decided to contact Dolby and Middleton to let them know of his new position, but to his dismay he discovered he'd again left his wireless on his dead batman. He lay down and watched the shelling as it continued to fall on the village. When it eventually petered out there was urgent shouting from 11 Platoon. The plainest cry of all was: 'Bug out!' As the survivors broke from the cover of the village, so came the sound of Burp guns. Wilson watched their muzzle-flashes advancing into the northern end of the village. Occasionally, Stens and Brens replied, but without conviction – 11 Platoon were deserting the village as fast as they could. Wilson kept willing them on, desperate that they should get well forward of his line of fire before the Chinese closed in on them. Gradually, they got clear. Behind them the village was teeming with Chinese.

'Fire!' yelled Wilson.

Results were immediate and spectacular. The Chinese reacted like startled rabbits, sprinting hither and thither, darting about in blind terror as they searched for cover. The pursuit of 11 Platoon stopped dead and it was some time before the Chinese returned Wilson's fire; even then it was no more than a gesture. They were pinned down for a long time and whenever one of them broke cover he was either shot or sent scurrying back.

Wilson began to worry about his next move. He knew his success wouldn't last indefinitely. The Chinese would soon call up reserves. Even as he lay there, debating the issue, he heard shouts and more bugle calls. Then, unexpectedly, the American gunners gave the village a vicious pounding. For ten minutes shells plunged into the village. When the shells stopped there was the usual hiatus, the smell of cordite hanging like a wet blanket. For perhaps another ten minutes very little happened, just the 'popping' sound of flares igniting in the sky. Then came a rumbling sound that rapidly became louder. Soon it was like a stampede and literally hundreds of Chinese appeared at the far end of the village. Wilson ordered everyone to get ready to move. They slipped away quietly and rejoined the MSR two hundred yards south of the village. They made good progress and just as Wilson thought they were out of danger they came across two wounded men from 11 Platoon. They'd been abandoned in the monsoon ditch. Wilson said: 'We'll carry them back. I'll take one. Denzil, you take the other.'

Wilson heaved one man on to his shoulders in a fireman's lift position and once Denzil had done likewise they set off with their burdens whilst the others hurried on ahead. Within fifty yards Denzil was staggering around in exhaustion and Wilson soon found he was doing the same. Then, at last, he heard McCleod yell, 'Stretcher bearers!' and before long McCleod came back with medics. As the wounded were eased onto the stretchers, Wilson, Denzil and McCleod went on to the village. They contacted a standing patrol and a corporal shouted: 'They're all waiting on the far side of the village.'

It wasn't until a quarter of a mile beyond the village that they came across the rest of the company. Some were standing around on the side of the road but most of them were sheltering in the monsoon ditches. As Wilson passed through them they stared at him with hostility. Beyond them was a line of American troop-carrying vehicles. By the first of these massive trucks was Middleton's jeep. The major and several others were clustered around it. Among them was Captain Southern, the company second-in-command who Wilson hadn't met before. Sykes was also there, talking to Corporal Turner.

Wilson flopped against the side of the jeep, fighting for breath. 'Thank God you're back,' said Middleton. 'Where the hell have you been?'

'We murdered them, sir,' exclaimed Wilson, his state of shock clear to all the others. 'Hundreds of them . . . we just shot them down . . . and the shelling . . . perfect, sir . . . couldn't have been better—'

Wilson looked around, mortified to see that everyone was indifferent to what he was saying. No one even said, 'Well done!' Sykes and Turner were regarding him in disgust and Middleton had the look of a man on the verge of losing his temper. 'Where the hell are those bloody stretcher bearers?' he demanded. He paced about and then turned on Wilson. 'You are supposed to have brought back two wounded men?'

'We did! They're coming.'

'Then where are they?' Middleton didn't wait for an answer. He looked at his watch and muttered: 'Come on! Come on, for God's sake, come on!'

'What exactly is happening, sir?' asked Wilson.

'We're bugging out. These trucks have been laid on for us. And ROK reinforcements are on the way to relieve us. We've been trying to call you back in for over an hour. Why didn't your batman answer?'

'He's dead, sir.'

'Then where the hell is your 88 set?'

'Still on him. We were pulling back—'

'Never leave your 88 set behind. I told you that before. And that shelling was laid on to cover your withdrawal. Surely you realized that?' Middleton broke off. Further down the road there was a lot of shouting and he hurried off to see what was happening. 'Here they come,' he called back. 'Put the wounded in the first truck and get moving. Everyone aboard.'

The men of Dog Company swarmed out of the monsoon ditches and into the trucks. Middleton said to Wilson: 'You're in the leading truck. The driver knows the form. Don't stop until we reach the field hospital.'

Wilson hurried to the rear of the leading truck and made sure his men were all aboard, with the wounded as comfortable as possible. Once again, he was conscious of open hostility. At the back of the truck an infantile argument was raging between McCleod and Fogarty.

'You great Scottish git! Why didn't you bug out like everyone else?'

'Because I'm no a bloody coward.'

'No, just a bleeding pillock.'

'I'll no just turn and run like you, Fogarty.'

'You were supposed to turn and run, you half-witted Haggis. We're in retreat. That means going bloody backwards . . . it's called tactics—'

'I know your tactics. A quick screw and then run for your miserable life.'

Further down the road there were frantic cries of, 'Get moving!'

Wilson clambered into the cab. The truck jerked forward. He was surrounded by noise, but heard nothing. He was totally spent. Behind his closed eyes was a kaleidoscope of vivid images: exploding shells, Shaw's body, the butchered Korean girls, and Chinese corpses littering the valley. The incredible thing was that he had survived, and whatever others might think, he'd done well. He could be proud of his first serious action. His body relaxed and contentment flowed through him. Then the images of war were replaced by the face of Fogarty's girl as he made love to her. He saw again the supreme joy and gratification as she embraced life's greatest sensation. When his head slumped forward in sleep, for all the death and destruction he had seen, it was the girl's expression of joy and fulfilment that dominated his mind.

CHAPTER FIVE

The Borderers were in reserve, a mile south of the River Imjin in a wide valley that had numerous re-entrants leading off it. When they arrived shortly after dawn, large dumps of tents were awaiting them. Also, brand new space-heaters and dozens of 42-gallon drums of petrol. There were cries of enthusiasm. They were going to be warm at last. Wilson gave precise instructions on how he wanted the platoon lines laid out, but the men were in no mood to listen. Tents sprang up at a prodigious rate and Wilson watched in silence. Then he made himself thoroughly unpopular by ordering them to be dismantled and re-erected in straight lines, as instructed. He went around scratching lines on the ground with a bayonet, indicating exactly where each tent must be. Even then, men proved incapable of satisfying him. Numerous tents were ordered down again, to be shifted this way or that. Fogarty's tent was ordered down twice. On the second occasion he stuck his head out of the flaps and shouted: 'We've only just put the bugger up!'

'Then you're only just going to take the bugger down again.'

Fogarty ducked back inside the tent, muttering obscenities. Wilson went in after him, grabbed him by the back of his collar and thrust him outside. Then he yanked the front tent pole out, making the tent collapse. The whole platoon watched, intrigued.

'What's this, then?' demanded Fogarty. 'It's time you realized that we don't go in for bullshit in Dog Company.' Then, realizing that those watching were expecting him to assert his natural authority, just as he had always done with their previous platoon commanders, he pointed a finger at Wilson and added: 'You and me are going to find it hard to get along together.'

Wilson laughed derisively. 'Fogarty! I don't have the slightest intention of getting along with you. No one, least of all me, has to get on with you. You just do as you're told. Or else your life will be hell. Now get that tent moved!'

Whilst the rest of Dog Company was relaxing in the tents, enjoying free-issue beer and cigarettes, 12 Platoon was still inching tents about, uprooting pegs and banging them in again, and then pulling on guy ropes until tents were upright and perfectly in line. When Wilson was finally satisfied, 12 Platoon made all other platoon lines look like gypsy encampments. Wilson would have had a problem erecting his own tent had not McCleod volunteered to help him. When it was up, McCleod said: 'You're needing a new batman, sir. What about me?'

'If that's what you want, OK.'

'Thank you, sir. From now on you can leave everything to me.'

Within half an hour McCleod had produced two chairs and a table, and shortly afterwards he entered again, this time with a camp bed, blankets, pillows, and a hurricane lamp. When it was all installed, he said: 'Message from Major Middleton, sir. He would like you to join him for drinks this evening. He says the company officers' mess will be ready by then. The major has parties all the time, sir. But watch him. He'll drink you under the table. And he'll expect you to pay a full share for all his guests.'

Wilson laughed. 'McCleod, you're a real Scot!'

'Aye, sir . . . and let's hope you are too.'

Major Middleton soon had the officers' mess and his personal living quarters remarkably well organized. He'd got hold of two easy chairs and he and Captain Southern were soon sprawled out in them, making a good start on the gin. Southern was a sandy-haired man aged twenty-six with a friendly face and an abundance of freckles. The two officers were in a light-hearted mood, their conversation punctuated by frequent laughter.

'Come on in, Wilson,' called out Middleton as he saw his subaltern hesitating in the doorway. 'Just in time for a drink.'

Wilson was served with a cold beer by a mess waiter. Then Dolby entered. He smiled gushingly at Middleton and Southern and nodded at Wilson. The two subalterns sat on hard chairs and weren't encouraged to join the conversation. Dinner was served at a long trestle table and as Middleton and Southern continued their dialogue it became increasingly obvious that they were on their way to getting drunk. The mess waiter refilled their glasses with gin after gin and no matter what they discussed they remained flippant and cynical. Eventually, Middleton turned to Wilson. 'So, Wilson! Got your tents up nice and straight . . . like a Guards battalion. Perhaps I should have told you. We don't go in for bullshit in Dog Company.'

Wilson blushed. Fogarty's words exactly. 'It's not bullshit, sir. It's just as easy to put tents up in straight lines as it to have them all crooked.'

'Is it, by God!' exclaimed Middleton. 'Yes, I suppose it must be. Do you know, that point has never occurred to me. Can it really be true?'

'If it is, how come we've never managed it?' laughed Southern.

'Probably because we're always too pissed.'

They laughed again, as though it was hilariously funny. When they calmed down, Middleton turned once more to Wilson. 'What do you make of it all?'

'Pretty hectic so far, sir.'

'Splendid. Make a real soldier of you. Know many of your men yet?'

Wilson rattled off a few names, deliberately omitting the hard cases.

'And Fogarty as well, I take it? Biggest crook in the army, that man. And as for that old bastard McCleod, I suppose you know what he carries around in his kitbag? Quite apart from all his loot, he's got a full ceremonial uniform of an Argylls piper. Even bagpipes. And he's a good piper. We've had great fun with McCleod on his pipes.'

'Why did he leave the Argylls, sir?'

'They kicked the old bastard out. Bloody insult sending him to us. We're not a garbage bin for bloody Jocks.'

Wilson's cheeks coloured. He was terribly sensitive to derogatory remarks about the Scots. 'There's nothing wrong with McCleod when it comes to fighting, sir. He's done wonders over the last couple of days.'

'Really? Still blazing away with that Bren of his?'

'Not any longer, sir. I've just made him my batman.'

Middleton, Southern and Dolby all exploded with laughter. Even the mess waiter joined in. Southern was so overcome that his drink went down the wrong way and came streaming out of his nose in an unsightly mess. Wilson watched them in amazement. When they'd calmed down, he asked: 'Isn't he suitable, sir?'

'I would hardly think so,' replied Middleton, still laughing.

'But like I said . . . he's done wonders . . . and he volunteered.'

'Did he indeed,' laughed Southern. 'Must be up to his usual tricks.'

'Is there something I should know about McCleod?' asked Wilson.

'No, no,' replied Middleton. 'It's just that he's not the batman type.'

Wilson felt mystified and hurt. He had never expected his company commander to be like this. Middleton became more serious, sensing Wilson's discomfort. 'Maybe it will work out well. One never knows.'

It had gone midnight when Middleton went to the side entrance of the tent and pulled the flaps back, allowing cold air to rush in. 'Come and look at this,' he said. The others joined him. The re-entrant rose above them gradually, with the company lines fanning out on either side. Despite the cold, most of the men were outside, clustered around petrol fires. Those circling the largest fire were singing 'Mobile', one of their favourite songs.

'One of the joys of active service,' said Middleton. 'The comradeship that follows a real dust-up. Let's wander around and see how morale is.'

They pulled on their greatcoats and followed Middleton up the re-entrant. Wilson was the only one wearing a beret with a Borderers cap badge. The others were in their usual balaclavas. They stopped at each group of men and Middleton had a few words with them – 12 Platoon was around the main fire, the centre of the singing, with Fogarty conducting. As the officers approached, their song died and there was a respectful silence. Middleton knew 12 Platoon well. He understood them. Rabble or not, they had character. The last thing these rogues wanted was a string of platitudes. He stepped forward, cleared his throat, and announced: 'A short recitation – "Dangerous Dan McGrew".'

Middleton's recitations were as famous as his manuscript and he gave them a full version. The last verse went:

And the little green-eyed Goddess
Took a grip of Dan McGrew
And thrust his cock right up her
To the east of Kathmandu.
And so he came to realize
As he got what was given to so few
That in the little green-eyed Goddess
He's bitten off more than he could chew.

The end was greeted by wild cheers and laughter. When the men were quiet, Middleton said: 'Muster parade at 1030 hours. No one to be late.' Then he strode off, Southern, Dolby, and Wilson following. When they got back to the mess, Corporal Turner had more drinks lined up for them and Wilson realized it was going to be an all-night session. The enthusiastic reception of 'Dangerous Dan McGrew' had whetted Middleton's appetite and he was all set to go through his entire repertoire. He started with his favourite, 'Eskimo Nell', only pausing for the laughter of Southern and Dolby. Wilson forced an artificial smile. If there was one thing he couldn't stand it was filth for the sake of filth. He just couldn't understand how a man of Middleton's age and rank could get pleasure from it.

Sudden relief came for Wilson when they heard the first, wavering notes of McCleod's bagpipes. Middleton broke off in the middle of a dirty joke, irritated by the interruption. Even so, he led the way outside. The noise of the company died away and the sound of the pipes became clear and true, searing through the crisp, night air with a haunting quality, music that stirred the blood and made the flesh tingle. When McCleod appeared out of the half light, Wilson could hardly believe his eyes. Gone was the sooty, smoke-engrained and dishevelled Jock. Instead, there was an immaculate highlander, as proud and erect as a startled stag. He was approaching in full regimental regalia, a uniform that put all others to shame. It was a blaze of colours: a tartan kilt of a hundred hues, disciplined by a sporran of contrasting black and white; thick, chequered stockings complete with skean dhu; snow-white spats; and – as a crowning glory – the famous red and white diced Glengarry of the Argylls with its monster cap badge gleaming brightly.

McCleod marched proudly down the hill, pipes skirling, kilt swinging; and as he passed, men pressed forward, deeply moved by the familiar air they knew as 'Scotland the Brave'. When McCleod reached the officers' mess he halted and played several tunes for them, finishing with the Argylls, regimental charge, 'Monymusk'. When he started up the hill again they applauded him, and as he gradually melted into the night his pipes became muted, blending with the wind to form a plaintive cry. To Wilson it was like an echo from past battlefields; a salute to bygone Scottish triumphs which made tears of pride well up in his eyes.

Middleton led the way back into the mess. Without saying a word about McCleod he resumed his dirty joke exactly where he had left off. The punch line was unbelievably crude. After McCleod's stirring music it was, to Wilson, the ultimate in bad taste. He finished his drink in one gulp and stood up. 'If you don't mind, sir, I'll turn in.'

'Really? Very early yet. Never mind, plenty of other nights.'

Outside the air was beautifully cold and invigorating. The men were in their tents, settling down for the night. At the top of the hill he could see a light burning in his own tent. When he went inside, McCleod was sitting at the table, still in his highland uniform. 'Great effort, McCleod.'

'Thank you, sir. A wee welcome from one Scot to another.'

'Thanks. I appreciate it. It saved my evening. I find the major rather like a commissioned Fogarty.'

'Aye, sir. I ken. He wouldna make corporal in the Argylls.'

'He gave us thirty verses of Eskimo Nell – thirty foul verses – I just hope to hell I never have to sit through anything like that again.'

'You will, sir. The major and Mr Carter spent hours on his manuscript.'

Before long McCleod left the tent to fetch two mugs of coffee. He then settled down on one of the chairs, his legs apart, his kilt hanging in a fold between them.

'You've washed and shaved as well, McCleod.'

'Aye, sir. You willna see me different when I'm properly dressed.'

'I've got a kilt with me – Macdonald tartan. My mother is a Macdonald. She made me promise to carry my kilt at all times. A lucky charm.'

'God bless her, sir—'

'It was her father's. He wore it in South Africa and never got a scratch.'

'May I see it, sir? Why not put it on?'

Wilson delved into his officer's valise and produced a crumpled and threadbare kilt. He began to undress and McCleod watched closely. 'Sticking to an officer's privilege I see, sir.'

Wilson laughed. 'The pants? Yes. I lack the confidence to go without.'

'Its bonny, sir. And you've got even bonnier legs to go with it. Turn round and let's have a proper look.'

Wilson swirled around. Then he sat down, tucking his kilt between his legs, like McCleod. 'All the others were very surprised that you should be my batman.'

'Don't see why, sir. They hardly know me.'

'Why were you transferred from the Argylls?'

McCleod skirted over the question, changing the subject. 'I wish we could have served together in the Argylls, sir. This Sassenach regiment is rubbish. The perfect set-up would be for us to be in a brigade consisting of the Argylls, the Camerons, and the Gurkhas. I served alongside the wee men when I was in Italy, sir. The Jocks got on famously with them. One Christmas we were in reserve with them. Our CO thought it would be a grand idea if we treated the Gurkhas to traditional Christmas dinners. So he came into my bunker and said: 'McCleod, how would you like a Gurkha for Christmas?' I thought for a moment, then said: 'Och, no thanks, Colonel. I've already got a chicken'.'

McCleod and Wilson laughed heartily. McCleod's cigarette jolted about in his mouth so much that a long column of ash fell on to his kilt. Then he added: 'Pity we're not up against the Krauts, sir. With these Chinks it's like grouse shooting. The ideal campaign would be against the Krauts with a few battalions of Londoners on their side. Sassenachs like

Fogarty, Chadwick and Gaunt. I'd fancy those bastards at the end of a bayonet charge.'

'Oh, come off it, McCleod. They're not that bad.'

'Och, they are, sir. You'll see. Right slimy bastards. And when you have trouble with them, just let me know. I was a sergeant in the Argylls throughout the war, so I ken all about hard cases.'

Wilson hesitated, but he couldn't resist returning to the subject which now intrigued him. 'Why were you transferred?'

McCleod smiled. 'All in the past now. Best left there, if you dinna mind.'

At dawn, Wilson was washed, shaved, and smartly dressed, having piled all his blood-stained clothing in a corner of his tent for McCleod to deal with. He wandered about the platoon lines for a time and then went to the top of the re-entrant and branched off to his left and into the valley parallel with the one they occupied. He was delighted to see a substantial river running the length of it. It was about thirty yards wide and flowing swiftly, with grass banks leading up to thick woods. He followed its course and after nearly half a mile he emerged at the clearing which housed battalion HQ. When he returned to his platoon he decided where he would set up the ablutions and also where he would site slit trenches, as a defensive measure against infiltrators. During the night there hadn't been anyone on guard in Dog Company, which was nothing short of suicidal and typical of Middleton.

The company's morning muster parade turned out to be such a farce that as soon as it was over, Wilson ordered Sykes to assemble 12 Platoon outside his tent. He then had a proper muster parade. He kept them standing rigidly to attention for nearly half an hour as he addressed them on their turn-out and their future behaviour. It was nothing but a tirade and it set the pattern for 12 Platoon's period in reserve. Even during the first two days, which the colonel had designated as a period of rest, with duties confined to basic essentials such as setting up cookhouses and latrines, 12 Platoon was chased from pillar to post. Their second muster parade dragged on for over an hour, with numerous men being sent away to get properly washed and shaved. Wilson even ordered a foot inspection, an unheard of occurrence in Dog Company. He also ordered a laundry area to be constructed alongside the river, and he laid down that all clothing that wasn't actually being worn should be washed.

However, there were compensations, even for 12 Platoon. The long-awaited American parka overcoats and cold, wet-weather boots were issued, and a Naafi van toured the battalion, selling the basic necessities of life, including footballs. These proved a godsend and throughout the battalion teams were picked and challenges issued between companies. Wilson kept clear of the football and spent his time making plans for the rest of their time in reserve, his sole aim being to attract the attention of the colonel. It didn't take him long to find the perfect answer. On his early morning walks in the neighbouring valley he saw the potential for creating an assault course. Twice, he took McCleod with him, seeking his opinion. 'A lot of work for the platoon, sir.'

'I wasn't just thinking of the platoon. What about Gook labour?'

'Aye, sir. Good idea. And the Pioneer platoon as well.'

On their third day in reserve, Colonel Wainwright called a meeting of all officers. It was the first time Wilson had seen the colonel and he was greatly impressed. Most of his address was concerned with the need for better training. 'What it comes down to is this. We are in a platoon commanders' war. So our training will be at platoon level. And platoon commanders must learn to be assertive. For a start, you will all be responsible for devising your own training programmes, subject to approval, of course.'

When Wilson and his fellow officers got back to Dog Company lines, CSM Randle was issuing new picks. 'What a waste of time,' commented Dolby. 'They'll only break like all the others.'

Middleton ignored him. Pick handles were a sore point with everyone. 'We'll have a meeting at 1600 hours,' he told them. 'Have your training programmes ready.'

When Wilson got back to his platoon, he called Sykes and the section commanders to his tent. He explained the situation and added: 'The first thing to do is clear the ground where you play football and make it into a parade square. We'll start as soon as we've got the new picks.'

'I'm afraid the ground will be too hard for digging, sir,' said Sykes.

'Oh yeah?' scoffed Wilson. 'We'll soon see about that.'

Within minutes of work starting on the square, two pick handles were broken. Wilson was further up the valley with McCleod when loud cheers went up. 'Pick handles,' said McLeod. 'They do it deliberately. Hold them at the top, swing hard, and away they go. Hold them lower and it never happens.'

'Then how about cutting them off halfway?'

'Aye, sir. Good idea.'

Wilson soon had all the pick handles sawn off halfway. He then tossed one across to Chadwick. 'Let's see you break that.'

Chadwick could never resist a physical challenge. He swung the pick with all his might. Frozen earth flew in all directions but the pick handle remained intact. Eventually, Chadwick exhausted himself and broke off for a rest.

'Right,' said Wilson. 'That solves that problem. There will be no more broken pick handles. And take a look at the hole Chadwick has dug. So much for all this talk about the ground being too hard.'

'Hang about a bit,' protested Fogarty. 'Chad was going flat out.'

'And that's what you are going to do from now on, Fogarty – go flat out.' Fogarty muttered insolently, but Wilson ignored him. 'And I'll tell you this once and once only. You'll have tasks to do and you'll stick at them until they're finished. Whether you do them quickly or slowly is up to you. But you won't get any rest until you are finished. You'll stay out all night if necessary.'

At the company orders group Middleton was highly critical of the suggested training programmes and ruled that they must all be the same. Wilson was furious. It defeated the whole object of the exercise and he didn't let it escape anyone's notice that Middleton's final plan was based on his ideas. When the meeting ended, Wilson asked Middleton for a word in private. 'What's the problem?' asked Middleton, expecting a long moan about Fogarty.

'No problem at all, sir. I'm after the loan of twenty Korean porters.'

'Twenty Gooks? What the hell do you want them for?'

'I want to build an assault course, sir.'

Middleton looked up sharply. 'An assault course! Wilson, if the colonel wants an assault course he'll no doubt make his own arrangements.'

'But the colonel wants platoon initiative.'

Middleton eyed Wilson with distaste. The fellow was positively transparent, nothing but a glory-seeker, an attitude Middleton despised. 'Now just look here, Wilson—'

'I'm only asking if spare porters are available—'

'I'll think about it. But you'd do better to forget all these fancy ideas of yours and stick to basics. What is your platoon doing now?'

'Digging in, sir. Making slit trenches for the sentries.'

'Sentries? What bloody sentries? Christ, Wilson, where do you think we are? Buckingham Palace?'

'They're in case of enemy infiltrators.'

'Infiltrators!' laughed Middleton, as if they were as unlikely to show up as submarines. 'And how many pick handles broken so far?'

'Two. But there won't be any more. I've sawn all the handles off halfway.'

'Christ, Wilson! You're a great one for destroying WD property. Those pick handles are like gold dust.'

'But it's impossible to break them now—'

'Bloody impossible to use them as well—'

'Not really, sir. And all those broken handles were a con.'

'And who told you that nonsense?'

'McCleod, sir. And he should know. He's broken dozens of them.'

'I'll bet he has, the old bastard.' Middleton resumed studying the training programmes, suddenly tired of Wilson and all his rot.

Wilson waited for a time and then asked: 'So what about the porters, sir?'

'I've told you – I'll think about it.'

When Wilson returned to 12 Platoon he examined the progress on the square and slit trenches. The former had progressed quite well, but the slit trenches were no more than impressions on the ground. He consulted his watch and said: 'I estimate you'll be finished around 0500 hours.'

They didn't know whether to take him seriously, but they soon found out. After a break for their evening meal, Sergeant Sykes got them back to work. When those on the square finished, Wilson sent them to help with the slit trenches. When it grew dark he ordered hurricane lamps to be taken out. For the rest of the night Wilson made regular trips from the officers' mess to see how they were getting on. He always carried a stick, on which he had made a notch at exactly four feet. Without a word to anyone he would dip the stick into the trenches. Then he would shake his head and depart. In the mess, the others watched his comings and goings with ever-increasing curiosity. Eventually, Southern asked: 'What exactly are you doing with that stick?'

Wilson explained what was happening. 'This is my dip-stick.'

'I see,' said Southern. 'Well if I were you, old boy, I'd concentrate on dipping your wick rather than your stick.'

Middleton laughed uproariously, but Dolby was too outraged to be amused. 'You can't keep your men out there all night,' he protested.

'Of course I can. They'll do as I say.'

'And are you staying up all night?' asked Southern.

'Naturally.' Wilson saw them all exchanging glances. 'It's the latest technique in industry. All tasks have an ETC, with piece-rates paid.' This was greeted by silence. Southern and Dolby expected Middleton to comment, but he didn't. Turner passed among them, re-filling glasses. As he topped up Wilson's he said: 'In industry, ETCs are agreed with the unions. But there aren't any unions in the army.'

'Bad luck on the army,' laughed Wilson.

'That's the attitude that made unions necessary in the first place.'

Wilson jumped to his feet and towered over the corporal. They all thought he was going to hit him. Instead, he hissed: 'You ever speak to me like that again, Turner, and your feet won't touch the ground for a week.'

The others looked away, too embarrassed to know what else to do.

When Middleton headed for 12 Platoon the following morning he was determined to put Wilson right on a few points. He knew he should have done it at the time, but reprimanding an officer in the mess was hardly the done thing. He looked around 12 Platoon carefully. He tried to find fault but couldn't. The tents were perfect and the turn-out of the men was a revelation. It made Middleton ashamed of his balaclava and he made a mental note to ditch it as soon as he got back to his tent. When Wilson saw his company commander, he hurried over.

'Morning, Wilson. Platoon area looks reasonable.'

'Thank you, sir.' Wilson fell in step alongside Middleton.

'Poor show in the mess last night,' said Middleton.

'Yes, sir. Corporal Turner is far too familiar at times.'

'Not him, Wilson. You! The way you told him off. If there's any telling off to be done in the mess it's up to me. Not you.'

They walked in silence to the head of the re-entrant. Wilson pointed out the slit trenches which were now occupied by sentries. A little further on, Middleton was amazed to see an ablutions point and a long clothes line straining under the weight of a mass of washing. He still made no comment and started to retrace his steps. Wilson held his ground. 'Over here is where I intend to put the assault course, sir.'

'Ah, yes! The assault course—'

Wilson led the way down the adjoining valley, explaining his ideas. Middleton showed no interest and asked no questions. When Wilson ran dry, Middleton said: 'Quite out of the question. Far too elaborate.'

When the platoon training programmes got underway, 12 Platoon soon concluded that they would have been better off back in the front line. Wilson was a fanatic. He chased them, harried them, nagged them, and threw every aspect of military training and discipline at them. His specialities were bayonet charges, early morning PT, alarm drills, and ten-mile runs in full battle order. It was the ten-mile runs that 12 Platoon hated most. Wilson used them to show off his superb fitness. Other platoons were often out doing similar stints and Wilson regarded them as a direct challenge. 'Right lads!' he would shout. 'We're going to overtake that platoon in front and show them what we're made of.' The other platoons didn't give a damn what they were made of and let them rush past to the accompaniment of jeers and cat-calls.

Wilson's greatest passion remained the assault course. Even though Middleton had rejected the idea, Wilson refused to accept that as final. On their second morning of training, Dog Company had a visit from Colonel Wainwright. In 10 and 11 Platoons things hadn't gone too well, but 12 Platoon was different. Everything was immaculate and Wilson made an immediate and favourable impression. He was full of confidence and spoke out clearly, anxious to show things off rather than hide them. After Wainwright had been shown the ablutions area, he took Middleton to one side. 'If this is your problem platoon, Roy, we can do with a few more problems like it.'

'Thank you, sir.'

'I'm not praising you, Roy. It's Wilson who deserved all the praise.' The colonel led the way back to the others. 'Thank you, Mr Wilson. Very good!'

The colonel's words were a clear dismissal but Wilson stood his ground. 'May I show you something else, sir? An idea for an assault course.'

Middleton shot Wilson a look of contempt. 'I've looked into this, sir. Completely impractical I'm afraid.'

Wainwright eyed Wilson curiously. 'Keen on assault courses, I take it?'

'Rather, sir. The Marines one at Lympstone is the best I've ever seen.'

Without further ado Wilson led the way into the next valley, explaining his ideas as he went. He kept it brief and to the point. It was some time before the colonel responded. 'A good idea, Wilson. But it would take well over a week to build.'

'Exactly what I said, sir,' remarked Middleton.

'No, sir. Not that long. No more than three days.'

'There are other things to do beside build assault courses, Mr Wilson.'

'Precisely, sir,' agreed Middleton. 'Exactly what I said.'

'But building an assault course would be training in itself, sir. Especially for the Pioneers. And anyhow, my men would be only too pleased to do the bulk of the work. Out of training hours, of course.'

'Your platoon would? 12 Platoon?'

'Rather! And when it's completed we could have an inter-platoon competition. I'll back 12 Platoon to beat anyone.'

'Who's been putting all these ideas into your head?'

'You, sir. The need to be assertive.'

'Very well. I'll let you know shortly. Now return to your platoon.'

Wilson saluted and sprinted away. 'Sorry about that, sir,' said Middleton.

'What the devil are you sorry about, Roy? That's exactly the attitude I'm trying to foster?'

'Yes, sir . . . but all that arguing.'

'He wasn't arguing. He was presenting his case. I'll give him three days.'

Once Wilson had the go-ahead with the assault course he changed his tactics with regard to punishing men. At the slightest excuse, he said: 'Assault course duty. Report to me after training.' At the end of each day's training the whole platoon would be outside his tent. When the Korean porters and the Pioneer platoon arrived, Wilson had a detailed plan awaiting them. However, it was the way Wilson drove the 12 Platoon punishment squads that resulted in the assault course being finished at lunch on the third day. Within minutes of completion, 12 Platoon was assembled at the top of the valley, awaiting Wilson's order to try it out.

It proved a lot tougher than Wilson had imagined. By the time they finished by swinging across the river on a Tarzan rope, they were exhausted. What made it even more testing was that the Tarzan rope was sited in such a way that unless it was tackled aggressively, with an enthusiastic launch off the catwalk leading to it, men only had a slim chance of clearing the water and landing on the far bank. Otherwise, they were bound to take a ducking.

On their first time over the course, Fogarty finished last. When he appeared at the end of the catwalk, the rest of the platoon, the Pioneers, and the Korean porters were all on the far bank, watching. They cheered as he sauntered along the catwalk. At the end of it, Fogarty grinned and bowed in an attempt to infuriate Wilson. However, when he put his mind to swinging across the river, his heart sank. The Tarzan rope was suspended from a bough of a tree and unless it was swung back by the previous man – the proper method – it was a tantalizing distance from the catwalk. As Fogarty stared at the rope, then the drop below into the river, he was scared stiff.

'Come on, Foggy,' shouted Denzil. 'Fly like a bird!'

Everyone cheered and Fogarty knew he could not be seen to funk it. He leapt into space and caught the rope, but he grabbed it too high, which meant that he lacked forward momentum. When he realized he had no chance of reaching the far bank he retained his grip, hoping to swing back to the catwalk for another try; but he didn't make it back to the catwalk. Instead, he swung to and fro several times and finally came to rest suspended over the middle of the river. Everyone watching was in hysterics. Fogarty was bound for the big drop and a soaking.

Fogarty shouted for help, but eventually, and inevitably, he dropped into the water. Furthermore, he completely disappeared. They all thought the river was only waist deep, so when Fogarty suddenly vanished it made it all the funnier. Their amusement reached a crescendo when Fogarty surfaced. His hair was over his eyes, he was spluttering for breath, he was shivering convulsively with cold, and his steel helmet was upside down and floating down stream, bound for battalion HQ. Fogarty waded to the bank and his eyes rested on Wilson. 'Never again! You can stick it up your arse!'

Wilson heard the words but ignored them. He ordered Sykes to fall them in and march them back to the platoon lines. As they plodded along, Sykes went to the rear of the platoon. Fogarty was squelching along, swearing revenge. For the first time, the platoon heard what was to become a familiar cry: 'I'll get that bastard if it's the last thing I do.'

Sykes was fascinated to know what would happen next. The crunch would come soon enough. Knowing what had happened with their previous platoon commanders, Sykes's money – if not his active support – was on Fogarty.

CHAPTER SIX

McCleod saw them all assembling. It was like a gathering of the battalion mafia. They were clustered around a huge fire on the edge of the square, supping their free-issue beer. McCleod joined them surreptitiously and then remained on the fringe, inconspicuous. Corporal Turner was doing most of the talking. He was relating recent events in the officers' mess. He claimed that a crisis was approaching and that unless Middleton took firm action, Wilson would end up dominating everything. He told how Wilson had snapped his head off for a perfectly innocent remark and how Middleton had done damn all about it. Also, how Wilson had subsequently complained to Middleton about the mess staff stealing drinks. 'And Middleton just accepts it all. So now we've got to get signatures for every drink we serve. But we're not bloody standing for it.'

Talk eventually turned to the assault course. That was the heart of the matter. 'What's it like, then?' asked a man in Able company.

'Ask Foggy,' quipped Denzil. 'He's had the closest look at it.'

There was general laughter and all eyes turned on Fogarty. 'It's bloody diabolical. I'll get that bastard Wilson if it's the last thing I do.'

For nearly an hour they continued to grumble. When a lull came, McCleod edged forward, as though announcing his presence. 'You Sassenachs are so full of bullshit I can hardly believe it. What you need is action, not all this moaning.'

'Like what?' demanded Chadwick. 'All you do is lick his boots.'

'Aye, but only because it gets me a cushy job. You willna see me leaping about on yon assault course.'

There were cries of derision and Fogarty shouted back: 'All right, Haggis. Since you're so bloody clever, let's hear what you would do.'

McCleod moved into the centre. 'Easy! Use military law. Several of you should get put on a charge by Wilson. Serious enough to go before the colonel. Then you have the legal right to state your grievances.'

'And a fat lot of good that will do us with old Wainwright.'

'Aye, the first man willna get much sympathy,' conceded McCleod. 'But when four or five of you have testified that Wilson has gone berserk, Wainwright will check with Middleton. And we all know that Middleton is already pissed off with him. So that will be the end for Wilson.'

'Better get yourself put on a charge then, Haggis,' advised Fogarty.

'Och no!' laughed McCleod. 'I'm the barrack-room lawyer. Not the hero in the dock. It's you who says you're going to sort the bastard out.'

'That's true enough,' agreed Denzil. 'You can't deny that, Foggy.'

'You shut your moaning hole. I know McCleod's game. He's trying to get me shut away in Pusan Detention Barracks.'

McCleod smiled. 'Aye, I wouldna object to that. But have you no thought that you might be better off in the glass house? Imagine Wilson when we're back in the line? And you could be safe and sound in Pusan.'

To many, McCleod's words made sense. There was nothing to lose. Only a lot to gain. Perhaps their lives. 'What about it then, Chad?' asked Fogarty.

'Like Smokey says, we've got bugger all to lose.'

'Right! The old strike routine again, then.'

Wilson entered the mess smiling broadly, visualizing Fogarty's ducking, but his good mood soon vanished when Middleton's batman handed him a beer and didn't ask him to sign for it.

'Major Middleton says there will be no more signing of chits, sir.'

'Rubbish! We've only just started the system.'

'And he's only just this minute stopped it, sir.'

'I'm afraid that's right, Wilson.' Middleton's voice came from the far end of the mess. 'With all these guests we'll be entertaining, Captain Southern and I don't see the point of chits.' Middleton lowered his voice and added: 'But we take the point about other activities.'

'You mean the waiters stealing drinks, sir?' replied Wilson, making sure Middleton's batman heard.

'Well, yes . . . I'll look into that. But chits are definitely out.'

Southern was sitting beside Middleton and made a point of changing the subject. 'What were you smiling about when you came in?'

Wilson laughed. 'Our first go over the assault course. Tremendous fun. Fogarty made a complete hash of it. Ended up hanging over the river on the Tarzan rope. And when he fell in, he completely disappeared.'

'A success then?' asked Middleton.

'Absolutely! It's tremendous. But really tough.'

'I thought it might be,' said Dolby.

'What it really needs,' continued Wilson, 'is fire simulation. Live rounds just over our heads. Or hitting the ground just behind us.'

'This assault course won't make you popular, Wilson,' said Middleton.

'Well, I certainly haven't done all that work to win popularity.'

'Not much!' said Dolby.

'Guest night tonight,' stated Southern, trying once more to avoid unpleasantness. 'Should be a good evening with the Duke coming.'

When the guests arrived they were already half-sozzled and as the party got underway Dolby and Wilson were totally ignored. They stood together, hardly talking. Dolby made his dislike of Wilson so clear that he confined his conversation to 'yes' and 'no'. To Wilson, the party dragged on for ever and even when their guests had departed Middleton and Southern had a long discussion about what a success it had been. Wilson excused himself as soon as possible. Outside, it was a clear night and in the north artillery was thumping and grumbling. When he got back to his tent, McCleod was waiting for him, the usual pot of coffee ready. 'I need to have a word with you, sir. There's a lot of unrest in the platoon.'

Wilson laughed. 'Really! You astound me. With the work-shy, bolshy, bastards I've been landed with, I would hardly expect otherwise.'

'Serious unrest, sir. They're planning to land you in the shit. They aim to get themselves put on charges. One at a time. And serious enough to be remanded for the CO. That way they are allowed their say to the colonel, about how you've been pushing them beyond reason—'

'Beyond reason! That's a joke. What do they think they're in? The Girl Guides?' Wilson sat on the end of his bed, took a swig of coffee, and then removed his boots. 'Don't worry, McCleod. The golden rule with hard cases is never to put them on a charge . . . just dish out extra duties.' Wilson began to strip off and McCleod watched him, admiring his physique. 'You worry too much, McCleod. Fogarty hasn't got the guts to try anything.'

'I wouldna be too sure of that, sir.'

'Well I would. I'd soon sort out that little squirt and he knows it.'

As Wilson slipped into his sleeping bag, McCleod sat on the end of the camp bed. 'You never did hear what happened to Mr Carter, did you, sir? With respect, I think you'd better listen. Then you'll ken never to underestimate these Sassenachs.'

For the men of Dog Company it was one of their best nights, with a rousing sing-song taking over from all the moaning. When they eventually returned to their tents they were pleasantly drunk. Chadwick and Gaunt soon fell asleep but Fogarty's mind was tormented by the suspicion that the talk about sorting Wilson out was nothing but a con on the part of McCleod. After all, although Wilson made life very unpleasant, Fogarty had known worse – Colchester Detention Barracks, for a start. McCleod's other main point, about going back into the line, was the biggest con of all. The longest they'd ever get inside was twenty-eight days, and the war wasn't going to be over in that time. Fogarty decided he'd got everything out of perspective. No doubt, Wilson would continue to make their lives hell in the day time, but once it was dark Wilson, like all the officers, disappeared into to their mess and left the camp wide open.

Fogarty leaned out of his sleeping bag and shook Chadwick and Gaunt. 'Do you blokes realize it's a week since we had a woman?'

'So what do you want then?' yawned Chadwick. 'An anniversary card?'

'Very funny,' scoffed Fogarty. 'But I'm not joking. Hasn't it occurred to you pillocks that this camp is wide open? Once it's dark we can do what we like.'

He reminded them of the bizarre things that went on along the MSR in reserve areas, and when he stressed that these attractions certainly wouldn't be open to them if they had a confrontation with Wilson and ended up in Pusan, his two sidekicks became convinced. They got dressed and emerged from their tent cautiously. There was no sign of life, apart from a hurricane lamp burning in Wilson's tent. They slunk away, keeping well clear of the 12 Platoon sentries. Within ten minutes they were on the MSR and heading south. The first vehicle that came along offered them a lift. 'Where you guys heading?' asked the American driver.

'Where there's some action,' replied Fogarty. 'Some jig-a-jig.'

The driver laughed. 'No problem. Dozens of places along the MSR.'

The American took them to a village just off the MSR. He stopped outside what was obviously a brothel. It had all the hallmarks: hideously decorated with lanterns and streamers, bright lights, blaring music, raucous male laughter, feminine squeals of delight, and even a couple of drunks staggering about outside. Several young girls came out to greet them and inside, at the bar, two girls and a Muma-san were pouring drinks for several customers. The girls were very professional, their small mouths daubed with bright red lipstick, their cheeks caked by cheap powder, their bosoms jacked up to maximum elevation, and their hair back-combed and brittle with lacquer. They wore long silk dresses slit up to their hips, showing generous flashes of stocking tops, suspender belts, smooth flesh, and miniscule underwear. They were experts at provocative poses, flirtatious glances, and remarks of sexual innuendo. Their pungent perfume pervaded the room, creating an atmosphere in which the three Londoners were immediately at ease.

They had a great time. They were soon in a state of slobbering merriment in which they didn't care how they behaved, oblivious to everything except carnal desires. They chatted up the girls with a flow of obscenities and lewd suggestions, mauling them lecherously as they spoke, running their hands up their legs, beneath their dresses, and into their knickers, steadily working themselves and the girls into a state where there was only one thing left to do, and that was to disappear into the cubicles set aide for copulation.

They hitched a lift back and arrived at the Borderers as reveille sounded. Several of their friends sensed they'd been up to something. At first they denied everything, but the truth soon came out. After all, the whole significance of their victory over Wilson would be lost unless it became known.

'You still going to stage a confrontation with Wilson?' asked Denzil.

'Sod confrontations,' said Fogarty. 'Apart from those like last night. This way we get more than get even. Just so long as you blokes don't tell McCleod. All that talk of his was a trick to get us put away in Pusan. Change of policy now. We'll toe the line during the day and then enjoy ourselves every night.'

Morning training passed without incident. Wilson was ever-watchful, determined to meet any trouble swiftly and harshly. Having heard the details of the Carter incident, he was more determined than ever not to stand any nonsense. Indeed, it now went deeper than that. He was furious that these men had treated an officer in such a despicable way, and that Middleton had done nothing about it. Subconsciously, he was itching to provoke a showdown.

His chance came when he noticed that the assault course was not being used. Since the announcement of an inter-platoon competition, Major Thompson had been put in charge of it, and 12 Platoon had to take its turn like everyone else; but he decided to take a chance and put his men over it again, this time with live fire. After their drill session with Sykes, he assembled the platoon at the top of the valley. 'Right! This morning we are going to do it against the clock. I'll go first and Sergeant Sykes and McCleod will provide the live fire with Brens, alternating your positions as I go down the valley.' As Sykes made his way down the course he was more convinced than ever that Wilson was heading for trouble. Wilson turned back to the rest of the platoon. 'As I progress along the course, you all follow me. And watch for all the points I've mentioned. And Corporal Higgins, you time me.'

Wilson went off like a greyhound and when he got opposite Sykes, the sergeant opened up with short bursts, placing them about six feet behind Wilson. When McCleod took over from Sykes he narrowed the distance appreciably. The platoon watched with grudging admiration. When Wilson did a perfect landing on the far bank, he demanded: 'What was my time?'

'Six minutes and twenty-five seconds, sir.'

As they reassembled at the top of the valley they all knew what was coming next. 'Right, a volunteer!' No one stirred. 'Well, come on. Someone has to go next.' Still no one stirred. 'How about you, Fogarty?'

'Not with live ammunition being fired.'

'Don't be so pathetic. Step forward, or I'll drag you out.'

Fogarty stepped forward. There was a mixed reaction from the platoon. Some groaned with disgust and others laughed at the prospect of Fogarty being chased down the course by live ammunition.

Fogarty started off at a ridiculously slow speed. Wilson shouted at him, but it made no difference. Fogarty just ambled along, determined to demonstrate his contempt for Wilson. 'Don't strain yourself, Foggy,' yelled Denzil.

Wilson clipped a magazine on to his Sten. He slipped the safety catch forward to automatic, and squeezed the trigger. The bullets landed a few inches behind Fogarty's heels. For a split second Fogarty couldn't make out what had happened. Then he was convinced his last seconds had come. He reacted instinctively. He leapt forward like a frightened rabbit.

When the rest of the platoon saw Fogarty's reaction a roar of delight went up. Wilson maintained his bursts even when Sykes and McCleod joined in with their Bren guns. Soon, there were so many bullets biting into the ground just behind Fogarty that the simulation of battle conditions could hardly have been more realistic. When Fogarty reached the Tarzan rope he didn't hesitate. He leapt at the rope and grasped it, but he failed to swing his legs forward. He landed just short of the far bank, going into the water up to his knees.

'What's going on here?' Everyone turned in surprise. It was Major Duke Thompson, advancing from the direction of battalion HQ. Behind him, strung out in platoons, was Able Company. Sykes called 12 Platoon to attention. Wilson hurried forward and saluted.

'Wilson! You know perfectly well I am now in charge of this facility.'

In the 12 Platoon ranks, Fogarty bent down to release water which had been trapped in his trouser legs above his anklets.

'Stand still that man!' Thompson stalked towards Fogarty and then circled him, regarding him with disgust. 'Well, well. If it isn't my old friend Fogarty. Was that you taking a ducking, Fogarty? Not very elegant, was it? Just as well you're not in Able Company. Was anyone timing Fogarty's effort, Mr Wilson?'

'Yes, sir. Corporal Higgins. How long, corporal?'

Higgins had no idea. He'd forgotten about timing Fogarty. He said the first thing that came into his head. 'Three minutes, fifty-nine seconds, sir.'

'Seems you've broken the four minute mile, Fogarty. No doubt those live rounds helped you along. Who was responsible for that?'

'I was, sir,' said Wilson.

'Good effort! I'll let Colonel Wainwright know of your initiative.'

CHAPTER SEVEN

A nervous truce settled over 12 Platoon. Everything was unnaturally quiet. Even Fogarty's cry of revenge was conspicuously absent. To Wilson it was quite simple. He had taken on the hard cases and won. Now, he could really go places. He knew he'd already made a favourable impression with the colonel. Whenever he showed top brass around he made a point of heading straight for 12 Platoon, pretending they were typical of the battalion. Soon, a close rapprochement developed between Wilson and Wainwright and 12 Platoon grew accustomed to the colonel calling out: 'Morning, Robert.'

The assault course became the hub of the battalion's training. The Brens giving live fire were bedded in on fixed lines and every platoon went over the assault course once a day with Duke Thompson timing them. The 12 Platoon times were consistently the best. In the officers' mess, it wasn't such a happy story for Wilson. He fell out in a big way with his fellow officers over the continuing theft of drinks by the waiters. To his fury he discovered a large dump of empty bottles at the back of the mess, clear evidence of just how much drink was being stolen. It worried him so much that every time he went to the mess he looked around the back and counted them, keeping a tally in his platoon book. He often drew odd looks from the others when he slipped into the mess through a joint at the back of the tent. Eventually, Southern asked: 'Why do you keep coming in through the tradesmen's entrance, old boy?'

'If you must know, I've been counting the number of empty spirit bottles out there.' Wilson looked around defiantly. He felt perfectly justified in bringing the matter into the open. His money was involved.

'Don't tell me,' laughed Dolby. 'Your friend McCleod has found somewhere down the MSR giving refunds on empties.'

They all sniggered. Wilson was so furious he retorted: 'Very funny! But it so happens that since yesterday this mess has consumed five bottles of gin and three of whisky. And that can only mean one thing—'

'You're drinking far too much, Phillip,' quipped Middleton.

'Perhaps we'd better start marking the bottles,' suggested Dolby.

'I already have. Between today's lunch and this evening, five-eighths of a bottle of gin and three-quarters of a bottle of whisky have disappeared. The waiters are obviously decanting it and selling it around the company.'

Middleton eyed Wilson with exasperation. 'Oh, come off it. They're only having a few free drinks. After all, they do look after us all hours. I'll speak to them. But then I don't want to hear another word about it.'

Middleton duly had a word with the waiters but they didn't take any notice. Instead of leaving the bottles lying around, they dropped them down the latrine. They assumed that even Wilson wouldn't look there. Nor were they slow to retaliate. They ostracized Wilson. They served him very grudgingly and at meals they practically threw his food at him, with portions that were so small they threatened to disappear altogether.

On evenings when there were no guests, there were long sessions on Middleton's manuscript. He made endless enquiries, such as, 'What rhymes with crotch?' or, 'Give me a line that goes with, 'The spiral stairs were covered in curly hairs'?' Wilson never attempted to answer and those supplied by Southern and Dolby were sheer drivel; and what infuriated Wilson was that Middleton had a habit of saying, 'Damn pity Barclay isn't still in the land of the living. He would have made a great contribution to the manuscript.'

Before long Wilson dreaded going anywhere near the mess. He confined his presence to meals and once he'd eaten his meagre rations he excused himself. He preferred the company of McCleod. His batman always had coffee and sandwiches for him, and their evenings together were something they both enjoyed. Yet ironically it was McCleod who sparked off more trouble in 12 Platoon. He soon realized that the change in attitude of Fogarty, Chadwick, and Gaunt was too good to be true, so he watched their every move and concluded that women were involved. With Fogarty, they always were.

McCleod decided to check out his suspicions. He knew Wilson would be back late after another party, which gave him an ideal opportunity. He waited until after midnight and then checked Fogarty's tent. All three of them were missing, having attempted to disguise their absence by stuffing their sleeping bags with clothing. As McCleod went back to Wilson's tent to await his officer's return, he chuckled gleefully. Wilson got back at 0130 hours and tucked into his sandwiches and coffee. McCleod watched with affection as he wolfed them down. Then he said: 'The phantom strikes again, sir. Our friends are out of camp. Screwing women.'

'Screwing women? Where?'

'Any village down the MSR. But no need to vex yourself, sir. Just leave them to me. It's easy to outwit the Sassenachs.'

The following morning, when Wilson went through the platoon lines to take the muster parade, he was astounded to see that Fogarty's tent was missing. All that was left were tent pegs, a space-heater, and an assortment of sleeping bags and kit. When he reached the square he searched the ranks. Fogarty, Chadwick, and Gaunt were in their usual place in the rear rank. Wilson did his inspection and then, instead of telling Sykes to dismiss the men, he said: 'Glad you're still with us, Fogarty. I thought you'd gone. Where's your tent?'

'Been stolen, sir. Last night.'

'And where were you when it was stolen?'

'Inside, sir. We're very sound sleepers.'

'And a damn poor liar. What have you done? Flogged it to some locals?' Wilson turned to Sykes. 'Did any of the sentries see or hear anything?'

'No, sir. Not a thing.'

'Very well then. Dismiss the platoon, Sergeant.'

As the men dispersed, Sykes asked: 'What are you going to do, sir?'

'Nothing! They either find it, buy a new one, or go without.'

'Everyone knows McCleod took it, sir. Even though he denies it.'

'What's your theory then? That McCleod took their tent down and carted it off whilst they were still inside, asleep?'

'Perhaps they weren't in it, sir.'

'In that case you'd better find out where they were. And until you do, three extra guards will patrol the platoon all night. And the section commanders will check on them every hour. And you will check on them every three hours. And I'll keep checking on the lot of you.'

The disappearance of Fogarty's tent caused a major furore. Those in authority were not amused. The QM refused to supply them with a new tent or even sell them one, and Middleton lost no time in venting his wrath on Wilson. 'Another of your bloody cock-ups, Wilson. What happens now?'

'Perfectly simple, sir. They'll have to sleep in the open.'

'But supposing it rains? Or snows?'

'Then they'll either get very wet or very cold. Or both.'

The news of the trio's brothel crawls soon leaked out and the consensus of opinion among the other ranks was that they were now one up on Wilson. Fogarty's stock once again rode high. Sleeping in the open was a small price to pay for such a triumph – until the wind turned back to the north and produced temperatures of -12 degrees Fahrenheit. Then, it was a different story. Snow fell every night and the sight of three snow-covered sleeping bags huddled together around a lone space-heater – which had invariably been blown out – was enough to soften the heart of anyone, bar Wilson and McCleod.

Leave was announced. A crash programme was embarked upon in an effort to give every man five days rest and recuperation in Tokyo before they went back into the line. Platoon commanders were told to have five men ready to leave first thing the following morning. Most of the platoons made out their leave rosters on seniority but Wilson did his on merit. Bottom of his list were Gaunt, Chadwick, and Fogarty. This brought an immediate protest. Normally, Fogarty would never have given an officer the satisfaction of seeing him complain, but five days in Tokyo was different. He tackled Wilson as he was on his way to a company Order Group.

'Sir, I wish to protest about being last on the leave roster.'

Wilson was stunned by his nerve. Then he relented. 'Yes, perhaps I have been unfair. Maybe you should be above Chadwick and Gaunt.'

'I wasn't thinking along those lines—'

'Not above your mates . . . but above everyone else. Is that it?'

Fogarty stared at Wilson with loathing. Eventually, he said: 'It's not that at all. You're just trying to do me and my mates out of our rights—'

'Fogarty, how many more times do I have to tell you? You have no rights. And I know you've been slipping down the MSR for women. If you want to go to Tokyo, try returning your tent.'

When Wilson arrived at the company Order Group he sensed straight away that something big was afoot. Middleton had been drinking and whilst this usually made him cheerful and flippant, now he looked worried, even scared. When everyone was present, he poured himself another gin and said: 'I've just got back from battalion and now know the score—'

'China 5: United Nations 0,' quipped Corporal Turner.

'Oh shut up, Turner! If you think this is funny you'd better think again. As you all know, north of here is the River Imjin. And that's where we're going to stop the Chinese once and for all. There are two hills dominating the Imjin. One is Old Baldy and the other is Bunker Hill. Bunker Hill is the more vital and that's where Dog Company will be. We have been especially selected for the task by the brigadier . . . due to our enthusiasm during training—'

Middleton let the innuendo sink in. They all knew what he meant. Then he added: 'The Chinese are expected to reach the Imjin in about ten days. They will then not only be confronted by a considerable natural hazard but by very heavily fortified defences on the south bank. Another advantage in our favour is that new British Centurion tanks have arrived out here and they are ahead of anything else. And part of the plan is that Old Baldy and Bunker Hill will have Centurions stationed on the top of them. And you don't have to worry about them being sitting ducks. The Chinese have nothing to even dent their armour. Tomorrow, all officers and NCOs will do a recce. The rest of 27th Brigade will be on our flanks and in reserve will be units of the US Cavalry—'

'Thank God for that,' interrupted Turner.

'Why do you say that?'

'Well, sir, with the US Cavalry in reserve, if we get into trouble they can gallop to our rescue . . . like in the films.'

'Oh, for Christ's sake shut up, Turner! There will be no rescue . . . no relying on the US Cavalry. Our orders are very clear . . . we fight to the last man!'

Within an hour the story was common knowledge. They were on a suicide mission. That night, three men from 10 Platoon deserted.

Wilson was thrilled by everything he saw on Bunker Hill. It was like a gigantic building site. There were bulldozers and earth-moving equipment everywhere, and so many American engineers and Korean labourers that the position had the hustle and industry of an ant hill.

At the top of Bunker Hill were magnificent views. 'The colonel says this is like a rhino's head,' said Middleton. 'Company HQ will be here, on what you might call the rhino's forehead. Then there are two mounds to either side, like the ears. Each will be a platoon position. And directly overlooking the Imjin is that peak. That's the rhino's horn. In fact, that's its code name: the Horn.'

They walked across a plateau to the Horn and saw its potential as a defensive position. It was Korea's Monte Casino, with clear views up several valleys on the far side of the Imjin. Directly in front of them the hill fell away steeply before blending into the more gentle slopes which in turn merged into the fertile plain of the Imjin, a perfect killing ground. A deep trench circled the Horn and on the very top an area had been blasted flat to accommodate two Centurion tanks. Every twenty yards or so along the trench, deep bunkers had been constructed, each sited to ensure interlocking fields of fire.

Once they had had a good look around the Horn, they returned to one of the rear platoon positions and before long they were joined by Colonel Wainwright and the brigadier. The brigadier was a big man, best known for twenty Welsh rugby caps in the vintage days of Jenkins and Wooller. As they stood in one of the half-completed bunkers, the brigadier said to Wainwright: 'Marvellous position. But don't let them sneak up between you and Old Baldy.' Then, for the first time, the brigadier turned to the others. 'You'll manage up here all right won't you, Middleton?'

'Yes, sir. We won't let you down.'

'Good man. And how about you platoon commanders? Happy?'

'Yes, sir,' chorused Dolby and Wilson. Then Wilson added: 'They'll never get beyond here, sir. No matter how many there are of them.'

The brigadier laughed, always ready to welcome keenness. 'Wilson, isn't it? And you're hoping to get the Horn, I take it?'

'Yes, sir. That would be terrific.'

'Capital! Give him a go then, Middleton.'

The Borderers were gripped by assault course fever. Interest in the inter-platoon competition was so great that morale rose miraculously; but it wasn't the act of going over the course that men found so fascinating, far more the 'book' which had been opened up by Private Billings as to which platoon would win. Early on, a plan was devised by Turner by which men bet against 12 Platoon winning, knowing that the competition was going to be thrown. His motive was to revenge himself for having been branded a thief by Wilson. At the same time, of course, he wasn't averse to making some money. Neither was the rest of the company and they all flocked to participate. The plan also incorporated a diversionary tactic. Men were primed to place tiny bets on 12 Platoon to win, but at the same time handed over much larger sums to Turner as part of a syndicate bet. The syndicate's money would then go on 3 Platoon, it being well-known that Major Thompson's latest ploy to secure victory was to transfer all his fittest men into 3 Platoon.

The success of the idea depended on Fogarty, Chadwick and Gaunt. They were the only ones with enough guts to throw the competition.

On the day 12 Platoon had no difficulty in reaching the final against

3 Platoon, and an hour or two before the big showdown, men converged on the valley, anxious to secure vantage points. There was an air or excitement, almost a carnival atmosphere. Wilson had his platoon arranged in a special order, the weakest men in the middle and the best at the back, apart from himself, as he intended to lead from the front. The trio were among those in the middle.

Wilson won the toss and elected to go second; 3 Platoon set off amid cheers and were soon making steady progress. Some were in early trouble through trying too hard, but they soon settled down and progressed steadily. One by one the obstacles were cleared and Wilson waited anxiously to hear their time. At last, it was shouted up the valley: twenty-four minutes ten seconds, a time 12 Platoon had never failed to beat.

Then 12 Platoon got off to a flying start and all attention was on Wilson as he blazed the way towards victory. Only the members of the syndicate were aware that further back Fogarty, Chadwick and Gaunt, although originally well spaced out, had joined forces and were falling behind, deliberately causing a bottle-neck which impeded others. By the time they reached the second plank wall, they were near the end of the platoon. They made their first attempt at the wall look like a narrow failure, but when Sykes appeared, bringing up the rear, he realized what was happening. He wasn't surprised, nor was he unsympathetic, but he certainly wasn't going to get involved. As Fogarty made another half-hearted jump at the wall, Sykes thrust the butt of his rifle up Fogarty's rump and heaved upwards, forcing him over.

Sykes continued to hurry them along but once they were crawling beneath the camouflage netting they were out of his control and they made sure their weapons got tangled up in the netting. Meanwhile, Wilson was seeing the leaders over the Tarzan rope, but the number of them appearing along the catwalk suddenly dried up. Wilson sprinted back and by the time he reached the stragglers they were crawling through one of the tunnels. He went in after them like a ferret after rabbits. When they emerged they saw Colonel Wainwright watching and since they had no wish to incur his wrath they set off again in haste, looking good. When they reached the Tarzan rope Wilson went first. He was followed by Chadwick and Gaunt. Both did perfect touchdowns. When Gaunt swung the Tarzan rope back to Fogarty they were still within 3 Platoon's time.

Fogarty's leap was deliberately premature but to everyone watching it looked like a case of overeagerness and they sympathized when he lost his grip and plunged into the river. When Fogarty reappeared, spluttering and gasping, the men with money on 12 Platoon to win urged him on. Fogarty soon got a foothold on the river bed and started to wade towards the bank. At the same time, Sergeant Sykes launched himself off the catwalk and started his swing across the river on the Tarzan rope.

It was a pure accident that Fogarty waded straight into Sykes's path. The sergeant raised his legs as high as he could but he had no chance of missing Fogarty. His boots caught him smack in the back of the neck, sending him sprawling face-first into the river. Laughter roared out. Even Colonel Wainwright guffawed. Eventually, as Fogarty floundered about, genuinely dazed, Wilson went into the river and literally dragged him across the finishing line. The laughter and shouting continued for a long time and Regimental Sergeant Major Duckworth had trouble in getting silence for Colonel Wainwright to announce 12 Platoon's time. It was twenty-five minutes exactly.

So 3 Platoon had won by fifty seconds.

Wilson was first into the mess that evening. He felt he had to get away from his platoon, even though he realized he would get no sympathy from his fellow officers. Middleton arrived with Dolby. He offered luke-warm commiserations. 'Good effort to come second.'

'Coming second doesn't do much good,' snorted Wilson.

Middleton glanced at him in despair. 'You might still have won if Sykes hadn't kicked Fogarty back in. Still, that was marvellous. Vintage Harold Lloyd. It was the first time the colonel's laughed in five years.'

Dolby was very condescending. 'Pity your platoon flopped, old boy. After all that practice, you should have done much better.' When Southern entered the mess he offered his expert opinion. 'You went wrong by having Fogarty at the back. You should have split your hard cases. Scattered them about in the middle. I know all this talk of Fogarty being the battalion record holder, but he should never have been at the back.'

'He wasn't at the back originally. And I did split up the hard cases. Still, at least you realize that they threw the competition.'

'Surely not!' said Middleton. 'Don't you go around saying things like that.'

Wilson sat through dinner in silence. Middleton and Southern then went off to a party and Wilson returned to his tent to write to his parents. His platoon had a huge fire going on the square and as he settled down he was aware of more and more men assembling. Soon, it seemed as though half the battalion was there, making an awful racket. Just before midnight, McCleod stumbled into Wilson's tent. He was so drunk he could hardly stand up. Wilson watched with distaste. 'What are the celebrations all about?'

'The Sassenachs! They've been celebrating their big win. Corporal Turner had a syndicate going and they won a big bet on 3 Platoon winning.'

'Trust Turner to cash in.'

'It wasna just him, sir.' McCleod paused. From the outset he had sworn he would not mention a word about the syndicate to Wilson; but now, with alcohol clouding his judgement, and the prospect of landing Fogarty in the shit, he couldn't resist the opportunity. 'Turner was the front man for the syndicate, sir. Our famous three were in it as well. And most of the others. They tried to hide it from me, sir . . . but you ken me, sir.'

'How much did they win?'

'Thirty quid each, sir.'

'And you as well?'

'I had a wee flutter, sir. But I lost. I had a fiver on the platoon to win. It came as a great shock to me when Fogarty and his lot threw it.'

Wilson grinned bitterly. He knew damn well that McCleod hadn't lost any money. If he had lost so much as a brass farthing he would have been moping around with a face as long as a pull-through, not hopelessly drunk. Wilson cursed himself for having been so naïve. With the others he wasn't in the least surprised, but McCleod's betrayal was a cruel blow that hurt him deeply. He suddenly realized what an artful old villain McCleod was. He gained in all directions. He had won a splendid bet and enjoyed a skinful of beer, and now he was shopping the rest of the platoon in order to get fresh punishments heaped on his enemies. The only count on which he lost out was on Wilson's friendship and that obviously meant nothing to him.

'Would you like some coffee, sir?'

'No. And don't bother coming back again in the evenings.'

At the muster parade the following morning, Wilson read out the names of those due to leave for Tokyo over the next week. The names of Fogarty, Chadwick, and Gaunt did not feature. Before the first session of training, the trio approached Wilson. This time, Chadwick was their spokesman.

'About this leave, sir. It's a diabolical liberty that we're missing our turn—'

'You're not missing your turn, Chadwick. You're missing out altogether. None of you is going to Tokyo – ever!'

'You can't bloody do that—'

'Can't I? Would your syndicate like to place another bet on that?'

'At least we have a right for an explanation—'

'Good God! You men and your rights! Chadwick, you have no rights. And I'm not going to waste my time arguing with a would-be barrack-room lawyer like you. If you don't like it, go and see your company commander.'

'Right. We'll do just that. Don't you bloody worry.'

'Good. And when it's arranged, let me know. I'll come too. And I'll make sure Billings is there. And Turner. And McCleod. And whilst we're about it, I'll bring up some previously undisclosed facts about Mr Carter.'

Wilson waited for further comments, but none came. The mere mention of Carter was like slamming a door.

In what seemed like no time at all, men began to return from Tokyo. They came back in a pitiful state; scruffy, eyes bloodshot, heads pounding. Their verdict on Tokyo was unanimous: fantastic, debauchery on an unprecedented scale. Wilson made the grave error of thinking that because he heard no more from Chadwick, the matter of their R and R was concluded. He didn't even take any notice of fresh warnings from McCleod. He put all further remarks by McCleod down to an attempt to re-establish their friendship. For his part, Wilson was not prepared to go along with that and he ordered McCleod around like a skivvy, telling him that he was sick to death with all his theories about Fogarty. Yet, for the first time in his young life, Wilson felt the pain of loneliness. Their rift was finally resolved when McCleod made a formal, written, request for an interview. When Wilson had him into his tent, McCleod said: 'I wish to apologize most sincerely, sir. About that bet. And my disgraceful disloyalty. I dinna know what overcame me.'

'Greed, McCleod. Pure, old fashioned, greed.'

'Aye, sir. And I am very sorry. Sorrier than I can possibly express.'

Wilson looked him up and down, uncertain how to react. In one way he wanted to bawl him out and make him suffer; but at the same time he realized that he needed McCleod's companionship and support. He was missing him terribly. He liked McCleod. He stretched forward and gave his batman a friendly punch on the shoulder. 'That's a handsome apology, McCleod.'

'Thank you, sir. It willna happen again, sir. I swear by my mother's grave that I'll always stand by you in the future – whatever!'

Wilson laughed. 'No need to get that dramatic about it.'

McCleod laughed as well. The relief etched into his craggy features radiated pure happiness. 'I'll get some coffee, sir.'

Following McCleod's betrayal of the platoon, he was declared a scab and sent to Coventry and any chance of finding out what was going on in the platoon disappeared. The trio, far from accepting defeat, concentrated on two things. Firstly, how to get to Tokyo despite Wilson, and secondly, how to make the most of the considerable sum of money they had won off Billings. They solved the latter easily enough through a stroke of luck. After the assault course competition, the colonel ordered that all afternoons should be devoted to sport. This, in effect, meant football, and since most of the officers were rugby players, they kept well clear and took the afternoons off. Wilson was among these, which meant that from the end of morning training until their evening meal, no checks were made on the men's whereabouts. So the trio smartened themselves up and once again sallied forth down the MSR. They encountered early difficulties. On their first visit the brothel was closed and they had trouble knocking up the Muma-san to convince her that there was nothing immoral or unnatural, or unprofitable, about fornicating in daylight.

Getting to Tokyo was not so easy. They established that all those leaving for Tokyo were picked up by battalion transport at company HQ at 1500 hours, having been checked aboard by CSM Randle. The transport then returned to battalion where the driver reported to the orderly room. RSM Duckworth did a head count, but he never checked men against a list of names. Consequently, the trio reckoned that all they had to do was hang around at the battalion orderly room and then, whilst the driver was inside, swap places with three young reinforcements who had been bribed and bullied into letting the trio replace them.

However, it all came to nothing. Two hours before the plan was due to go into operation, the Chinese launched an offensive. All Tokyo leave was cancelled. Order Groups were called and within hours the Borderers were mustered in companies. At 1500 hours, instead of Fogarty, Chadwick, and Gaunt winging their way to Tokyo, they were marching towards Bunker Hill.

CHAPTER EIGHT

At dawn the following morning, Wilson had his platoon hard at work on the defences of the Horn. They were split into three teams, some filling sandbags, others helping with the timber work on uncompleted bunkers, and the majority of them helping to shape the trenches in preparation for deep head cover, converting the hill into a warren of tunnels.

The American engineers, who were in overall command of the preparations, devised a series of 'cut-offs' in each tunnel. These consisted of timber supports which could be knocked down easily to collapse the roof and seal off the tunnels so that if the Chinese established themselves in the underground system they could be denied access to other areas. They also built an escape hatch in each platoon area: a trap door in the roof of a tunnel which, when unbolted, allowed a reduced amount of head cover to fall in and leave a small hole through which to escape. All tunnels also had zigzags to prevent a clear shoot down a long, straight stretch of tunnel.

There were problems, of course: principally the latrines. Holes were dug and pungent-smelling chemicals tipped down, but even after only limited use the smell of excreta spread everywhere. Rats were another problem. They were part of the furniture in all front-line positions, but at Bunker Hill they were different. Due to earlier battles fought on the hill, the rats had fed on human remains and become monsters. They were slow, sluggish, and easy to kill, but their numbers were awesome and their audacity incredible.

The storage of ammunition, food, and drink was catered for by building a large bunker in the middle of each position. This housed all necessary supplies and also acted as a rest centre. The forward slopes of the Horn received Wilson's particular attention. He had row after row of barbed wire laid and it became a joke that he wouldn't be happy until they reached down to the Imjin.

Throughout these preparations the sound of battle never ceased. During hours of darkness men looked out through the weapon slits of their bunkers, across the broad Imjin valley, and watched the flashes of guns and the multicoloured Very lights and flares soaring into the sky, the latter drifting about for minutes on end, bright and peaceful, like descending stars. Artillery duels never ceased and were inevitably followed by the chatter of small-arms fire.

Wilson was always keen to build additional bunkers. First of all he had an Observation Post constructed in the centre of the front tunnel, but then he failed to convince Middleton of the need for two bunkers facing backwards across the Bunker Hill plateau. When Wainwright visited the next day, Wilson remarked: 'We should never forget what happened at Singapore, sir.'

'I'm not likely to. I was there when it happened. What's your point?'

'Well, sir, our defences all face forward. What happens if the Chinese come from our rear? We need bunkers to face that way as well.'

'Good thinking. But can you build them in time?'

'No trouble there, sir. Thank you very much.'

The rest of 12 Platoon were far from grateful.

Whilst they were putting the finishing touches to these rear bunkers, an American gunnery officer presented himself to Wilson. He was standing in the tunnel and in the light of the hurricane lamps Wilson could see little of him, only that he was short and slight, with dark hair and sharp features.

'Lootenant Wilson?' the American enquired, a friendly hand extended and his accent betraying southern origins. 'I'm Captain Roland Pickles. Your new Artillery Forward Observation officer.'

Wilson welcomed him as best he could. As he helped him around to the OP Pickles remarked: 'Reckon we've got ourselves a real hot seat up here.'

'Not whilst your fellows hold them on the other side of the Imjin.'

'That won't last. They're due back by dusk, the day after tomorrow.'

It was just as Pickles said. The following morning they watched from the OP as the withdrawal got underway. The noises of battle became dramatically nearer and clearer. Smoke drifted south, with the pungent smell of cordite, and it soon became possible to identify individual noises: the rattle of Burp guns, the rasping of Brownings, and, of course, the incessant coughing of the 155mm guns which had been with them all the time. Through binoculars they had no difficulty in picking out men moving about on the hills ahead of them, and on one occasion they saw Americans bugging out after the Chinese had shelled them mercilessly. Then the Chinese appeared in pursuit, charging forward with their Burp guns blazing, only to be slaughtered by the American artillery.

They also spent a lot of time listening to wireless transmissions. Wilson was both fascinated and appalled by what he heard. He was tuned into the transmissions of the 9th US Combat Team who were operating directly ahead of them, often in hand-to-hand situations. The blasphemous language and obscenities outdid even Fogarty and before long he came to recognize the voices of various operators. He was able to piece together what was happening and his stomach turned as he heard cries such as: 'Here the sons of bitches come again!' and, 'Too many of the bastards this time!'

At other times Wilson watched the two bridges spanning the Imjin. The only vehicles going north were occasional Sherman tanks, or small, scurrying ambulance jeeps, sprinting forward to pick up yet another load of human debris. When night came, the battle raged spectacularly. The moon was full, casting mammoth shadows, making the Imjin shimmer and shine as it snaked down the pancake plain. The sound of Chinese bugles became commonplace and the flow of American jeeps, tanks, and lorries making for safety across the bridges never flagged. Traffic jams formed and white-helmeted military police swarmed like ants, trying to keep things moving and under control. When daylight approached, American infantrymen were pouring out of the hills like rabbits fleeing their warrens, bedraggled and combat-weary, many of them riding to safety on tanks or crammed into jeeps.

By noon the following day the number of troops coming back was reduced to a trickle, the rearguards finally abandoning their posts. At the northern end of each bridge machine guns had been established and beside each stood Sherman tanks, engines running, exhausts belching smoke, their turrets swivelling as they picked out targets. Later in the afternoon several dinghies with outboard motors made their way across the river, edging alongside the bridges. They stopped at regular intervals, allowing engineers to attach explosives to the main supports. Then, under the cover of fresh artillery concentrations, the dinghies pulled back. The machine guns on the far side were dismantled and loaded into jeeps. There was a roar of engines as the jeeps pulled back across the bridges, past a few remaining infantrymen plodding along. Finally, the Sherman tanks lumbered back.

A strange stillness settled over the Imjin. No men were left. No radio transmissions crackled. No guns fired. Not even an engine roared. Then, with uncanny precision, the two bridges were blown. With one accord they leapt into the air. Two lines of spray stretched from bank to bank and when the water settled, and the boiling foam subsided, there was nothing left, apart from splintered wood bobbing about in the water. Wilson stared down at the mighty Imjin. It was all that stood between his platoon and the Chinese.

The idea came from two Americans. They were signals engineers fitting a field telephone in the mess. As they worked, the three hard cases and some of their friends came in for a smoke. At first, the Americans remained silent, but when Fogarty and the others began bitching about their officer they recognized kindred spirits and joined in. Soon, a friendly, competitive spirit developed, with both sides spinning the most exaggerated yarns and gripes. The Americans listened with interest to the details of the trio's Tokyo disaster, but dismissed it as of little consequence, claiming that there was plenty of sex to be had in Korea. Then they related their own sexual experiences and the extraordinary antics of other nations. They claimed that the Turkish brigade maintained a harem which followed them wherever they went; how the French had Vietnamese prostitutes flown up from Saigon and circulated them among their units on a roster system, ensuring fair shares for all; and how ROK units took women into the front line quite openly. 'You guys have no idea what these other countries are like,' said one of the Americans. 'The less civilized they are, the more sensible they are about women.'

The Americans went on to describe what had happened recently in several American front-line units. It amounted to smuggling women off the MSR into company positions dressed as porters, or pretending to be houseboys. Fogarty became intrigued and his devious mind went into overtime: bizarre plans began to formulate. He saw the main problem to be getting off Bunker Hill. He put this to the Americans but they could see no problem. 'Just walk off,' said one. 'We do it every day. No one ever checks on us.'

Fogarty considered this too risky. Since the desertions in 10 Platoon, anyone stepping outside battalion lines without permission was automatically classified as AWOL and seen as a potential deserter; and desertion in the face of the enemy was no light matter.

'All right then,' offered one of the Americans. 'I'll ask your officer for a couple of men to help us cart supplies down to the MSR.'

They tried this, but Wilson foiled them. He detailed two recent replacements and they wanted no part in any of Fogarty's crazy schemes.

Wilson was sitting in his Command Post when the newly installed field telephone buzzed. It was Middleton. 'Wilson, a pleasant surprise for your platoon . . . a visit to the Mobile Shower Unit down the MSR.'

Wilson could hardly believe his ears. 'Is this a leg-pull, sir? The Chinese could attack at any time. This is the silliest idea yet.'

'It happens to be my idea, Wilson. And I'm sick to death of your know-all attitude. Have your men ready to move at 1500 hours.'

Wilson relayed the message to his men. They could hardly believe their luck and Fogarty immediately concocted a plan to exploit the situation. He came up with an idea which was so hare-brained that even his mates saw it as an act of desperation; yet since they couldn't think of anything better, and time was so limited, they agreed to give it a try. The idea was that once they got under the showers, Fogarty and Chadwick would stage a fight, and under its cover, Gaunt and Abrahams would get dressed and make good their escape down the MSR. They would then procure a whore, hitch a ride back to the Borderers, and smuggle her up the hill with Korean porters.

The plan failed miserably, but the repercussions made it well worthwhile. When they reached the Mobile Shower Unit, Fogarty and Chadwick duly staged a fight and the whole platoon was soon involved in a bogus punch-up, during which Gaunt and Abrahams sneaked back to the changing tent. There, to their astonishment, they found McCleod waiting for them. Gaunt lost his temper and lunged at McCleod, but the Scotsman was too quick for him. He grabbed a rifle and put a bullet through the roof.

The shot brought the platoon's free-for-all to an abrupt halt. It also brought Wilson and the American captain in command of the unit rushing into the changing tent to see what had happened. There was general relief when they found it wasn't a suicide, but when they tried to unravel events all they got was a lot of shouting and arguing. In the end, the American captain expelled 12 Platoon, assuring Wilson that by the time he got back to his unit his CO would be fully conversant with their outrageous behaviour. However, 12 Platoon sang lustily all the way back. Their plan had been thwarted, but they rejoiced in the knowledge that Wilson was bound to catch it in the neck from Middleton.

As anticipated, Middleton was furious. He saw it as final proof that Wilson was completely incapable of controlling his platoon. As Wilson stood in front of him, with Sykes a pace behind, Middleton shouted at him so loudly that he was heard throughout company HQ. 'I just don't understand what bugs you, Wilson. You've disgraced the battalion, and I demand an explanation.'

'Well, sir. McCleod fired a round because he caught Abrahams and Gaunt well and truly in the act—'

'The act? What act? Not buggery?'

'Buggery? Good Lord no, sir. Desertion. McCleod caught them as they went back into the changing room to get dressed.'

'And that makes them deserters? Getting dressed?'

'Yes, sir. No doubt about it.'

'And the fight?'

'A diversion, sir. To cover their desertion.'

Middleton's reaction was one of total stupefaction. 'For Christ's sake, Wilson! What sort of fucking balls are you talking? Sergeant Sykes, can you give me a sensible explanation?'

Sykes snapped to attention. 'Sir, the fight started because Chadwick turned Fogarty's shower to freezing cold. The American orderly in charge then switched all the showers to cold from a central control. Routine procedure in the events of unruly behaviour. And that caused a general punch-up. Gaunt and Abrahams, rather than get involved, went back to get changed. As for McCleod firing a shot through the roof . . . I can't explain that, sir.'

'I see.' Middleton turned back to Wilson. 'What do you say about that?'

'Absolute rubbish. And Sergeant Sykes knows it damn well.'

Middleton sighed with exasperation. 'Wilson, you're simply not shaping up at all. You have no idea how to maintain discipline in your platoon.'

'Maintain discipline! My God, when I took over they were a rabble—'

'That's rubbish! Why must you fight your men the whole time?'

'Me? It's not me . . . it's them!

Middleton exploded furiously. 'Your bloody conceit is incredible. And I'm sick to death with it. One more slip out of you and you're out! Gone! And your precious short-service commission with it. Dead as a dodo.'

The day after the mobile shower fiasco, Middleton held another orders group. He announced that the American engineers and Korean labourers would be going for good that evening. All finishing touches to the position would be the responsibility of platoon commanders. He also gave details of a new scheme to reinforce all units of the 27th Brigade. Every platoon was to have four private soldiers from an ROK Training Division seconded to it.

Sykes voiced their main fear. 'Will they be able to speak English, sir?'

'No, I don't suppose they will.'

'Then, with respect, sir, the whole thing will be a disaster.'

'I agree,' said Dolby. 'The Gooks may be OK as labourers—'

'One thing you'd better all get clear right from the start,' interrupted Middleton. 'No one is ever again to refer to them as Gooks. They are to be known as Katcoms. Anyone who dares to refer to them as Gooks from this moment on will be severely punished. And I don't care who it is.'

'What does Katcom stand for, sir?' asked Dolby.

'I haven't the faintest idea, Edwin. And it doesn't matter a damn.'

'Sounds like another piece of political meddling,' said Dolby.

'Maybe. And that doesn't matter either. Just look on it as a way to help the Gooks.'

'Katcoms, sir,' corrected Corporal Turner.

'Thank you. Katcoms. It's an attempt to bring their men up to standard. And it's no good you lot bitching about it. The scheme is going ahead whether you like it or not. The Americans have been doing it for ages and it's been a great success. Tomorrow, at 1430 hours, each platoon will send back two men to divisional HQ. And each pair will pick up four Katcoms for service in their platoons. And the two men who collect them will be responsible towards them. They will befriend them, as it were. So only send back reliable men. Is that clear?' They all nodded. 'Good. Now for the good news. Tomorrow the two tanks going on the Horn will arrive. They will be commanded by Lt Danny O'Leary of the Irish Hussars.'

'Will he be able to speak English, sir?' asked Corporal Turner.

The Chinese started to cross the Imjin shortly after midnight. It was an ill-prepared and badly executed manoeuvre. Because of the bright moonlight, Wilson and Pickles were able to watch hundreds of shadowy Chinese figures running down to the river's edge, dragging yellow dinghies behind them. Soon, they were milling about in confusion, trying to organize a crossing. Once, they even reverted to blowing bugles. Eventually, when they were fully committed, with the leaders in midstream, Pickles ordered flares to be hoisted. Everything was revealed in detail and Pickles lost no time in sending back firing instructions. A minute later air-burst shells exploded over the river and the dinghies disappeared amid smoke and spray. When the concentration finished, and the angry water subsided, the river was scattered with wooden paddles, lifeless bodies, and the yellow fabric of the dinghies.

After that, everything went still and silent.

Pickles and Wilson soon became good friends. They progressed from inanities such as, 'Not much happening,' or 'Pretty quiet . . . considering . . .' to talking about themselves, divulging intimacies and life ambitions. Pickles was a married man with a young daughter and he couldn't wait to get back to his family. He hankered after a quiet, suburban life centred around a local job, the country club, and relatives in every block. In contrast, Wilson aspired to a life of adventure, a full-time career in the army, with the prospect of troubleshooting in exciting far-flung corners of the world, clinging on to outposts of the empire. He also confessed his growing concern over his short-service commission, due to his rows with Middleton. Before long, he was doing most of the talking, unconsciously revealing his loneliness and isolation. When he spoke bitterly about the appalling behaviour of his men, he had no idea of how priggish he sounded to Pickles. Eventually, the American interrupted: 'You know your trouble, Rob? You need a woman.'

'Really? I can't see any connection.'

'Frustration! Frustrated people never relax.'

'I could have had one... Fogarty promised to fix me up.'

'Then why didn't you?'

'I don't know.' Wilson lapsed into silence. He saw once again Fogarty's mastery over the Korean girl in the first village: how his swollen organ had mesmerized her. It was by no means the first time he'd seen the incident in his mind's eye and eventually he said to Pickles: 'I'll never miss another chance. After we've sorted this lot out I'll have the confidence for anything.'

'You really think you're going to get off this hill alive?'

'Of course . . . don't you?'

'Hell, no! Not a chance.'

At dawn, the front line erupted violently. Chinese shells cascaded down along the entire length of the Imjin. Old Baldy, Bunker Hill, and Hill 375 were the main targets. It lasted for two hours, during which time men had no option but to cower in their bunkers. When the shelling tailed off, the Chinese laid a smokescreen in front of the river. At company HQ Middleton received so many conflicting reports about what was happening that he went round to the 12 Platoon OP to see the truth situation for himself. There, visibility was no better, and all he got was uncalled-for advice from Wilson. Middleton ignored him and turned to Pickles.

'Get your fellows to lay down a really heavy concentration right across our front. They're obviously crossing the river in swarms.'

'How about sending out a patrol, sir?' persisted Wilson. 'A small recce to go behind the smoke. Then they could direct the Gunners' fire.'

'Far too risky,' scoffed Middleton.

'I'll do it, sir. All I'll need is two men.'

Middleton was about to squash Wilson when Pickles said: 'It's not a bad idea. We'll never get good results firing blind.'

'All right,' conceded Middleton. 'I'll see what the colonel thinks.'

Colonel Wainwright agreed to the idea and twenty minutes later Wilson received a message from Middleton telling him that a patrol, headed by Captain Southern, was going out and that he was to monitor its messages over his 88 set. The patrol left from the 11 Platoon position and soon gave notice that they were on the far side of the smoke screen. It was a moment of considerable tension, but the next message was highly informative. It described how hundreds of Chinese dinghies were paddling across the river. Pickles soon had a map reference and when the shells landed Wilson received another message. 'Dog One. Fire effective. Suggest wider spread. Over.'

For over two hours the Gunners were able to chase the Chinese from one spot to another. When they took shelter in the lea of the foothills the patrol requested mortar fire instead. Not long afterwards came the cry of: 'Bandit! Bandit! Bandit!' They all knew what it meant. The patrol had been spotted. Confirmation came in the form of small-arms fire. The exchange was short and fierce. There was only one more message: 'We've had it!': then silence.

For the rest of the morning the three-inch mortars continued to pound the Chinese assembly area and the Gunners kept up a stream of shells on the southern banks of the Imjin. At lunch time the smokescreen cleared and at 1400 hours Wilson received a message that the Centurion tanks were on their way. Their arrival caused several complications. They found it impossible to make wireless contact with Dog Company and although plans had been made to rig up a telephone line with 12 Platoon by threading wires through conduit, this necessitated men moving about on top of the Horn, which was impossible in daylight. Another complication was the inability of the tank crews to get into the Horn without going back to company HQ. Eventually, it was arranged that O'Leary should take his tank back to company HQ and meet Wilson in the company CP.

By sheer coincidence, Wilson and O'Leary had met before at Eaton Hall OCS, so Middleton gave Wilson the task of showing O'Leary around. They went to the Horn first and Wilson showed off his responsibilities with great pride. What astounded him, and pleased him beyond measure, was the attitude of his men. They were still on full alert, standing to, but there had been a transformation among them. Gone were the sour looks and sarcastic remarks. For some reason they were cheerful, even happy. Men actually made jokes and laughed, and voiced sensible opinions about their situation and the way they were going to hold the Chinese.

O'Leary was most impressed, but in 10 Platoon morale was in a woeful state. In 11 Platoon things were even worse, and their last port of call – Dolby's bunker – demonstrated the true meaning of rock-bottom morale. Dolby moaned about everything, especially Middleton's bungling. 'He won't be happy until we're all dead. And as for that bloody silly idea of his to send out a patrol—'

'That wasn't his idea, 'said Wilson. 'It was mine.'

'Yours? Christ! I might have guessed. You really are the biggest shit on earth, Wilson. That patrol was nothing but plain murder. And as for fighting to the last man—'

O'Leary and Wilson were so embarrassed they left hurriedly. As they walked away, O'Leary asked: 'Are your orders really to the last man?'

'Oh, yes. No doubt about it. Aren't yours the same?'

'Far from it. We have to evacuate if things get too risky. We can't afford to lose brand new tanks.' For a moment O'Leary was thoughtful. 'If things get really rough it will be a bit hard to leave you blokes on your own.'

Wilson laughed confidently. 'It'll never come to that, old boy.'

'Fogarty and Chadwick have gone, sir!' McCleod's head was poking round the doorway of the OP. 'Deserted . . . like I warned you. It's a big joke in the platoon.'

Wilson cursed himself, suddenly realizing why there had been such a dramatic change in his men. They had been laughing at him behind his back, knowing full well what was happening and covering up for their friends. Wilson went in search of Sykes. He found him in the company CP, lying on Turner's bunk.

'Have you heard about Fogarty and Chadwick?' demanded Wilson. 'They've gone.'

'That's right, sir,' replied Sykes. 'I sent them . . . to get the four Katcoms.'

'The Katcoms!' exclaimed Wilson. He felt himself go hot and cold. He'd clean forgotten all about them. 'How long have they been gone?'

'Since 1430 hours. I sent them exactly as ordered by the major.'

'Why those two?'

'They volunteered. But they'll be back—'

'You hope! You could easily have sent two other men.'

'I could, but as I say, they volunteered, so what's all the fuss about? You forgot and if I hadn't sent them your short-service commission would be a real goner after what the major said.'

The two men glared at each other, Wilson searching for the last word. 'If those two men desert, sergeant, you're for it. A court-martial.'

The Chinese were expected to attack sometime before midnight. In the remaining hours of daylight the shelling of their assembly areas was kept up. Wilson left it all to Pickles. His mind was on other things. He kept looking at his watch, wondering what time the men would return from divisional HQ. Three times he rang Dolby to see if his men had returned. Dolby got so sick of it that he promised to ring Wilson back as soon as they arrived. He eventually rang back half an hour before dusk. As always, he was full of bitterness. 'I've got four fifteen-year-olds,' he stormed. 'Members of the Syngman Rhee Youth I wouldn't wonder.'

Wilson waited anxiously for Fogarty and Chadwick to show up but there was no sign of them. Eventually, Middleton telephoned. 'Wilson, everyone's back from division except your men. What's happening?'

'I don't know, sir. They must have been delayed.'

'I take it you sent two reliable men?'

'Two volunteers, sir.'

'Then what's happened to them? Let me know as soon as you hear.'

A thick mist was gathering in the valley, gradually creeping up the hills, ideal conditions for a Chinese attack. A silent, tangible tenseness settled over the battle zone. Throats were dry as men stared out of their weapon slits into the wafting mist. Hearts beat faster and hands became dank. Weapons were gripped in readiness, cocked, with safety catches off, fingers coiled about their triggers. The usual assortment of flares kept soaring upwards, bursting brightly and hanging lazily, but revealing nothing. Then the Chinese unleashed a ferocious artillery concentration. The Horn shuddered under its impact. When it was over, nothing else happened. The sound of bugles never came. Wilson did a round of his platoon. All was in order, except that each time he entered a bunker the men forgot their anxiety and reverted to their silly mood, taunting him openly with smiles and laughter and infantile jokes about the absence of Fogarty and Chadwick.

He returned to the OP and another hour passed. Then another, and still nothing happened: utter, eerie silence all around them. Eventually, Middleton ordered stand-down to fifty per cent. Men breathed more easily. More time passed. In the OP Wilson kept his eyes flickering across the slope in front of him, watching for the first signs of movement. Once again the seemingly endless silence was broken by the telephone. It was Middleton. 'Wilson! Your men are back with four Katcoms. You told me you'd sent reliable men—'

'Volunteers, sir—'

'Reliable volunteers, you said. Not Fogarty and Chadwick. You lied to me. Only a crass idiot would have sent those two back. Now they're hours late and have been drinking heavily. I want a full report. And maintain fifty per cent stand-to. Things are still very likely to happen.'

A couple of minutes later the silence in 12 Platoon was shattered by moronic and drunken cries. 'We're back, lads! We're back!'

Cheers and whoops of delight echoed from every bunker. Wilson realized there was nothing he could do. They would love it if he dashed out and made a scene. It would make them even greater heroes without achieving anything.

McCleod suddenly burst into the OP. 'They're back, sir!'

'I know, McCleod. Believe it or not, I've heard them.'

'They're stinking drunk, sir. But they've got four Gooks with them. Dirty wee bastards.'

'That's enough, McCleod. See if you can rustle up some coffee.'

When McCleod returned with coffee the drunken celebrations were still going on. Wilson continued to ignore the row even though Pickles kept flinging him anxious glances, unable to believe that these hate-inspired Limeys could so blatantly advertise their positions and endanger everyone, merely to score points in a childish vendetta.

Before long, activity along the line increased. Artillery duels raged. Then came the dreaded sound of small-arms fire. It was coming from Old Baldy. The top of the hill was now free of mist and as the small-arms fire persisted, so waves of Chinese emerged into the open, their Burp guns spitting venomously and crackling like a bush fire. The bunkers on Old Baldy were soon firing flat out in reply. It jerked 12 Platoon back to reality, to deep silence, with every man straining eyes and ears.

Then Chinese shells pounded the Horn viciously. It was so intense it seemed impossible for it to last for more than a few minutes. Half an hour later, when it did begin to tail off, Wilson heard someone sprinting down the tunnel leading to the OP. He grabbed his Sten and swivelled around in alarm. It was McCleod. 'You'd better come quickly, sir. It's bloody Fogarty.'

'What's he done?'

'One of the Gooks he's brought back is a woman.'

Wilson led the way back to the CP, running. The woman was standing in a corner. Corporal Higgins was standing guard over her. Her helmet had been removed and her long hair was hanging below her shoulders over an ill-fitting combat jacket. Her face was round and plain, almost entirely flat, like a cowpat which had had features drawn on it with a stick. Tears were streaming down her cheeks. All the shelling had clearly terrified her.

'What's going on, Corporal?' demanded Wilson.

'It was when the shelling started, sir. Fogarty called me round and when I got there one of the Katcoms was a girl. I pulled her helmet off and there she was . . . a woman. So I brought her round here . . . nothing to do with me, sir.'

'What did Fogarty and Chadwick say?'

'Nothing much. Except to laugh about it. They've had a few, sir.'

'Does she speak any English?'

'She won't say a bloody word, sir. Not even in Korean.'

'Do any of the Katcoms speak English?'

'No, sir.'

Wilson turned to McCleod. 'Go and get Sergeant Sykes and then Fogarty and Chadwick.' When Sykes appeared he was only moderately surprised, even though he pretended to be amazed. 'That's what comes from sending those two back,' stormed Wilson. 'Now what do you say?'

'You'd better see what explanation they've got, sir.'

'Don't worry. I will.'

They soon heard Fogarty and Chadwick approaching. They were singing one of their favourite songs, 'The Harlot of Jerusalem'. They stopped in the doorway and leered in. 'Well?' demanded Wilson. 'Just what the hell do you think you've been up to?'

'Not nothing to do with us,' retorted Fogarty. 'We just collected four Gooks. We were bloody amazed when we realized what she was. We just took what they gave us. We didn't consider it our duty to sex them. We thought they were hairy-arsed soldiers. Not day-old chicks.'

Fogarty and Chadwick laughed and Wilson sensed that Sykes and Higgins were having difficulty keeping straight faces. Only McCleod was unamused. 'You two are entirely responsible for this—'

'Bugger all to do with us,' protested Fogarty. 'We never saw nothing wrong with her. Neither did anyone else. Not even Major Middleton. He saw her. And so did Sarge, here.'

'Then why were you two hours late getting back?'

'Shortage of transport. Not our fault.'

Wilson had to restrain his temper. Eventually, he said: 'How the hell could you sink this low? To bring a young girl up here?'

'That just proves our innocence. We'd never do nothing like that. And if you don't mind me saying,' added Fogarty, 'it's obvious what happened. I've heard of it happening before. As soon as a Gook hears he's being sent to some death-trap, he gets his nearest female relative to double for him. Then, while he deserts, she gets discovered and sent straight back. By which time the real Gook is bloody miles away. Back in his village. Up to his knees in the paddy field, churning out next year's crop of Uncle Ben's Long Grain Rice.'

Chadwick, Sykes and Higgins all laughed. Wilson trembled with rage. 'Stand outside, Fogarty! And you, Chadwick. We'll see what Major Middleton has to say about this.'

Wilson cranked the field telephone. Middleton answered. 'What is it? Be brief. There's a hell of a flap on. Duke Thompson has just been killed on Old Baldy. What do you want?'

Wilson explained what had happened. There was a stunned silence from the other end. Eventually, Middleton demanded: 'Am I hearing you right, Wilson? Whilst Old Baldy is under attack, and us liable to be attacked as well, and you've got a Gook woman in your CP?'

'That's right.'

'And you fucking mad? Have you completely lost your marbles?'

'It's not my fault. I'm trying to sort it out—'

'Of course it's your fucking fault. You sent those two men back—'

'No I didn't. Sergeant Sykes did.'

'Don't start blaming others. First of all you lied, and now this. I'm holding you entirely responsible.'

'Right. I'll send her straight back.'

'No you bloody won't! I haven't got time to clear up your fucking mess.'

'But we can't keep her here.'

'You'll do as you're fucking told. And I'll throw you out of the battalion for this. Now put a guard on the bloody woman and stuff her somewhere safe until I can cope with her. And when trouble comes, try to redeem yourself.'

The line went dead. Fogarty and Chadwick edged back into the bunker, glorying in every word of Wilson's balling out. 'Just listen to this,' snapped Wilson. 'The girl is to stay here for the moment. Corporal Higgins, you will escort her back when we get the word. Meanwhile, she'll be guarded at all times. If anyone tries anything with her, I'll deal with them personally. Sergeant Sykes, get everyone standing to. McCleod, you go round to the OP. You other two stay here.' Wilson waited until he was alone with Fogarty and Chadwick. Then he added: 'You two are under open arrest. You'll be charged with being drunk and disorderly and procuring a female for immoral purposes. That'll mean a court-martial for you both. Probably years in detention. You both deserve it and I'll make damn sure you get it.'

CHAPTER NINE

Fogarty and Chadwick returned to their bunker and Wilson contacted McCleod, ordering him back to the CP. 'You've got to guard this girl until she's sent back. Get her out of the way on the top bunk.'

Once McCleod had her put on the top bunk, Wilson went round to the OP. Pickles was too busy to listen to what had happened. The whole line was alarmingly volatile, threatening to erupt in numerous areas. The first indication of an assault on the Horn came, not from bugle calls, but from the machine guns of the Centurions. When they opened up they made everything in the OP vibrate. They'd only been firing a few seconds when O'Leary came on the telephone. 'Robert! I don't suppose you can see them yet, but hundreds of Chinese are in your wire. Hang on a sec and your lads will have a field day.'

Within seconds the Chinese emerged out of the mist, struggling through the barbed wire; 12 Platoon joined the slaughter eagerly. Wilson did a round of the platoon, urging men on. He kept ranting at them to sustain their fire. When it was all over there were hundreds of Chinese strewn over the hillside, many of them hanging on the barbed wire in grotesque postures.

For the rest of the night Old Baldy and Hill 375 were under continuous attack, but no more Chinese ventured up the slopes of the Horn. The only man to report any further contact was Chadwick. He claimed to have seen vague shapes moving between Old Baldy and Bunker Hill. When he fired at them they disappeared. It was an unconvincing report which Wilson dismissed as Chadwick's imagination.

At dawn, the full horror of their encounter with the Chinese unfolded in grisly detail. Wilson was so appalled by the sight of so much torn flesh and the putrid smell of death, that he occupied his time touring the platoon. When he entered Fogarty's bunker he was surprised to see Sykes there. 'Take a look at those four Chinese on the wire, sir. They're very different from those out front. These are highly camouflaged. The others aren't. And these are obviously heading to our rear. Like the other ones Chadwick saw. It can only mean one thing. Last night's attack was a diversion. Most of the Chinese went between us and Old Baldy. They're probably laid up in that copse below 11 Platoon.'

Wilson hurried back to the CP and cranked the field telephone. Corporal Turner answered, but he was in one of his facetious moods. 'You've called at a bad time, sir. The major has just left, planning a major evacuation—'

'Evacuation?' repeated Wilson incredulously. 'We're pulling out?'

'No such luck. The major is evacuating his bowels. With Drake everything stopped for his bowls. But with Middleton everything stops for his bowels.'

'Turner! This is urgent.'

'He's having a shit, sir. Honest he is.'

'Then get him to ring me back. Top priority.'

The telephone didn't ring for ten minutes. When Wilson explained the situation, Middleton replied: 'OK. Hold on. We'll look into it.' Then he called out to Turner: 'Has the company cook returned from the stream, down by the copse? Find out. Quickly!' There was a long pause. Then Turner's voice said: 'They've spotted the cook. Halfway down to the stream. He's dead.'

Middleton repeated the news to Wilson. 'Standing-to! Ready for anything.'

Wilson grabbed his Sten and several magazines and ran through the tunnels to Fogarty's bunker. Before long, Middleton brought down 2-inch mortars on the copse, but the result was negative. Still doubtful, he despatched a patrol from 11 Platoon. They were still some way short of the copse when they came under small-arms fire. They had no chance of getting back. They scattered wide, but one by one they were cut down. Then a mass of Chinese infantry emerged from the copse and within seconds the whole of Bunker Hill came under intense artillery fire, with another front attack launched on the Horn.

It was like a replay of the night attack: noise, confusion, exhilaration, and fear, with everyone concentrating on their own sector, intent on killing the Chinese. Wilson dashed from bunker to bunker, shouting orders until he was hoarse. Men were arcing Brownings and Brens like firemen using hoses. A solid wall of Chinese was struggling through the remains of the barbed wire in front of the Horn, shouting and yelling and firing their Burp guns from the hip; all of them pathetic, doomed men, faced by another thirty yards into a curtain of bullets. Yet they were undeterred. They belched forth, an endless supply of cannon-fodder pouring over the crest of the hill. A mound of dead began to accumulate amid the wire and those coming up from the rear had to climb over them, only to die themselves and tumble forward, making the mound inch its way up the hill.

Eventually, the frontal attack withered away and the men's tension and fear were replaced by the usual elation, men rejoicing at being still alive and not among the multitude of dead. Wilson couldn't drag his eyes off the Chinese. The carnage was beyond belief. He was so absorbed by it that it was some time before he realized that there was still a battle raging to their rear. He went to Fogarty's bunker and what he saw made him realize that they were doomed. A large party of Chinese were wandering unchecked about the plateau by 11 Platoon; and in front of 10 Platoon they were crawling up to the weapon slits and tossing grenades in. There were so many of them that the fire power of the rear bunkers had no chance of keeping them in check. Wilson couldn't understand why Middleton did not bring down air burst on them. He ran back to his CP to make the suggestion but when he contacted Middleton over the telephone, the major was in no mood to listen. 'Just keep your men firing, Wilson. The Chinese are in the position. Collapse the main tunnel! It's your only chance. And don't argue. Just do it! Now!'

Wilson slammed down the phone. 'McCleod! Get the nearest two men. We've got to collapse the main tunnel. The Chinese are in it.'

McCleod soon reappeared with Galloway and Jones. They sprinted to the tunnel leading off towards company HQ. The hurricane lamps were still burning, but the atmosphere was so dust-laden that visibility was practically nil and when they reached the first zigzag they piled into each other. They negotiated the second zigzag successfully but when they were still some way from the area of the tunnel designed for collapsing, they heard Burp guns firing further down the tunnel. Wilson didn't dare go any further. He turned back, seeking shelter behind the zigzag. As they hurried along, Chinese bullets ricocheted off the tunnel walls just behind them. Galloway suddenly cried out as he was hit. They grabbed him by the arms and dragged him along until they were behind the zigzag. Wilson told McCleod to hold off the Chinese whilst he went back for explosives with which to blow in the tunnel. He got the necessary explosives from the platoon mess and then dashed back, sweat pouring down his face. Jones and McCleod had managed to hold off the Chinese. Twice, McCleod had waited until they were right on top of them and then leapt round the zigzag and emptied an entire magazine into them. Since then, there had been no sign of others.

Whilst Wilson worked frantically with the explosives, McCleod and Jones carried Galloway down the tunnel. Wilson soon followed them, the fuse wire trailing behind him. Once around the first zigzag he lit the fuse. They lay flat, waiting for the explosion. The blast was so powerful that it lifted them off the ground. Further down the tunnel, the crashing and splintering of timbers confirmed that the tunnel had been sealed off. They were on their own.

Galloway was in a terrible state. They took him to the CP and laid him on the bottom bunk. He had been shot several times in the back. Two bullets had gone right through him and another had somehow managed to come out at his right hip. Raw flesh and torn clothing were mangled up together and he had lost an enormous amount of blood. Whilst Jones returned to his bunker, Wilson and McCleod smothered Galloway in shell dressings but they failed to staunch the bleeding. Wilson injected him with morphine.

McCleod contacted company HQ over the 88 set, knowing the telephone link would have been destroyed. Middleton answered, in a state of panic. He ignored proper wireless procedure and gabbled so quickly that McCleod could hardly understand him. 'Position untenable ... being overrun ... evacuating—'

'Dog three. Roger. Further instructions requested. Over.'

'Stay put, McCleod. You know your orders. Stay bloody put!'

McCleod threw the headset aside and shouted across to Wilson. 'The major is bugging out. But we must stay.'

'Bugging out! But what about to the last man?'

'To the last man is an order you give to others. Very few do it themselves.'

'The bastard!' Wilson suddenly became aware that he was shivering. He tried to control himself but he couldn't. His body was shuddering so violently that he felt ashamed, especially since he knew that McCleod had noticed. 'I've got the wind up,' he blurted out. 'I'm shaking like a leaf.'

'Isna fear, sir. A wee touch of shock. When the body is in shock, it shivers, the way you are. When you're really frightened you get an erection. It's the way the body works. Shock equals the shakes. Fear and intense anger equals an erection. Unless you're like Fogarty. Then everything equals an erection.'

Wilson laughed, but he didn't stop shaking. He felt he had to get away from McCleod, away from everyone, until he could control his condition. 'I'm going round the platoon,' he said. 'You stay here.'

The platoon was still in remarkably good shape. Incredibly, Galloway was their only casualty. Wilson wandered around aimlessly for a time, determined that no one should notice his shakes. When he returned to the CP he was greeted by the repugnant smell of a dying man. It made him feel even more on edge. McCleod was still in the bunker and he watched his young officer surreptitiously. He was a man in crisis: at a watershed, the ultimate test of moral fibre. Now, it was all down to character: either he would emerge as a true soldier or an empty martinet. McCleod had seen it happen before and he knew it was something a man could only work out for himself. He slipped out of the bunker quietly. Wilson was glad to be alone. He flopped down at the table and for a time did nothing. Occasionally, he glanced across at Galloway. A large pool of blood had formed beneath him and a steady trickle came from his mouth. Wilson went to his side again, searching in vain for words of comfort. Galloway's eyes suddenly opened and flickered sideways, fastening on Wilson's. His lips moved and he muttered: 'You bastard!' Then he died.

All of a sudden Wilson found the odour in the bunker overpowering. In death, Galloway had lost control of his bodily functions and the stench hit Wilson like a physical blow. He dashed into the trench. 'McCleod!'

His batman soon appeared. Sykes was with him, fearing a new crisis. 'Galloway is dead,' said Wilson. 'Take him out of here.'

'We'll put him in the tunnel,' said Sykes. 'Beyond the platoon mess, We'll put all the dead there. And we'll use the mess as a dressing station.'

They took Galloway along the tunnel, past the platoon mess and then beyond the first zigzag, realizing the importance of getting the bodies some distance away. The smell was one thing, but they realized that as soon as the dead were left lying around rats would increase dramatically.

'Our new morgue,' said Sykes. 'See if you can rig a blanket across the tunnel. We don't want men wandering in here unnecessarily.'

'I have a feeling we'll all end up here, necessary or not.'

'For Christ's sake don't you start. Wilson's cracking up, isn't he?'

'A wee touch of shock. He needs time, that's all.'

'Time to grow up,' commented Sykes. 'Time to mature.'

McCleod sniffed the air. 'I fancy we'll all end up mature in here.'

*

Sykes made a point of visiting the CP at regular intervals. Wilson was always in an identical position at the table, staring ahead vacantly. Sykes realized he had no alternative but to take control. He roused Wilson and suggested a platoon meeting. 'We ought to let the lads know about the prospects of relief. And our general admin . . . food . . . ammo—'

'Good idea. You organize it.'

Half an hour later men went round to the CP, leaving just one sentry in each section. Soon, the bunker was crowded. They were in relatively high spirits, expecting to hear a plan for withdrawal. Sykes did the talking. Wilson sat at the table, watching the reaction of the men carefully. He was feeling a lot better. McCleod had given him a couple of coffees heavily laced with rum. His hands had stopped shaking and his resolve had stiffened.

Sykes went through details of administration but when it became clear that there was no plan for withdrawal, the men became restless. Sykes reverted to a blatant 'pep' talk, appealing to them on a personal level, stressing how often they'd come through difficult situations before.

When Sykes finished, Denzil asked: 'How bad were the others?'

'It sounded grim,' replied Wilson. 'The Chinese were in the trenches. We only stopped them coming down here by blowing in the tunnel.'

Fogarty cleared his throat. For once he was in a serious mood. 'It makes all this crap about fighting to the last man a load of cod's wallop.'

Wilson met Fogarty's defiant stare. 'What's your point, Fogarty?'

'Quite simple. If we stay, we've had it. Let's cut and run like the others.'

'Our orders are to stay . . . until relieved by a counter-attack.'

'What a load of bullshit,' cried Chadwick. 'I agree with Foggy.'

'Really, Chadwick! You amaze me. The day you don't agree with Fogarty will be a day to remember. Any more questions?'

Fogarty spoke up again. 'Are you seriously telling us that we're just going to bloody sit here and take any shit thrown at us?'

'That's precisely what I'm saying. Those are our orders. We obey them.'

There was a lot of muttering, but Wilson's determined manner indicated that the matter hadn't been thrown open to debate. Then Gaunt called out: 'How's the Korean girl getting on?'

The question came as comic relief. There was laughter and cheers and Wilson was temporarily wrong-footed. He'd forgotten all about the girl. He glanced up at the top bunk where she was lying flat, hardly visible. He ignored the question. 'Everyone back to their bunkers. And good luck!'

'Hang about a bit,' persisted Gaunt. 'That was a serious question.'

There were shouts of agreement and those men who had already left the bunker pushed their way back in, frightened of missing something. 'I think that what my comrade Private Gaunt has in mind, sir,' said Fogarty with exaggerated politeness, 'is that the presence of a sympathetic young lady, and her willingness to distribute a few choice slices off the joint, might well be of considerable benefit towards the fighting spirit and general morale of the platoon in the difficult and testing times that lie ahead of us.'

There were roars of raucous laughter. Wilson became pale with anger. His eyes flickered from man to man. They disgusted him beyond words. Fogarty started to speak again but Wilson cut him short. 'Silence! And just listen to this. The girl is going to be guarded against you animals. She is my responsibility and I will shoot dead any man who touches her.'

With Wilson confining himself to the CP, Sykes spent an increasing amount of time with Pickles. They soon struck up a good understanding. When Sykes explained what had happened at the platoon meeting, with Wilson threatening to shoot men, he suggested that Pickles should take command. Pickles agreed and they soon decided to adopt Fogarty's idea of breaking out. Neither Sykes nor Pickles had any faith in a counter-attack. They contacted O'Leary and, although he wasn't so pessimistic, he made it perfectly clear that if the situation did not improve his tanks would have to leave once it was dark. This made Sykes and Pickles determined to leave at the same time, regardless of anything Wilson might say. The men had to have the chance of survival. One thing was certain: the Chinese would not let them sit there. Sooner or later the blow would fall.

It fell sooner than anticipated. An hour later, the battle of Old Baldy started. Wilson was checking ammunition reserves and hauling out a carboy of rum for distribution around the platoon. He was feeling much better. After the platoon meeting he had had a short sleep and it had done him the power of good. So too had more coffees from McCleod.

He had a grandstand view of the battle. It was a magnificent but horrifying spectacle. For thirty minutes the hill was shelled mercilessly and as soon as it slackened off masses of Chinese appeared from the lea of the forward slopes, swarming upwards, screaming like banshees, bursting unhindered through the remnants of the barbed wire. Wilson ordered his men to support Old Baldy with their Brownings and Brens and above them the Centurions opened up with their machine guns and the full might of their armoured-piercing 20-pounder shells, lethal missiles which hissed across the valley like angry hornets and then crunched into Old Baldy.

The battle raged for over an hour but eventually the Chinese prevailed. In the final analysis there were simply too many of them. With a determined surge they reached the line of bunkers and then swarmed all over them. Wilson kept a close watch on the rear of Old Baldy where the covered trench emerged into the open and he soon saw men sprinting out of the covered trench, not realizing that the area abounded with Chinese. For the first time Wilson witnessed hand-to-hand fighting. He saw men killing by any means possible: men clawing, kicking, bludgeoning, and stabbing, full of hate and desperation. Worst of all, he saw the men of Able Company being systematically massacred. Once they'd been bayoneted or clubbed to death, the Chinese advanced into the underground defences, into the very heart of Old Baldy. Then Wilson saw a group go up to the Old Baldy Centurion and place satchel charges at the base of the turret. They hardly had time to jump clear before violent explosions made the tank leap into the air. When the smoke and dust cleared it was lying on its side, the turret half blown away, hanging like a tooth in mid-extraction.

Finally, the Chinese turned to the bunkers, some of which were still spitting out defiance. They placed satchel charges outside the weapon slits and one by one they were blown sky-high, each erupting like a miniature volcano, rocks, splinters of timber, sheets of corrugated iron, and even bodies flying high and wide. The final act came when men broke out of their escape hatch and ran for their lives. The Chinese shot them down without mercy. Old Baldy had fallen.

Hill 375 fell soon afterwards. It went down fighting, just as Old Baldy had. When it was all over Wilson just stared across at the usual devastation. The hills were thick with Chinese bodies, like a crazy pattern on a brown carpet. Eventually, Corporal Higgins appeared and told him he was wanted urgently in the OP. Sykes and Pickles were there. Pickles was speaking over the telephone to O'Leary. When the conversation ended, Pickles turned to Wilson.

'O'Leary and his men are going. They've got some technical trouble, caused by the shelling. But as soon as they can get the tanks started, they're off.'

'In broad daylight?' queried Wilson.

'As soon as possible. From choice, they would have gone already.'

Sykes moved to the doorway and said: 'I'll get everyone organized.'

'What do you mean?' Wilson called after him. 'Organized for what?' Sykes ignored him and kept going. Wilson turned back to Pickles. 'What the hell is going on?'

'As soon as O'Leary is ready, we're going with him. On the tanks. It's our only chance. Sykes, O'Leary, and I all agree.'

'We won't get off the plateau. We'll be sitting ducks on the tanks.'

A lot of shouting suddenly came from the tunnel, approaching the OP.

'What the hell is Sykes up to?' demanded Wilson.

'Getting everyone ready to leave. I've ordered evacuation.'

Confirming Pickles's words, men moved past the OP, making for the escape hatch. Wilson leapt out of the OP and barged his way in among the men. 'Stop!' he yelled, but they took no notice of him. In desperation, he elbowed his way through them until he was at the head of the line. Then he reeled around on them. They halted uncertainly.

'No one leaves. We stay here.'

Men still hesitated. From the back, Sykes roared out: 'Get moving!'

There was a general movement forward, but the men at the front remained still, causing the line to concertina. Wilson pointed his Sten straight at the leading men. 'No one leaves!'

There were shouts and curses from the rear and then lots of scuffling as Sykes pushed his way through. When he reached Wilson he snapped: 'Captain Pickles has taken command. And he's ordered us to leave.'

'Pickles is not in command. I am. Everyone back to their bunkers.'

No one stirred. Sykes stepped right up to Wilson. It was now strictly between the two of them. 'Captain Pickles is the senior officer. We are acting on his orders. I thought he'd made that clear to you.'

'I'm in command! Obey me or you will all be guilty of mutiny.'

No one knew what to do, including Sykes. They had no desire to cause a mutiny. All they wanted to do was escape from the Horn before it was too late.

McCleod was in the CP when he heard Sykes order everyone out. He moved with frantic speed. He stuffed things into his kitbag and checked that his most valuable items of loot were properly packed. At the same time he shouted at the Korean girl to get ready to leave. When he heard the rumpus in the front tunnel he dropped everything and went to investigate. He smiled as he realized that Wilson's internal conflict had been resolved, that the decisive commander had emerged supreme. McCleod pushed his way among the men and called out: 'Mr Wilson is right. Go on like this and it will be mutiny. Section 31 (a) of the Manual of Military Law. Mutiny in connection with operations against the enemy. Maximum penalty on conviction, death by firing squad. And you've all had a final warning from your legitimate commander. And I've witnessed it. Go back or you'll all be finished.'

Sykes knew he was beaten. Neither he nor Pickles had intended the situation to develop like this. They had sought to lead Wilson, not defy him. 'You heard your officer,' he shouted. 'Return to your bunkers.'

The men did not respond. There were angry protests. Sykes gave the order again, and someone yelled back: 'I'll shoot the bastard and be done with it.' Others also shouted threats, but they lacked conviction and gradually, one by one, they turned and shuffled back to their bunkers. Sykes and Wilson were left alone. 'Sorry, sir. A misunderstanding.'

'Misunderstanding my arse! You tried to usurp my authority.'

'No, sir. I thought it was best for Captain Pickles to take command—'

'Balls! It's a court-martial for you, Sykes.'

Wilson returned to the CP. McCleod was waiting for him with a mug half full of rum. Wilson gulped it down. 'Thanks for your support, McCleod. It was getting pretty ugly out there.'

'Aye, sir. A wee bit of panic creeping in. Nothing like a relevant section of military law to restore order.'

'Was it really the relevant section?'

'Aye, sir. I can quote you chapter and verse of anything you want.'

Wilson gave a despairing sigh. 'What do we do now?'

'They're right in a way, sir. But it would be best to persuade your friend O'Leary to hang on until dark. Then we'll make our own way back. Let the others act as a decoy. We'll head for the Imjin – the opposite direction anyone would expect – then cut back down stream.'

'Right,' agreed Wilson. 'I'll go and have a word with O'Leary.'

He was halfway to the OP when he heard odd noises. He stopped, wondering what they were. Then he realized it was one of the Centurions trying to start its engine. He was still listening when the engine fired, only to die again. He sprinted forward in alarm, amazed that O'Leary intended to leave the position without consulting him. He'd only gone a couple of paces when the machine guns of the Centurions opened fire. Then his own men started firing and warning shouts came of another frontal attack.

The Horn reverberated to the sound of small-arms fire. Wilson went into several of the bunkers to assess the situation. The usual slaughter was going on, but it wasn't until he reached the rear bunkers that he realized that this time there was a vital difference. The number of Chinese attacking from the rear was daunting. Fogarty and Chadwick were firing flat out, with Gaunt feeding them new magazines, but their efforts were puny. Wilson dashed back into the trench, overwhelmed by the desire to run: to run anywhere, as fast as he could. He sprinted down the tunnel screaming: 'Keep firing! Keep firing!'

Very soon there were two enormous explosions. They came simultaneously, from above. They were so violent that they tossed him off his feet and he landed in a heap, stunned. As he regained control of himself he realized that it was a repeat of Old Baldy. First the tanks, and then the bunkers. His thoughts were immediately confirmed. There were several more explosions in quick succession, just as vicious as the first two, only nearer. Within seconds, explosions were coming from all directions. He lay on the ground, his arms wrapped about his head, trying to keep out the fearsome noise. It was useless. The explosions continued, one after the other, so many that they merged into a continuous roar. Each time there was another devastating 'BANG!' his body was jerked off the ground and his breath knocked out of him.

The explosions stopped just as suddenly as they had started. Wilson's ears were ringing loudly but it didn't prevent him from hearing cries of anguish. They became louder, more urgent, more hysterical and confusing, coming from all angles. It was bedlam. An appalling cacophony of human protests, sounds which confirmed hell on earth and which would echo in his mind for ever. He kept telling himself to get up, to find out what was happening and to help the stricken; but his limbs refused to respond. He just lay there, motionless and useless, wondering how it would all end. When he eventually recovered from his inertia he saw that several yards down the tunnel a bunker had been blown in. The debris was half-blocking the tunnel. One of the most persistent cries of help was coming from it. He heaved himself to his feet and went to investigate. The bunker was no more than a tangled mass of splintered wood. There was no sign of any one, just a forlorn voice, getting fainter all the time. He spoke back to the man, promising aid, but he knew there was nothing he could do and he passed on. He came to two more bunkers in an identical condition. In a third bunker he saw a body protruding from the wreckage. An arm was missing and the head looked like a half-crushed melon. Yet the man was still alive, moaning piteously.

When Wilson reached the remains of the OP he heard voices ahead of him. It was a party of six men. One of them was Sykes. He had a torch and flashed the beam into Wilson's face. 'Mr Wilson! We're making for the CP. All the bunkers down here are blown in.'

The CP was in chaos. Four wounded men were lying on the floor and a fifth was on the lower bunk. One of those on the floor was little more than shredded remains and the man on the bunk looked as though he was already dead. McCleod was there, working frantically, slapping shell dressings on to a man's stomach wound. His hands and arms were covered in blood but he wasn't in the least perturbed. He even smiled at them as they entered. Sykes and Wilson did everything they could to help but they went about their task knowing that most of their efforts were in vain. When they'd done their best they stood back, soaking up the futility of it all.

Eventually, Sykes said: 'We'd better get organized. We'll go round the bunkers in pairs to look for others. Take plenty of dressings and morphine. McCleod, we'll bring any we rescue back here to you.'

The men moved off. Wilson took a torch from his valise and hurried to the OP to see if he could locate Pickles. He peered into the broken timbers, flashing his torch about. Then he heard a voice. It was no more than a whisper. 'I'm here. I can see your torch. I'm upside down.' Wilson pulled and heaved at the timbers, tugging this way and that. 'Hang on,' he kept saying. 'Hang on!' but nothing moved. The men working with Sykes found several men who had clawed their way to safety. Fogarty and Chadwick were among those who abandoned their bunker when they heard the first of the satchel charges. Four other men were dragged out of bunkers, relatively unharmed. Otherwise, it was a matter of extracting dead bodies or abandoning bunkers.

By the time Sykes got back to the CP it was no more than a gory hell-hole. Wounded men were scattered about and blood was everywhere, spreading over the earth floor and leaving dark stains. Wounds were gaping open, awaiting attention, but no matter how many dressings were applied nothing stemmed the flow of blood. They watched life slipping away from men without being able to do a damn thing about it. Some more wounded were brought in. One was Gaunt, but he died immediately. Another was one of the Katcoms. His stomach had been ripped open, his entrails spilling out.

Two hours later they had done all they could. The wounded were laid out in an orderly manner on the floor of the mess. As they died, so they were taken round to the morgue. Sykes went through their pockets first, removing their personal effects and identity disks. Only two men were known to be alive in the bunkers: Pickles, who seemed in reasonable shape, and Denzil, who was clearly in a bad way. Sykes put Fogarty in charge of those trying to release Denzil, and Wilson and two others worked on the OP. Then Sykes went round the entire platoon again, checking for oversights. He noticed that the air in the position was becoming increasingly foul. There was no circulation of fresh air.

Having completed his inspection, Sykes took stock. Ten men alive, fifteen dead, and thirteen wounded, several of them quite beyond hope. Then he went to the morgue to double-check on the dead. The blanket McCleod had put across the entrance was heavily blood-stained and when he drew it aside and flashed his torch over the bodies, there was sudden movement. Sparks of light glinted in his torch beam: rats' eyes. Rats were like sharks, thought Sykes. A whiff of blood and they appeared in droves.

He went back to the mess and looked around the wounded. He crouched down and spoke to several of them, some of the old hands: Corporal Higgins, who would be the next to die, half his back blown away. Sykes was still talking to him when he did die. He told two men to take the corporal round to the morgue. 'The bloke in the CP is dead as well,' said one of the men.

'OK. I'll go around.'

When Sykes got to the CP he was surprised to see the Korean girl standing by the table. He smiled, trying to reassure her, but she stared back blankly. On the bottom bunk a blanket had been pulled across the dead man's face. Sykes lifted it. It was Jones, the quiet Welshman. Sykes undid his collar and removed his identity disks. Then he went though his pockets, searching for personal effects. There were none. Sykes was surprised. There was usually something, if only a wallet and pay book. Probably left them in his bunker, thought Sykes. Then he glanced questioningly at the Korean girl. She was back on the top bunk. Sykes shrugged and thought no more about it. He stuffed Jones's tags into his pocket and dragged him off to the morgue.

Later on, Sykes made a point of taking Wilson around the bunkers, explaining that there was no fresh air getting in, and that without it they would slowly suffocate. 'I think we ought to break out, sir,' said Sykes. 'We must look after the wounded. Our only option is to surrender. The escape hatch should still be working. We simply go up with a white flag. One man at a time. McCleod's the man to go up first. I'll get the white flag organized.'

Sykes briefed the survivors and told Fogarty, Chadwick, and McCleod to go round to the escape hatch. Then he made up a white flag, attaching handkerchiefs to a rifle and bayonet. Finally, together with Wilson, he joined the others at the escape hatch. 'You go up first with the flag, McCleod,' ordered Wilson. 'The rest of us will follow one at a time once you've been seen by some Chinese. Sergeant, you stay in the position until the Chinese come down in order to show them the wounded. Right! Let's get going.'

Wilson stretched up and undid the bolts of the escape hatch. Soil cascaded down, daylight flooded in, and beautiful fresh air engulfed them. McCleod couldn't reach the sides of the escape hatch to pull himself out, so Wilson gave him a lift on his shoulders. Once McCleod had heaved himself out, Fogarty called out: 'What's it like up there, Smokey?'

'Dead Chinks everywhere. Bloody hundreds of them.'

McCleod suddenly crouched down. 'The flag! Quickly!' For a moment no one could find the white flag. Wilson had put it to one side while undoing the bolts of the escape hatch. 'Hurry!' urged McCleod. 'They've seen me.'

They found the flag and passed it from hand to hand, but before Wilson could thrust it through the escape hatch there was a burst of fire from a Burp gun. McCleod fell to the ground, disappearing from view; but then his boots and legs reappeared and he fell back through the escape hatch. He was bleeding, but still very much alive. Wilson thrust the flag up again, but it didn't reach above ground level. There was a lot of shouting from above and bullets suddenly zipped into the side of the escape hatch.

'Back down the tunnel,' yelled Wilson, knowing that grenades would soon follow. The others obeyed instantly and Wilson sprinted after them. Two concussion grenades were dropped into the tunnel and their blast ripped past them, not powerful enough to kill, but sufficient to set their ears ringing and numb their senses. What Wilson hadn't expected was for two Chinamen to jump down into the tunnel. They landed awkwardly but still managed to fire down the tunnel. Wilson heard bullets crack overhead. Others hit the tunnel wall. He could see the Chinese plainly, silhouetted against the daylight streaming through the escape hatch, and he knew it was his only advantage – the Chinese would be comparatively blind, looking into the darkness.

Wilson still had the rifle and bayonet in his hands. As the Chinese stopped firing he jumped up and charged forward, yelling as loudly as he could. He went for the one on the right, lunging at him, his feet off the ground as in a flying tackle. His face was twisted and distorted, a mask of fanatical hatred. As the bayonet sank into the man's stomach, his eyes and tongue protruded and he collapsed to the ground, dragging Wilson down with him. Wilson expected to be killed by the other Chinaman, but there was a blood-curdling scream and when he glanced up Fogarty was beating the man with his rifle butt, crashing it up and down. Wilson jumped up, snatched his bayonet free, and then plunged it into the Chinaman. When the Chinese were dead beyond doubt, they stood over them, looking at what they had done. Then they heard more voices above, closing in swiftly. 'The bastards got Chad,' cursed Fogarty.

'Get back!' cried Wilson. 'Behind the zigzag.'

Sykes and McCleod were waiting on the far side. Chadwick had been shot through the head and his body was sprawled out alongside them. They flattened themselves against the side of the tunnel and listened. They heard more noises, but no more Chinese dropped into the tunnel to rout them out. For some time nothing happened. Minutes passed and no movement came from the other side of the zigzag. 'The bastards are playing with us,' said Sykes. 'Waiting for our nerves to crack.'

Sykes was wrong. The Chinese were waiting for fresh satchel charges. As soon as they had them they dropped them down the escape hatch. There was a devastating explosion and ten yards of the tunnel either side of the hatch caved in. Wilson and the others were flung back several yards by the blast and ended up in a heap. When they disentangled themselves they retreated down the tunnel. Two men were standing guard at the junction by the OP. Sykes told them to collect Chadwick's body and take it to the morgue. When they got back to the CP, McCleod was put on the lower bunk, his trousers removed and cast to one side. His long legs were covered in blood but his wounds weren't serious, mere creases. Once they'd been dressed, McCleod dismissed offers of morphine and walked round to the mess. As Sykes left the bunker he said to Wilson, 'Now's the time to pray, if you're that way inclined.'

CHAPTER TEN

Darkness closed in. On Old Baldy, Bunker Hill, and Hill 375, the Chinese were clearing away their dead. To the south, a decisive phase of the Chinese offensive was raging. The reserve companies of the Borderers, together with other units of the 27th Brigade, were hanging on desperately.

In the Horn there was silence. Men were either asleep or dead.

After six hours, Wilson was the first to wake. For a moment he had no idea where he was. Then it all flooded back to him. The hurricane lamp was still burning, flickering uncertainly and throwing out wisps of smoke. He looked around in desperation. He had a premonition that he was the only one alive. He was certain the mess would be full of dead bodies. He felt compelled to find out. He had to convince himself that he wasn't alone, buried alive by himself.

The mess was in darkness. A sickly smell emanating from it. He flashed his torch beam around. Bodies were lying neatly against the walls. In some cases it was impossible to tell if they were asleep or dead. McCleod was nearest the door, a soft snore confirming his health. He looked comical without trousers but still with his socks and boots on. Sergeant Sykes was sitting on an ammunition box, his legs splayed out in front of him, his head slumped on his chest in total exhaustion. Wilson lingered in the doorway, soaking up a host of details. Then he became aware of something moving by his feet. He swung his torch beam around. It was a rat: a huge, fat one. He kicked out and sent it hurtling down the tunnel.

Wilson loathed rats. Usually, he did his utmost to keep well away from them, but on this occasion, quite inexplicably, he felt compelled to follow it down the tunnel. He went slowly and hesitantly. When he reached the morgue he eased aside the blood-stained blanket. This time the smell was different, dominated by evacuated bowels and bladders. He shone his torch straight ahead. The place was teeming with rats. It was the most horrific scene he could ever have imagined. The dead were strewn about haphazardly, arms and legs sticking out at all angles, with monster rats roaming all over them. Some remained motionless, staring back audaciously, silver tails thrashing. Finally, Wilson's torch settled on a rat that was gnawing at the base of a man's nostrils. It was too much for him. He turned and ran. That was how he would end up. Buried alive, suffocated, then devoured by rats. He burst into the CP and flung himself down at the table. He was shaking all over. He gripped the sides of the table in an effort to control himself. The whole table shook. He glanced into his shaving mirror hanging on the wall. His reflection revealed a pitiful sight. His eyes were streaming tears and his whole face was distorted in self-pity, the expression of a terrified child. Several loud sobs escaped him. Then he thought of his parents and felt ashamed. What would they think if they could see him now? They would expect him to be brave, to face up to death like a soldier – like a Scotsman! He recalled the last words his father spoke to him on seeing him off on the troopship: 'Show them the colours of your tartan, Rob!'

He found himself repeating the words out loud. He knew he had to pull himself together. He must not disgrace himself, even if there was no one there to witness it. He poured himself some rum and drank it in such haste that most of it splashed over his chin. Then he remembered the conversation he'd had with McCleod while in reserve: how he also had a kilt with him, and his mother's insistence that no harm would come to him whilst he wore it. He decided to put it on. He would bow out as a Scotsman.

He reached under the bottom bunk and pulled his kilt out. It was crumpled and dirty, but the very feel of it comforted him. He was like a child, finding solace in a familiar piece of blanket or flannel. He stood up, undid his belt, and let his trousers fall to his ankles.

He was amazed to see that he had an erection. It was the biggest and hardest erection he had ever known. It was enormous, and now he was aware of it, it throbbed and ached. For a time he stared at it, then he grabbed hold of it and laughed hysterically. It was just as McCleod had said: shock equalled the shivers, fear equalled an erection. So now he really was frightened!

His hysterical laughter increased as he looked down at it, as though wondering what to do with it. Then he heard movement above him. He looked up, startled. It was the Korean girl. She was watching his every move, peering down from the top bunk. He had forgotten all about the bitch. Instinctively, he snatched his trousers back up to cover himself. She kept staring and he stared back, their eyes locked. Her tear-stained face was expressionless, her level teeth gleaming in the half-light. Without thought, he leaned forward and grabbed her around the neck. Then he pulled her towards him until she was nearly off the top bunk. He thrust his face against hers, pressing their lips together. Her skin was beautifully smooth and warm and all of a sudden she was far more than a Korean girl who had been foisted on them. She was soft, tender, and inviting; she was consoling, someone he could hold and take refuge with, someone to help him erase the sight he had seen in the morgue – someone to die with!

He put a foot on the lower bunker and hoisted himself up. He wasn't conscious of any thoughts. He wasn't capable of any. He was totally obsessed by his desire to abate his fear. For several seconds he simply hugged her. Then, in a vivid flash, he had visions of Fogarty's Korean girl in the first village, and the next thing he knew he had the girl on her back and he was grappling with her clothes. He removed her ill-fitting combat jacket and pulled her trousers and underwear down her legs, dropping them over the side of the bunk. He was acting instinctively, a zombie, with no concern for her reaction. When they were both naked he clung to her, luxuriating in the feel of her from head to toe, glorying in a luxury he had never before experienced, and as he parted her legs and thrust his penis into her all his fears miraculously dissolved.

Sykes woke at 0630 hours and he was immediately aware of two things. The air in the position was far worse and he could hear distinct sounds of gunfire. He hadn't heard such well-defined noises since the end of the battle, so it could only mean a counter-attack was underway.

Sykes felt hungry. He decided to go to the CP where supplies were kept under the bottom bunk. When he got there, the hurricane lamp was still flickering. He peered inside, but Wilson was nowhere to be seen. Sykes was puzzled. He hurried back down the tunnel, anticipating that Wilson would be at the OP, making another attempt to rescue Pickles, but everything there was in total darkness. He retraced his steps, still mystified. Then it dawned on him. The sly young bastard, he thought.

He slipped back into the CP and looked up at the top bunk. Wilson and the girl were well hidden, snuggled up together, sleeping peacefully. Sykes watched them, wondering what to do. His first reaction was to wake Wilson and create merry hell, but he dismissed the idea, knowing it would gain nothing. Wilson had only done what the rest of them would have done given half a chance; and why not?

Sykes had no intention of making an issue of the matter, but he had every intention of letting Wilson know he had been caught in the act. He felt under the lower bunk and pulled out some C-rations and opened a tin of chicken hash. Then he heard someone approaching: the slow, uncertain steps of someone groping their way along in the dark. He watched the blanket as it was drawn aside. Fogarty's plump face appeared, split by a wide grin.

'Heard the guns, Sarge?'

'Never mind the bloody guns. Look up there.'

Fogarty's face remained blank for a second. Then it registered amazement and anger. 'I don't bloody believe it!'

'Quiet,' hissed Sykes. 'Let's wait and see what happens next.'

For some time nothing happened. Wilson and the girl went on sleeping. Eventually, Sykes grew tired of waiting. He picked up his empty chicken hash tin and threw it against a timber support. The noise made Wilson stir without alarming him. He stretched and yawned. As he awoke more fully he sat up and looked down at the girl. A momentary frown cross his brow, but then he smiled as he recalled the details of the night. He slid back into the sleeping bag and snuggled up to the girl.

'Morning, sir!' cried Sykes. 'No time for more of the other.'

Wilson jerked into a sitting position. He stared down at Sykes and Fogarty in alarm. His embarrassment could not have been more acute. 'It's not what you think! Nothing happened . . . nothing at all—'

Sykes laughed. 'Say no more. We're both men of the world. Well, you are now. I just thought you'd like to know what is going on outside.' The sounds were unmistakeable: the thudding of artillery and softer, coughing noises Wilson's could not place. 'Sherman tanks, sir,' said Sykes, reading Wilson's thoughts. 'And getting closer. With luck they'll reach us before we pass out.'

Wilson snatched up some of his clothes lying on the top bunk. 'No time to waste, Sergeant,' he said excitedly. 'I really thought we'd had it.'

'I'm bloody sure you have had it,' snorted Fogarty. 'Several times!'

Sykes laughed, but Fogarty's army humour was lost on Wilson. He could only think of being rescued.

Rescue came at 1840 hours. They had been buried alive fractionally under 24 hours. It was just as Corporal Turner had predicted: rescued in the nick of time in the best traditions of the US Cavalry.

In the hours which elapsed before the rescue, 12 Platoon had never worked harder. Sykes led a party trying to rescue Denzil but when they reached him he was dead. Wilson and others worked on the OP. They were still unable to release Pickles but they were able to establish that he was alive. The greatest blessing came when they reached Denzil. They were able to force a way through to daylight. It was a hole no bigger than a fist but through it came a blast of icy wind: a taste of fresh air!

Fogarty was working with Wilson at the OP. For a long time they strove in silence. When they were forced to take a break their eyes met and they smiled. Then they laughed without knowing why. 'Never thought we'd end up like this, sir. Mind you, it'll probably land me right in the shit.'

'You mean the girl being on the position?'

'Yes, sir. We never meant her any harm. We thought she would be sent back right away.'

'She would have been, but for Middleton.'

'Yes, sir. And we reckoned we were doing her brother a bloody great favour. Mind you, sir . . . you're a crafty sod! Getting your leg over like that.'

Wilson laughed. Allowing Fogarty to call him 'a crafty sod' was a measure of their new comradeship. It could never have happened before.

'You couldn't put in a good word for me, I suppose, sir? After all, we all deserve bloody VCs for what we've been through.'

'I know what you mean. Maybe it's a good time to start afresh? Why not give it a try? Stop buggering about and start again. On the same side.'

Fogarty went back to work. He was too old a soldier to miss the chance of safeguarding his future. 'Good idea, sir. Just so long as you put in a good word in for me when they ask questions about the girl being up here.'

'OK, Fogarty. You have my word.'

There was a fierce battle before the Americans were able to clear the Chinese off Bunker Hill. When 12 Platoon heard the first Sherman tanks clanking towards them, they stuck a rifle through the hole in Denzil's bunker and waggled it about to attract attention. When it was spotted a tank was called forward. Hawsers were attached to the broken timbers and a huge gap was soon opened up.

After that, it was all excitement and hysteria. Wilson was so charged emotionally that events became a blur in his mind. He remembered shaking hands with his rescuers, hugging Americans with stubbly beards. The Americans going into the Horn and re-emerging to call for stretchers.

The wounded coming out. Bloody and tattered, but all happy. Sykes standing there, as cool as a block of ice, checking men against his platoon book. The Korean girl appearing amid cheers from the 12 Platoon survivors and looks of amazement from the Americans.

Even greater amazement as the last of the living emerged: Smokey McCleod, limping out, reunited with his trousers. The laughter, the cheers, the tears of joy and whoops of delight that greeted the old Scotsman. How he stood there looking like nothing on earth, a freshly lit cigarette dangling from his mouth, his jikkay frame on his back, his bagpipes cradled in his arms. Then the discord of his first notes, followed by the stirring wail of 'Scotland the Brave', which set everyone's blood tingling. Stumbling back across the plateau, through the ranks of advancing Americans who, to a man, turned and stared. Swaggering behind their piper, shamelessly exhibiting their pride in having won the day. Their glory at having held the Horn.

PART TWO

Captain George Saville

CHAPTER ONE

Captain Dan Rimmer of the United States 1st Army HQ was accustomed to chasing around Korea on various assignments. Usually, it was in his jeep, sometimes on trains. Once, it had been on foot, at the double, with bullets flying around him as he fled from a motor convoy ambushed by North Koreans. As Rimmer lay in a monsoon ditch, pretending to be as dead as the legless man beside him, he decided he could never be a man of war. He was a gentle soul, an intellectual who should have been pleading a case in a court of law, not grovelling about in a Korean ditch, upholding the bloodied flag of the United Nations on the frontier of the free world.

Rimmer was a Jew, his appearance strictly traditional: a sallow complexion, a prominent nose, black hair, heavy eyebrows, and close-set eyes that sparkled from within dark hollows. He was one of a rare breed, a Jew without an inferiority complex, a man who ignored discrimination and insults and never objected to being called a 'Yid', content with what he was. He was a man of great determination with an unshakeable confidence in his own ability. He was certain that so long as he exploited his talents diligently he would rise to the very top of his chosen profession, the law. His vocation in life was the study, application and manipulation of the law, outwardly to uphold justice, but inwardly as a device for outwitting others and by so doing to become rich and famous. He had an absolute conviction that he would become one of American's greatest lawyers.

He had joined the army after graduating from Georgetown Law. He reasoned that the Judge Advocates General Department was the best way of gaining swift experience; and he was right. As soon as he arrived in Japan responsibilities were thrust upon him. He had acted as trial counsel, prosecuting GIs for an enormous variety of offences. The cases made him marvel at the ingenuity of human beings, their seemingly endless ability to get themselves into all manner of unpredictable scrapes.

In Korea, things were different. In Japan, offenders had been either stupid, greedy, careless, or bored. In Korea they were desperate. Rimmer called them 'desperadoes', men so sickened by the senseless barbarity of war that rational behaviour had deserted them; and whilst common sense demanded that they should be treated with compassion, the army – ever fearful of lax discipline – prosecuted them with haste and vigour. Rimmer soon had a long succession of triumphs to his credit. He had even won praise from his CO, Colonel Barns. He referred to Rimmer as 'That young smart-ass of mine!'

Gradually, it dawned on Rimmer that he was on the wrong side. He found himself sympathizing with the underdog and his conceit about his legal expertise made him long for the chance to defend these desperadoes. He toyed with the idea of discussing the possibility with Colonel Barns but he soon dismissed the thought. He knew it would only provoke a lecture on his duty to bring wrong-doers to justice and thereby preserve army discipline. So Rimmer held his tongue, knowing that Korea was only a short phase in his career, part of his training towards the day when he would be able to pick and chose his cases.

1st Army HQ was a vast, tented area, billowing and flapping in what was reputed to be the windiest valley in South Korea. On the northern fringe of the HQ Rimmer shared a tent with a young marine lieutenant named Ed Hooper who was on a public relations assignment. His job was to tour the combat zone and write stories of derring-do for the *Stars and Stripes* newspaper. His stories were hopelessly amateurish, teeming with clichés such as, 'All hell was let loose' and 'Enemy hordes charged straight at them'. Once, he even wrote: 'Suddenly, from nowhere, hordes of the enemy were everywhere.'

At 0830 hours on the morning of 12 January 1951, Rimmer was already behind his desk when Colonel Barns showed up. He stopped in front of Rimmer. 'Morning, Dan. Got a special job for you. General Kershaw has a problem with a British unit. He's told me to send along the best man I've got. And we all know who that is, don't we.'

Rimmer smiled. 'When do I get to see him, Colonel?'

'Right away. I've no idea what it's all about, but whatever it is, you make damn sure you solve it. You know Kershaw's reputation.'

Rimmer certainly did. He was a dynamic little bastard, not the sort to keep waiting so Rimmer went back to his tent to pick up Ed Hooper, knowing he would welcome a chance to get out of camp. They drove to Corps HQ and while Hooper parked their jeep Rimmer was shown straight into General Kershaw's tent. It was very austere. The only spark of colour came from a huge map propped up against the side of the tent.

'So you're Colonel Barns's top man,' observed General Kershaw from behind a large desk with nothing on it bar a telephone. 'Take a seat. And listen carefully. I'm going to be brief. Ever heard of a British press correspondent named Cameron? Or a British weekly magazine called *Picture Post*?'

'*Picture Post*, sir. But never Cameron.'

'Well, you're lucky. He's a son of a bitch. A typical left-wing Limey. As soft as shit. He seems genuinely amazed that the Gooks go around the place murdering people. Do such things surprise you, Captain?'

'No, sir. They've been going on right from the start.'

'Well, it seems the Limeys are very sensitive about these things. Especially this man Cameron. He came across some South Korean police ill-treating North Korean prisoners, obviously on the brink of shooting the bastards. So he wrote an article full of horror and indignation for his magazine, *Picture Post*. The article was suppressed by the London proprietor, but someone – probably Cameron himself – leaked it to the *Daily Worker*, a communist propaganda rag in London. So right now, the whole of the UK is going mad about the atrocities committed by the South Koreans. To make matters worse, our shitty friend Syngman Rhee has poked his nose into things. He claims the Limeys are nothing but communist fellow-travellers under the influence of Moscow. So relations between the Koreans and the Limeys are at rock bottom.'

'It'll blow over, surely, General?'

'Maybe you don't understand the Korean mentality, Captain. They won't forget these Limey accusations and insults. They've lost face. And the one thing they can't stand is losing face. So now they're looking for a way of hitting back at the Limeys. And it seems they've found a way of doing just that.'

General Kershaw swivelled in his chair and pointed at his map with his favourite pool cue. 'The Limey unit in question was right there, on Bunker Hill. The hill was overrun by the Chinese but a handful of survivors were buried alive for twenty-four hours and then rescued by a counter-attack. And here's where all the trouble starts. Among the survivors was a Korean female. A young woman.' General Kershaw watched Rimmer's expressionless face. 'You don't seem surprised.'

'General, out here surprising things happen all the time. And we've had a couple of cases of Korean women standing in for ROK reinforcement to US units. It's a desertion ploy. But surely this is a British problem?'

'Don't get too smart too soon, smart-ass. You haven't heard the half of it yet. The Korean female went on to Bunker Hill on the very night of the battle. She was soon spotted, but for some reason she wasn't sent straight back. And the Limeys are putting forward the same reason as you have. A desertion ploy. So it all checks out. But here's the crux of the matter. After the Limeys were relieved, the father of the Korean girl turns up at 2nd Div and claims that while on Bunker Hill his daughter was raped, that once the position had been overrun the platoon commander raped her. And here's where the real complications set in. Because of the Cameron report – and the way the Koreans lost face – their press and their government are demanding that the Limeys hand over the accused officer to them to face a civilian trial.'

'No can do, General. Cases are never handed over for civilian trials.'

'I know that, Captain. And we've told the Koreans that a hundred times. But they demand that from now on, starting with this case, they must be. That all cases concerning Korean civilians must be tried in Korean courts. The Limeys told them to get lost. In fact, they've already convened a field court-martial. But the Koreans refused to let matters rest there. They maintain it's a matter of principle. It all resolves around—'

'I know what you're going to say, General. The same old problem. No agreement or treaty between the Koreans and the British to cover cases involving civilians. When the war started no one cared about legalities.'

'That's the nub of the problem, right enough,' agreed General Kershaw. 'But it's not the whole story. While the Limeys are hanging on to their man, the Koreans are still raising hell. They've even taken their case to the UN. It's this little shit Syngman Rhee behind it all. And whilst we're sticking to our guns, and refusing to budge, the Limeys – in typical fashion – have just agreed to a compromise. They'll go ahead with their field court-martial. But if the accused man is found guilty, they'll hand him over to the civilian authorities for a second trial. Under British military law that can happen. But if the court-martial finds him not guilty, then nothing further happens. End of story. And the Koreans have to forget all about it.' General Kershaw broke off and studied Rimmer. 'You get the significance?'

'Sure, General. Two things. First, if guilty, he'll face a Korean court and be sentenced by the Koreans, not the British. Second, it'll set a precedent.'

'Exactly! The thin edge of the wedge. Next thing you know, the Koreans will be insisting that every nation out here – including us – must hand over our men to them for civil offences.'

'So it all depends on the British court-martial?'

'That's the size of it.'

Rimmer sat forward, intrigued. 'So what happens now?'

'Very simple. You make damn sure there is a not guilty verdict.'

Rimmer was appalled. 'Me? What the hell can I do?'

'Cut out the bullshit, Captain. You know as well as I do what field courts-martial are like. Dumb soldiers playing at being lawyers. Most of them won't even know when to stand up or sit down. But you're a goddamn professional. So all you have to do is make sure you keep your hundred per cent record.'

'Surely you don't intend me to defend the man?'

'No. No question of that. If I had my way, you would. But under British military law you can't. The deal is this. The British will allow a Korean lawyer to be present in court as an observer and adviser to the prosecution. So someone from the Judge Advocates General Department will be there in the same capacity for the defence. All perfectly legal under the British system, but advisers have no right of audience.'

'And what about this man – the accused?'

'He admits sexual intercourse, but denies rape. He says the girl was a willing partner. You know what the Korean punishment for rape is?'

'Same as ours, I guess. A capital offence.'

'Right. And the Gooks can't wait to shoot this poor bastard.'

'General, we're in deep shit, here. A man's life is at stake and I don't know a damn thing about British military law.'

Kershaw laughed. 'Deep shit, OK! But don't worry. There won't be too much difference between their law and ours. Ours is probably based on theirs anyhow, going way back. And here's the good news. The Limeys have dug up a qualified lawyer of their own in Japan. He's going to be the defence counsel. He's already been flown out here to organize the defence. Maybe he's a real smart-ass like you. In which case you can just sit back and take all the credit. But just in case he isn't, then you're going to be there to sort things out.'

'Sounds like a great assignment!'

'Don't worry, Captain. You'll get by. Professionals like you always do. And the military establishment will be right behind you. And you don't need me to tell you that the establishment has an uncanny knack of always getting its way. But just in case thing start going wrong, I want you there as well.'

'To get this man off . . . even if he's a hardened rapist!'

'Did I ever say that? I don't think I said that.'

'But that's what you meant.'

'My word, Captain! You really are a smart-ass.'

Dan Rimmer left General Kershaw's tent feeling thoroughly confused and more than a little ashamed. Why, he asked himself, was he already looking for excuses? Surely it was the big chance he had been waiting for? An opportunity to defend a classic desperado. A chance to show everyone, especially himself, exactly how good he was. Yet a gut feeling told him he was on to a hiding to nothing. For a start, he was only an adviser to an unknown Limey, with no right of audience; and rape was the worst crime of all to defend. It invariably came down to one person's word against another's, and it was such a loathsome crime that the victim – especially if young and virginal – was guaranteed the benefit of any doubts. To cap it all, the Limey officer admitted intercourse in the heat of battle, so rape by fear would be a cinch to prove.

Rimmer realized that there was only one thing for the defence to do. They would have to dig up as much dirt about the girl as possible: paint her whorehouse red and hope that it stuck.

Rimmer was still ruminating about these things as he wandered around the HQ looking for Hooper. Eventually, he found him in the officers' mess. They grabbed a cup of coffee and then set off in their jeep for the British 27th Brigade HQ. 'What's wrong, Dan? You look worried.'

'A tough case. I've got to get a Limey officer off a rape case.'

'Defending? Man, your big chance! Not chicken already?'

'No, not chicken,' laughed Rimmer. 'It's just that the case is going to have some tricky points of law. Not even our law – British law.'

'Here come the excuses,' scoffed Hooper. Then he saw Rimmer shoot him a glance of annoyance so he said no more.

It took them some time to locate the 27th Brigade. The brigadier saw them personally and he told them that arrangements had been made for them to stay overnight. 'Anything else I can do, meanwhile?'

'I'd appreciate a copy of your King's Regulations and your Manual of Military Law, sir,' said Rimmer. 'I've got a lot of study to catch up on.'

In the evening they had a good dinner. Immediately afterwards, Rimmer left Hooper to look after the socializing and disappeared into a corner of the mess to concentrate on reading the two manuals he'd been given. He was relieved to find a basic similarity between British military law and their own, but he didn't relax his concentration, knowing that the case could stand or fall on a technicality. In the Manual of Military Law he read Paragraphs 15 and 17 of Chapter VIII, relating to rape, but it was the familiar wording – 'Without her consent by force, fear, or fraud.' The word 'fear' was mentioned frequently, just as Rimmer had dreaded.

When Rimmer and Hooper arrived at the Home Counties Borderers the battalion was out on a training exercise, the accused among them. The adjutant, the 2 i/c, and a few orderlies were the only ones left in camp. The two British officers were expecting Rimmer. 'See if you can't sort this bloody nonsense out, old man,' said the 2 i/c, a fat, blustering major. 'Never known such tommyrot. Hardly a heinous crime to poke a Gook woman, surely?'

'How do you rate Wilson's chances? Your general view?'

'Don't like the look of it,' admitted the 2 i/c. 'An old pal of mine is prosecuting, Bunny Ashby. First-rate fellow. Whereas the gormless idiot they've sent us from Kure . . . well, God help us! Bloody national serviceman—'

'Wilson's defending officer is a little odd,' said the adjutant. 'The theory is that he's so odd there's something special about him. Perhaps you'd better meet him. He's in the mess, reading magazines. Been there since breakfast. As fellow lawyers, maybe you'll get on OK.'

When they entered the officers' mess, Rimmer and Hooper looked curiously at what little could be seen of Captain George Saville. He was horizontal, slumped very low in his armchair with his feet extended out in front of him, resting on the seat of another chair. Only the portion of his legs between the chairs was visible, together with the top of his head, his dark, wiry, hair standing up proudly like clumps of well-manured meadow grass. He was holding a magazine above his head and even as they watched a podgy hand came up and turned a page.

'Captain Saville!' shouted the 2 i/c.

Saville shifted slightly. Then his face appeared over the arm of his chair. His eyes were magnified several times by his pebble-lens spectacles. As he recognized the 2 i/c he began to clamber laboriously to his feet.

'Visitors for you, Saville,' added the 2 i/c. 'Captain Rimmer and friend.' Then the two British officers left, washing their hands of further involvement.

Saville flopped back into his chair, adopting an identical position to before. He resumed reading his magazine, totally ignoring the Americans. Rimmer moved forward, determined to stamp his authority on the situation.

'Captain Saville, I believe?'

'That's what the man said.'

Rimmer laughed uneasily. 'I'm Captain Daniel Rimmer. Call me Dan. The corps commander ordered me over from the JAGD.'

Saville looked up peevishly, allowing his magazine to drop to the floor amid a pile of others. Then he sighed deeply, resigning himself to the fact that he wasn't going to be allowed to enjoy any peace and quiet. 'Ordered you over from where, old boy?'

'The Judge Advocates General Department.'

'Good show!'

'Weren't you expecting us?'

'Heard something about a visit – from one person.'

Hooper moved forward in a friendly manner, his right hand extended. 'Ed Hooper, US Marines. I'm attached to Army HQ. Just helping Dan out.'

Saville ignored the proffered hand and scanned Hooper with distaste, especially his crew cut. Then he gave Rimmer the same treatment. Finally, having decided that neither of them was worth bothering with, he stretched over the arm of his chair, retrieved his magazine, and resumed reading.

The Americans exchanged glances. Hooper was on the point of laughing. This was a Limey as he'd always heard them described. Rimmer pulled up a chair. 'Mind if we talk?'

'A free country, old man . . . or so they say.'

'Sure thing. I've been asked to offer my services with the defence of this officer who is being court-martialled.

'Prick Wilson—'

'Is that a hyphenated name?'

'No. Wilson is his name. Prick is purely adjectival.'

'Pardon me?'

'Adjectival. A descriptive word, old boy. Wilson is like a prick.'

'I see. Well, like I said. I've come to offer my services.'

'Very civil of you, old boy. I'll let you know if anything crops up.'

Rimmer hesitated, genuinely puzzled by Saville's attitude. He decided on a fresh approach. 'I'd like to assure you, Captain, that I find this just as embarrassing as you do. But I can assure you that I won't interfere.'

'Ditto, old boy.'

'Pardon me?'

'I said "Ditto". A word of Latin derivation. By using it I seek to convey to you that I can also assure you that you're not going to interfere.'

'I see.' Rimmer fought back his mounting anger. He wasn't going to take that kind of crap from anyone. His voice took on a harsher tone. 'Captain, I'm here on the direct orders of General Kershaw.'

'Who the hell is he?'

'Commanding general, 1st Corps.'

'Well what the hell has it got to do with him?'

'Your regiment is under his command.'

'My regiment, old fruit – the dear old Duke of Welly's – is in Malaya. Stuffing the commies out of sight . . . which is a bloody sight more than I can say for your shower out here.'

'I mean Wilson's regiment. The Frontiers.'

'The Borderers.'

'Pardon me. The Borderers. I'm afraid you'll have to excuse me—'

'Certainly, old boy. Always happy to make due allowances.'

There was another pause in the conversation. Rimmer was lost for words. It took him time to get going again. 'Well, as I was saying—' but he had forgotten what he was saying and his voice trailed away.

'You were alluding to General Curtains.'

'Kershaw. He's most anxious about this court-martial.'

'Aren't we all, old boy?'

'Well, yes. Of course.'

'Splendid.'

'Now look here, Captain—' Rimmer's voice rose to a shout. 'General Kershaw has many reasons for being concerned about this trial. He wants the best possible defence. He wants to make certain—'

'It strikes me, old boy,' interrupted Saville, 'that your General Curtains is trying to pervert the course of justice. And if he tried that in the British army, Curtains would be a very appropriate name.'

'His name is Kershaw and he's not trying to pervert anything. It's just that this case has grave complications and possible repercussions, especially with regard to Korean jurisdiction and international law—'

'Bollocks! Bugger all to do with international law. It's nothing but a field court-martial, for Christ's sake.'

Rimmer shifted on his chair. He could see Hooper grinning, trying to suppress laughter. 'So that's how you see it? A straightforward case?'

'Precisely, old boy. Very interesting in one respect . . . lots of extenuating circumstances. Battle fatigue and all that hog's wash. And badly let down by an inexplicable delay in the American counter-attack.'

Rimmer managed a sickly smile. He wasn't going to rise to the obvious bait. 'What about the alleged rape?'

'The alleged rape – as you so quaintly put it – has precious little that is alleged about it. Prick Wilson just hoiked out his great fat chopper and stuffed it straight up her. Didn't even have the manners to say "Excuse me, Madam".'

Hooper was unable to control his laughter any longer, but Rimmer was far from amused. 'Then how come Wilson is pleading not guilty?'

'He's not. He's pleading guilty.'

For a moment Rimmer was speechless. Then he protested: 'That's not what General Kershaw said.'

'Really? Fat lot he knows about it, then.'

'But a guilty plea is impossible.'

'Then ask Prick Wilson yourself, old boy. He'll be back soon from playing soldiers in the barren wastelands. My tactics are simple. Wilson pleads guilty and I go flat out for mitigating circumstances. That's why there is nothing for you to do. Hopefully, it will all be over by lunch. Then you can go back to General Kershaw and I can return to Japan to attend to more pressing matters. But hang around if you want to. You might pick up some useful tips.'

Rimmer couldn't stand any more. He got up and stalked out of the mess. Hooper followed close behind, glancing back at Saville every few paces as though to apologize for Rimmer's abrupt departure. Outside, Rimmer lit himself a cigarette. He rarely smoked but he always carried a pack of Lucky Strike for moments of stress, and this was a moment of stress. As he lit it, his hands were shaking with anger. He needed time to think. In the last twenty-four hours a whole pile of shit had been dumped on him and he certainly hadn't bargained on meeting someone like Saville, nor a plea of guilty. That was absurd. It had to be. It made the whole thing a farce.

Rimmer went back to his jeep and flopped into the driver's seat, smoke drifting from his nostrils. 'That Limey sure is a dandy lawyer,' said Hooper, trailing after him. 'If he ties up the prosecution the way he tied you up, then he'll get this Prick Wilson guy off whatever he pleads.'

'Don't tell me you were impressed? Winning this case happens to be vital.'

'OK, Dan. Take it easy, man. It's just that you're always on about defending people and yet now—'

'Get lost! I'm going for a drive. Go keep your Limey pal company.'

Rimmer drove off down the MSR. He had to get away from everyone in order to clear his mind. He went back to basics. He assembled the few facts at his disposal and started to building a proper defence strategy. He soon concluded that he had to do five things. First, ignore Saville and make an appointment to see the Borderers' colonel. Then see Wilson and tell him to change his plea to not guilty. Third, to advise him to ditch Saville and find a new counsel. Fourth, study a copy of the Summary of Evidence. Finally, to send Hooper back to Corps HQ with instructions for Sergeant Hammond and his Provost staff to locate the Korean girl and then investigate her.

When Rimmer returned to the Borderers, he was more confident. At least he had somewhere to start. He was still sitting in his jeep, making notes, when Hooper approached. 'Man, that Limey really is a freak,' he said. 'When I tried to get on first-name terms he insisted that all Americans call him by his nickname: the Commonwealth Kid!'

'Oh God! That's all we need. The Commonwealth Kid!' Rimmer got out of his jeep. 'Hang on here, Ed. I'm going back to their orderly room to see if their colonel is around yet. First thing I do is see him. Then I get hold of Prick-Wilson and tell him to ditch that little bastard.'

Rimmer and Colonel Wainwright met briefly. It was not a smooth meeting and it convinced Rimmer that his greatest difficulty would be getting along with, and understanding, the British. Right from the start, it seemed to Rimmer as though Colonel Wainwright was being deliberately remote. He never smiled and his clear blue eyes never stopped staring at Rimmer in apparent hostility. When he spoke his voice was clipped and abrupt and he made it clear that he was far too busy to bother with any pleasantries or smalltalk. When Rimmer opened proceedings by saying how much General Kershaw admired the fighting spirit of the Borderers, the colonel reacted as though his regiment was so internationally renowned that flattery, even from an American general, was totally superfluous.

Despite their lack of rapport, they progressed on businesslike lines. They agreed on four outstanding issues: that Rimmer must have an immediate sight of the Summary of Evidence; that he should have an early meeting with Wilson; that he should endeavour to supply the court with the names of any new witnesses he might want called; and that Rimmer, as an adviser without audience, should be permitted to interview any of the witness, defence or prosecution.

As the meeting drew to a close, Rimmer mentioned Wilson's intention to plead guilty. Wainwright was astounded. First of all, he queried Rimmer's information and then he made a conscious effort to steer a neutral course. 'As the convening officer it is not my place to comment. The plea is up to the accused and his defending officer. But he'll take your advice, naturally. That's why you're here.'

When the interview was over, Rimmer collected a copy of the Summary of Evidence from the adjutant's office and settled down at a table to read it. He soon discovered that Saville's view was not so outlandish after all. The Summary was a damning document: every witness piled up evidence against Wilson. Then Rimmer recalled the golden rule with all Summaries of Evidence. They were no more than surface evidence, produced by laymen. No professional questions had been asked, no motivations examined, no honesty doubted, and in this case no enquiries had been made about the girl.

Rimmer stayed in the adjutant's office for nearly an hour, thinking about the Summary and rereading parts of it. Then he used the telephone to contact 1st Army HQ. He was soon shouting at the top of his voice to Colonel Barns. 'It doesn't look good, Colonel. Rape by fear. The girl was so terrified she just let him get on with it. But the main problem is the defending officer. He's persuaded the accused to plead guilty.'

'That's no damn good.'

'I know that. And I'll work things out, just so long as I can get all the help I need from your end. It so happens I've got Ed Hooper with me.'

'Hooper? That gold-bricker? The last thing we want is coverage in the *Stars and Stripes*. This is a low profile job.'

'I know that, Colonel. He's helping me. And he's coming back first thing in the morning with a list of things I want checked out.'

'OK. Just don't forget that my neck is on the chopping block, same as yours.'

CHAPTER TWO

Rimmer and Hooper met Wilson over dinner. British mess etiquette discouraged 'shop' being discussed so they confined themselves to small-talk. Rimmer was glad. It gave him a chance to size up Wilson, to make sure he wasn't another British nut case.

They got on well right from the start. Rimmer found that, in stark contrast to Saville, Wilson was polite and friendly even though, like so many men accused of serious crimes, he was subdued and lacked confidence. The last thing he resembled was a rapist. After dinner they went to the Dog Company orderly tent where they were free to discuss the trial without interruptions.

'I hope you don't mind me coming to help?' asked Rimmer.

'Good heavens, no. I'm absolutely delighted.'

'Captain Saville says you were badly let down by an American unit?'

'What absolute rot. Your blokes were marvellous. And Captain Pickles became a good friend of mine.'

'Maybe. But what he says in the Summary won't help you. How are things going so far?'

'Awful. I've made my usual mess of things.'

'Captain Saville says you are going to plead guilty?'

'That's right.'

'Are you guilty?'

'I honestly don't know. I was in such a blue funk that I didn't know what I was doing. But she certainly didn't try to stop me. If she had, I'd never have done anything.'

'Sure. The prosecution will say it was rape by fear.'

'So Saville said.'

'About Captain Saville—' Rimmer paused, hoping for a voluntary response. He didn't have to wait long.

Wilson's cheeks coloured. 'Look, I may as well tell you this right away. I know George Saville of old. We shared a cabin on the troopship coming out here. And to be honest, we didn't get on. He's got a really low opinion of me. He is convinced that I raped the girl. But there's more to it than that. Since he's been in Japan he seems to have changed. On the troopship he was a raving extrovert. The type who wouldn't give a damn how many Korean women were raped. But now he's different. When we met again he kept on about whilst he's been in Japan, saving girls from prostitution by giving them jobs at Headquarters British Commonwealth Forces in Korea, I've been raping Koreans. Then he tackled me about six men from my platoon he'd come across in the Kure Base Hospital. He kept on about them only having four legs and three arms between them – as though it was my fault.'

'So what about him as your defence counsel?'

'Well, I certainly don't have any faith in him.'

'Good . . . then we'll get shot of him.'

'It's not as easy as that,' countered Wilson. 'When I heard that Saville was being flown out from Japan, my first reaction was to refuse him. But Colonel Wainwright has gone to tremendous trouble to find someone who is legally qualified. And believe it or not, Saville is qualified. An Oxford graduate. The only qualified British solicitor in either Japan or Korea. So after all the efforts the colonel has made, I can hardly turn him down. That's why I was so pleased to hear that you are going to mastermind things. At least you'll be able to make sure he bucks his ideas up.'

Rimmer took his out pack of Lucky Strike and lit one. He closed one eye to prevent smoke curling into it. 'So what about this plea of guilty?'

'Saville says that by co-operating I will gain sympathy from the court, which will be a big help when he goes for clemency. He's not saying that I won't be found guilty. But it'll be a formality . . . a dishonourable discharge.'

'Oh, boy!' exclaimed Rimmer. 'What utter crap! This man Saville really is something! Believe me, he's talking straight out of his asshole. It won't be a British court that sentences you. You'll go before a Korean civil court and they'll sentence you. Hasn't anyone explained that to you?'

'Yes, the colonel did. And Saville knows all about it as well.'

'Well, a Korean civil court is never going to give you a dishonourable discharge, for God's sake.'

'Perhaps not, but Saville says the Koreans aren't ogres . . . that I can forget all this talk about a capital offence and firing squads.'

'Robert, whatever crap this comic character Saville has been feeding you, you'd better get one thing straight. The Koreans have been raising merry hell to get their hands on you. This is politics. And politicians don't give a shit about individuals. You're just a pawn. You are totally – but totally – insignificant . . . and just as disposable. If you're found guilty they'll execute you. Ogres is exactly what they are. Haven't you heard of their record in World War II? And haven't heard about the South Korean police?'

'Yes. I've seen them in action. During the big retreat I saw them shoot fifteen refugees. Simply because they were in the way.'

'There you are then. So for God's sake be realistic.' Rimmer got up and strode around, fighting his impatience. Eventually, he sat down again and he became calmer. 'Let me put it this way. Qualified though Saville may be – Oxford and all that crap – he is nothing but a screwball. And you do have two basic rights. To decide what you plea. And to sack your counsel. So forget about Colonel Wainwright and all his efforts. It's your life that's at stake. Worry about avoiding the firing squad. Not offending your colonel.'

Wilson stared down at his hands. Rimmer could see frustration driving him close to tears. 'There's no one else I can get,' said Wilson. 'None of the subalterns in the Borderers wants anything to do with me. Originally I had two very good friends. But they were both killed.'

'You can't be all that unpopular.'

Wilson laughed bitterly. 'Oh yes I can! Awful, isn't it? Apart from the colonel, I've upset just about everyone. I just don't understand it. They all think I'm an absolute shit. Although all I've ever done is handle my platoon the way they taught me.'

Rimmer suddenly realized how lonely and vulnerable Wilson was and he felt desperately sorry for him. 'I can't explain the unfairness in life, Robert. But I can use my skills to get you off this charge. Let's forget Saville for a moment. The first thing – and something I absolutely insist on – is that you change your plea back to not guilty. Come shit or shine, and no matter what Saville or anyone else says, you're not guilty. And you stay that way.'

'Saville won't like that.'

'I don't give a fuck what he likes. You're not guilty. Right?'

'Righty-ho,' agreed Wilson.

They discussed the case into the early hours of the morning. They went through the Summary of Evidence line by line and then Rimmer listened to Wilson's story from the day he landed in Korea. The only time Rimmer interrupted was when Wilson mentioned that one of his jobs after the battle was to sort out the personal effects of the dead. With one man there weren't any. He'd queried it with Sergeant Sykes, who told him that when the man died on the lower bunk in the CP he had been alone, apart from the girl.

'You think the Korean girl went through his pockets?' asked Rimmer.

'Possibly. She did get off the top bunk very occasionally. Does it help?'

'Maybe. We'll keep it in reserve. An insurance policy.'

Rimmer asked more questions about the girl but the answers he got were vague and eventually Wilson became impatient and said that really, the girl was quite a decent type. Rimmer threw his pencil down. 'For crying out loud! Just cut out all this British crap. This decent type has got you well and truly by the balls. And I'll tell you this. The odds are that she's the local tart. I've never known a Korean woman yet who wasn't sexually available when it was to her advantage. These people are desperate. You've been telling me how your men had local women in every village they ever went to. So what suddenly makes the one you screwed a decent type? And how can you be so certain than none of your men didn't screw her as well?'

'Because I had McCleod guarding her.'

'McCleod! My God, you talk about McCleod as if he was the archbishop or something. He just happens to be one of the star witnesses for the prosecution. He has nothing good to say about you, any more than your friend Pickles.'

'I know. That did surprise me, I must say.'

'Well, for Christ's sake get one thing straight. Everyone who ever appears in court has one overriding consideration – to look after himself. If he can tell the truth as well, then so much the better. But his first consideration is always himself . . . and it doesn't matter who it is.'

'You as well?'

'You betcha!' Rimmer sent his chair skidding backwards as he got up again and resumed pacing about. He realized he may have overstated the point, so he added: 'OK, as a lawyer I also want to see truth prevail. I want to see justice done. But I'm also acting in your defence and my job is to get you off. For your sake. But for my own as well. I'm a professional with a hundred per cent winning record. I'm top of the pile. And I intend to stay that way. And I'll tell you this. I'm damned if I'm going to let that little bastard Saville get in my way. Nor your perverted British sense of fair play and decency.'

For several seconds Wilson stared at the American, amazed by his outburst, trying to fathom the full implications of what he had said. He wondered how he had ever got himself into such a mess. He just couldn't credit how everything had conspired against him. When he handled everything by the book, he was regarded as a disaster, yet when he behaved like his men, he suddenly became a rapist, facing the death penalty. To cap it all, it seemed that his trial wasn't about proving his innocence. It was everyone looking after their own interests. He suddenly had an overwhelming longing for the presence of his parents.

He stood up and said: 'If you don't mind, I would rather like to go to bed.'

Breakfast at the officers' mess was a hectic time. The officers were eating centrally, rather than in companies, which meant that the cooks had to prepare around fifty mixed grills, to say nothing of various fruit juices, endless rounds of toast, and tea served in individual pots. Breakfast was served between 0730 and 0830 hours and if anyone was late the mess sergeant had full authority to turn him away.

Saville always arrived at 0825 hours precisely. On his first visit, the mess sergeant refused to serve him, but Saville created such a stink, knowing he was in the right, that the adjutant was summoned and intervened on his behalf. From then on, whenever Saville arrived for breakfast, he poked his head into the kitchen and yelled: 'Synchronize watches! 0825 hours precisely. I'm about to take my seat for breakfast.'

This behaviour did not endear him to the kitchen staff and they were just waiting for the opportunity to send him away with an empty stomach. Their chance soon came. Despite a valiant sprint from his tent, and even though he hadn't bothered to wash or shave, and in army vernacular was half undressed, with numerous buttons undone, Saville failed by a minute to get to the mess on time.

The mess sergeant watched Saville's sprint into the tent. Then he smiled as Saville plonked himself down at a table and drummed his fingers, as though he had been waiting for ages. The mess sergeant strode into the dining tent, consulted his watch, and called out: 'Synchronize watches! It is now 0831 hours precisely. Breakfast has been served and you've missed it.'

'Don't be so damned impertinent,' yelled Saville.

To the amusement of the few officers still in the tent, the sergeant returned to the kitchen. Saville followed him, but despite another row he got nowhere. 'Right,' Saville concluded. 'I will sit in the dining tent until you do serve me.'

'Then you'll sit there all day and all night, sir. Breakfast is finished.'

In Japan, where Saville was Camp Commandant, and in charge of all messes in HQBCFK, the mess staff would never have dared to treat him like that. What's more, Japan had taught him the importance of not losing face, so he resumed his seat in the dining tent, determined to prevail. For some time nothing happened. Then orderlies came in to clear away the dirty dishes. They regarded Saville with amusement, deliberately leaving him surrounded by greasy plates. Finally, one of the orderlies approached him. 'Would you like some breakfast, sir?'

'I would indeed. And I'm not leaving here until I get some.'

'Of course not, sir. Leave it to me.'

The orderly shuffled off. He went into the kitchen and rummaged around in the waste bins and among discarded plates. Very selectively, he picked out a tomato here, a couple of sausages there, and even a rasher of bacon and an over-cooked egg which had been severely stabbed but otherwise unmolested. He piled these relics on to a clean plate and pushed them about until they somehow resembled an appetising meal. Then he reheated the plate and collected together some toast, marmalade, and a pot of stewed tea. When Saville was presented with what looked like a freshly cooked breakfast, he smiled for the first time since leaving Japan. The orderly stood alongside him as he ate, hovering in the best traditions of a professional waiter. As soon as Saville finished his mixed grill the orderly pressed toast and marmalade on him and poured him a cup of tea.

'Splendid!' cried Saville when he'd finished. 'A fine breakfast, my man.'

'Glad you enjoyed it, sir.'

Saville suddenly became aware of the orderly leering at him in a most disconcerting manner. 'We shouldna be seen together, sir,' said the orderly.

'Shouldn't we?'

'No, sir. And certainly not talking to each other.'

'Why not? Are we suspected of being lovers, or something?'

The orderly's leer developed into a chuckle, which did nothing to reassure Saville. 'Och no, sir. I dinna think we're the types for love.'

'Speak for yourself. I get more than my fair share.'

'You dinna understand, sir. I'm McCleod.'

'Well a splendid breakfast, McCleod. Congratulations! Men have been awarded the Victoria Cross for less than that.'

'McCleod, sir . . . witness for the prosecution—'

'Prick Wilson's batman? Then you're right. We shouldn't be talking.

Bugger off! But thanks for the breakfast.'

McCleod had a firm grip on the back of Saville's chair, making it difficult for Saville to pass. 'I ken it's highly irregular, sir. But I must have a word with you. It's vital for Mr Wilson.'

'About the trial?'

'Aye, sir.'

'Impossible, McCleod. Quite impossible.'

'But it's vital, sir. Mr Wilson is in terrible trouble.'

'You're telling me!' laughed Saville. 'I've got to defend the silly sod. So what kind of trouble do you think I'm in? The difference is that he deserves it and I don't. Now if you don't mind, I'd like to pass. I'll eat your breakfasts any time – absolutely splendid – but there's nothing else I can do for you.'

Saville was still in the mess lounge when other officers drifted in for their morning coffee. As always, he ignored them and went on reading. However, this time he wasn't reading magazines. He was studying a copy of the Summary of Evidence. During the morning Wilson had told him he wasn't going to plead guilty after all. Saville was most indignant, knowing that the Yank had got after him, but nothing he said changed Wilson's mind. It meant that Saville had no option but to take the trial more seriously. He would have to think up searching questions for the prosecution witnesses. Then he could rest content. Wilson would still be found guilty, of course, but Saville knew that if he could give the impression of professional competence it would enhance his chances of returning to Japan without delay.

Japan had had a tremendous impact on Saville. Because of an air crash over the South China Sea, in which British officers bound for Kure perished, Saville had been promoted acting captain in order to take over the post of Camp Commandant. He flattered himself that he'd done rather well at it, but his friendliness towards the Japanese had got him in to all kinds of trouble with several field officers, notably the senior chaplain, Padre Muldoon. In fact, it was through Muldoon's conniving with his friend Wainwright (both veterans of Changi) that Saville had ended up in Korea. He had left behind a personal problem the like of which he had never expected to encounter and which, unless he got back to Japan quickly, would scar his life for ever.

As the only qualified solicitor in the theatre of operations, Saville understood the reason for his posting, but what bugged him was the precise nature of it. It actual read: 'Temporary secondment to the

Borderers', but no one would confirm that this simply covered the period of Wilson's trial. When he arrived at the Borderers and sought clarification, all the adjutant said was: 'No doubt Colonel Wainwright will let you know of his plans in the fullness of time.'

While Saville reclined in his chair, ruminating over these things, Rimmer entered the mess. He was also a worried man. He had just had a very rough ride over the telephone from Colonel Barns. He had told Rimmer that if the defence counsel was incompetent or refused to co-operate, then he was to be gotten rid of. It left Rimmer with only one course of action. He had to have tough words with the colonel, even though he didn't relish the task.

When Colonel Wainwright entered the mess with the adjutant at his heels, everyone snapped to attention or leapt to their feet. Even Saville managed to get halfway out of his chair before the colonel called out: 'Carry on, please, gentlemen!' Rimmer waited until the colonel had a cup of coffee and then caught his eye. To his surprise, Wainwright and the adjutant approached him. 'You look worried, Captain. Problems?'

'One basic one, sir.'

'Captain Saville?'

'Yes, sir.' Rimmer anticipated that the colonel, having so astutely identified the problem, would say something else, but he didn't. 'I appreciate that you're in a delicate situation,' said Rimmer. 'Being the convening officer, and all. But you should know that Wilson is in big trouble with his defence counsel. I've sorted out the plea, but there's still hostility between Saville and Wilson. They go way back together and have never gotten along. Saville has no sympathy towards the case. He's just . . . well, fouling things up.'

Again, there was no response from Colonel Wainwright so Rimmer turned, bringing the adjutant into the conversation. 'It's like you said when I arrived. Saville isn't interested. He spends all his time reading magazines. He's done nothing to examine the background of the girl. For all he knows, she might be a well-known whore.'

Rimmer paused, letting the accusation sink in. He thought it was of such fundamental importance that it would impress the British officers, but it had no impact. It was as though any slur on the girl was in very bad taste and against the spirit of fair play. 'Look, Colonel,' resumed Rimmer, 'my job has taught me to recognize the real criminals. And I'll tell you this. Wilson is no rapist. One squeak out of that girl and he wouldn't even have held her hand. Yet Saville can't see that. Maybe he hasn't had experience in cases like this.'

'He comes highly recommended,' said Wainwright. 'He read law at Oxford and gained an honours degree. One can hardly ask for more than that.'

'Well I'm sorry, Colonel, but if his heart isn't in the case, and he doesn't believe in Robert Wilson, degrees of any sort won't do him any good.'

'We haven't had any complaints from Wilson,' said the adjutant.

'And you won't. He's frightened of causing offence.'

'Offence to whom?' asked the colonel.

'You, sir. When I told him to ditch Saville he turned the idea down flat. He thinks that if he sacks Saville it will incur your wrath.'

'Well, I certainly wouldn't be very pleased.'

To Rimmer, the colonel's reply was the final straw. Anger edged through. 'Colonel, I don't give a shit where Saville has been flown in from. If he's no damn good it's high time someone said so . . . and got shot of him. Colonel, Wilson's life is at stake. Doesn't that mean anything to you?'

'It means more than you'll ever realize,' replied Wainwright. 'But it's too late to replace Saville. In three days we go back into the line, on to Hill 425. And I don't have to tell you what's going on there. If the court-martial is delayed, the prosecution could end up with witnesses killed. And we certainly aren't going on to Hill 425 without some of its best men, just because you have no faith in Captain Saville.' Then, with a suggestion of sarcasm, Wainwright added: 'Don't worry. There will be a fair trial. British justice will be done. And be seen to be done. And bear in mind that we have not only secured a qualified British lawyer, but I've secured your services as an adviser.'

'Great! Just great!' Rimmer laughed bitterly at the thought of advising Saville. 'OK, Colonel. I'll do whatever I can. But when you find yourselves handing over Wilson to the South Koreans, don't say I didn't warn you. Now, if you'll excuse me, I'd better get back to work.'

As Rimmer stomped out of the mess the adjutant said: 'Odd bloke, sir. Very volatile. But I'm inclined to agree with him.'

'You haven't read the confidential reports on Saville, so just trust my judgement, Geoffrey. When this break is over, give me twenty minutes to reread the reports and then tell Saville I want to see him.'

Saville wasn't surprised when summoned before Colonel Wainwright. He had seen the coffee break conference with Rimmer and his ears had been burning like a couple of slices of neglected toast. When he entered the colonel's tent he gave his usual sloppy salute, something Wainwright would never have tolerated from one of his own officers. 'Sit down, Captain Saville. I think we should have an informal chat.'

As Saville settled on a wooden chair, Colonel Wainwright reopened one of the files. Having reread them, he had a very clear picture of Saville: a brilliant academic, but a man of moods and unpredictable behaviour; a man with a Mensa rating bordering on genius, but the sort of Old Etonian who revelled in financial independence and who loved to flaunt his over-inflated ego; spoilt rotten from birth and now arrogant and lazy, allowing his talents to go to seed. Above all, a completely non-physical person who would dread the prospect of commanding a front-line platoon in Korea. Anyhow, that was what Colonel Wainwright was banking on. He was not normally a devious man, but in this case he had every intention of taking advantage of Saville. It was the final comment in Brigadier Tewson's report which decided him on his course of action. The comment said: 'Saville has the potential to become a brilliant staff officer. But what he lacks, and needs urgently, is motivation.'

Colonel Wainwright had very firm ideas about motivation. To him, motivation in the army was perfectly simple. Motivation was fear. The greater the fear, the greater the motivation.

'You are probably wondering what I want to talk about?'

Saville shrugged. 'Something to do with the court-martial?'

'Oh, no. You haven't got any queries about the trial, have you?'

'No. All straightforward as far as I am concerned.'

'All boned up on *mens rea*, I take it?'

Saville frowned, but said nothing. The remark reeked of innuendo and he was amazed that Wainwright had ever heard of *mens rea*.

'Good. Then let's forget the trial. I'm concerned about your future—'

Saville stirred uneasily. The words of his posting, 'temporary secondment', flashed through his mind. He decided his best bet was to pretend the possibility of staying on in Korea had never occurred to him. 'I don't follow. My posting is a temporary secondment in order to defend Mr Wilson.'

'Oh, no. Your immediate future is with us, here in Korea. Do you have a movement order back to Japan?'

'No.'

'Quite so. You came on a one-way ticket.'

Saville worst fears had come true. The bastards had conspired to keep him away from Katsumi-san. His alarm could not have been more obvious. It was the reaction Wainwright had anticipated. 'Not that I have anything definitely earmarked for you. As you'll appreciate, in today's army we try to fit men into the right jobs. How exactly do you see yourself fitting in with the Borderers?'

Saville felt like saying that he wanted damn all to do with the Borderers, that his one desire was to return to Japan, but he knew that it would be disastrous to let his true feelings show. 'It's difficult to say—'

'You're right, Mr Saville. Very difficult. Intelligence Officer comes to mind, but we've already got a first-class officer doing that.'

For several seconds the two officers stared at each other, Saville with distrust and Wainwright with a mocking smile masking his anger. Saville had not once called him 'Sir', an insult Wainwright had never suffered before. Eventually, the colonel nodded to the two files on his desk. 'As you can see, I've been well briefed. It seems you led a very dissolute life in Japan. Are these reports from the Provost Marshal true?'

'Not having seen them, I can't really say. But I expect so.'

'It seems you've been up to just about everything . . . from rugby trips to Tokyo on RAAF transport planes, complete with girl friends, to creating spurious jobs for Japanese girls related to your chief clerk. To say nothing of letting your men sleep out of barracks with their girlfriends. True?'

'Yes.'

'And you've become heavily involved with your Japanese housegirl? And are about to apply for permission to marry?'

'That's right,' admitted Saville wearily.

'An application which won't meet with approval and no doubt explains why your services were so readily offered to us after the court-martial?'

'Yes. That's exactly the way I see it.'

'And is your Japanese girlfriend pregnant?'

Saville stiffened. Even Tewson and Muldoon hadn't asked that. 'Not that I'm aware of. But Padre Muldoon made sure I haven't see her for some time.'

There was a long silence. The longer it lasted the more obvious it became to Saville that his only chance was to take the ultimate gamble: to tell Colonel Wainwright the truth and hope to gain his sympathy. 'Actually, sir,' he said, his tone suddenly respectful, 'I wasn't entirely truthful just then. There is no chance at all of my fiancée being pregnant. Not that we haven't cohabited. But medically it is impossible. She is what the Japanese call one of the 'Exposed'. As a schoolgirl she was caught in the Black Rain at Hiroshima. And the radiation in the Black Rain destroys female fertility. On top of that, she could go down with radiation poisoning at any time.'

Wainwright was stunned. His expression became grave. 'Does Padre Muldoon know that?'

'No, sir.'

'Why didn't you tell him?'

'With his attitude towards the Japanese, it would have been pointless.'

'Yes, I can imagine. Sadly, the Padre has very fixed ideas about the Japanese. And . . . if she gets radiation poisoning, is it normally fatal?'

'Invariably. They still have no idea how to treat it.'

'Oh dear.'

'The Americans have just completed a brand new clinic for those afflicted. So if she does succumb, there is still some hope.'

'Quite so.'

'One of the consequences of war, sir—'

'Yes . . . well, I do hope it doesn't turn out that way.'

'Thank you, sir. I keep praying—'

Wainwright felt gutted, utterly ashamed, especially in view of the way he was about to manipulate Saville. For a moment he even considered abandoning his plan. He gathered the files together and placed them in a drawer, playing for time, trying to evaluate this new development. 'I take it you are absolutely serious in your attachment to this girl?'

'Absolutely, sir! I've no doubts at all. Nor has she.'

Wainwright knew Saville was longing to beg to be allowed to return to Kure and normally he would not have stood in his way; but he had already made up his mind on how to handle him, and on a matter of principle he could not allow sympathy for an individual to sway his judgement. His first duty was to the Borderers. The regiment came before everything; and anyhow, in a curious way, Saville's predicament made it even more vital for him to stick to his tactics. It would seem detestably callous to Saville, but if it transformed his negative attitude towards the court-martial, everyone would benefit, Saville most of all.

Eventually, Wainwright said: 'I really do sympathize, Captain. And maybe I can help. I don't wish to cause offence, or belittle you, but the fact is that you are not suitable as an officer in the Borderers.'

Saville made no reply. He was too stunned.

'The Borderers is an elite regiment, renowned for our officers. And there is another point. If it had been up to me, your temporary secondment would be simply to defend Mr Wilson. Keeping you here might be the brigadier's way out of the difficulties you've caused in Japan, but in the Borderers I have a policy that problems must be sorted out at source. We've just had a typical case in one of our platoons. But we didn't post the troublemakers to another unit. We improved the leadership of that platoon. In fact, it was 12 Platoon, Mr Wilson's platoon which distinguished itself on Bunker Hill.'

'Really, sir?' During the past few seconds Saville's spirits had soared.

'Yes, thanks to that policy 12 Platoon has become the finest in the battalion, whatever you may hear to the contrary. And when we go back into the line in three days – on to Hill 425 – Mr Wilson and 12 Platoon will again be taking the forward position.'

'Really, sir. Proof of the pudding, as you might say.'

'Quite so. And their example only convinces me that the problems you've caused in Kure must be sorted out in Kure. But I'm not just ignoring Brigadier Tewson's wishes. By chance, there are no vacancies in the Borderers. We've received our full quota of reinforcements after Old Baldy and Bunker Hill. So with the best will in the world, we can't make use of your services.'

'I see, sir.'

'And it can't be long before they set up a legal department in Kure. Perhaps you'll become the Captain Rimmer of HQBCFK—' Colonel Wainwright forced a laugh and Saville joined in with a much more convincing chuckle. 'I assume you're getting on well with Captain Rimmer?'

'Yes, sir. One or two little differences, but nothing serious.'

'Good. Very well, Saville, I'm glad we've cleared the air. As I've said, I think it best if you return to Kure as soon as the court-martial is over.'

'Right, sir.' Saville beamed with delight. 'Thank you very much.'

'Not at all. Just one final point . . . what you might call a warning order. Just in case something completely unforeseen happens. An accident, or an officer taken ill. If that happens, then naturally we would have no option but to call upon your services, just to see us through until we get another replacement. Not that it's likely. They all look healthy enough to me and our training is over. In fact, practically nothing will be happening. Most of us will be following your fortunes in court. I certainly will be.'

Mention of the court hit Saville like a physical blow. 'What about Wilson?'

'Mr Wilson? I don't understand – what about him?'

'His court-martial . . . the result!'

'Oh, I see. What happens if Mr Wilson is found guilty?'

'Yes, of course!' Saville's voice had risen to a shout.

'Well, if Mr Wilson is found guilty we'll have to hand him over to the South Koreans. And we'll be short of one officer, won't we?'

Saville made no reply. He just stared back at Colonel Wainwright.

'I would have thought that was obvious. But don't worry. I'm absolutely confident you'll get Wilson off. However, if you don't . . . well, I don't pretend for a moment that you would be my first choice as a replacement, but I dare say you'll get on well enough in command of 12 Platoon—'

'Of 12 Platoon!' exploded Saville. He jumped to his feet. 'Me? Command 12 Platoon? Those bloody cut-throats?'

'Captain Saville! Control yourself. I am only talking about possibilities.'

'No you're not! What you're talking about is a dead bloody certainty. Nothing but blackmail. Unless I get Wilson off, I get his bloody platoon. On the bloodiest hill in Korea. That's nothing but blackmail.'

Saville stared down at Wainwright, so angry he became speechless.

The colonel remained unperturbed. It was blackmail and he knew it, but he was certain it was the only way to motivate Saville, the only way to get him off his backside and make him fight like a terrier for Wilson's life and the reputation of the Borderers. He went to the tent flaps and drew them to one side. 'You forget that I have full powers to retain you, regardless of the court-martial. I consider that I am being eminently fair. That's all. Dismiss!'

CHAPTER THREE

Saville didn't bother to salute. He swept past Colonel Wainwright, through the adjutant's outer office, and out into the cold midday air. He was so livid he just strode about the battalion lines, cursing under his breath. 'Plain bloody blackmail. The two-timing bastard!'

Eventually, he found himself back in the officers' mess. He flung himself into his usual chair and picked up a magazine, acting out of habit, but he couldn't read. He couldn't think of anything other than commanding 12 Platoon, of being pushed on to the forward slopes of Hill 425. Everyone knew that was murder. It was attacked en masse every night. Sometimes twice nightly, like a bloody theatrical performance. He had visions of being shot, spurting blood in all directions; or being blown up by mortars, staring down at his hanging limbs; or standing in a trench with hordes of Chinese sprinting towards him with fixed bayonets.

The very thought of these things made him break into a cold sweat and even when his visions of Hill 425 dissolved through sheer repetition, they were replaced by fresh horrors, even greater horrors: Katsumi-san's predicament in Kure. He would never see her again. He would never even know what became of her. Not that it was difficult to imagine. Even if she remained healthy she would never get another job. No one would ever employ one of the Exposed who had already been dismissed by the Occupation Forces. Her only option would be to become a New Geisha, a polite name for a bar hostess. He would be dead and she would be a whore, being screwed by all and sundry.

Saville tormented himself with these thoughts until eventually he could stand them no longer. He got up and started to wander around again. Eventually, he walked into the dining tent. Most of the other officers had finished lunch, and when he sat down he received the usual stares from the waiters. He ignored them, knowing that they had no option but to serve him. By the time he started on his main course, he was the only officer left in the tent. Several orderlies came in to clear away dirty dishes. One of them was McCleod. As soon as Saville spotted him, he knew what he had to do. He might not have the guts to fight the Chinese, but he had the wit to make mincemeat of a military blockhead like Wainwright. If the colonel wanted to play it dirty, then so would he, and in the process he'd stuff the bastard out of sight. He had told Katsumi-san he would never leave her and he never would. His love for her was so genuine and profound that he didn't give damn what he did. He waited until McCleod drew near. 'Still want a word with me?'

'Aye, sir.'

'What are you doing next?'

'Washing up, sir . . . alone.'

'Right! I'll give you a hand. When the coast is clear, give me the nod.'

'Aye, sir. I willna waste your time.'

'You'd better not! I'll wait for your nod. You wash and I'll wipe.'

Rimmer was waiting for Hooper to return from Army HQ in the tent Colonel Wainwright had made available to him. During the morning he had interviewed the prosecution witnesses, Fogarty, McCleod and Sykes, but all he had discovered was that none of them had interfered with the girl. More and more it seemed that everything was dependent on Hooper and Hammond producing something sordid about the girl. Rimmer was still musing over these things when he felt something tapping on his shoulder. He looked around sharply. It was Saville, tapping away with his swagger stick. He was wearing a peaked cap and an enormous greatcoat. Rimmer was so surprised he took a moment or two to respond. 'Ah, the Commonwealth Kid!'

Saville ignored the sarcasm. 'Shouldn't we be getting on with some work, old boy? We can't afford to sit around on our fannies all day.'

Rimmer was stunned. 'I'm waiting for Ed Hooper.'

'You might just as well wait for Godot, old man.'

The remark was lost on Rimmer. 'How's the reading going?'

'Fine, old boy. Just finished their magazines. So now I'm all set.' Saville removed his greatcoat and settled down in front of the space-heater, stretching his stubby legs out in front of him so that the soles of his boots almost touched it. 'I don't know about you, old fruit, but I have no intention of going back to Japan as a loser.'

Rimmer's mind began to race. This was a very different Saville from the one he had met before. He was genuinely cheerful and confident. 'What about the guilty plea? Doesn't that make winning a little difficult?'

'Forget that, old boy. Just a little ploy of mine. Testing out Prick Wilson. But credit where credit is due. The old Prick stuck to his guns. Showed character. As far as I'm concerned, he's not guilty and it's going to take a brilliant man to prove otherwise. I'm a fighter, not a quitter.'

'Well, you certainly had me fooled.'

Rimmer waited, wondering what kind of plan Saville would disclose, but Saville just sat there, smiling pleasantly as he watched steam rising from his damp boots. He seemed fascinated by the sight and it wasn't until the boots were on the verge of bursting into flames that he withdrew them. He loosened the laces, removed his feet, and said: 'Ah, the sheer luxury of hot, smelly feet.'

Rimmer was tempted to comment on the smell but thought better of it. He stuck to the matter in hand. 'So what do you suggest our tactics should be?'

'What do *I* suggest? To be frank, I was banking on hearing your ideas first. You're the adviser, so let's be having some advice out of you.'

Rimmer explained his views, skirting over their precarious situation by emphasizing his confidence that Hooper and Hammond would come up with good evidence against the girl. He was still expounding his hopes when they heard a jeep draw up outside. Rimmer guessed it was Hooper and hurried out. Straight away he saw there was good news. Hooper was clearly bursting to tell Rimmer what had happened, but Rimmer forestalled him.

'Listen, listen! Let me put you in the picture. This place is a nut house. And the biggest nut of all is Saville. I complained about him to the colonel and now he's a different man. Full of enthusiasm. Come on in. We're discussing our approach. And tell me your news. I can see it's good by your grin.'

It was Guest Night at the Borderers officers' mess and as Rimmer followed Wilson into the dining marquee he was amazed. It was resplendent: wine glasses sparkling, cutlery gleaming, smart waiters stationed at regular intervals along the marquee, and down the centre of the long table a magnificent display of regimental silver, choice items which had been looted from all corners of the globe in the heyday of the regiment. The meal went into seven courses and Rimmer thoroughly enjoyed it. He got no worthwhile conversation from Wilson so he spent the meal in the role of an observer. The revelation of the evening was George Saville. He was without a care in the world and evoking great mirth among his companions. He had purchased several bottles of Beaujolais and his generosity meant that his sphere of influence spread along the table, bringing at least a third of those present under his spell. Rimmer could just hear his anecdotes and there was no denying that he was a born raconteur. He was so amusing that Rimmer – against his natural inclination at first – found himself warming to the man. After one particular story about Saville trying to seduce the MO's daughter on the billiards table at Raffles, Wilson nudged Rimmer. 'That's the real George Saville. One smutty joke after another.' Wilson's voice reeked of contempt, but to Rimmer the real Saville was a vast improvement on the cantankerous little bastard he'd first encountered.

When the meal was over, Rimmer made a point of rounding up Saville, Wilson and Hooper in order to finalize their tactics. Saville wasn't keen to get involved. He was enjoying himself far too much with his new friends. However, Rimmer refused to be thwarted and eventually the four of them settled down inconspicuously in a corner of the mess so that they could talk shop without causing offence. As Rimmer explained his views his hands played with a pack of Lucky Strike. He stressed that Hooper and Sergeant Hammond were making good progress with probing the girl's background. She lived with her parents in a tea house and there was a strong possibility that it might turn out to be considerably more than tea house. Then he went on to more general points: how he expected the case to proceed, the accusations the prosecution would make and how they should react. He drilled into Saville the need to handle the girl gently and to keep the trial as clean as possible. He explained that nothing upset members of a court-martial more than unnecessary and explicit sexual details, so any claims about the girl's promiscuity must be avoided until backed up by hard facts. The defence had to establish how reasonable it was so that when they did drop their bombshell about the girl's notoriety, their previous fairness towards her would lend credence to their case and not be seen as more irresponsible ranting.

Rimmer concluded by reminding them that the girl's background wasn't the only unknown quantity. They must never forget what Rimmer referred to as the 'X-Factor': the money and personal effects which had mysteriously disappeared from the man who had died on the lower bunk of the CP when the girl was known to be the only one present.

Apart from a derisive snort when Rimmer mention the 'X-Factor', Saville listened in silence. He was marvelling at the Yank's brazen cheek; the way he reckoned he'd got the right to breeze in and take control. He hadn't even marshalled his facts properly. He obviously had no idea that money had also gone missing from McCleod's trousers when they were removed from him when wounded; but Saville certainly wasn't going to enlighten him.

Despite his annoyance, Saville refrained from interrupting. He had had a beautiful meal amid splendid company, and all he wanted now was to sit back, take it easy, and puff away on the King Edward the adjutant had given him. He was at peace with the world, happy in the knowledge that in his tent, tucked at the bottom of his wad of notes on his clipboard, was a complete strategy for establishing Wilson's innocence: a comprehensive, systematic exposé that made Rimmer's vague hopes pathetic by comparison.

Jock McCloud, despite a personal odour of greasy plates and unchanged underwear, had turned out to be a barrack-room lawyer of pure genius. Saville wasn't so naïve as to consider McCleod's plan foolproof, but it was brilliant. He had been staggered by the Scotsman's cunning and his detailed knowledge of what had happened in Dog Company. Also, his suggestions on how to destroy witnesses was masterly, and the way he intended to exploit his own role was positively Machiavellian. He even had an alternative strategy which put a whole new slant on the legal definition of rape by fear. The sly old devil had devised an option he called a 'sympathetic extenuation'. It was the only point on which Saville wasn't entirely clear, but McCleod had told him not to worry, that it would never come to that anyhow.

Saville would have remained silent through Rimmer's pep talk had not Rimmer suddenly said: 'OK, Kid? You realize what I'm expecting of you?'

'You . . . expecting of me?'

'Sure. Are you happy with everything?'

'Perfectly. But the only way I'm going to handle things is my way.'

'But Kid! Don't you understand? Until Sergeant Hammond—'

'Wally Hammond can do what the hell he likes,' countered Saville. 'And if he comes up with a last-minute sensation that Liami Wo Pak is one of Syngman Rhee's Comfort Girls, then I'll be the first to make capital out of it. But in the meantime I've got to conduct a coherent defence, not sit on the fence and pray for the miracle of Brand X.'

'Then how are you going to handle the prosecution witnesses?'

'Simple, old boy. I'm going to prove them all to be bloody liars.'

'But you can't do that.'

'Why not?'

'Because they aren't all bloody liars.'

'Bollocks! The Koreans are bound to lie. So will Middleton. And that sergeant bloke, Sykes. And as for Fogarty and McCleod . . . my God, those two bastards wouldn't know the truth if it sat up and hit them.'

There was silence. The others stared at Saville, wondering why he had suddenly gone sour on them again. Eventually, Rimmer said: 'Kid, there is no way you can prove those witnesses to be liars. The facts speak for themselves.'

'Bugger your so-called facts,' scoffed Saville. 'I'm going to destroy their credibility. Then your so-called facts will take on a very different look. That's the key to this case, old boy – credibility. Not facts. Not even Brand X.'

Rimmer lit a Lucky Strike. 'Look, Kid. Please believe me. I know! For three years I've handled courts-martial and I know from experience.'

'Rimmer, old fruit, you don't have exclusive rights on experience.'

'All right! Just tell us how much Goddamn experience do you have?'

Rimmer's voice had risen to a shout so that everyone in the mess heard him. Colonel Wainwright was sitting with several guests, one of whom was a tall, bald-headed major named Rupert Ashby. He was the prosecuting counsel. Out of politeness, Ashby and the other guests pretended they hadn't heard Rimmer's outburst, but it was so obvious that Colonel Wainwright was unable to ignore it. 'The defence appear to have a few differences to iron out.'

'Yes, sir,' replied Ashby. 'I know how they must feel. Even if the defence was united, young Wilson still wouldn't stand a chance.'

CHAPTER FOUR

The sombre setting for the field court-martial could not have been more appropriate. Dawn was struggling to break, with a uniform murkiness easing out total darkness. A large marquee had been erected adjacent to battalion HQ. Attached to it were two smaller tents, one for the use of the members of the court and the other for providing refreshments during adjournments. Further away there was a fourth tent for the witnesses.

The president of the court was Lt-Col C.V. Jameson, MC. He was a tall, handsome man with an extravagant moustache. He strode into court carrying a briefcase containing the Summary of Evidence, the charge sheet, King's Regulations, and a copy of the Manual of Military Law. The four other members of the court – consisting of three captains and a major – were already there. Colonel Jameson wasted no time and they went through a ritual of legal requirements. They established that they were all qualified to serve as members of the court and had been properly authorized. Finally, they read through the charge sheet and verified that it had been signed as correct by the convening officer, Lt-Col P. Wainwright. Colonel Jameson then ordered the court to be opened. Regimental policemen ushered in the interested parties: the prosecution team headed by Major Ashby, together with his Korean adviser; George Saville and Dan Rimmer as the defence team; the interpreter; and the RASC shorthand recorder. When they were all seated, Robert Wilson entered the court, flanked by two brother officers. Finally, all the witnesses were called in for the swearing in.

When the formalities had been satisfied, Wilson stood to attention at the side of the defence table. Colonel Jameson then read out his full name, rank and number and asked: 'Are you that person?'

'I am, sir.'

'You are charged with committing a civil offence under Section 70 of the Army Act, that is to say wilful rape contrary to Section 1 (1) of the Sexual Offences Act, in that you, Second-Lieutenant Robert James Wilson, on a defensive position known as Bunker Hill, on 11 December 1950, had sexual intercourse with one Liami Wo Pak without her consent. How do you plead? Guilty or not guilty?'

'Not guilty, sir.'

Wilson remained standing until he felt Rimmer tug at his sleeve. He sat down and Major Ashby rose instead. 'Sir, I am the prosecution counsel. Before I outline the case against the accused I would point out that this is a case fraught with complications and I seek the court's indulgence in pointing them out at the outset.'

Ashby then described the dispute over jurisdiction and the agreed compromise. He also mentioned that both sides were availing themselves of advisers who had no right of audience. 'Matters are further complicated,' added Ashby, 'by the unusual circumstances surrounding the alleged rape. I refer, of course, to the presence of a Korean female civilian on a British front-line position. This has been the subject of a Court of Enquiry by the Home Counties Borderers and it was found that the girl in question, Liami Wo Pak, was forced into her predicament by her brother, who is now officially listed as a deserter. Allegations that certain British soldiers abducted the girl were not substantiated. However, I submit, that the reason for the girl's presence on Bunker Hill is not relevant. The only function of this court is to determine whether or not Liami Wo Pak was raped by the accused.'

Ashby then went on to outline his case, saying he would be calling six witnesses. Eventually, he called his first witness. There was a lot of shouting from one regimental policeman to another, as though they were determined to play their full part and capture the atmosphere of the Old Bailey. Everyone waited with interest for the appearance of the girl's father. He turned out to be small and fat, a toad of a man, dressed in a shabby, double-breasted suit of impressive vintage which had absorbed considerable local colour during its service. He made an affirmation to tell the truth and then, working through the interpreter, he confirmed his name and address to Ashby. Ashby then instructed him to tell the court what happened on the evening of 12 December.

There was a delay whilst this was translated. When the answer came it had the ring of well-rehearsed patter. 'On the date mentioned I was at home. We were anxious about my daughter. She had been missing ever since she went to see her brother off to combat duty as a Katcom. It was dark when an army jeep came up to my house with my daughter. She told us that she had been taken to Bunker Hill by two British soldiers, then raped by a British officer.'

'What action did you then take?' prompted Ashby.

'I sent her to a doctor for examination. He said there had certainly been sexual intercourse. Sog reported the matter to the UN Forces.'

'Please explain to the court why you took this action.'

'Because it was an outrage. And she is no longer a virgin. And in Korea a girl must be a virgin to secure a good marriage. Now, my daughter's only hope of a good marriage is to have her name cleared. And anyhow, my daughter was violated against her will. That must be punished.'

Major Ashby asked no more questions and sat down. Saville rose slowly, studying a list of notes on his clipboard. Outwardly, he looked casual, but inwardly he was plagued by nerves. Despite his legal qualifications, and his boasts to Rimmer, his experience in court was nil. He realized his performance would depend to a large extent on what kind of an opening he made. As though that wasn't test enough, McCleod had insisted on an enormous gamble at the start. 'It's no more than a wee bluff, sir. These people willna have any idea of what they're up to. Gooks and amateurs, that's all.'

Saville hoped to hell McCleod was right.

He started in a clear, ringing, voice. 'You have explained to the court your daughter's reasons for bringing this charge of rape, yet among those reasons you did not mention compensation. If the accused is found guilty, you will claim compensation?'

The girl's father was clearly puzzled. 'Compensation? I don't know anything about compensation.'

'Then can I take it,' asked Saville very deliberately, 'that in the event of a guilty verdict, you will definitely not exercise your daughter's unquestionable right to apply for financial compensation?'

When the interpreter had finished the translation, the girl's father looked across at the Korean solicitor, seeking guidance. In turn, the solicitor went into a whispered conversation with Ashby.

Eventually, Saville cut in, addressing himself to Colonel Jameson. 'In the absence of an answer, sir, perhaps I should make my point clear. In the event of a guilty verdict, Korean law provides for punitive damages. Similarly, as I am sure you are aware, British military law provides the machinery for a guilty member of His Majesty's Forces to meet awards made against him. I refer to Chapter Ten, para (c) of the Manual of Military Law where it states: 'In cases of compensation being awarded against a guilty party, appropriate deductions will be made from the pay of the said party.'

This generosity on the party of British military law surprised everyone. Saville paused to let it sink in. Then he added: 'What I therefore seek to establish is whether or not the charge against the accused is motivated by the desire for financial compensation. If so—'

'We see your point, Captain Saville,' interrupted Jameson. 'But it is a matter of accuracy. Major Ashby, do you contest this information?'

'Sir, this whole question of compensation is a complete red herring—'

'That's nonsense, sir,' protested Saville. 'This is a question of motivation. If the trial is being brought in the hope of compensation – about which I do not question the legality – then it should be divulged. In just the same way as counsel listed the other points.'

'Quite so,' agreed Jameson.

'But sir,' countered Ashby, 'I think it is only right to point out that the witness feels most strongly—'

'Major! The witness is under cross-examination. He must answer for himself.' Colonel Jameson instructed the interpreter to tell the witness what had been said. When this had been done, he told Saville to proceed.

'Is it your intention to apply for compensation on behalf of your daughter in the event of the accused being found guilty?'

'Well, that depends . . . if she is entitled to compensation . . . then surely she is entitled to claim it . . . surely?'

'Absolutely,' agreed Saville. 'So we can now amend the reasons you gave regarding your daughter's reasons for bringing this charge of rape as being as follows: loss of virginity, damage to marriage prospects, being despoiled against her will, and compensation.'

'No. That's not right. My daughter seeks justice, nothing else. She did not bring the charge for money.'

'Thank you for that clarification,' said Saville with the air of someone being excessively reasonable, 'I quite understand. Heaven forbid that money should raise its ugly head. Now then, let's press on. You've given your address to the court, but please explain where you live in relation to the 38th Parallel.'

'Very near the 38th Parallel.'

'North or south?'

'Virtually on it. It is very difficult to be exact.'

'Are you saying that in the same way as you had known nothing about financial compensation, you are also ignorant of whether you live north or south of the 38th Parallel?'

The witness didn't answer, so Saville turned to the president. 'With respect, sir. Would the court please instruct the witness to answer directly and accurately. It's a very simple question. Rather like asking an Englishman if he lives north or south of the Watford Gap.'

'Answer the questions properly,' said Jameson. Then he glared at Saville.

'North or south?' persisted Saville, unabashed.

'North.'

'So you and your family are North Koreans?'

'No. We're Koreans. Just Koreans.'

'But North Koreans in that you come from north of the 38th Parallel?'

'I don't recognize artificial frontiers.'

'Answer truthfully and sensible,' snapped Jameson.

'Are you North Koreans?' repeated Saville.

'Yes.'

'On the outbreak of war, were your sons in the North Korean army?'

'Yes.'

'Yet we learn from the prosecution that one of your sons is now posted as a deserter from the South Korean forces. Would you please explain that?'

The witness gave a very confused explanation.

'So what you are telling us,' said Saville with unrestrained amusement, 'is that your sons were first of all conscripted into the North Korean army. Then they deserted. Then they joined the South Korean army. Now your elder son is missing, presumed dead. And your second son – the one indirectly involved in this case – deserted from the British army when he became a Katcom. When he should have joined the Borderers, his sister took his place and he disappeared and hasn't been seen since. Can all this really be true?'

'It's not as simple as that. My sons were on garrison duty in Wachon and when the town fell to the South Koreans my sons were captured. And like all others they had the choice of joining the South Korean army or being shot.'

'Then we can assumed they changed sides pretty quick-sharp?'

'Yes.'

'And did you support their desertion?'

'Well . . . yes.'

'You don't see anything wrong with desertion?'

'Not from the wrong side.'

'So does your second son, the deserter, think he's on the wrong side again? Does he knows something we don't? Maybe he's joined the Chinese?'

There was a ripple of laughter around the court. The Korean's face distorted in anger and he shouted back belligerently. 'I can't answer for my son. And people change sides the whole time.'

'I'm quite sure they do. And I'll bet you and your daughter are just the same. That you change loyalties and jobs at the drop of a hat.'

Ashby jumped to his feet. 'Sir! That is totally unjustified.'

Jameson didn't bother to consult his fellow members. He peered over his glasses at Saville. 'We are all fully aware of the difficulties presented by a civil war, Captain Saville. Please keep to relevant questions.'

'Very good, sir.' Saville studied the questions on his clipboard and turned back to the witness. 'Do you, as part of your livelihood, run a tea house?'

'Yes. That's right. My wife looks after that.'

'And does your tea house receive visits from American soldiers?'

'Yes. Frequently.'

'And what do they do when they call in?'

'They drink tea.'

'Really? Don't they have something a little less genteel in mind? Isn't it true that your tea house has now become a house of ill-repute? A brothel?'

The Korean glared at Saville furiously. 'Never. That is a lie.'

'I suggest that your tea house is not only a brothel, but that your daughter is one of its main attractions . . . nothing but a jig-a-jig girl? Is that true?'

The witness erupted. He shouted back at the interpreter, so incensed that he sprayed saliva all over the place. Ashby again leapt to his feet in support. 'This is outrageous, sir. The defence has no grounds—'

'I'm only asking a question,' snapped Saville.

'Sir, what the defence must realize—'

'I'm perfectly entitled to ask a straightforward question—'

The president thumped his gavel. 'This court will be conducted in an orderly manner. Resume your seats. The court will consider the objection.'

Jameson went into a whispered conversation with his members. Then he turned to Saville. 'How do you justify this aggressive questioning?'

'I wouldn't agree that it's in the least aggressive, sir. And I will certainly justify my questions by quoting the Manual of Military Law. This makes the matter of cross-examinations, and what can and cannot be put to witnesses, very clear. Sections 126 and 127 of Chapter Five on Evidence. Both sections state that any questions can be put in cross-examination to test accuracy, veracity and credibility of witnesses. Indeed, Section 126 (a) states that leading questions and ones without direct bearing may be put and must be answered. So I would suggest, sir, that these sections give the defence sweeping powers of cross-examination in order to establish innocence. What they have in mind is the danger of trumped-up stories, a real possibility in this case. And with respect, sir, I would suggest that it is pointless for the prosecution to object every time I put a question they don't like. Whether or not the Wo Pak tea house is a brothel is, I submit, absolutely fundamental to the entire case. If his daughter is a whore, there is simply no case to answer. My questions only sought to clarify that.'

The members went into a further huddle. Jameson then announced a recess. Everyone stood up as the members went into their rear tent to check Saville's claims. They soon reappeared. When everyone had settled once more, Jameson said: 'The objection is overruled. The question will be repeated.'

By the time the recorder had read back the question, the girl's father was much more composed. 'It is a ridiculous lie. My house is the same as it ever was. A normal tea house. And my daughter is highly respectable.'

Saville accepted the answer and then asked: 'Are you aware that the American Military Police have shown considerable interest in your tea house and placed it out of bounds?'

'I know of no such thing.'

'But surely you've seen their notice board?'

'No. I've never seen or heard anything about any notice boards.'

'Really?' mocked Saville. 'In that case you'd better be very careful when you next go home in the dark. You might trip over it and have a nasty accident. The board measures three foot by four foot, has red letters on a black background, and is driven into the ground on a metal stake directly outside your front door.'

The interpreter started to translate, but Saville sat down and called out: 'No need to translate. That was a statement. Not a question. If he does trip over it, he'll only have himself to blame. No more questions.'

Saville's flippancy caused a stunned silence. Among the court members there was a tangible feeling of outrage. They could hardly credit his cockiness and arrogance. Jameson glared at him with frightening hostility. Behind Saville, Rimmer hissed: 'That's exactly what I told you not to do. You didn't have a damn thing on that witness, and Hammond only put that notice board up there this morning—'

'Did I ever say anything any different?'

'And where did you dig up all that about Korean compensation?'

'Pure guess, old boy. Probably complete balls.'

Rimmer looked as though he was about to explode with anger, so Saville turned away. He refused to get rattled. He may have offended the court's sensibilities, but he was damn sure he had also sown seeds of doubt in their minds. Anyhow, what really mattered was that his cross-examination had flowed. He'd enjoyed it. It was like old times at Oxford, blasting away in the Union.

The next witness was Liami Wo Pak. She was dressed in traditional costume: a colourful kimono, obviously brand new and beautifully embroidered, depicting flowers and waterfalls. She wore a mere hint of make-up, so expertly applied that it made her look incredibly young and innocent. Her hair was hanging to her shoulders, also calculated to foster the 'little girl' look. She even managed to mince through the marquees with her eyes demurely downcast. To Saville, it was all so artificial that any sympathy he might have felt disappeared. He just hoped to hell that McCleod's reading of her character was correct: that quite apart from being a thieving little bitch who had stolen money from his discarded trousers, she was an empty-headed youngster who could be easily confused and frustrated, and forced into inconsistencies, errors and lies.

Major Ashby went straight on to what happened upon her arrival on the hill. 'Did you have any idea of the dangers to which you might be exposed?'

'Not really,' she replied through the interpreter. 'I was quite sure that once an officer knew of my presence I would be sent straight home.'

'Tell us what happened when your presence was first discovered on account of your uncontrollable tears brought on by the sudden shelling.'

The girl gave a brief and accurate summary and concluded: 'All the time the officer was very angry and shouting. I was put on the top bunk and there was someone with me, guarding me. Always the same man.'

'Did he ever leave you?'

'Sometimes. But only briefly. And then the officer would be there.'

'Did you find that a comfort?'

'Yes. I was frightened that without someone there to guard me, the other men would misbehave.'

'In what way?'

'The usual way. By having sex with me.'

'But did anyone, besides the accused, molest you in any way?'

'No. The officer was the only one.'

'At any time, during your journey to Bunker Hill, or on your arrival, or on your stay there, would you have willingly had sexual intercourse with any of those men?'

'No. Of course not.'

'Now please relate the sequence of events leading to the alleged rape.'

The girl described the meeting in the CP and then recalled the way the fighting had intensified, with wounded and dead men being brought in. Then she said, 'By this time I was completely terrified. And things got even worse. Eventually, there were lots of very loud explosions. Then more wounded men came in, with sights of unimaginable horror. Eventually, the last wounded man who came in was the old one who had previously been guarding me. After they took him away, the officer was the only one left with me. He was in a terrible state. He was drunk and getting more and more drunk. Anyhow, at length he went to sleep and so did I. The next thing I knew, I was woken by the officer rushing back into the bunker. He was in an even more terrible state. He was frightened out of his life. As though he had seen evil spirits. He was shaking all over. And crying like a small boy. At one stage he looked into a mirror and laughed and cried at his own image. As though completely mad. Then he suddenly stood up—'

The girl stopped speaking and looked appealingly towards Ashby and the Korean solicitor. 'I am afraid you will have to continue,' said Ashby.

'When he stood up he lowered his trousers and exposed himself. He exposed his penis. It was standing straight up in the air. He had a very, very big erection. He looked down at it, as though in amazement. Then he started to laugh again. Even more crazy. Then he grabbed it in his hands, as though angry and frustrated. He was getting more and more crazy all the time.'

'And what exactly were you doing?'

'I was terrified. I was peeping over the edge of the top bunk. And suddenly he looked up, straight at me. For a moment he froze. Then he leered at me. A gloating look, very cruel. His eyes were crazier than ever. All white and evil. Then he grabbed me around the neck and kissed me. Then he leapt on to the bunk beside me. He got on top of me, his legs astride me, pinning me down. He unzipped the sleeping bag and tore my clothes off me. Then he tore his own clothes off. And all the time he was laughing. I tried to resist, but he was too powerful. And then he raped me. He forced his way into me and hurt me very much. After that, we were so exhausted that we went to sleep. I don't know for how long. When I woke again I thought he was going to rape me again. His leg went across me. But the sergeant's voice suddenly sounded. When I looked down, the sergeant and another man were there, watching us. They all spoke together for a short time and then the officer suddenly became very happy. He put his clothes on and jumped down from the top bunk. After that, several hours, I suppose, we were rescued.'

'One final question,' said Ashby. 'Before you went on Bunker Hill were you, in any way – no matter how slightly – experienced in sex?'

'No. In no way whatever. I was a virgin.'

All the way through Ashby's examination, Rimmer was in a dilemma. He watched Saville making copious notes, and he was terrified that he was going to pursue his avowed intention of proving the girl a 'bloody liar'. Rimmer's common sense told him to keep quiet, but the temptation to intervene was too great. He scribbled a note and pushed it forward to Saville. It read: 'If you bully her, you'll only make the court more sympathetic towards her.'

Saville gave the note a cursory glance. He had already compiled a list of questions and he was so convinced he had good ammunition against the girl that he screwed Rimmer's note into a tight ball and stuffed it into a pocket.

'Liami Wo Pak,' began Saville, working through the interpreter, 'you said that when you were taken into the command post, a guard was placed over you. And that you found that a comfort.'

'Yes.'

'Well then, thus comforted, did you try to speak to the officer?'

'No. As I've said, I can't speak or understand any English.'

'None at all? Not even "yes" or "no"?'

'No. Nothing.'

'So you made no effort to insist on being taken off the hill?'

'No. I knew no one would understand me. And I was too shocked.'

'I suggest that you didn't say anything because you knew full well your brother – the deserter – needed time to make good his escape.'

'That's not true. I've told you, I was too frightened. All I could do was cry.'

'So you went through this horrendous battle without saying a word – in any language. Then, when the officer in charge suddenly lowered his trousers for no apparent reason and revealed what you so graphically describe as a "very, very big erection", you still said nothing. You didn't even scream!'

'I keep telling you – I was too scared and shocked.'

'But that's exactly when people do scream . . . when they're confronted by something that terrifies them. Unless, of course, what you saw didn't really terrify you at all. That you've seen plenty of other men in that condition.'

'You're lying. I was too shocked. You don't know what it was like.'

'Oh yes I do,' protested Saville. 'You thought you were going to die. That you were going to be suffocated, or even worse. And was it not the case that you were so terrified of dying that you were prepared to accept his presence, that in your need for comfort and reassurance, you decided not to resist?'

'No. He was too strong for me to resist—'

'I accept that, but resistance would at least have warned him off.'

The girl offered no answer.

'And if you had screamed, others would have come to investigate—'

Again, there was no answer.

'And how is it that having suffered this alleged rape at the hands of this crazy, wide-eyed, maniacal monster, you went to sleep in his arms?'

'Not in his arms.'

'Well, it couldn't have been far short . . . in the same sleeping bag. And how about in the morning, when you woke to find him leaning over you? Why didn't you resist him then?'

'I didn't have a chance. No sooner had I woken than the sergeant's voice sounded. Then we heard guns and the sergeant, the other man, and the officer all left. I didn't see anyone else until we were rescued, some hours later.'

'So there was a time when you were left alone? Some hours.'

'Yes. But that was at the very end.'

'Before, you said it was for brief moments, now it's for hours. Which is it?'

'I was wrong before. But I was only left alone for any time at the end. That was different. Most of the men had been killed or wounded. And those left only had one concern, and that was to be rescued.'

'Right. At least we've got that sorted out,' said Saville, crumpling another note into his pocket. 'In truth, you were unguarded for hours.'

A smile spread across Saville's mouth as he studied his clipboard again. It was the type of smile Rimmer had come to dread. 'Earlier on, you testified that you were frightened that men in 12 Platoon might misbehave. And when asked how, you said, "In the usual way. By having sex with me." So does not "the usual way" imply that men are either in the habit of having sex with you or making passes at you?'

'No, it does not!' The girl shouted her answer as soon as the interpreter got the words out. 'It doesn't mean that at all.'

'Then tell us what it does mean.'

'It means that's the way men behave. Especially soldiers. They all wanted sex with me. Foreign soldiers think all Korean girls are easy.'

'Are you talking from experience? Have you had sex with foreign soldiers?'

'No! I keep telling you I haven't.'

'Well how many soldiers have tried to have sex with you?'

'None!'

'Then why are you so certain all British soldiers want sex with you?'

'Because all soldiers want sex. With any girl—'

'Do they indeed! All British soldiers want sex with any girl?'

'Yes. I know those men wanted sex with me by the way they were talking.'

'Then you do understand some English?'

'No, I don't. I said by the way they were talking.'

'I see. The tone of their voices told you that they were lusting after you? But none of them actually touched you. Not even on your way up to Bunker Hill?'

'No.'

'But tell me this – if all British soldiers think Korean girls are easy, you must have known full well when you went on to Bunker Hill that you were liable either to be molested or have sex thrust upon you? And you were happy to take that risk?'

'It was a possibility. That's all. I didn't expect to stay there long enough for anything to happen.'

'I put it to you that your reason for going on to Bunker Hill – to save your brother – was so important to you that you were quite prepared to have sex with British soldiers in order to achieve your ends?'

'No. Definitely not.'

'I'm not saying that you specifically wanted sex, just that it was a sacrifice you were prepared to make, if necessary?'

'That's not true. I expected to be sent off the hill right away.'

'But why should sex-starved British soldiers, panting to have sex with any girl, send you back? When you suddenly turned up, of your own free will, surely you expected them to make the most of their opportunity?'

'No.'

'But you've already said you expected that,' cried Saville in exasperation. 'You are contradicting yourself.'

'All I knew was that they couldn't keep me on that hill. That as soon as an officer knew, I would be sent back.'

'An officer? Why should an officer be any different? You told us that *all* British soldiers lusted after any girl.'

'But not officers. They are different.'

'Really? Yet here you are accusing an officer of having raped you.'

The girl didn't answer. She couldn't understand why everything was being unfairly twisted. Her words were being spun around in circles until they were meaningless and then tossed back at her. She glanced across to the Korean solicitor, utterly bewildered. Tears welled up in her eyes. She started to sniff and then, as tears appeared, she wiped them away on the sleeve of her kimono.

'And do you have no sense of responsibility?'

'I don't understand. What sense of responsibility?'

'Well, do you see nothing wrong with a young girl breezing into a front-line position and inflaming the passions of sex-starved soldiers facing death?'

'I was raped!' screamed the girl. 'I wasn't tempting anyone. And he was brutal . . . an animal . . . like the devil. I've never seen anything like it. Never.'

'Never in all your experience?'

'No, never.'

'So you do have experience in these matters?'

'No! No!'

The tears spilling from the girl's eyes cascaded down her face. She went on protesting in Korean, but she was gabbling so quickly and so hysterically that the interpreter made no attempt to translate. Saville assumed a despairing expression. When she calmed down, he resumed as if she was a delinquent child. 'If the accused was like the devil or an animal, how were you able to sleep with him for the rest of the night in the same sleeping bag?'

The girl made no reply, just continued to cry.

Saville waited once more, shrugging his shoulders to the members of the court. Eventually, when the girl quietened a little, he continued: 'Cast you mind back to when the officer dropped his trousers to reveal what you describe as 'a very, very big erection'. By saying that it was 'very, very big' it implies a degree of judgement, as though you are familiar with the size of erections—'

Major Ashby leapt to his feet again. 'Sir! This is preposterous. Nothing but harassment. You really can't allow this line of questioning—'

As Ashby made his protest, the girl's tears increased and all around the marquee sympathy for her became tangible. A buzz of conversations came from the spectators and three of the court members were leaning towards Colonel Jameson, anxious to make their views known. Rimmer squirmed about on his chair. The whole thing was a nightmare to him. He was ashamed to be part of it. He just couldn't imagine how anyone could be as infantile as Saville. He leaned forward and hissed, 'Cut it out, you stupid bastard.'

Colonel Jameson removed his glasses and pointed them accusingly at Saville. 'Is this type of questioning necessary?'

'It is absolutely essential, sir,' retorted Saville. 'A principal argument of the defence is that this girl is not in the least sexually innocent. It is entirely the witness's choice that we are involved in this highly sexual case, so she must be prepared to face the consequences of her actions. And my quest for the truth is certainly not going to be put off just because she chooses to turn on the tap to avoid awkward questions.'

Saville's tirade caught the court off balance. They expected him to be defensive, even apologetic, not unleash a virulent broadside, accusing the girl of trying to manipulate the court. Everyone studied the girl, trying to decide if she was putting on an act. As she sensed attention focusing on her she made an even greater palaver of dabbing her tears away, playing straight into Saville's hands, blissfully unaware of what had been said.

Eventually, Jameson said: 'No one is trying to stop you doing your duty, Captain Saville. But the witness is not to be bullied. There will be a short adjournment whilst she recovers herself.'

When they resumed, Saville changed his tack. 'What work do you do?'

'I have no job.'

'Isn't that unusual? Don't most young Korean women get jobs?'

'Yes. Many do. I worked in a shop. But the job disappeared with the war.'

'So what do you do now?'

'I help at home.'

'You earn money in the tea house?'

'Yes.'

Saville put his clipboard to one side and regarding the girl earnestly. 'Liami Wo Pak, there is something I must ask you. A question with a yes or no answer. There will be no need to elaborate. And I can assure you that everyone is obliged to accept your answer. Now then! Please tell me this. Are you employed by your father in his tea house as what is known throughout Korea as a jig-a-jig girl?'

As soon as the question was put to the girl the last traces of composure vanished. She lurched forward in genuine distress, burying her face in her hands as she sobbed loudly and bitterly in staccato bursts. Ignoring the translator, she cried out: 'No, no! Never happen. Not jig-a-jig girl! Not true.'

She continued to cry. Her sobbing became pitiful. Tears ran down her face and dripped off her chin. Everyone watched her in silence, shocked by her extreme reaction. Only Saville remained immune to her distraught condition. He stirred irritably. Then he turned on the interpreter. 'Translation, please!'

The interpreter stared back blankly.

'Come on, man . . . translation!'

The only answer came from Colonel Jameson. 'Captain Saville, the witness spoke in English.'

'Really, sir?' cried Saville in mock amazement, adopting a falsetto voice. 'In English? My goodness! Well I do declare! So she speaks English after all. No more questions of this witness, sir.'

CHAPTER FIVE

Major Middleton was the next witness. Under Ashby's direction he gave a full, meticulous, and superficially fair account of events. At the end of it, Ashby asked: 'And did you make it clear to Mr Wilson that a guard was to be placed over the girl at all times?'

'I did, sir.'

'And did you make it clear to him that he was responsible for her safety?'

'I did indeed, sir.'

'So what was your reaction when Mr Wilson was charged with rape?'

'I was amazed. It was so out of character. He'd always made himself difficult. And he had no idea how to control a platoon that was full of warring factions, but I had the utmost confidence in him regarding personal matters.'

'Thank you, Major Middleton. No further questions.'

Saville approached the task of cross-examining Middleton with rare determination. He knew Middleton's evidence would be a fulcrum: break him and the balance would tip in their favour; let him off the hook and the case for the defence would collapse. Saville was well aware that the points he'd scored against the girl and her father lacked substance, but equally he knew that if he broke Middleton, McCleod's tactics would fall into place, assume relevance, and suddenly expose a conspiracy against Wilson.

'Major, am I correct in saying that as soon as Mr Wilson knew Liami Wo Pak was in his platoon position he informed you and asked for permission to send her straight back to company HQ?'

'Yes, sir. He did.' Middleton replied firmly and clearly, using 'sir' in the approved manner, even though Saville was his junior. He was acting the veteran: a Sandhurst-trained regular, supremely confident and capable.

'And you said no?'

'Well, that's not quite fair. I did say no. But we were at the start of a major battle. I was in no position to deal with the girl at that stage.'

'In what way did you have to deal with her?'

'Well . . . to sort her out.'

'Sort her out? All you had to do was send her back to battalion?'

'That, sir, would have been a lot easier said than done.'

'Why?'

Middleton looked dumbfounded. 'Why? Surely that's obvious?'

'Not to me it isn't. By my reckoning it would have taken one man ten minutes to be rid of her. Couldn't you have spared one man for ten minutes?'

'Far from it. That's the whole point. You may not realize it, but every man in a rifle company has a specific and vital job to do. And unless that is adhered to, the whole structure crumbles.'

'But didn't you order Mr Wilson to place a guard over the girl?'

'Well, yes, I did.'

'So whether or not every man was vital, and whether or not he had a specific job to do, the man guarding her couldn't have done much fighting, could he?' Saville paused, waiting for an answer, but none came. Middleton was clearly shaken. Saville persisted: 'Well, come on, Major. Could he or couldn't he? It's a perfectly simple question.'

'I suppose not.'

'So if the forward platoon could spare a man, you could certainly have spared one at company HQ, couldn't you?'

'I suppose so.'

'But you did nothing. You gave Mr Wilson a straight refusal, didn't you?'

'Yes.'

'So although Mr Wilson wanted rid of the girl, you wouldn't permit it. You made sure he was landed with her on the Horn. Correct?'

'I've already told you that I was trying to run a major battle.'

'Weren't you also determined to embarrass him? To rub his nose in it?'

'Certainly not. That's ridiculous.'

'But you blamed him entirely for the girl being there, didn't you?'

'Yes, I did. And it was his fault.'

'And did you say you weren't going to clear his mess up after him?'

'I don't recall that.'

'Well, do you recall saying that you'd fling him out of the battalion?'

'Yes.'

'Do you have the authority to sling officers out of the battalion?'

'Not strictly speaking. But I can recommend.'

'And are you seriously suggesting that Colonel Wainwright would have flung out the junior officer with the best fighting record in the battalion?'

Middleton stared at Saville with mounting distrust. It had never occurred to him that he would be subjected to hostile questions. 'No comment.'

'No comment! Major, this isn't a press conference. You are in a court of law. With possibly a man's life at stake. So you will answer my questions.'

'Yes, all right. I knew he wouldn't be flung out. But Wilson, with all his righteous superiority, and his contrived heroics, had pushed me to the limits. I'd had as much as I could take from him. He was continually—'

Middleton stopped abruptly, realizing that he had lost his temper. He made an attempt to get a grip of himself. Then he added: 'I threatened to kick him out in the heat of the moment . . . in extremely trying circumstances.'

'Right, Major. Let's keep calm. These words you used to the prosecution counsel – "Warring factions in 12 Platoon". Please explain what you meant by "warring factions".'

'Nothing, really.'

'Nothing? Do you usually say things that don't mean anything?'

'Of course not—'

'Then what did you mean by "warring factions"?'

'Just that there were continuous rows in 12 Platoon.'

'Don't you mean the whole platoon was like a cauldron, seething and boiling over with hatred?'

'Certainly not. There was never any hatred.'

'Major, tell the court why 12 Platoon was always right at the front during clashes with the enemy, and always at the rear during retreats?'

'Because of all the volunteering Wilson did.'

'And his volunteering no doubt caused rows within the platoon?'

'I believe so.'

'And do you know why he kept volunteering?'

'Yes. Out of ambition. He aimed to impress everyone so much that he would gain a short-service commission. Then a regular commission.'

'So he deliberately endangered his men's lives for his own ambition?'

'Yes. Definitely.'

'And did they all realize that?'

'Of course.'

'And was that the reason they came to hate him?'

'Undoubtedly.'

'Then you admit there was hatred?'

'All these things are relative ... and must be seen in the correct context.'

'Don't play with clichés, Major. There was hatred, wasn't there?'

'There may have been ... with some—'

'But you denied there was any hatred. You deceived the court.'

Major Ashby cleared his throat and interrupted. 'Sir, I can't for the life of me see what relevance all this has on the alleged rape.'

Jameson's eyes switched to Saville. 'Does it have any relevance?'

'Very much so,' protested Saville. 'It is central to my entire defence. And these matters were raised in examination by the prosecution.'

Colonel Jameson looked at his watch. 'The court will adjourn for lunch. But I will see both counsels privately first.'

Ashby and Saville followed the members into the adjoining tent. They remained standing while the members sat at the table. 'Gentlemen, I'm becoming increasingly concerned about relevancy. It would be nice to know where it's all leading. Captain Saville, would you like to comment.'

Saville explained as best he could, feeling inhibited by Ashby's presence. 'It is our contention that there was a united campaign of hatred against Mr Wilson. And this has led to the fabrication of evidence which goes very much against him. We intend to prove that the survivors of the Horn know very well it wasn't rape. What's more, we intend to show that members of 12 Platoon are deliberately withholding evidence. So I therefore have to establish that there was hatred towards Mr Wilson. From Major Middleton down.'

The members listened carefully but none of them asked any questions. Jameson turned to Ashby for comments. 'We will refute that entirely, sir. There has been no fabrication. And even if there was hatred towards Mr Wilson it has nothing to do with the alleged rape.'

'Well, gentlemen, I will allow warring factions and hatred towards Mr Wilson to be further explored. But not indefinitely. I look forward to early developments. An interesting morning. Let's have lunch.'

In the refreshments tent an attractive buffet had been laid out. Saville followed after Ashby and members of the court and as he watched them helping themselves he noted how they were all determined to have a good lunch out of the court-martial if nothing else. He didn't skimp himself, either. Once his plate was overflowing, he joined Rimmer and

Wilson. 'Warring factions and hatred have been deemed relevant.'

'Good,' mumbled Wilson.

'More than good. They'll win us the case.'

'I don't see how,' said Wilson.

'You don't have to.'

'Nor do I see how,' challenged Rimmer.

'You don't have to either.'

'Now look here, Kid—'

'Just a joke.' Saville raised his hands in appeasement. 'Keep your hair on, old boy.'

Rimmer bit back his anger. He'd already written Saville off as a total disaster. He'd come across some deplorable defending officers in his time, but none so juvenile as Saville. He reckoned that if he carried on as he had done with the girl and her father, the whole thing would disintegrate into farce. He had half a mind to pull out and be done with it; but when he thought of the fury of General Kershaw and Colonel Barns if he returned before the trial was over, he realized that he had no option but to stick with the obnoxious Limey.

When the court restarted, Saville went into the attack. He made Middleton give an account of the defence of the three villages, forcing him to admit how he'd been infuriated by Wilson's tenacity. Then Saville extracted an account of the episode with the 12 Platoon tents and how they'd been ordered up and down until in perfect dressing. 'And was that when dislike became hatred?'

'Could well be.'

'Upon arrival in reserve, the accused also insisted that his men were properly dressed and smartly turned out, didn't he?'

'Yes, sir. He did.'

'What headgear were you wearing at the time, Major?'

'What the devil has that got to do with it?'

'Just answer the question.'

'A balaclava.'

'What colours?'

'Yellow and black.'

'Horizontal stripes?'

'Yes.'

'Yellow and black horizontal stripes,' repeated Saville incredulously. 'How very fetching . . . and was this wasp-like garment standard issue?'

'Of course not. Don't be absurd.'

'And how about all your men? Were they in fancy dress as well?'

'It wasn't fancy dress. They were worn due to the extreme cold.'

'Didn't the accused feel the cold?'

'Of course he did.'

'Then why didn't he wear fancy dress?'

'It wasn't fancy dress!'

'Could it be that he had too much respect for army discipline?'

'I've no idea.'

'But his strict discipline certainly led to greater hatred, didn't it?'

'Yes. Wilson couldn't grasp that we were a front-line unit. He seemed to think he was still strutting around a regimental depot. He picked fault in everything he saw . . . or anything his men did. And the worst thing of all about his bull was that—' Middleton halted in mid-sentence.

'Go on, Major. What was the worst thing about his bull?'

'It doesn't matter. The answer to your question is yes.'

Saville wound Middleton up like a clock, until his nerves were as taut as a fully extended spring. Every point he made illustrated how deep the hatred was towards Wilson and how it grew greater by the day, with Middleton opposing him every inch of the way.

'And did Fogarty, Chadwick, and Gaunt throw the assault course contest?'

Middleton swallowed several times. Everyone saw his Adam's apple bobbing up and down. 'Yes, I now realize the competition was thrown.'

'And what disciplinary action did you take?'

'None.'

'None! Then perhaps you were glad it was thrown. You certainly told him to keep quiet about it being thrown, didn't you?'

'Did I? Yes, I might have done . . . yes. I did.'

'So although Mr Wilson was doing a first-class job of soldiering, all he got was a total lack of support from you and hatred from his men? In fact, I suggest that you hated Wilson just as much as his men did.'

'Of course I didn't. That's preposterous.'

Saville brought up more points, such as the drinks episode in the mess, and when certain he had convinced the court that there was serious and unprofessional acrimony between Wilson and Middleton, he changed his line of questioning abruptly. 'Tell us about Fogarty's vanishing tent.'

Middleton related the incident, explaining why Wilson had made three men sleep in the open and then struck them off his R and R list. 'So these three men had a special reason to hate Mr Wilson?'

'I suppose so.'

'And were you aware that one of these men was going around the company openly swearing revenge on the accused?'

'Yes . . . but only vaguely.'

'And do you recall – however vaguely – what the threat was?'

'I know the phrase,' admitted Middleton. 'Although I only heard it once. And then in the distance. It was: "I'll get that bastard if it's the last thing I do".'

'And who did you hear shout that?'

'Private Fogarty.'

'And what disciplinary action did you take against Fogarty?'

'None. One can't take action against casual barrack-room talk like that.'

Saville then got Middleton to explain how 12 Platoon got the Horn position. 'And due to your indiscretion everyone in Dog Company had early knowledge that Bunker Hill was to be defended to the last man, didn't they?'

'Yes.'

Saville eyed Middleton contemptuously as he fidgeted in the witness box. 'The order "to the last man" is a clear and decisive, wouldn't you say?'

'Yes.'

'But not an order which some people are prepared to obey.'

'What the devil do you mean by that?'

'I mean you didn't fight to the last man, did you?'

'Now listen here . . . I'm not going to stand here—'

'Sir!' yelled Ashby in protest. 'Major Middleton is not on trial here.'

Colonel Jameson intervened. 'Captain Saville, that is a very serious allegation. You would be well advised to rethink your line of questioning.'

'Sir, I make no guarantee that when the real truth emerges it will not be highly embarrassing for Major Middleton. My question is perfectly simple and I insist that it is answered.'

'I see. Objection overrule. But if you carry on like this I will stop you. Answer the question, Major.'

'No. I didn't fight until the last man.'

'And when you deserted your post, against orders, what were your final instructions to 12 Platoon?'

'To stay where they were.'

'In effect, to fight to the last man!'

'Yes.'

Middleton's head sank forward in shame. Saville watched him without sympathy. He leafed through his notes, determined that everyone should have time to absorb that Middleton was not only a coward, but had treated Wilson abominably. Then he asked: 'Major, in view of the threats you'd heard being made against the accused, and knowing only too well the character of the man making them, how did you think these threats would manifest themselves?'

'I never considered the matter in that light.'

'Are you saying that men in your company were openly threatening one of your officers, and you never thought it would lead to anything serious?'

'Exactly. Troops forever grumble but don't do anything about it. You may not realize it, but grumbling is traditional in the army. Always has been.'

Saville hesitated and then spoke very calmly. 'I'd like to clarify this point beyond all doubt. Are you saying that, despite your knowledge of the villainous nature of certain men in 12 Platoon – and the personal threats you heard, namely "I'll get that bastard if it's the last thing I do" – you never for one moment thought these men capable of turning their hatred into acts of revenge? Are you saying that?'

'For about the third time, that is exactly what I am saying.'

'I see.' Saville paused, making a note on his clipboard. He resumed in his own good time. 'I would now like you to cast your mind back several weeks. To the death of Mr Carter—'

Middleton blanched noticeably. He clutched the rail of the witness box.

'You remember Mr Carter?'

'Yes, I remember Carter.'

'He was killed on patrol, wasn't he?'

'Yes.'

'Please give the details of that patrol.'

'I can't. The full details were never established.'

'Don't trifle with the court, Major. I can bring witnesses to relate exactly what happened. Are you going to force me to do that?'

Saville stared at Middleton for what seemed an eternity. The atmosphere in the court was charged with curiosity. Eventually, Saville said: 'Well, I'll refresh your memory, Major. Is it not true that Mr Carter's patrol came across a much larger North Korean patrol and when he ordered his men to charge they totally ignored him? That they remained motionless on the ground while Mr Carter jumped up and charged alone into the enemy? And that Mr Carter was shot dead without any of his patrol firing a shot?'

'I believe so.'

'And having seen him shot down in cold blood, that patrol turned and ran back to your company position. Is that true?'

Middleton was a ghostly figure. He seemed to be shrinking. 'Yes.'

'But that's not what you thought had happened to start with, was it?'

'What the hell has all this got to do with Wilson?' demanded Middleton, his temper suddenly flaring. 'I object . . . strongly object.'

'You can object all you want. But you'll answer my question. That's not what you thought had happened, was it?'

'No.'

'Then what did you think?'

Middleton tried to force words out, but they wouldn't come. All he could do was keep repeating: 'I thought . . . I thought—'

'You thought he'd had been shot in the back by his own men, didn't you?'

Middleton didn't answer. He just stood there, nodding. A loud murmur went around the marquee. Saville glanced about dramatically, his eyes finally settling on Jameson. 'You thought Carter had been murdered, didn't you?'

'Yes . . . but I was completely wrong.'

'Maybe. But you thought it was murder. And which man did you accuse – in front of witnesses – of deliberately shooting Mr Carter?'

'You know damn well. What are you trying to do to me?'

'Who?'

'Fogarty.'

'So a few weeks ago you openly suspected, even accused, Private Fogarty of murdering his officer? The very same man who you heard threatening Mr Wilson with the words "I'll get that bastard if it's the last thing I do"?'

'Yes.'

'I see! Very interesting.' Saville reverted to more glances around the court. 'I am now going to repeat a previous question. With your knowledge of the villainous nature of certain men in 12 Platoon – and the personal threat you heard, namely "I'll get that bastard if it's the last thing I do" – you never for one moment thought these men capable of turning their hatred into acts of revenge? Are you still saying that?'

Middleton looked down, not daring to face anyone. His tongue kept darting in and out of his mouth, licking his lips, and it seemed as though his answer would never come. 'Yes. I knew anything was possible.'

'Then for the second time you've lied to the court.'

'No! Not deliberately. Only because you twist things.' Middleton's glared round the marquee. 'I resent that suggestion . . . I repudiate that entirely—'

'You can repudiate what you like, but it's true. You knew perfectly well that those men were capable of anything. Even murder!'

'But not deliberately—' Beads of sweat were trickling down Middleton's face. His good looks had deserted him and all that was left was a devious and puny apology for an British army officer. Saville knew he was a broken witness. That he could now be made to say virtually anything.

'As their company commander, with your intimate knowledge of them, you wouldn't have put it past them to take a whore up there, would you?'

'No. . . . No . . . I wouldn't.'

'And you knew how Fogarty and the others would react to a whore?'

'Yes.'

'That they would all make damn sure that they had sex with her?'

'Yes.'

'And would go to any lengths, tell any lies, to get Mr Wilson convicted?'

'Yes.'

'And when you refused to get rid of the girl, you told Wilson you weren't going to sort out his "effing mess", didn't you?'

'Yes. I did.'

'And do you now accept that if you hadn't been so vindictive towards Wilson, none of this would have happened?'

'I suppose not.'

'No more questions of this witness, sir.'

Saville sat down, leaving Middleton shaking in the witness box. He was a pathetic figure. He knew he had been proved a shameless liar and that his army career now lay in tatters around him. He turned to the president and bleated: 'I'm sorry, sir . . . I was deliberately misled—'

Jameson's contempt for Middleton was so great that he ignored him and turned to Ashby: 'Re-examine if you wish, Major.'

Ashby started a futile re-examination which only made matters worse for Middleton. Rimmer slipped another note forward to Saville. It asked: 'Where did you get all that new stuff?'

Saville took his pen out and wrote: 'I'm not just a pretty face!'

CHAPTER SIX

Captain Pickles entered in a wheelchair, being pushed by a male nurse. His legs were joggling about helplessly with the movement over the rough ground. He remained seated beside the witness box. After Ashby had established that Pickles had been the FOO on the Horn, he put his first question of any consequence. 'While you were in the Observation Post with the accused, did you have long talks? Sometimes about sexual matters?'

'Yes. We had long sessions together, keeping watch. Sometimes we talked about women. He told me of some of the things the men in platoon had gotten up to. And once he became pretty personal and asked me about my sexual experiences. But on the whole it was obvious something was bugging him. That he'd never had a woman. And the way things were, he never would. He looked pretty sad and said: 'Yeah, I've certainly missed some chances. But I'll never miss another.' Those were about his exact words, as I recall.'

Saville only had a few questions lined up for Pickles. He asked about the personal relationships within 12 Platoon and the only new light Pickles shed was that Sergeant Sykes refused to stay in the OP in the company of Wilson.

'Did that sort of thing go on all the time?'

'Sure. Right up to the mutiny.'

At first, Saville missed the significance of the remark. Then it dawned on him. 'The mutiny! What mutiny?' He laughed, genuinely amused. 'This is quite something. We've had an alleged rape. Desertions by the dozen. Warring factions. Hatred. Suspected murder. Raw lust. Threats galore. Blatant lies. And now mutiny. Tell the court about this mutiny, Captain.'

'Well, after Old Baldy fell our only chance was to make a run for it under cover of the tanks. We could still have gotten through the escape hatch. The only thing holding us back was Robert Wilson. So Sergeant Sykes suggested that I should take command. The tanks were already trying to get started so we went ahead with a plan to break out with them. Just as all the men were lined up in the tunnel, Robert Wilson appeared and ordered everyone back. There was a stalemate for a time. Everyone stood there, refusing to move.'

'So what did you do? You'd seized command.'

'I know. But Wilson said I had no authority. Anyhow, all of a sudden McCleod appeared. He quoted military law at everyone. He said they were making a mutiny. Sykes seemed to agree and ordered them all back. So they obeyed, even though there was a lot of shouting and rebellious threats.'

'What kind of rebellious threats?'

'Well, a man named Chadwick shouted: "He won't be happy until we're all dead." Another man shouted: "I'll shoot the bastard and be done with it".'

'Who was that?'

'I don't know. Lots of men were shouting. It was very confusing.'

'And was the feeling toward the accused one of pure hatred?'

'It sure was. I've never known anything like it.'

'And what about your feelings?'

'I was sore too . . . still am . . . I survive, but others were blown to bits.'

'So presumably you wouldn't be surprised if this vehement hatred towards Mr Wilson still exists today?'

'I'd put my shirt on it. Their hatred for Robert Wilson will never die.'

When Sergeant Sykes's name was called he rose eagerly, only to have his confidence dampened when the policemen by the entrance said: 'Watch out for Saville, Sarge. He's just crucified Middleton.'

Sykes assumed a smart, military bearing in the witness box and Ashby went through the usual procedure of identifying him. Then he asked: 'Who arranged for Privates Fogarty and Chadwick to go back to divisional HQ to pick up 12 Platoon's Katcoms?'

'I did, sir. Mr Wilson forgot to detail anyone.'

'And why did you select those men?'

'I called for volunteers and they were the only ones to step forward.'

Ashby took Sykes through the sequence of events involving the girl. Then he asked: 'What was the attitude of your men to all this?'

'There was considerable amusement, sir. At a platoon meeting it was suggested it would be a good idea to have sex with her. And everyone laughed and agreed. It was all in good fun. Unfortunately, Mr Wilson took it the wrong way and threatened to shoot anyone who went near her.'

'Was that a typical reaction?'

'Yes, sir. Mr Wilson could be very unstable.'

Under further questioning, Sykes gave his account of other incidents, including the 'mutiny' which he made out to be very insignificant, a mere misunderstanding. He went on to describe how most of the men had been killed in their bunkers and how their plan of escape had gone wrong. When asked for details of the following morning, he replied: 'When I woke the air in the position was poisonously bad. Our hours were definitely numbered. But in the distance I could hear gunfire – getting nearer. I decided there was no point in waking the others and maybe raising false hopes. I felt hungry so I went round to the CP where the rations were kept. When I got there, there was no sign of Mr Wilson. I looked for him in the OP but he wasn't there either. It wasn't until I got back to the CP that I saw him on the top bunk with the Korean girl.'

'Did you notice anything about the bunker in general?'

'There was clothing scattered about, as though there had either been a struggle or they were very keen to get at each other.'

'And what did you do then?'

'I sat there and ate my meal. Then Fogarty came along and I pointed to the top bunker and told him to keep quiet. When Mr Wilson woke, he stretched over and kissed the girl. Then he fondled her breasts, obviously keen to have more sex.'

'Whilst she was still asleep?'

'Not really. His movements woke her. And she immediately pulled back. And at the same time I called out: "Good morning, sir!" '

'And how did he react?'

'Very guiltily. He said: "It's not what you think. Nothing happened".'

'And did you believe him?'

'No, sir. Of course not.'

'And what happened in the hours before you were rescued?'

'We all got a new lease of life. Especially Mr Wilson. We all worked on trying to rescue Captain Pickles and Private Denzil.'

'Did you see any more of the girl before you were rescued?'

'Only briefly, sir. When she came out of the position. The Americans carried her out on a stretcher. She was all right, but crying.'

'Sergeant Sykes, did you ever have sexual intercourse with the girl?'

'No, sir. Certainly not.'

'And as far as you know, did anyone else besides Mr Wilson?'

'No, sir. I'm positive no one did. They never got a chance.'

'Sergeant Sykes,' said Saville, opening his cross-examination. 'Your two volunteers, Fogarty and Chadwick. Had they ever volunteered for anything before?'

'Not that I recall.'

'Then weren't you suspicious?'

'No.' Sykes realized he'd uttered his first lie to Saville. He swallowed hard and cursed himself. By way of self-justification, he added: 'I would never have sent them if I had been suspicious of anything.'

'Really? Even though you knew them to be the most notorious hard cases in the Borderers?'

'I can't accept that—' Sykes cut himself short, his voice trailing away. It was his second lie.

'Then you had no fears of what Fogarty and Chadwick might get up to?'

'I asked for volunteers. They stepped forward. That's all.'

'Volunteering seems to have been a feature of 12 Platoon, Sergeant. What did you think of all Mr Wilson's volunteering?'

'I advised him against it. It wasn't fair on the platoon.'

'And was it the main reason why he was so disliked. Hated, perhaps?'

'Yes, sir. Hatred was just about it.'

'And who did the main hatred come from? Fogarty and Chadwick?'

'Yes. From them. And others.'

'And were you aware that Fogarty was in the habit of shouting threats against the accused?'

Sykes smiled. 'I assume you mean he often used to say, "I'll get that bastard if it's the last thing I do"?'

'I do indeed. And did you punish him for that?'

'No. But I warned him against it.' It was another lie.

'When Fogarty and Chadwick volunteered to go back to divisional HQ, were you aware that there was a plan afoot to discredit the accused with Major Middleton and thereby ruin his chances of a short-service commission?'

Sykes hesitated noticeably. He realized that at some time someone – probably Fogarty – had been shooting his mouth off and that the defence counsel already knew exactly what had happened. His immediate impulse was to admit everything and safeguard himself, but some deep, underlying loyalty to his fellow rankers stopped him. 'No,' he said, lying to Saville for the fourth time. 'I was totally unaware of any such plot.'

'But you must have realized that the girl's presence on the Horn would be the death knell for his short-service commission?'

'Yes, sir. We all realized that.'

'And did you overhear Major Middleton refuse to take the girl off your hands . . . and then tell Mr Wilson to sort out his own effing mess?'

'Yes, sir. I overhead all that.'

Saville decided to put Sykes under pressure on a personal level. He referred to the three villages and asked him if he had had sex with one of the local girls. When Sykes admitted it, Saville demanded: 'And how do you justify that?'

'I don't have to. It's not an offence to have sex with a consenting female.'

'Well, did this kind of thing happen often in 12 Platoon?'

'Yes, sir. Whenever there was a chance.'

'Are you seriously telling the court that whenever 12 Platoon located some consenting women they had sex with them?'

'Yes. So long as there was time.'

'Really! And were Fogarty and Chadwick leaders in these exploits?'

'Yes. You could say that.'

'And do you think it was why Mr Wilson cancelled their Tokyo leave when their tent disappeared? Using Tokyo leave as an ultimate punishment? Just as they sought to discredit their officer by taking a girl on to the position?'

Sykes smiled wearily and lied again. 'I know nothing of that, sir.'

When Saville's little trap failed, he was wrong-footed. He stared at his notes until he came across the word 'Mutiny!'. 'Now then, Sergeant. The mutiny! The incident in the tunnel after you had usurped Mr Wilson's authority. When you had the men lined up, ready to escape on the tanks, what was their reaction when ordered back?'

'A lot of muttering and cursing, but they did as they were told.'

'Were there threats against Mr Wilson?'

Against his better judgement, Sykes lied again. 'I heard no threats.'

'But the court has been told that Mr Wilson's decision not to escape on the tanks cost 12 Platoon dearly in deaths and horrific mutilations. Do you agree?'

'I do,' shouted Sykes. 'And very strongly. It's something I'll never forget or forgive. It cost around twenty dead. Completely unnecessarily.'

'Oh dear! As many as that. Then I understand why you'll never forgive.'

Sykes stared straight ahead. He knew he'd already said too much.

'The court has been told,' added Saville, 'that there is a quest for revenge against Mr Wilson. Do you know anyone wanting Mr Wilson to be found guilty?'

There was a long silence. Sykes's mouth actually opened as though to make a denial, but no words came. He was out of his depth now, metaphorically drowning. The trappings and formalities of the court bore down on him and the solemnity of the occasion overpowered him. He was terrified of lying again. He had an uncanny feeling that Saville knew the answers to all his questions before he asked them, and that he was just waiting for one lie too many before crucifying him, just as he had Middleton.

'Well, do you?' demanded Saville.

'Yes . . . Private Fogarty . . . he told me so about an hour ago.'

'Did he indeed! And has he ever admitted to you that he took the girl on to the Horn to land Mr Wilson in trouble?'

Sykes was stuck with his original lie. 'I know nothing about that.'

'But when Fogarty and Chadwick reappeared on Bunker Hill with a woman, did you assumed they'd smuggled up a whore from the MSR?'

'I had no idea.' Sykes felt himself go clammy, his clothes sticking to him. His one aim was to get out of the witness box as quickly as possible.

'Well, do you think the men in 12 Platoon considered her a whore?'

'How should I know.'

'Sergeant, don't try to be smart. You've already testified that it was suggested that the whole platoon should be allowed to have sex with her. And they laughed and cheered. So surely they all regarded her as a whore?'

'Yes. Yes, they did.'

'And did you?'

'Yes. I wasn't thinking straight just now. We all knew she was a whore.'

'So when you saw Mr Wilson on the top bunk with her, it never occurred to you for a single moment that he had raped her, did it?'

'No.'

'Did the girl behave – or even look – as if she had been raped?'

'No.'

'Did she make any protests to you? Or appeal to you for help?'

'No.'

'And if you'd had the slightest suspicion that she had been raped, would you have done anything about it?'

'Of course I would. But I simply assumed Mr Wilson had got one over the rest of us and kept her for himself? Done what we would all have done.'

'Have you ever expressed that opinion to anyone?'

'Yes, sir. Often. Even to Fogarty at the time.'

'And did he agree with you?'

'Yes, sir.'

'And do you still think she was a whore?'

'Yes, sir.'

'And how close a watch did you keep over her on the Horn?'

'Not a close watch at all. I was more concerned with other things—'

'And would you ever have trusted McCleod to look after the girl?'

'No. Never. He's the last person I would have trusted.'

'Then you can't be certain that no one else had sex with the girl, can you?'

'Not if you put it like that.'

'Well I do put it like that! And it means you've told the court a pack of lies. You said you were positive no one else in the platoon had had sex with her. But now you've contradicted that.'

'Yes . . . but—'

'But nothing!' roared Saville. 'Since all your men regarded her as a whore, they would have pulled any trick to have had sex with her, wouldn't they? Just as they have done since their first day in Korea?'

'Yes, I suppose so.'

'Did you ever know Fogarty or Chadwick to miss out on sex?'

'No.'

'So they could well have had sex with her, couldn't they?'

'Yes, they might have—'

'Thank you, Sergeant Sykes. No more questions.'

'Private Fogarty!'

The cry of the regimental policemen echoed around the court. As Fogarty left the witnesses' tent one of the policemen said: 'You show 'em, Foggy!' It made him feel good and he grinned at the thought of seeing Wilson in the dock. He decided to give him a long stare and then a mocking smile. As Fogarty entered, he was conscious of heads turning, as though something special was expected of him. He gave Wilson his stare and mocking smile and even had time to cast an eye over the defence counsel. He looked a right little pillock. Then he faced up to his first question from Ashby. He didn't know it, but Ashby had decided to keep things as brief as possible. The more witnesses said, the more Saville twisted their words and he didn't intend to take any chances with Fogarty.

'Private Fogarty, please tell the court what happened from the time you woke on the morning of your rescue.'

'Everything was pitch dark,' began Fogarty, 'but I could hear gunfire. I struck a match and saw that Sarge wasn't in the mess, so I went looking for him. He was in the CP and as I went in he nodded at the top bunk. So I looked up and saw Mr Wilson and the girl smooched up together in her sleeping bag.'

'What was your reaction?'

'I was amazed. Especially after his threats to shoot anyone who touched her. Anyhow, Sarge said to keep quiet. To wait to see what happened. And as soon as Mr Wilson woke he got all randy. He'd got his leg across her with his backside humped when Sarge yelled out: "Morning, sir".'

'Then what did the accused do?'

'It was the girl who reacted first. She pulled away in fear. She looked terrified and disgusted. Then Mr Wilson denied that anything had happened.'

'And did you believe him?'

'Course not. Would you?'

'Tell the court what else you noticed about the bunker.'

'Well, for starters they were both stark naked. Not a stitch on. And their clothing was all over the place. Most of it on the floor. Including the girl's knickers. They were torn bloody near in half. It was as though there had been a hell of a struggle . . . a right dust-up if you ask me. I remember thinking—'

'I really think we can do without the opinions of this witness, sir,' said Saville, appealing to Colonel Jameson.

'Sustained,' growled Jameson. 'No opinions, Fogarty.'

Ashby took over again. 'Private Fogarty, I have to ask you this, just to make things clear. Did you ever have sexual intercourse with the girl?'

'Me, sir? God Lord no! Never got a chance. Mr Wilson made sure of that. He'd have shot me, even if I'd just touched her. He was quite capable of it.'

'Thank you, Private Fogarty.'

Saville rose for his cross-examination in slow motion. He then adopted an outrageously exaggerated Oxford accent, relaxing to the point of foppishness, pretending to be every private soldier's idea of an idiot officer. 'I'm counsel for the defence. Just a few questions if you don't mind. Won't keep you long.'

'Right, sir,' replied Fogarty. His confidence surged. Half his ordeal was over and Saville was obviously a first-class twit, just as he thought.

'This sudden and unexpected appearance of the girl on the Horn . . . nothing to do with you, was it? You didn't even realize that she was a girl, did you?'

'No, sir. We thought she was a Katcom.'

'Got a good army record, Fogarty?'

'Could be worse, sir.'

'Well, you're not a troublemaker or a hard case, are you? I only ask because it is part of my job to establish that you're a reliable witness. To establish that you're not a notorious liar. You're not a notorious liar, are you?'

'No, sir. Course not.'

'Splendid. And how did you get on with the accused?'

'OK. Just one or two differences. Routine niggles.'

'Seems there was hatred towards Mr Wilson. Did you hate him?'

'Blimey no! He wasn't my favourite officer, but I didn't hate him.'

'Good show. But not too keen on his beloved assault course?'

Fogarty looked wary. 'No, sir. No one was keen on that.'

'But weren't you a key member of the assault course team?'

'I don't know about that—'

'But surely you were the battalion record holder?'

'Yes, that's true. Although—'

'Splendid! Jolly good show, Fogarty. So you must have been terribly disappointed when 12 Platoon lost the inter-platoon competition?'

'Yes, sir. We all were.'

'Then there can be no truth in the evidence given by Major Middleton that you, Chadwick and Gaunt, deliberately threw the competition?'

'Never!' Fogarty licked his lips and looked around nervously. Then he added: 'Mind you, we had bad luck. Chad got cramp.'

'What wretched luck. Is that why you lost?'

'Yes, sir.'

'Bad luck indeed. Ever hear anyone go around the place making threats against Mr Wilson?'

'Threats? No, sir.'

'Previous witnesses have said that a threat often heard was 'I'll get that bastard if it's the last thing I do'. Know anything about that?'

'No, sir. Never heard nothing like that.'

Saville chuckled, as though apologizing for the absurdity of his next question. 'Then the court can be sure that you never made the threat?'

'Definitely never said that. Not me. Not that I remember.'

'Well, you'd obviously remember a thing like that, wouldn't you? I mean you couldn't go around the place yelling "I'll get that bastard if it's the last thing I do" and then forget about it, could you?'

'No, sir.'

'Then you definitely never said it?'

'No, sir.'

'Good show! Had much luck with the Korean women whilst you've been out here, Fogarty?'

Fogarty laughed self-consciously. 'Had one or two good moments.'

'But I take it that you're not one of these sex-maniac types?'

'Me? Good Lord, no! Me and my mates have always been very careful and selective, sir. Good-class tarts, that's all.'

'Then you would never have taken advantage of this unfortunate girl?'

'Course not. I'd never have done nothing like that.'

'Good show. Now, this matter of your tent. It seems some locals stole it whilst you and your mates were asleep inside?'

'That's right, sir.'

'Are you sure you weren't down the MSR . . . on a brothel crawl?'

'Brothel crawl,' repeated Fogarty incredulously. 'Certainly not, sir.'

'In that case you must have considered your punishment of losing your R and R in Tokyo to be very harsh?'

'Yes, sir. That's certainly true.'

'Was the accused usually unreasonable like that?'

'You bet he was.'

'And what did you do? Complain to your company commander?'

'Not likely. Don't believe in nothing like that.'

'So instead you and your mates plotted against Mr Wilson by taking a girl on to the hill? Right?'

'Plot? We never plotted nothing. We didn't even know she was a girl.'

'Right you are. Let's pass on. When you were all about to try to escape on the tanks, and you were ordered back, were there violent protests?'

'No, not really. Just a bit of grumbling.'

'Just a bit? But didn't most men consider it to be a death sentence?'

'Yes, they did,' yelled Fogarty. 'And for most of the lads it was.'

'And during this not very serious bit of grumbling, did you shout: "I'll shoot the bastard and be done with it!"?'

'No, I never. It wasn't me that shouted that.'

'Then it was shouted?'

'I never said it was.'

'Indeed you didn't. Don't get excited. Just tell me if anyone shouted it?'

'No. Definitely not.'

'Then you heard everything that was being shouted?'

'Course I did.'

'Even though men were shouting different things at the same time?'

'Yeah.'

'So there were approximately thirty men all strung out in a long line and you heard what each one of them shouted?'

'Well . . . yeah . . . sort of—'

'Sort of?'

'Yeah . . . you know . . . sort of.'

'But you didn't shout anything yourself? Presumably you were listening to everyone else . . . sort of?'

Saville didn't wait for an answer. He smiled at the members. 'I imagine you've heard enough from this witness, gentlemen. No more questions.'

There was an adjournment for afternoon tea. Saville made a point of sitting on his own. As far as he was concerned, the trial had reached its most decisive moment. He had to decide whether he had the courage to go through with it. Also, whether he had the nerve and ability to carry it off. Most of all, could he trust McCleod not to make villains of them both? He felt in his pocket for his photograph of Katsumi-san. The small face smiling back at him was as lovely as ever. Then, as though that wasn't inspiration enough, he visualized leading the likes of Fogarty and Sykes on Hill 425 and any doubts disappeared. The fact that on his very first appearance in a serious court he was going to throw away every professional standard didn't worry him in the least. If things did go wrong, he'd be most unlikely to get the blame. Solicitors rarely did. They were only ever misled by their clients, and McCleod wasn't even his client, he was one of the prosecution's star witnesses. So if the worst happened and there was a complete cock-up, it was McCleod who would catch it in the neck.

He had put this point to McCleod at the outset, but McCleod was perfectly happy to accept the risk and responsibility. Indeed, he laughed it off. 'You dinna have to worry about Jock McCleod, sir. You lead and I'll follow.'

CHAPTER SEVEN

As McCleod strode down the marquee the smoke from his final drag was still drifting from his nostrils. After the usual preliminary questions, Ashby said: 'Please explain your responsibilities as a batman while on the Horn.'

'I looked after Mr Wilson's personal needs. I manned the 88 set and the field telephone. On top of that, I guarded the Korean girl.'

'Why do you think you were selected for that last job?'

'Because I was the only trustworthy man in the platoon, sir.'

'I see. And did you carry out those duties conscientiously?'

'Aye, sir. Until I was wounded, I was hardly ever away from her. And no one went near her. They knew better than to tangle with Jock McCleod.'

'I see. But that does leave open the question of who guarded the guard. You must have had ample opportunity to have sex with the girl?'

'Aye, sir. All the time in the world. We used to sit there for hour after hour, just looking at each other. I often thought she fancied me.'

There were numerous smiles around the court, including a broad one from Colonel Jameson. 'Indeed,' commented Ashby. 'Then you'd better make it abundantly clear as to whether or not you had sex with her?'

'Och no, sir. The attraction wasna reciprocated.'

'And can you state, quite categorically, that no one, apart from the accused, had any physical contact with her?'

'That I can. There was no way anyone could have touched her. No one even tried. The behaviour of the men was impeccable.'

When Saville rose for his cross-examination, he knew exactly what he had to do: loosen McCleod up, get his tongue wagging, inflate his ego, encourage indiscretions, and thereby give McCleod the opportunity to make it all sound perfectly natural. 'McCleod, tell the court why you volunteered for batman.'

'Because being his batman had several advantages. Such as not going over Mr Wilson's assault course.'

'In other words, you were simply looking after number one?'

'I dinna deny that. I always do. As any honest man would admit.'

'Were you aware that the accused was highly unpopular? Hated?'

'Aye, sir. The whole battalion knew that.'

'How about you? Did you hate him?'

'No, sir. I dinna hate him. I've got more experience than the others. Until a few months ago, I was an Argyll. And in the Argylls everyone is keen. Just like Mr Wilson. A Scottish regiment is very different from an English one.'

For several minutes McCleod waxed lyrical about the virtues of the Argylls. He also criticized the Borderers outrageously. Saville let him ramble on, allowing him to become overconfident and relaxed as he condemned everything English. His favourite term of contempt, 'Sassenachs', began to feature two or three times in each sentence.

As soon as Saville sensed that the court had heard enough of McCleod's prejudices, Saville pulled him up in mid-sentence. 'Thank you, McCleod. Much as we appreciate your views, we must press on. Perhaps we could look at your personal record. As defence counsel I have to verify your reliability. To establish your veracity, as we like to say in the legal profession.'

'Aye, sir. I ken the terminology of the legal profession.'

'Good. Then you won't mind questions about your army record?'

'Not at all. As defence counsel you are entitled to know.'

'Thank you, McCleod. Then how is it – good?'

'Volatile, sir.'

'Been up and down the ranks a few times?'

'Aye, sir. Like a yo-yo.'

'And am I right in saying, McCleod, that you have a reputation – second to none, I'm told – as a barrack-room lawyer?'

'Aye, sir. There's nothing in the Bible I dinna ken.'

'The Bible?'

'The soldier's Bible, sir. The Manual of Military Law.'

'Oh yes. Of course. Pardon me.'

McCleod grinned around the court, delighted by the way he had put another Sassenach in his place. 'Aye, sir. I ken the Bible word for word.'

'And has this incredible knowledge stood you in good stead?'

'That it has, sir. During my service I've been court-martialled three times. And each time I defended myself. And each time they couldna find me guilty. No case to answer each time. Always demolished their cases with my cross-examinations. The first time—'

'We've no time for details, McCleod. But I'll just clarify one or two salient points if you don't mind. Am I right that your first court-martial was on a charge of buggery?'

'Aye, sir. That's correct.'

'And the second on a charge of bestiality?'

'Aye, sir. That is correct.'

'And the third on another charge of buggery?'

'Aye, sir. That is correct.'

'I take it, McCleod, that Mr Wilson was unaware of these charges having been brought against you when he put you in charge of the girl?'

'Aye, sir. I never told him.'

'Had he known how partial the Argylls considered you towards buggery and bestiality, do you think he would have had second thoughts?'

'Be fair, sir. Not guilty, each time. Never a case to answer, like I said.'

McCleod's face glowed with self-satisfaction. Such was his pride in having cleared his name so convincingly that the revolting nature of the charges didn't bother him. He grinned around, as though expecting applause.

'A truly remarkable record, McCleod. The best I've ever come across. You should be doing my job.'

'Aye, sir. That's what I've been telling everyone.'

This time McCleod laughed out loud, a queer, rasping sound which few besides Wilson had ever heard. It was an infectious laugh and several spectators joined in. Saville pressed on, keeping McCleod in his ebullient mood. 'You really know your military law, McCleod. No one has ever tripped you up, I'll bet.'

'That'll be the day, sir.'

'The barrack-room lawyer par excellence!'

'Second to none, sir. Like you said.'

'With a special interest in bizarre sexual offences, by the sound of it. You must find this case of great interest?'

'Not really, sir. Rape is usually one person's word against another's.'

'But you've missed the point,' exclaimed Saville. 'You disappoint me, McCleod. It throws doubt on your so-called expertise. Don't you realize that other charges could be brought against certain members of 12 Platoon? A charge of procurement, for instance? If evidence given to this court demonstrates that the Korean girl was taken on to Bunker Hill in order to be used for sexual purposes, then procurement is surely established?'

McCleod came back at Saville swiftly, making all eyes switch away from the defence counsel. 'Aye, sir,' he cried excitedly. 'But with respect, you're not being practical. Courts-martial must only be convened if there is a high probability of a conviction. And Section 20, paragraph (c) of Sexual Offences makes it quite clear that – and here I quote – "to prove procurement, persons cannot be convicted on offences mentioned on the evidence of one witness only". And where would you get more than one witness in this case?'

This time Saville stepped in quickly, causing heads to turn again. 'But you only half quote Section 20 of Sexual Offences, McCleod. Again, you disappoint me. Don't you realize that Section 20 goes on to say – and here I quote – "Unless that one witness is corroborated by some material particular". In other words, if it comes to light that the girl was paid money, that would corroborate the evidence of only one witness. And the act of bringing the girl on to Bunker Hill would be procurement.'

While members of the court were watching Saville, bemused by the legal quotes being bandied about, McCleod was bursting to interrupt. As soon as he got half a chance, he declared: 'No, sir! You misunderstand the wording of Section 20 entirely. The money we paid the girl would only prove complicity on her part. Section 20 says – and here I quote again – "if it transpires that the woman was, in fact, a willing partner and needed no procurement, there can be no conviction of this offence". And a woman who accepted our money like this one did would inevitably be regarded as a willing partner. There canna be any argument about that, sir! I ken the Bible!'

Saville remained stock still, staring sadly at McCleod. He watched the Scotsman as he continued to smile around the court, preening himself, basking in what he assumed was admiration. It was some time before McCleod noticed the stony expressions surrounding him. His smile faltered; his expression became quizzical, then positively bewildered. The silence in court seemed to go on for ever. It was eventually broken when McCleod turned to Saville and declared: 'Well, you canna argue with that, sir. Am I no right?'

Saville leaned forward on his desk and said softly: 'Absolutely right, McCleod. Congratulations! But hadn't you better tell the court what really happened during the hours when you were buried alive?'

'Aye, sir. I already have. Everything the prosecution asked me.'

'Every word you uttered was a lie, McCleod. And you know it.'

'Not at all, sir.'

Saville sighed impatiently. 'McCleod, during your lecture on military law, you became so overcome by your knowledge of your precious Bible that you didn't realize what you saying.'

'I just gave you the facts. I meant no disrespect to you or the court.'

'We're not talking about disrespect,' snapped Saville. 'We are talking about your confession. Your confession to having paid the girl money.'

'Confession!' cried McCleod. 'I no confessed to anything.'

'McCleod, you distinctly said, "money we paid to the girl would only prove complicity on her part". You also said, "a woman who accepted our money as this one did"—'

'No, sir. I dinna say that.'

'You most certainly did. It's on record. In the book.'

'I deny it. I dinna say it.'

Saville turned to the president. 'May I ask for the relevant sections to be read back to the witness, sir?'

'I dinna say that,' McCleod yelled at the president. Then his eyes switched to the other members. 'I tell you, I dinna say that.'

Jameson rapped his gavel. 'Silence. The witness will be quiet.'

Jameson turned to the major beside him, asking him if he'd caught what had been said; but he had been left in a daze, and when Jameson turned to the other members, they were equally confused. 'The recorder will read back the entire section about the procurement of women,' ruled Jameson.

The recorder read back the passage. He quoted McCleod as saying: ' "The money we paid the girl would only prove complicity on her part".' Then, ' "A woman who accepted our money, as this one did".'

As the words were read out, McCleod's former look of triumph was replaced by one of disaster. His mouth tightened in anger until it became nothing but a thin white line. Blood drained from his cheeks, his pallor acknowledging the extent of his indiscretion. No man ever did a better imitation of a pricked balloon.

At length, Saville asked: 'How much did you pay her, McCloed?'

McCleod looked down at his boots. 'I paid her all I had. Ten pounds, plus loose change. Far, far too much. But at the time it dinna seem to matter.'

'And who exactly is the "we" you referred to?'

'Fogarty, Chadwick and myself, sir.'

There was a sudden commotion in court. The Korean solicitor was on his feet, shouting. 'It's lies! It's lies!' Colonel Jameson banged his gavel angrily. 'Major Ashby, are you objecting?'

'No, sir. As far as I know, I've no grounds.'

'Then restore order! That man does not have the right of audience.'

Ashby turned to the Korean and exchanged harsh words with him. The Korean resumed his seat reluctantly. Jameson told Saville to proceed.

'Tell the court the whole story, McCleod. Exactly what happened.'

McCleod was slow to start. He oozed humility. 'We all knew what the form was with the girl, sir. But suddenly everything went wrong. Especially during the confrontation when Mr Wilson ordered us back to our bunkers instead of making a run for it. I was no in favour of disobeying Mr Wilson like Fogarty and the others, but all the same, we should have gone. Anyhow, when the bunkers were blown in it seemed that the few of us left were all doomed. For a time, everyone was dashing around, doing all kinds of things. Then things gradually calmed down. Only two men were left trapped. Denzil and Captain Pickles. It was hopeless trying to get them out. And there were too many people helping, so I went back to the CP for a wee dram.'

McCleod's voice became very faint, as though the nearer he got to the essence of the matter, so his shame increased. 'Anyhow, sir. After a time, Fogarty and Chadwick came round. Their mate Gaunt had already been killed. They were as cocky as ever and we got talking. And what Foggy and Chad were saying made sense.'

'What exactly were they saying?'

'That we should have sex with the girl.'

'And did you agree?'

'Aye, sir. It made no difference to me. So Fogarty did all the chatting up, like he always does with the Koreans.'

'But the Korean girl neither speaks nor understands English—'

McCleod laughed. 'She understood Foggy's Gook-talk right enough, sir. She was soon smiling and nodding. And when she saw the money, that clinched it—' McCleod broke off, looking down at his feet again.

'You must tell the court everything that happened, McCleod.'

McCleod raised his head and spoke more forcefully. 'Then we had a row, sir. About who should go first. I still had some pride and wasna going to soil myself by going after two Sassenachs—'

'Quite so. So what happened?'

'I went first. Then Foggy. Chad dinna mind going last. He was that type.'

'So you had what is commonly known as a gang bang?'

'Aye, sir.'

'And you all paid her?'

'Aye. Handsomely. In advance. That's my way. The others tried to get out of it. But I wasna going to let the Sassenachs get away without paying.'

'Naturally. But were you actually present when Fogarty and Chadwick had intercourse with the girl?'

'Aye, sir. We were all in the bunker the whole time. Although one of us stood by the doorway, keeping a lookout for anyone coming.'

'I see. And does anyone else know about this?'

'Only Foggy and me, sir. Chad was killed not longer after when we tried to surrender. So Foggy and me agreed to keep quiet about it.'

'Why was that?'

McCleod laughed bitterly. 'Well, we werena going to blab about it. Not after all the fuss Mr Wilson made. And I was supposed to have guarded the girl, not have a gang bang with her.'

'Are you telling us that you and Fogarty had a pact of secrecy?'

'Aye, sir. That's what it amounted to.'

'Even when you realized how serious the consequences would be?'

'That did worry me, sir. At the Court of Enquiry into how the girl got on to the position, we all did a hush-up job for Foggy's sake. Even Mr Wilson. And when there was a second enquiry into the alleged rape, it was too late to change our story. We dinna expect the charge of rape to stick. Not with a girl like that, straight off the MSR. Anyhow, when the news broke, Fogarty and I talked it over. And he convinced me that Mr Wilson had it coming to him.'

'He said that? "Had it coming to him"?'

'Aye, sir. One of Foggy's favourite expressions.'

'So in order to let Mr Wilson have what was coming to him, you and Fogarty settled on a cover-up story?'

'Aye, sir. When there are two of you involved it's very difficult to come clean. If you do, it means you drag your mate down with you.'

'Come off it, McCleod,' cried Saville in exasperation. 'You were only interested in looking after number one again. It's always number one with you, isn't it? You told us so!'

'Aye, sir. That's true enough. Having lied at the first enquiry I realized there was a possibility that we would end up on a perjury charge, that I'd end up in the Pusan Detention Barracks. At my age I couldna stand that.'

'Well, since you've now been forced to tell us the truth, McCleod, we may as well have the whole lot. Tell us what happened when the platoon was about to leave through the escape hatch under orders from Captain Pickles. Do you recall anyone shouting: "I'll shoot the bastard and be done with it"?'

'Aye, sir. That was Foggy. I was standing directly opposite him.'

'And another point. Were you surprised by the girl being on the hill?'

'No, sir. No one was. We all knew there was a plot against Mr Wilson. And with good reason. The Gooks once stole their tent and after that Mr Wilson made them sleep out in the open and each morning it was pitiful to see them. They were just like lumps of ice, frozen to the ground. It was the most inhuman thing I've ever seen in the army. So it was little wonder they planned their revenge. First, they tried to go AWOL to Tokyo, but when that fell through they decided to smuggle a girl on to the position. So they got Sergeant Sykes to send them back to division for the Katcoms.'

'But Sergeant Sykes called for volunteers—'

'Volunteers!' laughed McCleod. 'I wasna asked to volunteer. Like I said, it was part of a plan and there was a lot of laughing and joking about what kind of a tart Foggy and Chad would bring back.'

'And when they did return with a girl, what did you all think of her?'

'About par for the course, sir. A typical whore off the MSR.'

'And would you say that subsequent events proved you right?'

'Aye, sir. Of course.'

'Thank you, McCleod. No more questions.'

Colonel Jameson ordered an adjournment. Rimmer and Wilson were soon sitting together, sipping cups of tea. Wilson was totally bewildered. He knew perfectly well that McCleod had never laid a finger on the girl. Nor had Fogarty or Chadwick. The audacity of McCleod's lies left him flabbergasted. He remembered how McCleod had promised on his mother's grave to stand by him in the future, and he felt a great glow of affection towards him, but he was convinced he would never get away with it, that the whole charade would end in a spectacular disaster. However, Wilson decided not to say a word. As a diversion he asked Rimmer: 'Is bestiality the same thing as sheep-shagging?'

Rimmer didn't answer. He wasn't even listening. His eyes were fixed on the entrance of the tent, waiting for Saville to appear. He didn't have to wait long. The defence counsel bounced in rubbing his hands together joyfully. He headed straight for Rimmer and Wilson.

'What about that then, my old fruits?'

Wilson beamed with simulated delight. 'Great. Well done.'

Rimmer showed no such enthusiasm. He got up, grabbed Saville by the arm, and jerked him to one side. 'What sort of bloody stupid stunt was that, you Limey cretin?'

'What's bitten you, old boy?'

'I'll tell you what's bitten me. I've seen some corny, ham acting in my time. But that old Scotch bastard and you hit the jackpot.'

'Are you accusing me of something, old fruit?'

'Something! Christ, you've broken every rule in the book.'

'What the hell are you talking about?' demanded Saville, knowing he had no option but to bluff it out. 'It was a brilliant piece of cross-examination. Not many people could have cracked a cunning old devil like McCleod. Hang on a tick. I rather fancy a cuppa to wet the old whistle—'

Rimmer tightened his grip on Saville's arm. 'You're not going anywhere, Limey. Not until you've answered a few questions. Don't you realize they will have seen through that masquerade of yours? They'll realize there has been collusion between you and McCleod.'

'Collusion! What bloody collusion?'

'I know what you've been up to and I want no part of it.'

Saville shrugged his shoulders. 'Then piss off, old boy. Won't worry me. Your contributions so far have hardly added a new epoch to the field of military litigation . . . apart from Brand X, of course.'

'Now look here, shit-head—'

'No hard feelings, old man. But if you're going to become slanderous every time I crack open a dishonest witness, then fucking good riddance to you.'

Saville realized his defiance had Rimmer wavering. He pressed home his advantage. 'Just how the hell do you think I colluded with McCleod? Tell me! I'd love to hear. Especially since that was the first time I've ever clapped eyes on the old bastard. I've spent my whole time in the mess, reading magazines – remember? The whole battalion knows that. And I told you at the start that all the witnesses would be liars. And so they are. Apart from poor old Pickles. But at least McCleod has a reason for his belated honesty.'

'What?' demanded Rimmer.

'What? Oh, come on, old fruit. Wakey! Wakey! He's in love.'

'In love?'

'With Wilson, for Christ's sake! McCleod is as queer as a coot. He's been court-martialled twice for buggery, to say nothing of bestiality. The randy old sod will shag anything that's warm. Why do you think he volunteered to be Wilson's batman in the first place? He's been lusting after Wilson from the moment he joined 12 Platoon. And one has to admit that Prick Wilson is a nice-looking young boy. And very impressively hung, by all accounts.'

Saville broke away from Rimmer's grip as he felt it slacken. He realized he was back in control. 'Incidentally, isn't old Foggy a splendid villain. I like him. Hang on, I really must get myself a cuppa.'

Saville strolled across the tent and collected two cups of tea. When he returned he handed one to Rimmer as though they were the best of friends. Rimmer accepted it grudgingly. He was regarding Saville with a mixture of distrust and envy. Even if there had been collusion, Rimmer was astounded by Saville's handling of the Scotsman. It had demanded an extraordinary degree of skill. The same was true of his cross-examinations of Middleton and Sykes. Both had been devastating. So how could there have been collusion? With Middleton and Sykes it was out of the question. What's more, Saville's claim never to have seen McCleod before rang true. He had never stirred outside the officers' mess; and he had never had the chance to interview prosecution witnesses, so if McCleod had wanted to collude, he would have tackled Rimmer during their interview; but he hadn't. He'd been surly and evasive.

As the two officers drank their tea, Rimmer continued to stare at Saville, trying to work out what was going on. Eventually, Saville became aware of the scrutiny. 'I told you I was a winner, old boy.'

'You think you have all the answers, don't you, Kid?'

'I hope so.'

'In the States we have an expression for people like you.'

'Really? Something bloody rude, I'll bet.'

'Smart-ass!'

'Oh, I've been called lots worse than that.'

Major Ashby was highly suspicious of McCleod's evidence, but the thought of a fellow-officer being implicated in skulduggery never occurred to him. The Korean solicitor was not so easily fooled. He knew villainy was afoot, so much so that he ranted at Ashby, demanding that he should do something about it. He blamed Rimmer. He saw the whole thing as an American conspiracy. The Yank wasn't just sitting there doing nothing. He had master-minded every single development, using Saville and McCleod as pawns.

When the court reassembled, Jameson called Ashby and Saville forward. He said that the court would recall two witnesses: Liami Wo Pak and Fogarty. Saville took this as a clear indication that they had not been convinced by McCleod's rebuttal. Ashby pointed out that before anything else was done, he wanted the chance to re-examine McCleod. 'I don't intend to let his evidence go unchallenged,' he declared.

He soon got the court's sympathy and Colonel Jameson agreed to recall the two witnesses after McCleod had been re-examined.

Ashby was determined to cut McCleod down to size. After listening to the Korean solicitor, he was certain that McCleod's new evidence was no more than a loyal batman trying to save his officer's skin at the last moment. He started with questions designed to give McCleod the chance to admit this loyalty, but when this had no effect, Ashby became rattled. He tried to pour scorn on McCleod's evidence, then he tried to reason with logic. When this didn't work he threw in several trick questions, but whatever tactics he tried he was met by a brick wall. McCleod was more than his match. He remained calm and subdued, as though at last possessed by the purity that comes only to those who have confessed their sins and purged their guilt.

Eventually, Ashby had McCleod declared a hostile witness, but it didn't do him any good and in desperation he tried to blacken McCleod's character. That was what Saville had been hoping for. He got to his feet and turned to Jameson. 'Objection, sir. The prosecution can't get away with that. Section 125 paragraph (c) states that although a witness has been declared hostile, his character must remain unsullied. In other words we must, whether we like it or not, accept McCleod's veracity since he was put forward as a witness worthy of credit. We are therefore bound to accept every answer he gives.'

Ashby was ruled out of order and resumed his seat, clearly defeated.

The court then recalled Liami Wo Pak. Colonel Jameson put four questions to her, all seeking the same information: whether or not she had had sexual intercourse with anyone other than Wilson. Four times she declared most indignantly that he was the only one. Saville declined the opportunity to put further questions to her.

Fogarty was then recalled. He was terrified, his eyes darting from person to person as he stood in the witness box. Jameson regarded him sternly. 'I am going to put four questions to you, Fogarty. All simple and straightforward, requiring simple and straightforward answers. You are still under oath and perjury is a serious crime that will not be tolerated. Do you understand?'

'Yes, sir.'

'Good. The first question is this: when you escorted the girl to Bunker Hill as one of the Katcoms, did you realize she was female?'

'No, sir. No idea.'

'Did you ever have any sexual activity with the girl Liami Wo Pak?'

'Definitely not. I never touched her.'

Jameson noted the answer. 'And thirdly, do you know of anyone, besides the accused, who had sexual intercourse with the girl?'

'No, sir. No one.'

Jameson made another note. 'The fourth question is this: did you, either on your own or with Private Chadwick, ever approach Private McCleod in order to gain access to the girl?'

'No! Never went nowhere near McCleod.'

'Thank you, Fogarty. No further questions. But stay where you are. The defence counsel may wish to cross-examine you again.'

Saville rose swiftly. 'I do indeed, sir.' This was what he had been hoping for, the opportunity to polish Fogarty off once and for all. He gave Fogarty a sickly smile, but there was no foppishness about Saville this time. 'Private Fogarty, do you get on well with your platoon sergeant?'

'Yeah. Course I do.'

'Then it might interest you to hear that Sergeant Sykes has told this court that you are hoping that the accused will be found guilty?'

'That's rot! You're bluffing.'

'Not at all. He told the court you said it recently. Earlier today.'

'Rot. I never told him nothing.'

'Are you now saying the Sergeant Sykes is a liar?'

'He must be. I never said that.'

'Then you deny that you hope the accused will be found guilty?'

'Course I deny it. I'm just here to give evidence. Not to take sides.'

'The last time you gave evidence you said that you had a reasonably good army record. Tell us how many times you have been in Colchester.'

'Three times.'

'And you still claim to have a good character?'

'Why not? You should hear the records of some of the blokes in there. Anyhow, I'm just here to give evidence of what I saw.'

'And you still wish the court to believe you're not a notorious liar?'

'Certainly! Having been in Colchester doesn't make me a liar.'

Saville let Fogarty simmer for a while. He watched him as he bit his fingernails. 'Private Fogarty, the court has heard from other witnesses that you were in the habit of making threats against the accused. Yet previously you said that you got along with him quite well, that you didn't hate him, and that you never made any threats against him. How do you account for that?'

'I can't help what others tell you. If it was McCleod, it'll be lies anyhow.'

'Three witnesses have quoted you as having threatened the accused as follows: "I'll get that bastard if it's the last thing I do".'

'Who told you that?' demanded Fogarty. 'Bloody McCleod, I'll bet!'

'Did you ever make that threat?'

'What if I did? So did others. We all hated his guts.'

'And what about the assault course competition? Did you throw it?'

'Yes, we bloody did. And served the bastard right. He had it coming to him. I'd do it again, any day. It's all right for you, standing there asking questions, but you've no idea what he was like. He even tried to shoot me.'

'Good God!' exclaimed Saville. 'Shoot you? How?'

'On his assault course. He fired within inches of my heels. He followed me right down the course, firing at my heels the whole time.'

'Is that when you clipped three minutes off the battalion record?'

There was laughter from all corners of the marquee. The most unlikely people laughed: Rimmer, Wilson, Jameson, the members, and even Ashby. Fogarty glared around with universal loathing. As everyone continued to laugh, he yelled: 'It was no bloody joke! The bastard could have killed me.'

Jameson banged his gavel. 'Order! Order!' When the laughter died away, he added: 'And there is one thing I want to make quite clear to you, Private Fogarty. There will be no more swearing in this court. Understand?'

'Yes, sir,' muttered Fogarty.

Saville resumed his questioning. He put Fogarty under pressure on numerous points and at each turn Fogarty was proved to be a blatant liar. His cockiness was a thing of the past and he was reduced to shouts of rage and snarls of defiance, like a mangy dog getting the worst of a fight. When Saville had him well and truly softened up, he demanded: 'And do you still deny that you deliberately brought the Korean girl on to the position?'

'Of course I do. I didn't even know she was a bint.'

'So you've said. But it might interest you to know that in her evidence the girl said you and Chadwick were perfectly aware of her sex long before you reached Bunker Hill. How do you account for that?'

'She's a liar.'

'Another liar?'

'Yes. It's all a load of cobblers.'

Jameson was on the verge of intervening again but he refrained, simply glaring at the witness. Saville went swiftly on to his next point. 'Since your previous evidence, Fogarty, we've been told that when the platoon was waiting to go through the escape hatch, and Mr Wilson ordered you all back, it was you who shouted: "I'll shoot the bastard and be done with it".'

'Who the hell told you that?' roared Fogarty. 'What lying bastard told you that? McCleod, I'll bet! You don't want to believe anything that Scottish git tells you. He's a born liar.'

'Are you saying that because he's let you down?'

'That git lets everyone down.'

'But you in particular. Over your pact of secrecy about what happened?'

'Pact of secrecy?' scoffed Fogarty. 'What you on about? I don't know nothing about any pacts of secrecy. Look, don't you understand? McCleod is a liar . . . a born, bloody liar . . . and he hates my guts. He'd tell you any lies to get me into trouble.'

'And you haven't been lying to the court, I suppose?'

'Not on things that matter—' Fogarty groped for words. 'Look – I don't know what you are on about. My evidence is that I saw Wilson with the girl after he'd raped her. We caught him red-handed . . . about to have another go at her. All this other crap . . . I just don't know what you're on about.'

'I'm on about your lies. And especially your biggest lie of all . . . that you didn't have sex with the girl.'

'My God! I never did. What the hell is this? I swear to God I never went near the little tart. I keep telling you—'

'Then it might surprise you to hear,' interrupted Saville, 'that evidence has been given that you, Chadwick and McCleod all paid money to the girl for sex. That you had a gang bang.'

'Gang bang! Christ, you're never going to believe that.'

Fogarty's words came as half a scream and half a disbelieving laugh. In his anger, spittle flew everywhere. He looked around the court in amazement. Then his temper snapped. It burst like a lanced boil, spouting forth. 'That's McCleod, that is! That bloody old bastard told you that! I know that filthy old bastard. The bloody lying git. I'll get that bastard if it's the last thing I do—'

Colonel Jameson crashed his gavel down. Everything on the table jumped. The major beside him jumped as well. 'Contempt of court!' yelled Jameson. 'You're in contempt. I warned you. Contempt!'

Fogarty's chest was heaving up and down with outrage. 'That's bloody unfair, sir. I swear to God I never touched the little whore. It's that bugger McCleod . . . the lying sod. I'll get that bastard—'

'SILENCE!' thundered Jameson. 'No swearing in court. Contempt!'

The marquee buzzed with excitement. The president was puce with anger. Saville remained silent, waiting for things to cool down, but his sense of timing told him to call it a day, with Fogarty in contempt. In a subdued voice he said: 'No more questions.'

When the court settled down, Saville slipped a note to Rimmer. 'Shall we emulate McCleod and go for no case to answer?'

The note was intended to appease Rimmer, but it had exactly the opposite effect. It made him feel sick. He knew he should have welcomed it, but he didn't. He felt only anger at the possibility of Saville getting away with it: fury that the little schmuck had outwitted everyone. Worst of all, Rimmer realized how foolish it would make him look. He dreaded to think what those at Army HQ would think. There he was, screaming blue murder about a tough case, and how the British counsel was useless, and all of a sudden there was no case to answer. Rimmer wrote a note back saying: 'Your decision, Kid.'

A very demoralized Major Ashby re-examined Fogarty, but it got him nowhere. Fogarty just slipped further and further into a quagmire of lies and contradictions. Eventually, Ashby abandoned his witness. As Fogarty was led away, still swearing aloud about his innocence, and vowing revenge on McCleod, Ashby closed the case for the prosecution.

Saville then took great delight in submitting that there was no case to answer; that the evidence deduced did not disclose a prima facie case against the accused. He quoted paragraph 58, note 3, of Rules of Procedure, which stated that grounds for dismissal as being, 'If the witnesses produced by the prosecution were so unreliable that no reasonable court could believe what they said'. Saville claimed that that was precisely what had happened.

The members of the court were clearly taken by surprise. After a brief conference, Colonel Jameson asked for statements from both sides. Ashby responded strongly, stressing Wilson's admission of intercourse and the evidence of Liami Wo Pak. He claimed that MCleod's rebuttal was completely unsupported and no more than a batman showing loyalty towards his officer.

Saville claimed that the girl's background was extremely dubious, coming from an out-of-bounds tea house; that her motive in bringing the case was suspect; and that her presence on Bunker Hill put her character in doubt. Also, she had lied. He further claimed that Middleton, Sykes, and Fogarty had all been exposed as liars, with Fogarty actively seeking revenge on the accused. In contrast, he praised the belated honesty of McCleod. He also stressed that since the prosecution had put McCleod forward as a trustworthy witness, his final evidence must, under law, be accepted by everyone. They had no choice. It was an edict laid down in cold print. That being so, the court could only find that the girl was of such lewd character that she would have been a willing partner with the accused.

When Saville finished, he took his seat, convinced that he had won the day. The president and his members retired. An hour later they returned and ruled that there *was* a case to answer.

CHAPTER EIGHT

Rimmer was gripped by a feeling of impending doom. To him, the court's decision defied all logic. It reeked of prejudice. By ignoring Saville's insistence that McCleod *must* be believed, the court demonstrated that they were guided by sentiment and instinct, not justice, with no respect for the letter of the law. Saville reacted furiously. He flew into a foul temper and kept referring to it as a travesty, with the members of the court nothing but 'a load of amateur wankers'. When Rimmer sympathized with him it only made matters worse. Saville turned on the Yank as though his sympathy was either veiled criticism or self-satisfied gloating.

'All right then,' stormed Saville, 'if you're so bloody clever, you convince the amateur wankers. So far, all you've done is sit on my back. So here's your chance. From now on we'll do things your way. We'll see what your mate Hammond comes up with . . . and see just how good you are.'

With this challenge ringing in his ears, Rimmer had a restless night. He kept going over every detail of the trial. The basic truth was that Saville had shot his bolt. He was finished and he knew it. He'd played all his aces brilliantly, but they had failed. Now, he had nothing left. All he could do was dump his responsibility on his adviser. Such shitty behaviour didn't surprise Rimmer a bit, but he wasn't going to shirk the challenge. As a matter of personal pride he would never allow the Limey to humiliate him. As he'd always maintained, everything depended on Sergeant Hammond's investigations into the girl and what the Limey sneered at as Brand X.

At one point during the night Rimmer sat bolt upright in panic. A fresh possibility occurred to him, something no one else would ever think of. He suddenly realized that when Sergeant Hammond turned up in the morning after his raid on the Wo Pak tea house, his evidence might just as easily destroy their case as clinch it. It made it essential for him to intercept Hammond before he got anywhere near Saville or anyone else, and certainly before he took to the witness stand.

Rimmer also realized that if his fears were correct, he would be forced to give the law a helping hand. It would mean throwing overboard all his professional principles, something he would never normally have dreamt of doing: but this was different. He was merely an adviser in a foreign court and he certainly wasn't going to let the little schmuck Saville humiliate him. It would be risky, even with Hammond's co-operation, but that was the least of his worries. After all the aggravations of the trial, and the ignominy he had suffered at the hands of Saville, only one thing mattered: restoring his self-esteem and stuffing the Limey out of sight; proving to the swine the real meaning of talent.

Immediately after breakfast the defence had another set-back. The adjutant received a message that Hammond and Hooper had been involved in a traffic accident and would arrive late. Saville took the news badly. He kept repeating: 'No way am I going to examine Hammond cold and blind. I have to know what he's discovered. I'm not going into court until I've spoken to him.'

Rimmer made no comment, but he had no intention of allowing Saville anywhere near Hammond. They weren't going to meet until Hammond was in the witness box and everything had been settled.

As Saville made his way into court he was still in a foul temper and when the court got underway his fury increased when Jameson refused to grant an adjournment and ruled that Wilson should be called first. Then, if Hammond still hadn't appeared, he would grant an adjournment.

Saville had no option but to comply. Rimmer was delighted and slipped out of court, heading for the adjutant's office. Much as he wanted to see how Wilson got on in the witness box, it was far more important for him to catch Hammond as soon as he drove into camp.

Sooner than expected, a message came through from 27th Brigade to say that Hammond had borrowed a jeep and would be arriving in around fifteen minutes, leaving Hooper to sort out the accident problem at Brigade HQ. Hammond wasn't even that long. When Rimmer heard the jeep roaring into the Borderers camp he rushed out to greet it. Hammond skidded to a dramatic halt. 'Good news,' he called out. 'We've unearthed a minor treasure trove.'

Rimmer shrugged his shoulders. It was exactly as he had suspected. He slipped into the passenger's seat beside Hammond and offered him a

Lucky Strike. Then he gave him a crooked, conspiratorial, smile, the smile of old buddies. He'd never asked anything like this of Hammond before but he knew Hammond would play along. What's more, as a consummate professional, he would carry it off with panache and discretion, then pretend it had never happened.

When Rimmer resumed his seat at the defence desk, Saville was still examining Wilson. Rimmer wrote out a note and waited until Saville had instructed Wilson to tell the court what had happened in his own words before slipping it forward. Saville was none too pleased. He didn't even look at the note. He pushed it into his trouser pocket, and continued to concentrate on Wilson's evidence, knowing that he might have to interrupt at a moment's notice.

To start with, Wilson described events on the Horn reasonably well, but when he reached the point where the bunkers were blown in and they were buried alive, facing death, instead of remaining cool and factual, he became highly emotional. His recall was so total, so vivid, and so horrific that the court was spellbound. He ended his account by describing how he had fled from the morgue, back to the CP.

'Eventually, when I looked up and saw the girl, she made no attempt to look away, or pull back. So I took hold of her around the neck. She was beautifully warm and consoling. She offered comfort and reassurance... I can't really describe it . . . it was the mere presence of another human being . . . someone to die with. And I assumed by the way she looked at me that she felt the same way. So I climbed on to the top bunk and before I knew what was happening we were making love. She never tried to stop me. There was never any question of that.'

When Wilson stopped speaking no one stirred. His evidence had been a deeply moving account of human disintegration.

During the rest of his examination, Saville demonstrated how the girl, far from resisting Wilson, had accepted his presence: how she had gone to sleep in his arms without a murmur of protest, and how she had moved her body in sympathy with his during intercourse. Other questions he put enabled Wilson to emphasize the lack of difficulties normally associated with first-time sex; how the girl – a self-proclaimed virgin – needed no foreplay or arousal to enhance penetration and shed no blood.

From the start of Ashby's cross-examination it was clear he was keyed up for a major effort. He took Wilson through a host of details about his maniacal behaviour. He spared him nothing about removing his trousers and then his reaction to his own excited condition, demanding to know what kind of effect that would have on an innocent young girl. Whenever Wilson tried to deny something, or make a comment in his own defence, Ashby jumped in with the taunt: 'But you told the court you were acting instinctively, that you weren't conscious of what you were doing?'

Wilson was never able to refute this. It soon got to the state where he didn't know how to answer and was reduced to making absurd excuses.

'You've given the court a very graphic account of your experiences on the Horn,' declared Ashby, 'But you have never once mentioned the girl's feelings. Didn't you realize she would be even more frightened than you?'

'Of course I did. We were all frightened.'

'Yet you managed to alleviate your fear, didn't you?'

'Well, yes . . . I suppose so.'

'Then you had intercourse without regard for her? You simply used her.'

'No. That's not true.'

'And the following morning? Were you about to have sex with her again?'

'That's impossible to say. It would have depended on her.'

'But it didn't depend on her on the first occasion, did it? When you grabbed her, kissed her, then leapt on to the top bunk and forced yourself upon her . . . it didn't depend on her then, did it?'

'I suppose not.'

'Then you admit it. On the first occasion you forced yourself upon her, against her will. That is rape! You admit it, don't you?'

Wilson yelled back frantically. 'No, it wasn't rape. She didn't mind. I know she didn't. If she had, she would have resisted.'

Beads of perspiration flowed down Wilson's face and his eyes implored the members to believe him. Ashby's next question followed swiftly. 'I put it to you, Mr Wilson, that your advanced stage of sexual excitement – what your counsel loves to call a very, very big erection – is conclusive proof that your attack was premeditated, that you needed no encouragement. That from the moment you entered that bunker your one thought was to have sexual intercourse before you died, that nothing would stop you, even if it meant raping a defenceless, terrified, young girl.'

'No. I'd always been concerned for her. I'd tried to protect her.'

'Oh, really! Well, if you were so greatly concerned about the girl, tell the court what you said to Sergeant Sykes when you woke in the morning.'

'I'm afraid that I denied anything had happened.'

'You lied – through shame!'

'No, not shame—'

'Then why?'

'I don't know. Through guilt, I suppose.'

'Guilt of rape?'

'No! Of going against orders. My own orders.'

'And this professed concern of yours for the girl . . . when you realized the counter-attack was underway you immediately jumped down from the bunk and left the command post, didn't you?'

'Yes, sir.'

'You discarded her . . . totally ignored her. Isn't that true?'

'Yes.'

'And when did you next see the girl?'

'Yesterday morning when the trial started.'

'You didn't even bother to see her off the Horn safely, did you?'

'No, sir.'

'And when you were rescued, you not only ignored the girl but everyone else as well. Even your wounded. You just swaggered off the hill with your friend and batman, Private McCleod, whilst he was blowing his bagpipes. Like a couple of conquering heroes. Didn't you?'

Deep shame covered Wilson's face. 'Yes.'

Ashby was in full cry: angry, red-faced, his bald head glistening with sweat, his voice higher than ever. 'I say that on that fateful night you were determined to have sex before it was too late – to prove yourself to be a man – that you deliberately attacked this defenceless young girl knowing that she had no option but to submit, that you used her for your own selfish ends. Someone you could rape and then cast aside without a second thought—'

'No!' shouted Wilson. 'It isn't true. I swear she didn't mind.'

Ashby regarded Wilson with utter contempt. Then he sat down.

Saville realized that Wilson was all but finished. Ashby had excelled himself. He had made Wilson look shallow, callous, and selfish, only interested in experiencing sexual satisfaction before he died. He had also got as near as anyone ever could to extracting a confession from Wilson.

Saville had only one chance left. Whilst listening to Ashby taunting Wilson about alleviating his fear, and acting subconsciously, and not knowing what he was doing, Saville recalled McCleod's alternative strategy, what he had referred to as his, 'sympathetic extenuation'. If that meant what Saville thought it meant, it tied in with the obscure reference Colonel Wainwright had made to *mens rea* during their stormy interview. It was a gamble, but he had no alternative but to take it.

As Wilson started to leave the witness box, Saville surprised everyone by calling out: 'Don't go just yet, Mr Wilson. With the court's permission, I would just like to clear up one last point. Please cast your mind back to the period directly before the alleged rape. Think again of that ghastly scene in the morgue where your men were lying in a heap, being eaten by rats. That was too much for you, wasn't it?'

'Yes.'

'You fled. Ran off in abject terror. And as you ran, realizing that you would be overtaken by the same fate, was anything else on your mind?'

'No.'

'And when you burst back into the command post, did that sight still dominate your thoughts?'

'Yes.'

'And at that point, were you aware of the girl's presence?'

'No. I'd forgotten all about her.'

'Then how do you account for the fact that when you removed your trousers, prior to putting your kilt on, you found that you had an erection?'

Wilson was nonplussed. He didn't answer.

'Well, something must have caused that erection? And in evidence, you said you were amazed by it.'

'I was.'

'Well something caused it . . . and you just said that you hadn't seen the girl. And you didn't even realize she was there. So if she didn't cause it, what did? Had you been having sexual thoughts, or wild fantasies?'

'Good God, no!'

'And when you heard the girl move above you, what did you do?'

'I covered myself up in embarrassment.'

'So she could hardly have been the cause of your condition. And if she wasn't, then what was?'

For several seconds Wilson was silent, his face blank, as though he was completely lost. Then he recalled the conversation he'd had with McCleod when he'd suffered from the shakes. He began to answer, stumbling and stuttering over his words, marshalling his thoughts out loud as he went along. 'All I can suggest – even though it might sound far-fetched – is that my erection was caused by fear. By sheer terror. I was once told that terror and extreme anger can have that effect. A sort of reflex action. If you are in shock, you get the shakes. But if you are frightened, really frightened, you get an erection. Apparently it happens to men who are about to be executed.'

'So what everyone has so far assumed was an outward manifestation of your sexual lust, and your determination to have sex before you died, was nothing to do with sex, but a subconscious reflex, a reaction to your enormous fear?'

'Yes.'

'Mr Wilson, have you ever heard of a legal expression *mens rea*?'

'No.'

Saville looked across at the court members. Their puzzled expressions showed that they were equally in the dark. Saville turned to Colonel Jameson. 'Perhaps I should explain, sir. *Mens rea* concerns criminal intent. In normal cases of rape it never features. In plain English, no one normally rapes someone else unless they intend to rape them. But in this case we are not dealing with the normal. This is abnormal and unprecedented. So extraordinary that the question of intent, or *mens rea*, becomes highly relevant.' Saville faced Wilson again. 'So let's be quite clear about this. When you returned to your command post, did you have any sexual designs or ambitions with regard to that girl? Did you intend to rape her?'

'No. Absolutely not!'

'Did the thought of it ever cross your mind?'

'Definitely not. I was acting instinctively—'

'Yes, you mentioned that during your cross-examination . . . and the prosecution accepted it . . . that you didn't know what you were doing. So the question comes down to this: did you ever intend the girl any harm? Did you ever have the slightest intention of raping her?'

'No. Never.'

'Thank you. Nothing further.'

Colonel Jameson called another adjournment. It was just what Rimmer hoped for. While Saville had been ploughing through his bizarre theory of *mens rea*, he was bursting with impatience, anxious to explain what had happened with Sergeant Hammond. As soon as the members of the court made towards their tent, Rimmer blurted out: 'We're home and dry, Kid!'

'You think they'll accept that?'

'What?'

'*Mens rea*—'

'That fucking crap! You must be joking. But who cares! What Hammond and I have come up with is real evidence. Hard evidence.'

'Is the tea house a brothel then?'

'No.'

'Then how the hell can we be home and dry?'

Rimmer just had time to explain the details of what Hammond had found in the tea house when the members of the court returned, having checked on the exact meaning of *mens rea* and its relevance to the charge sheet. When they had settled, Jameson looked over to Saville. 'Has your final witness arrived yet?'

'Yes, sir.'

'Good. Then waste no more time. Proceed.'

Sergeant Hammond was an imposing, heavyweight figure. When he stepped into the witness box it creaked loudly. Saville established his identity, then asked: 'What were your duties last night as Provost Sergeant?'

'I was assigned to visit four different Korean establishments.'

'Was one of those a tea house in the village of Chowsong?'

'Yes, sir.'

'Is this tea house wellknown to you?'

'Yes, sir. It is an off-limits establishment under surveillance on account of it being the home of a known deserter. Kim Wo Pak.'

'Explain what happened when you visited this tea house last night.'

'We did a thorough search. We found one or two minor irregularities. But also some money.'

'Please tell the court about the money.'

'We impounded it, sir. Generally, we are not looking for money. There is no offence in having money. But this wasn't normal currency. It consisted of £1 baf notes, total amount 25 bafs. These baf notes are peculiar to the British Forces and are not freely negotiable. They are only negotiable in official British canteens, as laid down by the GROs of the theatre of operations.'

'So is it an offence for Koreans to have these notes?'

'No, sir. The offence lies with those who distributed them.'

'For an American you seem remarkably well informed on British law regarding baf notes. Can you explain that?'

Hammond grinned. 'Very simple, sir. All the information I've given the court is printed on the back of each note. When I read it, I contacted my superior officer. He told me to impound the money for 48 hours so that an investigation could be made into the offence of distribution.'

'Did you ask in the tea house where the money came from?'

'Yes, sir. Only the lady of the house was present and she didn't know. All she could tell us was that the bedding roll in which we found the money belonged to her daughter, Liami Wo Pak.'

'Have you got the money with you? If so, please hand it to the clerk.'

The clerk collected the money and placed it in front of the members. Once they had examined the money it was shown to the prosecution.

'Having impounded the money,' said Saville, 'what happened next?'

'I was instructed to find out which British units had been in the area. The location of Chowsong is unusual in that you have to cross either Teal Bridge or Crosby Bridge to reach it. So we checked the logs on both bridges and found that no British units have ever been logged across.'

'Then how do you account for the money being in Chowsong?'

'Sir, it could only have been obtained in another area and then taken back to Chowsong.'

'Thank you, Sergeant. Please leave the bridge logs with the court so that they can examine them.'

When Hammond concluded his evidence it seemed that the trial was effectively over. McCleod's evidence had been vindicated: the girl had received money for services rendered and that proved her to be of such lewd character that she would have been a willing partner with Wilson; but, of course, the trial had to stagger through its last rites. Ashby cross-examined Hammond but nothing could alter the fact that the baf notes found in the girl's bedding roll must have come from Bunker Hill.

Colonel Jameson then surprised everyone by recalling two witnesses: McCleod and Liami Wo Pak. McCleod was first. Jameson put to him a very simple question.

'When you paid money to the girl, what currency did you give her?'

The question was like a clap of thunder. The whole issue was in the balance once more: it was quite possible that McCleod could have used one of several currencies: yen, won, dollars, bafs, or ordinary sterling. Everyone watched McCleod. Rimmer and Saville realized that if he said anything other than bafs, all Hammond's evidence would be worthless.

McCleod faced the question confidently, once again the invincible barrack-room lawyer. 'I paid the girl in the only currency I had, sir.'

'I realize that, McCleod. But what currency was it?'

McCleod grinned, playing with the court. He knew to the last half-penny what had been taken from his trousers. 'One pound notes, sir. That is to say, special British Army baf notes, face value £1 sterling. The

Sassenachs gave her bafs as well, although I don't know how many.'

'Thank you, McCleod. Stand down.'

Liami Wo Pak was then recalled. Since she had had been accommodated at Brigade HQ throughout the trial, she had no idea of what had transpired at her home. Nor was she aware of the evidence that had been given that she had taken money from three soldiers in exchange for sexual intercourse.

She took the stand looking nervous and agitated. When Jameson explained that firm evidence had been produced indicating that she had been paid for sex by three men, she screamed denials, ranting at the interpreter. Even when Jameson explained to her that her bafs could only have come from Bunker Hill, she merely screamed that she had been raped and that everything else was lies. Eventually, Jameson manoeuvred her into a position where she had no option but to account for how she came to be in possession of the money.

It was then that she wiped away her tears and admitted the truth: that she had stolen the money from the pockets of a man who had died on the lower bunk and from the trousers of the man who had previously guarded her when his trousers had been removed from him when wounded.

It was the greatest irony of the trial that the only people who believed her, and knew her to be telling the truth, were the three men huddled around the defence table. They sat there, their eyes downcast, avoiding visual contact with anyone, especially each other.

Saville felt desperately sorry for the girl. It was all so totally unfair, but it was just as totally beyond his control. The girl was one of life's losers, a young woman trapped by her own stupidity and dishonesty and now branded a whore. He felt like shouting out the truth, and bringing everything to a dramatic halt; but of course he didn't. He had long ago learnt the basic lesson in life that to sympathize with the downtrodden is one thing, but to do something about it to one's own detriment is another proposition altogether.

So Saville ignored the girl. As she reverted to tears and protests, he occupied himself with preparing his closing address; and since he'd sold his soul to satisfy his cowardice and his love for Katsumi-san, he saw no reason why he shouldn't indulge himself and enjoy the fruits of his sins. His daydreaming was pulled up sharply when Jameson asked the girl another simple question. 'Did you steal anything else? Anything besides the money?'

Once again, everything was in the melting pot. Saville stirred in alarm.

This was a possibility that had never occurred to him, and he assumed it had never occurred to Rimmer either. He glanced back at Rimmer, but the American refused to raise his eyes.

As soon as the question was asked, and the girl realized its implications, her tears disappeared. 'Yes. I stole several things besides the money. I stole a leather wallet, a cigarette lighter, a pocket watch, and a silver cigarette case. I kept them with the money. I hid them at the bottom of my bedding roll. Wrapped in a silk scarf. It was all stolen. Nothing to do with any payments.'

Jameson consulted his members. During the pause, Saville leaned back to Rimmer and whispered: 'This could be disastrous.' Rimmer still didn't look up, let alone answer. With increasing bitterness, Saville added. 'You never bloody thought of that, did you, Yank?'

Rimmer knew better than to respond.

When the members of the court finished their whispering, Jameson recalled Sergeant Hammond. When the American took his place in the witness box, Jameson asked: 'When you found the money, was anything else with it?'

'No, sir. Just the money. And we did a very thorough search.'

'You say "we" Sergeant. Did you search with someone else?'

'Yes, sir. We search in pairs. My colleague can verify everything I've said.'

'Where is your colleague? Here?'

'No, sir. Army HQ. We became stranded on the MSR because of a minor accident. And whilst I borrowed a British jeep and came on here, he went back to Army HQ for medical treatment.'

'Did you get a signature for what you removed from the house?'

'No, sir. That's not our policy. Most of the Koreans are illiterate.'

'No signature,' pondered Jameson. 'One should always get a signature—'

'As I've said, sir, my colleague could verify everything I've said.'

Jameson still looked dubious and unhappy, but the other members seemed perfectly satisfied. Jameson shrugged and invited Ashby to cross-examine again, but he declined.

Rimmer leaned forward and said to Saville: 'Oh ye of little faith!'

The final phase of the trial came with the closing addresses.

Ashby stumbled over a sad little effort. When Saville rose he was ebullient, knowing that Rimmer had been true to his boast and clinched the case in the final round with Brand X. Saville spoke without notes, full of

The party in the officers' mess was a very happy affair. Colonel Wainwright was in a rare, affable mood. He welcomed everyone as they arrived and viewed everything with deep pride. Things could hardly have ended more satisfactorily. Soon, and quite rightly, the court-martial would be forgotten and the regiment would only be remembered for its brilliant campaign, sealed by the award of the American Presidential Citation; but on a personal level Colonel Wainwright knew he would never forget the court-martial. As the Convening Officer, he had a special reason for satisfaction. When the trial finished, he called the members of the court together to thank them for their services. When he accompanied Colonel Jameson to his jeep they had a brief discussion about the trial, colonel to colonel. Jameson admitted that initially they had had grave doubts about McCleod's rebuttal, and had been greatly relieved when Sergeant Hammond's evidence proved McCleod's evidence was indeed true, thus putting the issue beyond any doubt.

'That came as a great relief,' said Jameson. 'Otherwise, the trial could have ended up being very controversial. The truth is, even if Hammond hadn't come up with his evidence, and had failed to support McCleod's rebuttal, we would have acquitted Wilson anyhow.'

'Really?'

'Oh yes. Purely on the strength of the extraordinary circumstances and Wilson's obvious lack of any intention to commit rape.'

'*Mens rea*!'

'Precisely! We had to adjourn to look that up, and it was then, by pure accident, that we noticed the exact wording of the charge sheet. It was different from the specimen charges shown in the Manual of Military Law. Instead of the usual: "that is to say, rape contrary to Section 1 . . ." it said: "that is to say, *wilful* rape contrary to Section 1 . . ." A very significant difference.'

'Indubitably!' agreed Colonel Wainwright. 'How extraordinary. As Convening Officer, I should have spotted that.'

'Just as well you didn't,' laughed Jameson. 'That one word made all the difference.'

'Well I never!' said Wainwright. 'What a stroke of luck.'

Once the celebrations had warmed up, Wainwright drew Saville and Rimmer to one side. He intended to heap praise on them and give them full credit for a brilliant defence against all the odds. After all, the whole essence of the Establishment was that it worked in mysterious ways: discreet and covert.

Wainwright singled out Rimmer first. 'I'll let General Kershaw know of our gratitude for all your valuable help, Captain. A capital effort! I'll also put in a good word for Sergeant Hammond. I know how relieved General Kershaw will be with the outcome.' Then Wainwright turned to Saville. 'So, Captain! I am delighted with the way you responded to our stormy little interview. No hard feelings?'

'No, sir. Of course not.'

'We soldiers have to have a few tricks up our sleeves, you know. Just like you legal fellows. Anyhow, the adjutant has got your movement order for Japan. A one-way ticket. And Brigadier Tewson will be delighted to see you back in Kure. And a word of advice – stick to your guns with Muldoon. And when you get your girl back to England do us all a big favour. Forget the army and stick to the law.'

Saville laughed happily. 'Good idea, sir.'

The three officers were then joined by Wilson and Hooper and they spent several minutes discussing the highlights of the trial. Eventually, Wainwright put an arm around Wilson's shoulders and steered him towards the bar. 'I'm sorry you only got a Military Cross, Robert. You deserved far more. What you did on the Horn was way beyond the call of duty.'

Saville grinned at the two Americans. 'Christ, if screwing a Korean girl is way beyond the call of duty, what decorations will the old Prick get when he runs amok among the Tokyo whores?'

'The most lasting accolade of all,' said Hooper. 'The VD and Scar.'

Saville looked at the marine in amazement. Then he slapped him on the back. 'Well done, old boy. A joke! A very old joke, but nevertheless a joke. My God, things are looking up. This is going to be a memorable evening. Let's head for the bar and cadge free drinks.'

Saville's appetite for free drinks was soon satisfied. First of all, the 2 i/c bought a round of large whiskies, and then Wilson ordered jugs of beer and circulated throughout the mess topping up everyone's glass. The party soon became a riotous affair, the sort of evening a mess is lucky to experience perhaps once every ten years, with boisterous games which endangered life and limb, beer flowing like water, and wine glasses being flung to destruction amid flamboyant toasts. In the small hours of the morning, Rimmer, Saville, Hooper and Wilson were the only ones left in the mess. They were surrounded by clinging tobacco smoke, the eyesore of unfinished drinks, overflowing ash trays, and the smell of stale beer. They were in varying degrees of intoxication, with Saville well ahead of the field.

'So that's that!' said Wilson. 'I never thought we would make it.'

Saville unleashed a fruity belch. 'If you say that once more, Wilson, I'll brain you. Anyhow, I've had it. I'm going to bed.'

They followed his lead. Wilson thanked everyone once more and went towards his company lines. The others hurried through the cold night air in the opposite direction. Hooper was the first to duck down into his tent. As Rimmer unfastened the flaps of his tent, he looked back at Saville. 'Probably won't see you again, Kid. Good luck.'

'Hey, Dan! Thanks for all you did.'

'That's OK, Kid. We had our moments, despite our differences.'

'Christ, you can't mean that. But thanks all the same. You were great. It was Wally Hammond's evidence that clinched it. Bloody brilliant, old fruit. How were you so certain there'd be nothing else with the money?'

'Just a hunch. Forget it, Kid. Go to bed.'

'Can't turn in yet, Dan. Not without apologizing for having been such a first-class twat. I'm not really like that. Not when you know me.'

'I'll believe you, Kid. See you some time.'

Rimmer knew that for the rest of his life he would regard Saville as the biggest cheat and shit he'd ever met. He moved into his tent, but Saville wasn't that easily deterred. He pushed his way in uninvited and plonked himself on the end of Rimmer's camp bed.

'What about the girl, Dan? That poor, miserable girl?'

'She'll survive. She was no virgin. She may not get any compensation, but she saved the life of her brother. Never forget that the other Katcoms in Dog Company were all killed. So don't worry too much about her. There are worse fates in life than being screwed by Wilson.'

'Really? You could have fooled me.'

They were silent for a time. Rimmer began to undress. Then Saville said: 'Dan, can I tell you something?'

'Don't bother! Go to bed.'

'You ever been in love?'

'No, reckon not.'

'Well I am. I'll show you a photo.' Saville produced his picture of Katsumi-san, but Rimmer wasn't impressed. He never was by photographs of Nip broads. They only ever showed head and shoulders, never their bandy legs.

'I'll be back with her tomorrow night,' said Saville. Then he suddenly burst into an old army song.

I'd rather be in England,

Merry, merry England,
Shagging away from morning until night,
Cor blimey!

Rimmer had had enough. He grabbed Saville by the arm, yanked him to his feet, and thrust him out of the tent. 'Go to bed, Kid.'

He watched Saville stagger into the darkness, still singing happily. Rimmer completed undressing and slipped into his sleeping bag. He had a sudden craving for a cigarette. For a time he watched smoke drifting to the roof of the tent. He was thinking about the Korean girl. Maybe she had been hard done by, but there was nothing new in that. Rimmer had sent plenty of innocent desperadoes down the line. The law wasn't necessarily justice, and only a fool ever thought it was.

Rimmer stubbed his cigarette out in a gesture of annoyance. He knew he was only kidding himself – making futile excuses. He had allowed his pride and conceit to transcend everything. The realization that Saville had more talent in his little finger than he could ever aspire to had driven Rimmer to his first addictive step into corruption. He had taken the easy way out and in his heart he knew that the sweet, seductive taste of personal triumph would stay with him for the rest of his career.

Rimmer lit another cigarette, knowing he wasn't going to get any sleep. He would get his fair share of glory at Army HQ, but that was no consolation. He was sick to death of the whole thing. All he wanted to do was put the last few days behind him: to be rid of Saville, and rid of the British generally. Most of all, rid of his great triumph . . . the Bunker Hill court-martial.

Rimmer felt under his pillow and pulled out a small bundle. He unwound the covering silk scarf and examined the contents: a leather wallet, two cigarette lighters, a pocket watch, and a silver cigarette case. All exactly as the girl had described. He studied them for a time, still amazed by what he had done. Then he wrapped them up again and replaced them under his pillow. He knew he would have to get rid of them in the morning, and once rid of them he would pretend the whole thing had been a bad dream.

He decided that when he drove over Teal bridge he would throw them into the Imjin. There, they would be lost and forgotten for ever. The Imjin, in the shadow of Bunker Hill, would be a fitting resting place.

The following morning Saville slept late. He was eventually woken by loud shouting. 'Corporal! What the bloody hell is that tent doing still stood standing there?'

'Not my fault, Sarge. Captain Saville is in it. The solicitor bloke.'

'Well, my compliments to Captain Saville and tell him that his moments of glory are bloody over. And to move his idle body.'

When Saville emerged from his tent he helped the corporal to dismantle it. As they went about their task, Saville was amazed to see that the surrounding hills were now empty. The Borderers encampment had disappeared. The battalion was in the final throes of moving back into the line. Shouts of NCOs echoed around the steep valley as they sorted themselves out into formations, ready to march off. When Saville's tent was folded he gathered his kit together and went to the MT Section. He found his jeep easily enough. The driver was a cheerful young Cockney, the talkative type. 'I was beginning to wonder if you would ever turn up, sir. Let me give you a hand with your kit.'

They heaved the kit into the back of the jeep and drove off. They bumped along a track for half a mile before they reached the MSR. As the driver went to turn left, heading south, Saville asked: 'This the way the battalion comes?'

'Up to here, sir. Then they go north.'

'Pull over then. I'd like to see them march off.'

Despite the cold, they waited an hour. The driver talked most of the time but Saville hardly listened. He just grunted and smiled as he thought appropriate. He was thinking about the trial. He still couldn't get over the way Rimmer had eventually come up trumps. Then he thought about the deviousness of McCleod, and Wainwright for that matter. He smiled, respecting them for having stood up for what they really loved. He had done the same and had no regrets. When it came to justice for an unknown Korean girl or the happiness of the girl he loved and intended to marry, there was no choice. He had done what he had to do.

Eventually, they heard the Borderers approaching. Their bugle band was in full cry, blasting out their regimental march, *Pretty Polly Perkins*. The piercing notes echoed amid the cloistered mountain peaks which had stood in silence for centuries. It was a thrilling microcosm of military power and pomp, complemented by the steady pounding of over a thousand heavily laden feet. As the long column of fighting troops appeared, Colonel Wainwright was at their head, a lone figure with a hand-carved cromack in his left hand, a gift and tribute from the Argylls.

'Are you going to do the honours, sir?' prompted the driver.

'I suppose I'd better.'

They got out of the jeep. As Colonel Wainwright drew level with them, they stamped to attention and Saville flung up a smart salute. Colonel Wainwright returned it with vigour seldom seen among senior officers. 'Good luck, Captain Saville,' he called out.

'Thank you, sir. And the same to you and your men.'

As the battalion marched past they wheeled north. It was easy for Saville to distinguish the various companies. Among the men in battalion HQ was Jock McCleod, confirming that Wainwright had abandoned his policy of never splitting his troublemakers. McCleod was unmistakable. His jikkay frame was on his back, housing his legendary loot, and his newly won MM was pinned on his parka overcoat. He was also defying orders by wearing his Glengarry with the enormous badge of the Argyll and Sutherland Highlanders. He spotted Saville and waved. 'Keep looking after number one, sir.'

'And you keep studying the Bible.'

The next man Saville recognized was Wilson. He was leading 1 Platoon, directly behind Able Company's new commander, the successor to Duke Thompson. He was striding out effortlessly but the old swagger, which Saville had first seen only a few months before on the troopship *Devonshire*, was no longer there. Saville doubted if it ever would return.

When Dog Company marched past, Saville noticed that Middleton was missing. At the end of the company, the last in the battalion, was 12 Platoon. Their new commander looked incredibly young. As he passed by, Saville muttered to himself: 'There, but for Jock McCleod and Dan Rimmer, go I.'

Alongside 12 Platoon's new commander was Sykes. Saville wondered how he'd get on with his new officer, and what fresh adventures would befall the notorious 12 Platoon on Hill 425?

Saville was about to order the driver to start the jeep when he noticed the very last rank of 12 Platoon. The man nearest them was Fogarty. When Fogarty saw Saville he stopped dead. Then he made a rude, two-fingered gesture and let out a stream of foul abuse. As he rejoined the rest of the platoon, his comrades roared with laughter.

'Just listen to old Foggy!' exclaimed the driver.

'You know him?'

'Blimey, sir. I'll say. Everyone knows old Foggy. Great lad. But they say he's going to be done for perjury.' The driver noticed Saville's look of concern. 'Don't worry about old Foggy, sir. He'll soon sort out the screws at Pusan.'

At last 12 Platoon wheeled right on to the MSR, heading north. They began to disappear in the dust, becoming mere specks bobbing up and down. 'Stirring sight, don't you think, sir? The battalion marching off to battle? Bloody marvellous really, sir. I'm only a national serviceman, but you have to be proud of the lads, don't you? The American Presidential Citation and all that. Bloody fantastic.'

'Yes.'

'And Mr Wilson especially... . . . criminal he only got an MC.'

There was a short silence, but the driver had not finished. 'Does make you think though, doesn't it, sir? I mean not just about the Borderers. But the whole of British history. Lads just like us have been doing these kind of things for hundreds of bloody years . . . all over the bloody world.'

'Yes, I suppose we have. We've pillaged, raped, and put to the sword in most places, so I don't see why Korea should be an exception.'

'That's right, sir,' rejoined the driver, missing Saville's sarcasm. 'The 2 i/c says the Horn will go down as one of the great defensive battles of all times.'

'Really?'

'Yes, sir. Definitely. A modern-day Rorke's Drift. Wherever that was.'

'Natal. South Africa. There were eleven VCs at Rorke's Drift.'

'That's about the same as we should have had, sir.'

Saville glanced across at the driver. The youngster was still watching his comrades march north. Pride shone from his eyes. The myths were forming, thought Saville. The legends taking root.

They continued to stare after the Borderers for a time. Then Saville said: 'Come on! Back in the jeep. You'd better get me to Seoul.'

'Right, sir. Then where are you off to? Pusan?'

'Kure.'

'Blimey, sir! You're in luck. Japan's the place to be, so they all say.'

'Yes.'

'Know it well, sir?'

'Pretty well.'

'What exactly do you do in Japan, sir?'

'Nothing much. Just screw around, mainly.'

The driver laughed gleefully. 'Bloody roll on! I'm due for my R and R soon, sir. They say Jap girls are the best in the world.'

'Yes,' replied Saville. 'The very best.'

The driver revved the engine and the jeep leapt forward. Saville glanced back, hoping for a final glimpse of the Borderers, but the cloud of dust being thrown up behind them was so thick that it obliterated everything. It seemed to Saville as though the whole of Korea, and all it stood for, was blowing away in their wake.